Second Chance Inn

by
Marlayne Giron

"My tongue is the pen of a ready writer"
Psalm 45:1

D1214375

Second Chance Inn

Copyright
© 2023 by Marlayne Giron

All rights reserved. Except for brief excerpts for review purposes, no part of this book may be reproduced or used in any form without written permission. Quantity sales and special discounts are available to organizations and educational programs. For details, contact the author:

mmgiron@yahoo.com

ISBN 979-8-218-95377-5
ISBN 979-8-218-95378-2 (ebook)

This is a work of fiction. Names, characters, places, and events are products of the author's imagination, and any resemblances to actual events or places or persons, living or dead, is entirely coincidental.

Cover and interior design: Kimberly Denando

Printed in the United States of America

DEDICATIONS

To my Savior, Jesus, who returns beauty for ashes
and redeems the years that the locust has eaten.
(Joel 2:25)

To the memory of Barry (my first love).

To Michele – Barry's sister who has become my sister
and dear friend although we are in no way related.

To my true-life prince charming, Michael,
who healed my hurting heart and filled it with love.

…and to my sissy, Mary, who has been my greatest
encourager and champion in my writing career.
I couldn't have done any of this without you.
I love you dearly.

Marlayne Giron

TABLE OF CONTENTS

GLOSSARY

Bitte — please

Boppli — baby

dawdi haus — a small house or rooms separate from the main house where a grandparent or grandparents live out their retirement.

Danki — thank you

Daed — father

Der Herr — the Lord

Dochder — daughter

Englisch — a non-Amish person

Frau — wife

Guder mariye — good morning

Gut morgan — good morning

Kinner — children

Narrish — crazy

Nee — No

Ordnung — the written and unwritten rules of the Amish; the understood behavior by which the Amish are expected to live, passed down from generation to generation. Most Amish know the rules by heart. These may differ slightly district to district

Onke — uncle

Rumspringa — "running around", the term used to describe the period of adolescence Amish experience starting at around age 16 with increased social interaction and independence (alternate spelling: Rumschpringe)

Schwester — sister

Chapter One

The End of Normal

Rachel's heart clenched in fright "Barry, what's wrong?"

Her husband, Barry, was grasping his head with both hands, his teeth bared in pain. "Barry, are you having another one of your severe headaches?"

Barry nodded then stiffened, he was looking right at her, but his eyes were not focusing. "I can't see! I can't see! I'm blind!" He cried, then collapsed onto the floor, blood seeping from his ears.

"Karen!" Rachel shrieked, falling to her knees besides his inert body. "Call 9-1-1! Hurry!!" "Barry! Barry, can you hear me?" she was screaming at him, but he didn't respond. She put her ear to his chest, but his once pounding heart was just fluttering… Searing terror coursed through her veins. *What is wrong? He's as healthy and strong as a horse! This can't be happening!* Her head reared back, eyes seeking to tear open the ceiling to heaven. "God, no! Don't do this to me! Please help me! Please bring Barry back to me! Please don't take him away from me! I can't bear this, please!" She shook Barry's shoulders, wails erupting from her throat loud enough to shake the rafters. "Barry! Please don't leave me!"

She screamed and shook him for what seemed hours so it barely registered when the EMT's barged through the front door with all their equipment and pushed her to one side.

Karen pulled her out of the way. "Mom let them work, everything will be okay."

1

She was trembling uncontrollably and praying with all her might under her breath but inside she was screaming. *Please don't take him from me, Lord. He's my life, my soul mate, the only person left in this world that loves me. I'll do anything, pay any price…just please, please, please don't take him from me…*

They worked on him, taking readings, and putting an IV into his arm. Finally, after several minutes the EMT's stood to their feet and the room became deathly still. None of them would look her in the eye as they packed up their gear.

"Are you going to call it in then?" One of them said to another. The guy spoke into his mobile phone. "Patient is unresponsive, eyes fully dilated. Bleeding through ears indicates a massive aneurysm. Preparing to transport." He looked at Rebecca, his face sympathetic. "Mamm, we're going to take him to the ER do you wish to accompany us?"

Rachel nodded, unable to speak, unable to swallow. Karen shoved her purse into her numb hands. She watched in numbing pain as they loaded her husband's body onto the gurney and out the door to the waiting ambulance; they no longer seemed to be in any hurry. This alone spoke volumes. *They've given up trying to resuscitate him. God, pleeeee-ase….!* She was trembling so much that she could barely walk. Nausea swept over her as reality sank in. *I'm only 32 and I'm a widow…*

"*Noooooooooooooo,*" she wailed, crumpling onto her knees onto her front lawn. Then she passed out.

Karen's voice seemed to come from very far away. "Mom, Mom, wake up." Karen was staring down at her in naked fear, fighting to control her tears. The sight sent stabbing pains of terror through Rachel's heart. Karen *never, ever* cried.

This can't be happening; this must be a nightmare. Please God, not Barry, not now. I can't face life without him. The EMT helped her onto her feet and into the back of the ambulance. Barry lay on the gurney, a blanket covering his face. She had no strength left to do anything to wail her agony.

The thing she had always feared most in life had actually happened. Barry was gone...her life was over. She doubled over inside the ambulance clutching her chest as if to keep it from splitting open; aware that she was making a scene but unable to help herself. When the ambulance finally arrived at the hospital the EMT and Karen half-lifted, half-walked her into the ER and put her into a chair while Barry's body was wheeled past her and beyond her sight.

Rachel was inconsolable. Her sobs filled the ER waiting area, but her eyes were too swollen shut to see how uncomfortable she might be making the other people in the room. She went through an entire box of Kleenex and was on her second when a nurse approached her.

"Mrs. Winston?"

Rachel nodded, unable to speak, her body trembling uncontrollably.

"Please come with me," the nurse put her arms around Rachel's waist and assisted her to a standing position. Karen was immediately on her other side and together they supported her as she walked through the double doors. A doctor met them in the hall and his face was grave.

His downcast eyes held no hope for her. "I'm sorry, Mrs. Winston-" was the last thing she heard before the floor came rushing up to meet her.

Rachel slowly came out of her drug-induced fog and peered around her darkened bedroom. The first thing she noticed was the smell...it was overwhelming...and it was coming from her. She couldn't remember the last time she had been awake, eaten or drank anything or taken a shower. The blankets on the bed were a tangled mess. Slowly she sat up, shutting her eyes to wait until the room stopped spinning. She swung her feet onto the floor and felt a wrapper of some kind crunch under her heel. Her mouth felt as dry as cotton and her lips were cracked and peeling.

Her bedroom door opened at that moment. She looked up. In the doorway stood all four of her sister-in-law's: Debbie, Monique, Julie and Barry's sister, Michele. They looked around her bedroom in horror and pity then back at her in shock.

"This is an emergency intervention," Michele informed her, crossing to the window, and opening the curtains. The room flooded with light.

"I don't want an intervention!" her voice came out in a croaking whisper. She fell back into bed and drew the covers over her head. "Leave me alone!" she wailed, the hot tears starting afresh, her voice muffled by the blankets. "Just let me *b-b-b-beeeeeeeeeeeee!*" The crushing reality of Barry's death washed over her like a tidal wave.

"Because we love you, we can't do that!" Monique said, pulling the covers off her.

Several pairs of arms reached for her, gently but firmly pulling her out of bed and lifting her to her feet. Rachel tried to peer through squinted eyes, but the room was still spinning. They waited as she dry-retched then gently guided her to the bathroom. She heard someone turn on the shower.

"Her hair is all matted," said Karen's voice from the doorway.

"We'll do our best to get the tangles out, Karen," replied Debbie. "Why don't you help me with the bedroom while the others get your mom cleaned up?"

"Yeah, okay…whatever," Karen mumbled.

Rachel would have guffawed in derision if she weren't so miserable. Karen hated and avoided housework like it was the plague. When Julie and Monique reached to pull her sweat-soaked, smelly nightdress off her she shoved their arms away.

4

"I can do it!" she snapped, angry and resentful of their intervention. She lost her balance and almost crashed into the shower door.

"Obviously not," Monique replied, holding her upright in her arms while Julie and Michele pulled her night dress off over her head. "Just relax and let us help you."

"What day is it?" Rachel asked. She had lost all track of time.

"Daddy's funeral is today," she heard Karen say from the bedroom. Rachel's chest constricted, her heart thudding loudly in her ears. She opened her mouth to speak but all that would come out was a loud wail of anguish.

Rachel stared into her lap, studying her hands as her CPA continued to give her the bad news.

Judy had been painfully straight with her. "Rachel, even with the settlement from the life insurance company, I'm afraid your long-term financial outlook isn't very good."

Rachel stared at the petite Asian woman who had done their taxes for the past ten years. Judy was sympathetic but always painfully blunt and truthful. The news was devastating. Rachel wasn't expecting to get "rich" from losing Barry, but neither was she expecting her financial situation to be so dire.

"There's enough money to pay off your mortgage if you sell your home, but that leaves you with little left to live on since you currently have no income. The cost of living in California is just too high – I strongly suggest you sell your house and move out of state, somewhere cheaper where you won't have a mortgage. Or…"

Rachel's lower lip had trembled as she fought back her tears, "…or what?"

Judy's dark eyebrows knit together with obvious concern. "Move in with a friend or family member for a while. At least until you decide what to do long-term. If you were working full-time and had a steady income, this wouldn't be such a time sensitive issue, but you still have a lot of credit card and school debt. There simply isn't enough to support you and your daughter on a long-term basis without a substantial deduction in liabilities. Is there anyone who would be willing to take you both in?"

"Not without causing them incredible inconvenience," Rachel had replied, studying the saturated Kleenex wad in her lap. "My mother-in-law already has her daughter, son-in-law and their kids living with her; the only other relative nearby has three children in a modest house. There's really no room for us anywhere."

"What about your friends? Could any of them take you both in?"

"I would like to keep them as friends and not wear out my welcome as a refugee...so...*no.*"

"What do you think about moving out of state? Someplace where the home prices are significantly cheaper? Perhaps having that B&B you and Barry always talked about?"

She stared at Judy morosely. Selling her and Barry's home? Moving out of state? Running a business? *Alone?* It was all too overwhelming.

Judy leaned forward. "Rachel – it might be a very good move for you. It would provide you with shelter, an income and be a good tax deduction since it would be considered income property. You should really investigate it. You could finally put your culinary skills and hospitality degree to good use."

Rachel wiped her swollen eyes and blew her nose again. "You really think so?"

"It would also keep you very busy and interacting with people. It would be a lot better than sitting alone in that house, eating your heart out with grief day after day..."

Chapter Two

In Strange Territory

Rachel Winston watched the undulating, green Pennsylvania farmland roll past the glass train window, her heart leaden. The bucolic scenery was a stark contrast to the concrete jungle she had left behind in Southern California a few days earlier. The green fields were dotted with white farmhouses, picturesque barns, along with small herds of cows, goats, and sheep grazing peacefully.

She grimaced to herself. The only thing missing was large letters floating in the sky that heralded WELCOME TO AMISH COUNTRY. Occasionally, she would catch a passing glimpse of an Amish buggy waiting at a train crossing and wondered if any of them held the man who was to pick them up at the station in Strasburg.

Rachel turned her gaze from the window and glanced at her teen-aged daughter Karen, whose eyes were shut as she listened to her music. They had barely spoken for the entire three-day trip. Karen was still giving her the silent treatment, furious at being forced to leave family and friends behind. Rachel had waited until the end of the school year to pack up and leave but it hadn't made her daughter any happier about it. Rachel sighed in resignation. She had accepted the punishment as part of her motherly duty. She really didn't blame Karen for feeling the way she did. She would have pretty much felt the same way if her mom had forced her to leave everything behind and move across the country against her will too, but financially, there had been no other choice. Not after losing Barry…her husband and the love of her life.

A sob erupted from Rachel's throat, but Karen didn't notice. A little over a year had passed since Barry had died and the pain was barely tolerable. The more time that passed, the more real it became that she wouldn't see him this side of heaven. She brushed away the tears that seeped down her cheeks, struggling not to succumb to her grief. Once she started, she wouldn't be able to stop, and she didn't want to frighten Mr. Miller with the spectacle of a totally unglued "English" woman having a breakdown in his buggy.

The train braked suddenly, slowing down and a voice came over the loudspeaker. "We will be pulling into Strasburg station in five minutes. Passengers, please make ready to disembark if this is your stop."

Rachel tapped her daughter on the knee to get her attention.

Karen opened one eye and favored her with a grouchy look. "What?"

Rachel pointed to the overhead bin. "Get your suitcase down, we're almost there."

Karen didn't budge. "Yeah…yeah." She closed her eyes again and went back to her music.

Rachel stood up and yanked an ear bud out of her ear. "Now, Karen."

"Alright! Geez!"

Samuel Miller stood on the train platform and held up his homemade sign with the words "RACHEL WINSTON" on it, scanning the faces of the disembarking passengers. Dozens passed by him and moved on until a weary looking woman in her mid-thirties with brunette hair approached and stood before him with the saddest face he had ever seen.

"Are you Mr. Miller?" she asked. She set her heavy suit-case down and straightened slowly, grimacing. She looked utterly exhausted, and her deep-set brown eyes were red-rimmed, puffy and ringed with pain, a sure sign that she had been weeping recently. Creases from long-term emo-tional pain were etched between her eyebrows.

The woman turned and introduced the sullen teenag-er at her side. "This is my daughter, Karen." When there was no response she scowled at the young girl, brought her hands up to her ears and made a pulling motion, indicating that Karen should take out her earbuds and say hello.

Karen was not much taller than her mother, with long glossy brown hair, glasses, and a very petite frame. She rolled her eyes and obligingly removed one earbud, the mu-sic blasting out of the tiny speaker. "Hi," she deadpanned before replacing it.

Samuel said nothing. It was obvious the teenager would rather be any place other than Lancaster County, Pennsyl-vania.

"Please don't mind my daughter; she's not too happy about moving from Southern California." Rachel apolo-gized.

Samuel nodded. "Do you have much luggage?"

"Just these two, the rest are arriving with the moving van," Rachel replied, her eyes welling up again. She wiped them with a Kleenex. "I'm sorry," she sniffled, glancing away. "This is all just so traumatic for me...for us."

Samuel nodded, his heart moved with compassion, al-ready aware of the circumstances which had brought her to Lancaster. Words were woefully inadequate at times like this as he only too well knew; his own world had disintegrated just a year ago.

Samuel looked down into the wounded eyes of the *En-glisch* woman and recognized his own pain in her face. To his surprise, he found himself wishing he could pat her hand to let her know it was okay, but it was strictly forbidden. He was Amish, she was *Englisch*. Even a casual gesture of kindness was off limits, especially in public. "My buggy is this way," he said gently, hefting the suitcases and leading the way out of the Strasburg train station.

They followed him in silence, seemingly occupied with their own thoughts. Rachel dug some Kleenex out of her purse and blew her raw nose.

Samuel put the luggage into the back of the buggy and waited for them to get in.

The daughter stared at the buggy, wrinkling her nose as Samuel's horse passed waste right in front of her. She gagged as it plopped in great steaming heaps into a bag that sat just below its rump. "You don't have a car?"

"Karen – don't be rude, I explained to you about the Amish." Rachel snapped, turning red with embarrassment.

Samuel climbed in and offered Karen the reins. "Would you like to drive Dodger?"

"You're kidding, right? Me?" Karen replied, a ghost of a smile appearing on her face.

Samuel nodded, "*Jah.*"

Karen climbed in and accepted the reins. "What do I do?"

"First, unplug your ears." Samuel replicated the pulling motion he had seen her mother make. "You can't hear traffic if you're filling your ears with music. Then, you will need to back Dodger away from the rail. Pull gently on the reins until he steps backwards enough, then take the right rein and pull it to the left to take us out onto the road."

Karen put away her iPhone, pocketed her earbuds, and giggled nervously as she pulled back on the reins. Dodger didn't budge until Samuel clicked his tongue. Dodger nickered then backed up a few steps.

"Now pull the reins to the left," Samuel reminded her.

Karen swung the reins over to the left as he had shown her. Samuel clicked his tongue again. The horse obediently went left and soon they were trotting out onto the road.

Samuel kept a watchful eye, ready to assist whenever Karen faltered.

Rachel watched from the backseat, amazed at how well a virtual stranger was handling her daughter. *How is it that men are always so much more patient and calm teaching young women to drive than their mothers?* She forced down the sob in her throat. It should have been Barry teaching Karen to drive in the high school parking lot, not a strange Amish man in a horse-drawn buggy three thousand miles from home. Except for the traditional Amish beard, which was long and scraggly, Samuel Miller looked nothing like what she expected. He seemed close to her age, with thick, dark wavy hair that peeked out beneath his straw hat at odd angles. Despite the beard, he had a ruggedly handsome face and vivid blue eyes. He stood at least a head and a half taller than she and his body was trim and well-muscled, no doubt due to many years of heavy physical labor.

"Could we stop at a local market to pick up some items for our next few meals?" she asked.

Samuel looked over his shoulder at her. "What do you need?" he asked.

"Just some staples, milk…eggs…meat."

Samuel turned back to correct Karen's grip on the reins. "We have fresh eggs from our chickens, smoked meats, milk from my cows, fresh vegetables from the garden, fresh fruit from the orchard, and a pantry of canned produce. Is there anything else you need for your next few meals?"

Rachel stared at the back of his straw hat in surprise. She'd forgotten that she'd purchased a self-sufficient Amish farmhouse that provided much of its own foodstuffs.

"We could use some toiletries like shampoo, toothpaste, and deodorant," Karen replied.

"There is a Wal-Mart on the way home," Samuel replied.

"Thanks." Rachel sat back and sniffled, struggling to dismiss Barry from her mind. How had her life come to this? She closed her weary eyes, trying to concentrate on the soothing *clip-clop, clip-clop* of the horseshoes upon the road to lull her anxious mind…

"Mom, we're at Wal-Mart."

Startled, Rachel snapped out of her private ruminations and looked out, her throat constricted in pain. They were apparently parked on the Amish side of the large lot because she could see quite a few other Amish buggies parked near them.

Karen clambered out and stared. "That is the biggest Wal-Mart I've ever seen in my life."

Rachel joined her and turned to Samuel. "Are you coming in? Do you need me to pick you up anything?"

He seemed surprised that she would ask him. "*Nee, danki,*" he replied, shaking his head. "I'll wait here with the horse."

Rachel was completely exhausted from the three-day train ride in which she had hardly slept. It was good to be on her feet and stretching her legs again. She and Karen entered the Wal-Mart and ogled its massive interior once inside.

"Let's just get the essentials and get out of here, I'm tired," Rachel announced. Despite her best efforts to rein Karen in, they wound up with a cart full of toiletries, books, and snack foods. It was hard to say "no" to her daughter when she was ridden with guilt. The only thing she put her foot down on was buying DVDs since the farmhouse had no modern conveniences or electricity.

Samuel's eyebrows rose into his hairline when he saw the number of packages they had brought back with them but said nothing. He just helped load them into the back of the buggy and put the reins back into Karen's hands. It was another half hour ride before they pulled off the narrow country road into the driveway of their new home. At this point, Samuel took back the reins, guiding Dodger onto the pea gravel driveway and up to the front of the farmhouse. Rachel leaned forward and stared. The white farmhouse was bigger, much bigger, than she had expected and utterly charming.

It was a two-story white clapboard house with a grayish roof, and a broad, wrap-around porch with flower baskets hanging from beneath the wainscot ceiling. All the windows had window boxes, but the flowers were long since dead. Evidently, Samuel had forgotten to water them. The farmhouse stood on a little rise surrounded by lush green grass and large mature trees, all well-kept. To one side of the house was a large vegetable and herb garden and behind that was a small orchard. The red barn sat well back from the road and adjacent to the house was a small, detached in-law house.

The photographs didn't do it justice...it is idyllic, Rachel thought.

The spell was broken when Karen turned around and regarded her with an accusing look. "Is that an actual out-house over there?" she pointed. "Are you seriously telling me there are no indoor bathrooms...really? REALLY?" The novelty of driving the buggy had worn off, instantly replaced with seething teenaged fury.

Rachel blushed crimson at Karen's tirade, embarrassed by her rudeness.

Samuel came to her rescue. "My *daed* was very Old Order and never put one in. Rachel..." He paused, struggling to contain his emotions. "We were planning on installing bathrooms inside when I lost...when...I didn't see the point of the expense anymore..." He turned his face to hide his pain.

Rachel's heart plummeted. She watched in silence as he helped Karen down, then herself, ignoring the teenager as she shoved the earbuds back into her ears and cranked up the volume. Rachel followed Samuel into the main house with her arms full of shopping bags. He set their suitcases

13

on the floor just inside the front door. The entire downstairs was swept and scrubbed clean. His personal possessions had been moved into the *dawdi haus*, where he had taken up quarters as the property caretaker. The room smelled of Minwax and Lysol. His *schwester* and her *kinner* had done a thorough job of preparing the home for its new owner.

"It's so…*plain*." Karen griped, turning around in a circle in the family room. The furnishings were simple and utilitarian, with nothing on the walls and simple braided rugs on the hardwood floors. A large river rock fireplace stood on one side and in the kitchen was an actual wood-burning, vintage black iron stove and long farmhouse table. "So, where's the TV?"

"No TV, honey, I'm sorry. Remember I explained to you about this house? It's Amish, which means there's no electricity, no cable or satellite," Rachel murmured, already prepared for the blow-up.

"No indoor plumbing, electricity, or television?" Karen's voice went up an octave, her face registering complete disbelief. "Are you freaking kidding me?"

"Weren't you listening to me when I told you about all this months ago? No, there isn't," Rachel replied. She turned to Samuel, "thank you so much for all your help. The moving van is arriving in the next day or so. Would you be available to help me move some of our heavier things in?"

"*Jah*," Samuel nodded, heading for the front door of what used to be his house. "I'll just leave you to get unpacked." The door shut behind him. He heard Karen explode again the moment it closed behind him, her voice carrying well to the outside.

Karen glared at her. "How could you drag me all the way out here, away from EVERYTHING to a place that doesn't even have a decent toilet?"

"I'm sorry, I had no other choice." Rachel's voice was weary, defeated.

Rachel and Karen stared at one another. Karen was out-of-body furious, and Rachel was thoroughly exhausted and dejected. She set the grocery sacks down on the kitchen counter and began unpacking them, ignoring Karen who stomped upstairs with heavy footfalls, wandering from room to room, with a final slam of a bedroom door.

Karen threw herself on the bed and buried her face deep into the pillow to stifle her angry sobs.

This is so unfair. Why did I have to be dragged away from everyone I care about? I miss my dad. He never would have done this to me...He never would have moved us out here! I wish it had been— she choked back the thought, afraid of bringing down a divine curse upon her head but it only made her cry harder. She just couldn't connect with her mother. *She never listens to me, she's always angry and now she's ruined my life.*

Her mom's roller coaster emotions made her extremely uncomfortable. She just couldn't be the lovey-dovey kind of daughter her mom had been hoping to adopt. Hot tears soaked the pillow. Her dad was never coming back...her wonderful, funny, dependable dad...*never.* His loss hurt more than she could bear. She had lost the only parent who just accepted and loved her for the way she was, without conditions.

My life has become a living hell.

Samuel entered the *dawdi haus* and shut the door. He sat down heavily in his armchair and looked around. If life had gone as planned, he would not have moved into it until his eldest son had married and brought his spouse into the main house. Instead, his son lay six feet beneath the sod, never to know the joys of marriage and *kinner.*

After their funerals, Samuel could no longer bear to live in the large, empty house. Every inch bore memories that were too painful to endure. As an Amish man, he didn't possess even a single photograph of his *frau* and *kinner.*

There were no wedding photographs, none of his children as infants...nothing. He had nothing by which to remember their beloved faces. He had nothing left of them but memories. He would not see them again until they were reunited in heaven, providing God still allowed him in. He had not prayed, read his Bible, nor spoken to *Der Herr* since the accident. He had attended the bi-monthly Meetings, but it was mainly done for appearances sake and to see his *schwester's* family. He went through all the motions demanded of him, but his heart was filled with broiling anger for all he had lost.

Der Herr had betrayed him, and he wanted nothing more to do with Him.

Samuel remained in his chair, staring at nothing, not even bothering to light the kerosene lamp when it grew dark.

Rachel had put it off as long as she could, but time had run out and so had any room in her bladder. After the long train and buggy ride, she found herself staring at the door of the dreaded outhouse, the need for relief becoming exquisitely painful. The brightly painted red wooden structure with the crescent moon cut into the top half of the door seemed to leer back at her, as if anticipating its newest victim with relish. It looked clean and even cheerful from the outside (for an outhouse) but the bright exterior did not allay her qualms.

She had not used an outhouse since she was in Girl Scouts and the memory was not pleasant. There were always webs and bugs no matter how clean you tried to keep it and it smelled bad - that was just the nature of the beast.

Just get it over with already.

She marched up to the little structure, armed with Lysol, toilet paper, flashlight, and a clothespin. She took a quick look around to make sure no one was looking then clipped the pin on her nose and entered. A small cloud of insects flew out.

"Eek!"

She jumped up and down, waving her arms furiously, determined to scare every one of pests away so she could go inside in relative peace. After a few minutes of flailing, she had managed to scare most of them away. She sprayed some Lysol inside then shut the door behind her, pushing the simple wooden peg into the "locked" position, and set the flashlight on the floor near the door. She had to admit that it was the cleanest outhouse she had ever seen, but it was still an outhouse with all the smells and nuisances (like pesky bugs) that came with it. She wanted to get in, get it over with, and get out, but she was finding it almost impossible to relax enough to finish her business. By the time she found relief, a good six minutes had passed...five minutes longer than she wanted to take.

She exited the structure, pointed the Lysol can one last time at its interior and unloaded the remainder of its contents. If any insect was dumb enough to return and take up residence, it would surely meet a quick death by asphyxiation.

She turned around and almost bowled Karen over.

Although Karen was sixteen, she behaved like a five-year-old who had waited too long to go potty. Her knees were pressed together, and she was doing the "pee-pee" dance.

"What did you just spray in there?"

"Lysol."

"OMG – give me that clothespin!" Karen snatched it off Rachel's nose, placed it on hers, and ran inside, in too much in a hurry to bother locking the door. Rachel held it shut for her.

"Mom, you have got to get indoor plumbing. I can't take doing this for the rest of my life."

"I'm with you, honey. It's just going to take some time."

"OMG! OMG! There are bugs flying around inside here. *Eek...eek... EEEEEK!*"

Rachel grinned, unable to help herself.

The door opened and Karen jumped out. "What are you smiling about? *It isn't funny!*"

It was the first smile Rachel remembered having in almost a year and it was hard to get rid of. "Sorry."

Her daughter favored her with another filthy look then ran back into the house, letting the screen door slam shut behind her. Rachel followed slowly, her momentary good humor dissolving as she climbed the porch stairs and entered the house to find the master bedroom. It was located just off the enormous kitchen and family room on the first level. Rachel sat on the bed and stared accusingly at the simple cross on the wall. She'd been giving God the silent treatment for the better part of the past year, angry at Him. Grief descended upon her like a heavy blanket.

Lord...You promised that You would never give us more than we could bear, well, I've had about all I can take. What am I supposed to do now? I've never felt so alone in all my life! I wish Barry were here to hug me and comfort me, only he can't because his body is decaying 10 feet under the ground! And our adopted daughter hates me...

Rachel hugged the pillow against her chest, closed her eyes, and waited, hoping that just once she would get an audible response from the God who seemed so distant. As she waited and waited, she became aware that the smells and sounds were different from the home she had left in California. Outside, the birds were singing and there was the occasional moo of a cow, the snort of a horse, or the bleat of a sheep; other than that, it was very quiet. There were no sounds of car traffic and no sounds of children playing. She breathed in deeply; the room smelled of lavender.

She looked around and found a small china teacup filled with dried lavender flowers next to a kerosene lamp on the simple nightstand. Her gaze traveled down to the bed and the quilt upon which she sat. She looked closely, wondering who had made it. The colors were navy blue, maroon, hunter green, and black; not what she would have chosen, but the stitches were fine and even. She took in the simple yet well-built pine furniture, old fashioned washstand, bowl and pitcher and bare walls. There was no mirror.

Well, at least here she wouldn't be confronted with constant reminders of Barry and what she had lost every time she turned around.

Rachel shuddered, an invisible steel band of pain tightening around her heart. If it weren't for Karen, she would have swallowed all the sleeping tablets the doctor had prescribed after his death and never awakened, but she knew that Barry would have expected her to behave responsibly and see their daughter through to adulthood. Yet it was all she could do to get through each day. Karen had no plans to attend college when she finally graduated, so the two of them were "stuck" living with each other for the foreseeable future.

She and Karen had never understood each other. Rachel wore all her feelings on her sleeve and had been an emotional basket-case since Barry's death while Karen had been the exact opposite. She didn't behave as though she had just lost the only father she had ever known nor shed a tear since the day of the funeral. The more painful something was, the more Karen "shut down" emotionally, leaving Rachel felt completely alone in her grief. It especially hurt when Karen treated her like there was something wrong with her for not having "gotten over it" already.

Where are you, God, when I need You the most? Where is the peace that passes understanding that You promised? I could really use some right about now...

She didn't know what to do next. Opening a B&B in the lovely farmland of Pennsylvania had been a fanciful dream she had shared with Barry the last time they had visited Lancaster County as tourists, but now she felt a panic attack coming on. *What on earth was I thinking? Maybe I should have moved into my mother-in-law's home as Karen wanted?*

Rachel shook her head. *No.* Karen may have been happier there for a short while but living with them would have just provided her with the perfect excuse to remain an emotional wreck, stuck in her grief. All her friends had said she was crazy to pull up stakes and move across the country where she knew no one, but she had stuck to her guns, sold most of her belongings and done it anyway. Now, after only half a day and her first encounter with the outhouse, she was already second-guessing her decisions.

The proceeds from the sale of the house had been enough to purchase the farmhouse outright with enough left over to move in, make some renovations and live on for a while, but she would soon have to turn her attention to earning a regular income. The six-bedroom farmhouse was too large for just her and Karen, so she planned on converting it into an Amish style bed and breakfast inn with one of the bedrooms converted into two, communal "His" and "Hers" bathrooms for her future guests.

Work will be your "salvation" her friends had told her. Work will keep your mind too occupied to dwell upon the pain. Well, she had her work cut out for her if she was to make a success of it. Right now, she just couldn't think about it. The all too familiar wave of emotional agony swept over her again, paralyzing her with pain. Scarlett O'Hara came to mind with her trademark *"Fiddle-Dee-Dee"* mentality. She just wouldn't think about all that now, she'd think about it tomorrow.

Rachel turned over and buried her face in the pillow to muffle her wails of sorrow, having no idea that her daughter was doing the same thing one floor above her.

Oh God, I miss him so much. Please tell Barry I love him... please tell him that I miss him. How am I going to go on without him?

20

After helping them unload, Samuel had retired to his *dawdi* house, the mention of his family weighing heavily on him. He lifted his head and turned in the direction of the main house, listening intently. Through his window he could hear both the *Englisch* woman and her *dochder* sobbing. He listened for a long while as they gave vent to their grief and for the very first time since he had lost his own family, tears of sorrow slid down his own cheeks and into his beard.

Karen's eyes flew open. It was still dark outside. *What was that gawd-awful noise?* Something was just outside her window, and it was making a horrific racket. She stumbled out of bed, peered out the bedroom window but could see nothing. The crowing sounded again. With a loud moan of disgust, she flopped back onto her bed and pulled the pillow and covers over her head, but it only muffled the racket. She lay there for a few moments, gradually becoming more wide-awake. There it was again! She stumbled to the double hung bedroom window and struggled briefly before figuring out how to get it open, cursing under her breath the entire time.

Urrrr urrr urrr urrr urrrrrrrrrrrrrrrrrrrrr.

Whatever it was, it was on the roof just above her bedroom. She leaned out as far as she dared, twisted around, and looked up. Her eyes went wide. It was a rooster! An actual rooster!

"*Shuuuuuuuuuut uuuuup!*" she yelled. The rooster squawked and half flew, half plummeted to the ground far below. Karen ducked inside, banging her head on the sill. She cursed again then slammed the window shut intending to go back to sleep; however, the aggravation and surge of adrenaline had brought her fully awake. She looked at her ever-present cell phone: Four AM? She was living a nightmare! A faint light outside her window caught her eye. She pressed her face up against the glass and cupped her hands around her eyes so she could see better. A man with a lantern was leaving the little house next to theirs and going into the large red barn. Curious, and no longer able to go back to sleep, Karen grabbed her hoodie, pulled it over her head and slipped into her UGG boots before creeping downstairs. *Might as well go have a look; there's no going back to sleep now.*

She left the house, hugging her arms around her slender body to keep warm. Her breath came out in small white puffs in the cold, pre-dawn air. She muttered curse words under her breath. The crunching noise her UGGs made on the pea gravel driveway sounded loud in the stillness of the early morning. Not even the birds were awake yet, just the stupid rooster! She entered the barn and looked around just in time to see the glow of a lantern moving around a corner. The smell of hay and cow manure greeted her nose. She stopped and turned to go back to the house, but curiosity wouldn't let her. She'd gone this far; she might as well see what was going on. As she rounded the corner in the dark barn, the smell grew more pungent. She pinched her nostrils shut, wishing she still had the clothespin she'd used for the outhouse. Now she could distinctly hear cows mooing and sheep bleating.

In the dim light, Karen stumbled into the Amish man who was squatting on a little wooden stool next to a large cow. The lantern cast only a faint light from its hook in the ceiling, not enough to see him from several feet away. He paused and looked around, surprised to see her standing there with her fingers still pinching her nose. The sight brought a smile to his otherwise grave face.

"*Gut morgan,*" he nodded, turning back around.

"Are you actually milking a cow?" Karen asked, her voice sounding funny with her nose pinched shut.

"*Jah,*" he paused, then turned back around to regard her. "Would you like to try?"

"Who…me? Are you kidding?" She couldn't believe he was offering to let her, a stranger, do such a thing. Animals had always fascinated her, but her only experience had been with her two dogs, Beatrice, a Cocker Spaniel, and Buddy, a mutt combo of Dachshund and Corgi which her mother had liked to describe as a "*Dawgi*".

"*Jah*…you," he replied. He paused from his milking, stood up and beckoned to his stool.

Karen sat down and looked up at him expectantly. "Now what?"

"You can't milk a cow with your fingers pinching your nose shut like that," he reminded her.

"Oh…sorry." Karen sheepishly removed her fingers and curled them around the warm udders.

Samuel squatted next to her, gently took her hands in his and manipulated her fingers, showing her how to squeeze the milk from the top of the udder to the bottom so it would squirt into the pail.

"Cool," Karen smiled, immensely pleased with herself when she produced a full squirt.

Samuel stepped away and watched her for a few moments, then moved on to the next cow. They worked in companionable silence except for the hiss of milk squirting into the pails. A small clowder of cats collected on the sidelines and Karen giggled uncontrollably when he squirted milk into their faces as a reward for their patience. They lapped it up in mid-air.

"Mine's full, now what?" Karen asked him.

"Now it goes into these to be refrigerated," Samuel said, carefully lifting the pail and pouring the contents into large, galvanized containers.

"You don't pasteurize it?" Karen asked in shock.

"*Nee*, not for personal use. I sell some of the milk to my neighbors and the local Amish creamery and use the rest for myself." He walked over to an enormous propane-powered refrigeration room and put the canisters inside.

"What does it taste like?"

A ghost of a smile came to Samuel's face, but it was a sad smile. "*Gut*, would you like to try?"

"Maybe some other time" she said, just to be polite, but with no real intention of doing so. "What next?" she asked, hoping to change the subject.

He regarded her for a moment. "Would you like to feed the sheep or collect eggs from the hen house?"

"Can I do both?"

"Collecting the eggs will take quite a long time. We will feed the sheep first."

Karen followed him to another part of the barn where several sheep with woolly coats greeted him eagerly. Samuel handed her a pail of feed. "Put it into the manger there," he pointed.

"I thought a manger was only used for the baby Jesus," Karen retorted but instantly regretted it, feeling like an idiot. Mr. Miller ignored her comment and poured fresh water into another large container for the animals. She petted the sheep while they turned their faces up to nibble at her sleeve. He handed her a rake. "Rake out the old straw and put it into that wheelbarrow, then we'll put in fresh," he instructed.

Karen wrinkled her nose. "Isn't it full of sheep pooh?"

"*Jah*, that is why it needs to be changed," he replied, thrusting out the rake for emphasis.

Karen had nothing to say in response to that and since she had volunteered in the first place, she figured there was no getting out of the dirty job now. She raked and shoveled the smelly straw until the floor was clear then Samuel threw in half a bale.

"Spread it around *gut* with the rake."

She did as instructed, then looked up at him.

"Now we go to the hen house," Samuel said, grabbing the lantern and leading the way out of the barn to the enormous, walk-in coop. Karen pinched her nostrils shut again.

The smell from the chickens was even worse than the cows. It was so strong her eyes began to water.

She ogled the rows and rows of boxes. "How many chickens do you have?" She had been expecting maybe five or ten, but he had a small chicken warehouse. She turned back to Mr. Miller who was fighting down a smile, "About fifty."

"Fifty?" This was going to take all day. "What do I do?" she asked, her voice coming out funny again with her nose pinched tight.

Samuel took down a large wire basket padded with straw. Karen watched in amazement as he reached underneath a chicken, ignoring her clucking protests and fished out a large blue egg as though it were the prize at the bottom of a Cracker Jack box and put it into the basket.

She was sold. "Can I try it now?" she asked.

"You will have to stop pinching your nose in order to get the eggs," he reminded her again.

"Couldn't you hold the basket?" Karen wheedled but Mr. Miller shook his head. With a grimace, Karen released her nose and stuck her hand under the warm feathers of the chicken, which squawked furiously in protest. She jerked her hand out and looked nervously up at him. He gave her an encouraging nod. "I guess I'm a little scared," she admitted with an apologetic smile.

"*Ach*," he nodded. He took her hand in his large one and guided her fingers under the chicken.

Karen found the egg and pulled it out. It was another blue one. "I did it." She smiled up at him, pleased with herself.

"*Gut.* Now you gather from all the rest and bring them into the house. There are empty cartons to pack them in. When you have emptied the basket, finish the rest of the chickens, and bring about half a dozen inside for breakfast. There is nothing like fresh eggs."

"Then what?" Karen asked, moving on to the next chicken. She looked up when he did not immediately answer her.

His features had become sorrowful. She wondered why he looked so sad.

"Then we take care of the horses," he finally replied.

Karen's eyes lit up. She loved horses, but she had never been near one before until yesterday. She made her way down the row of chicken boxes, quickly filling the wire basket with eggs. She was swiftly getting the hang of it. It took several more trips between the chicken coop and the service porch, over an hour, before she had successfully collected all the eggs for the day.

"Can we do the horses now?"

"Take those into the kitchen first," Samuel reminded her, indicating the last basket of eggs, "and put the rest into the service porch refrigerator."

"Okay, but will you wait for me?" she asked with a hopeful smile.

"*Jah*," he nodded.

Karen half walked, half ran back to the house, holding the basket carefully so the eggs would not get jostled and crack. She stepped into the kitchen to find her mother standing in her robe next to the wood stove, stoking the fire with a poker while she waited for a pot of coffee to brew.

Mom actually knows how to use one of those things? Who knew?

Karen set the eggs on the counter as her mother's eyes opened wide, surprised to find her up so early. "Mom, guess what? I milked a cow, fed sheep, and actually got eggs out from under the chickens' butts. That Amish man—"

"Mr. Miller," her mother reminded her.

"Yeah...whatever, Mr. Miller, he said there's nothing like fresh eggs. Next, he's going to show me how to take care of the horses."

Karen waited for her mother to share in her enthusiasm, but all Rachel could do was to stare at her in shock. "Okay, who are you and what have you done with my daughter?"

Karen rolled her eyes. "*Mooooooooooooooom.*" She pushed the basket of still warm eggs across the counter to her mom.

"Would you make us some fresh eggs? Scrambled, just salt and pepper? I'm hungry. I'll be back after I'm done with the horses." She skipped out the screen door, letting it slam behind her. Before returning to the barn, she made a quick, but necessary, visit to the dreaded outhouse. The second visit was every bit as bad as the first.

Mr. Miller was waiting for her just outside the horse's stall. There were two horses and a small mule team.

"Ready," she announced.

He looked down at her UGG boots and shook his head. "If a horse accidentally steps on those soft shoes, your foot will be crushed. Go into the house and see if you can find a pair of leather shoes like this that will fit you." He held up his sturdy black leather-clad foot to show her.

Karen opened her mouth to argue but thought better of it. "Okay," she said and ran back to the house, taking the stairs two at a time. She went into one closet after another, finding several articles of plain clothing and finally a pair of leather shoes that looked like her size, never questioning who they might have belonged to in her eagerness. She sat down on the wood floor and put one on, hoping it would fit. It was a bit tight, but she figured she could stand it long enough to help with the horses. She would have to talk her mom into getting a pair that fit her better. She raced back downstairs and out the door, ignoring her mother's call that breakfast was almost ready.

"I'm back," she announced, standing at attention like a soldier reporting for duty.

"I heard your *mamm* call you for breakfast," he said, shoving hay into a hanging sack by the stable door.

"Yeah, but—"

"Then you go."

Karen stared at his resolute face, knowing there would be no arguing with him. "Would you come with me?"

Samuel stared at her and for a moment looking like he might refuse, but then he seemed to reconsider and nodded. "*Jah*, I will come. We can finish the mules after breakfast."

Karen walked beside him and reached for his hand. The friendly gesture seemed to surprise him, but he gave her a small squeeze before extricating his fingers and followed her into the kitchen. She watched as he inhaled the smell of hot coffee and scrambled eggs that greeted him.

"Mom – is it okay if Mr. Miller eats breakfast with us? *Please?*"

Karen saw her mom turn around and gasp in horror. She was still in her robe, pajamas, and house slippers, her brunette hair all askew. In her excitement over the animals, Karen had completely forgotten that her mom was not dressed for visitors. She watched her mom's face grow pale then cover her mouth with embarrassment.

"I will take my breakfast in the *dawdi haus*," Samuel said, quickly excusing himself. He averted his eyes and beat a hasty retreat out the screen door while her mother continued to gape at her.

"Have you lost your mind, Karen, bringing that poor Amish man in here when I look like this?" Rachel screeched, pointing to herself.

Karen flushed red with embarrassment, but she wasn't about to admit fault. "Well, I didn't know he would react like that! I mean, you *are* wearing a robe." She plunked down at the kitchen table. She had been having such a great morning, until now. She picked at a spot on the table while her mother scraped the eggs onto a dish and set them before her. "I'm not hungry now," she moped.

Her mother set the cast iron pan down on the stove with a loud bang. Karen knew she had crossed the line and pushed her mom too far, but she didn't care; her mom deserved it for all the misery she was putting her through. An eruption was imminent.

"Fine, do whatever you want. Take it over to Mr. Miller so it doesn't go to waste then." Rachel growled, turning her back.

"Fine, I will," Karen spat, springing back onto her feet. She snatched up the plate and marched it over to the little in-law house, letting the screen door slam behind her in a most satisfactory manner.

Karen entered the in-law house without knocking, carrying the plate of scrambled eggs before her. "Mr. Miller?"

He stepped into view, an ominous frown upon his face. The sight of his unexpected disapproval made her nervous. She set the plate of eggs down on the little table and backed away toward the door.

"I wasn't hungry so mom thought you might like to have these, so they don't go to…" her voice trailed off.

She watched as Mr. Miller glanced at the plate then back at her, his expression becoming grimmer by the moment. Karen shifted uncomfortably.

"*Nee*, I will not take any food from the hand of a *dochder* who treats her *mamm* so shamefully," he said, his words cutting her heart to the quick. "*Sei so gut*…leave."

"*Sei so gut?*" Karen repeated, fighting back her hot tears of embarrassment.

"*Please* leave," he translated.

She had never felt so shamed in her life. Karen ducked her head, ran out of the little house, and didn't stop until she was safely back upstairs in her room. She slammed the door shut behind her.

Rachel watched her daughter flee upstairs, more upset than she had ever seen her in a long time. *What had that man said to her to get her so upset?* Her motherly instincts shifted into high gear. She tied her robe snugly, marched out to the in-law house, and pounded on the front door, fuming, the need to vent her emotional spleen overwhelming.

Samuel opened it, obviously surprised to find her standing there. He averted his eyes from her uncovered hair, staring at the floorboards beneath his feet instead.

"What just happened?" Rachel demanded to know. "Karen is really upset!"

Samuel paused a long time before he answered her, obviously uncomfortable. "I told her that I could not accept food from the hand of a child who treated her *mamm* with such disrespect."

The wind instantly went out of her sails. Rachel blinked, her ire dissipating as she realized that he had taken up for her. It was the last thing she had expected to hear. "Oh," was all she could manage after a long pause. She couldn't remember the last time anyone had ever supported her over her daughter. Barry often didn't and it had been the primary source of contention between them in an otherwise happy marriage. She gazed at Samuel Miller and instantly recognized the all too familiar emotional pain etched into his own features. Until that moment, she hadn't given much thought to the circumstances surrounding her purchase of the farmhouse or why he, as the original owner, had been willing to sell it so quickly and at such a reduced rate. The only contingency was that he be allowed to live rent-free in the in-law or *Dawdi* house.

She thought of the six fully furnished bedrooms upstairs devoid of occupants. *Why is an Amish man in his mid-thirties still single? Why would he sell his farmhouse to a stranger with no regard for the price? Didn't they normally marry at a ridiculously young age and have twenty kids by now?* Comprehension dawned on her, hitting her like a ton of bricks. Something must have happened. Something truly awful. She felt sick to her stomach when she guessed what it might have been.

She bowed her head, unable to look him in the eye. "Thank you, Mr. Miller...I appreciate that." Rachel stuck out her hand.

He looked down at it and stared at it as though it were a forbidden object. He hesitated for the longest time then finally accepted it. They briefly shook hands. Rachel peered past him and saw the plate of eggs growing cold on the table then she looked back up at him.

"When's the last time you had a home-cooked meal?" she wondered aloud, noticing his drawn face. She slapped her hand over her mouth and stared up at him apologetically. "I'm sorry. I'm always too blunt for my own good. Barry always did say that I 'shoot from the lip.'"

Samuel cleared his throat. "Not since I ate at my *schwester's* last week," he admitted, "but I get by."

Rachel wasn't fooled. She knew a normal man's appetite. With all the physical labor Samuel must put in daily, between the fields and the barn, he could probably put away three times what Barry used to eat and still not gain an ounce. She looked down and saw his hand still hanging at his side. She grasped it again and gently pulled him out the front door toward the main house.

"I'm making you a decent breakfast." she informed him. She could feel him trying to extricate his fingers from hers, but she wouldn't let go until she had him inside.

"Mrs. Winston – I'm fine. It's not necessary—"

"Look, Mr. Miller. You're the main caretaker of this property and I can't put you to work with a clear conscience if I know you're not eating properly. Call it the Jewish mother in me, but I feel the need..." she paused, waiting for him to ask the inevitable question.

His eyes widened and he unknowingly took her bait. "Need to what?"

Rachel felt a brief smile ghost her lips as she recited her mantra. "*The need to feed.* Not only do I come from a long line of Jewish women with a celebrated history of stuffing

copious amounts of food into people's stomachs, but I have also been formally educated in the culinary arts."

It was obvious he was having a difficult time keeping up with her. "I don't understand. How are you Jewish and also a believer in *Der Herr*?" he asked, staring at the cross around her neck, still refusing to sit down at the table.

"That's a long story for another time, but right now I'm more concerned with seeing you well fed," Rachel replied.

"She means she's a great cook," Karen yelled from the upper landing, where she had been eavesdropping. "She is, please come in for breakfast, Mr. Miller."

"Have you apologized to your *mudder* yet?"

"No…" Karen admitted, taking the stairs one at a time and looking suitably remorseful.

Samuel crossed his arms and waited.

Rachel couldn't get over it. She looked at Karen then back at Samuel. *Imagine that…a strange man taking her daughter to task and Karen actually remorseful! Will wonders never cease?*

Karen cleared her throat. "I'm sorry, Mom," she mumbled.

"*LOUDER.*" Samuel and Rachel responded at the same moment, using the same tone of voice. They stared at one another in shock for a moment then shared a brief smile.

"I'm sor-reeeeeee," Karen obliged in an annoyed tone of voice.

"With true remorse," Samuel added.

"Don't hold your breath," Rachel whispered under hers. She could count on one finger the number of times Karen had ever truly sounded remorseful while apologizing. Kids with reactive, nonattachment disorder couldn't express genuine remorse.

"I'm very, VERY sorry."

Samuel exchanged a look with Rachel, which clearly told her that he still wasn't satisfied. He addressed Karen. "You wish to help with the horses, *jah*?"

Karen nodded, her head lifting with sudden hope.

"You wish me to stay for breakfast, *jah*?"

Karen rose to her feet with an expectant smile on her face.

"*Gut*, you come with me then." Samuel said, walking out the door to the barn. Rachel watched her daughter follow the Amish man like a loyal puppy dog and shook her head. Why couldn't she have this kind of effect on Karen?

Once inside the barn, Samuel put a halter over the first horse, led it out of the stall, and put it into a small paddock. Next, he handed Karen a large flat shovel and pointed to the smelly manure and straw in the stall. "Scoop this all into a wheelbarrow then put in fresh straw from that bale," he pointed.

"Look, I said I was sorry," Karen complained.

"*Jah*, performing this task will put the truth into your words," Samuel nodded. "When you are finished with this stall you shall do the other. When you come into your *mudder's haus* with a truly contrite heart and give her a real apology, you shall have breakfast."

Karen stared at him in defiance. "Who do you think you are? You're not my father!"

Samuel stared at her; his blue eyes filled with pain. "I once was to many *kinner*," he replied and left her gaping after him in the barn.

Chapter Three

Eggs and Commiseration

In the few moments it had taken Samuel to return to the main house, Rachel had already turned the kitchen upside down. There was bacon frying in the skillet, a package of cinnamon rolls opened on the table, and she was in the midst of whipping up a large vegetable and cheese omelet with the fresh eggs her daughter had collected earlier that morning.

Rachel heard the screen door creak open and found herself suddenly alone with the tall Amish man. She gestured to the kitchen table. "It won't be but a minute, please make yourself comfortable." She paused a moment to stir the vegetables simmering in butter then stared back at him when he didn't move.

Samuel Miller stood still as a statue, staring at the kitchen table and the empty seats surrounding it as though he were seeing ghosts.

"It's just breakfast," Rachel assured him, wondering what Amish rule he was worried about breaking. Samuel's face relaxed. He walked to the kitchen table and sat down.

Rachel brought a large mug and a pot of coffee over to the table, trying to keep things light. "Coffee?"

Samuel jerked as if she had startled him then nodded, his eyes darting over to the door as if he wanted nothing more than to escape back to the solitude of the little in-law house.

Rachel poured the hot coffee. "How do you take it?"

"With cream," he replied.

She poured the coffee three-quarters of the way up and went to the refrigerator. She held up a vintage looking glass container. "They still put milk in these?"

"I do," he replied, as she poured some into his cup then froze, her arm still in mid-air.

"Where did this milk come from?"

"From the cows in the barn."

"It's not pasteurized?"

"*Nee.*"

"Doesn't it make you sick?"

His face took on an air of offense. "Mrs. Winston, I have been drinking milk from my own cows since I was a *boppli*, it has never made me sick."

She conceded the point, he looked healthy as a horse, albeit a bit thin.

"The eggs, Mrs. Winston," he reminded her.

"Oh my gosh!" Rachel put the cream down on the table and rushed to the stove, lifting the smoking cast iron pan off the heat. "That was close."

She cut the enormous omelet in half, deftly slid it onto two plates, and returned to the table. She poured herself a cup of coffee and sniffed briefly at the raw milk before pouring it into her cup with a shrug. Samuel waited while she took a seat across from him. She found it odd that he did not bow his head or close his eyes to pray. She had always thought the Amish were very devout people. Samuel just sat there staring at his plate, the muscles in his jaw working as though he were at war within himself.

Rachel cleared her throat. It had been a very long time since she had thanked God for anything, but figured it was time she started again. She bowed her head and closed her eyes.

"God, I know it's been a long time," she sighed deeply, feeling his eyes upon her. "Thank you for this food and my new life. Please give me the strength I need for this day and thank you for Mr. Miller's help." At this, she paused for a long moment, fighting to keep her voice steady. "Please tell Barry I love and miss him. Amen."

"Barry was your husband?" Samuel asked softly.

Rachel nodded, toying with her food. "I haven't really prayed in almost a year..." she admitted, tears plopping onto her eggs. "Guess that makes me a pretty lousy Christian..."

"You lost him?"

Rachel nodded, a lump forming in her throat. She peeked up through her lashes. Samuel was still staring at her, a stricken look on his face.

"How?" he asked then looked immediately sorry he had said it.

"Brain aneurysm," Rachel murmured, tears streaming down her cheeks again and plopping onto her eggs. "He had been having a lot of headaches in the last few months then woke up with double vision the morning he died. He was looking right at me when he suddenly lost his vision then dropped to the floor. He was gone before he hit the ground. He was only 35 and the love of my life."

Samuel stared at her, his eyes wide with horror.

She put down her fork and buried her face in her hands. "Why would God give me such a wonderful man then rip him away from me like that?" she wailed, her feelings of divine betrayal overwhelming her. "A disease, a car accident, those I could blame on just bad *luck,* but this felt like God literally snatched him away from me! He had a ticking time bomb waiting to go off in his head and none of us knew until it was too late. The doctors said that even had they known ahead of time, there was nothing they could have done – it was too deep inside his brain. Why would God do that to me? *Why?*" her voice ended on a plaintive wail.

"I have asked myself the same thing, Rachel," Samuel replied softly, staring intently into her eyes.

Rachel struggled to compose herself, not wanting to give in to the bitterness that threatened to overwhelm her. "I was a total recluse for six months – I couldn't function…I just didn't want to live anymore."

At that moment, Karen reappeared in the doorway. Her shoes were caked with manure, and she was sweating profusely.

Rachel bolted up from the table and pointed a finger at her. "Don't you dare come into the house with those filthy shoes!"

"I'm really sorry, mom," Karen said through the screen door sounding sincere for the first time that Rachel could remember. "Please forgive me for being so disrespectful." For Karen it was as contrite and remorseful as she was ever going to get.

Rachel was content. "Apology accepted, honey. Leave those filthy shoes outside on the service porch and get cleaned up while I make you some breakfast. Are you hungry now?"

"Starving!" Karen replied.

Rachel turned back to her plate and to Samuel, who was eating quietly across the table from her, his eyes fastened on his coffee cup.

"This is very *gut*," he remarked, spooning another mouthful of eggs into his mouth.

"Thank you, Barry always did complain I was too good of a cook."

Samuel looked up; his brows furrowed. "How can a *frau* be too good of a cook?" It was obvious the very idea seemed preposterous to him.

Rachel explained. "He put on a lot of weight after we got married, especially while I was going to the culinary institute and trying out recipes on him. He sat at a computer most of the time and didn't burn it off by doing hard physical labor like you."

Samuel nodded and took another bite of his omelet. "My *frau* was a good cook, too," he murmured automatically then fell silent.

Rachel sat back in her chair and stared at him, swallowing hard. "You lost your wife?"

Samuel nodded, refusing to meet her eyes. He laid down his fork and hid his trembling hands under the table.

"…and your family?" Rachel whispered in horror. "How… how many children did you have?"

Samuel abruptly stood up and pushed his plate away. "Five…they are all in heaven with *Der Herr* now." He turned away and marched out the door, leaving her alone at the kitchen table. Rachel felt awful for opening her big mouth and pouring salt in his wounds.

Karen returned moments later to find her mother sobbing with her head on her arms, oblivious to her ringing cell phone. "I'm so stupid, stupid, stupid!" Rachel groaned in-between sobs banging her forehead on the table.

"Mom – your cell phone," Karen exclaimed, snatching it off the kitchen table. Rachel looked up in surprise. She had been too lost in her misery to hear it. She wiped her eyes on her apron and grabbed the phone back from Karen. "Hello?"

"Mrs. Winston, this is the dispatcher from the moving company. Our truck can't find your location, they're lost. Can you give them directions, please?"

Rachel moaned. She didn't know the way to the farmhouse any better than they did. She looked out the screen door to see where Mr. Miller had gone. "Mr. Miller," she called, running outside to catch up with him.

He paused and turned around; his face drawn with pain. "*Jah?*"

Rachel held the cell phone out to him. "I hate to bother you, but could you please give the dispatcher directions on how to get here? The moving van is lost."

To her disbelief, Samuel shook his head. "*Nee*, it is not permitted for me to use that device," he said, indicating her cell phone.

Frustration and panic filled her heart. She was coming dangerously close to an emotional melt-down. "Can you at least tell me while I tell them?" she begged.

He sighed then took the cell phone from her outstretched hands and held it up to his ear.

"Where are you?"

He listened. "You're on the right road, you just need to go about another five miles and turn right onto Pequea Lane. What? *Jah*, I know there are two of them...but...*ach.* I'll come out to get you." He handed her back the phone and went to retrieve one of his horses. Ten minutes later he was cantering bareback down the road.

❦

The van arrived thirty minutes later, having been obliged to follow behind Samuel Miller on his horse. Rachel yelled up the stairs. "Karen, can you come down and help unload, please?"

No response.

"KAREN."

Silence.

Never known for her patience, Rachel stormed upstairs and shoved open the bedroom door, letting it hit the wall with a satisfying bang. Her daughter looked up from the bed in surprise, her iPhone music drowning out all other noise. Rachel yanked the earbuds out of her ears and pocketed the phone. "The van's here; I need your help...*now.*"

"Okaaaaaaaaaaaay," Karen griped and rolled her eyes. She slid off the bed and trudged downstairs. "You didn't have to yank it out of my ears."

39

Rachel said nothing, but in the back of her mind, she could hear Barry's voice chastising her to be more patient.

Oh, shut up, she retorted mentally.

Karen stomped down the stairs ahead of her and froze when she saw Mr. Miller staring up at her daughter with a disapproving frown. He had evidently heard it all.

Rachel almost walked into her. "Keep walking, Karen," she urged, giving her a little nudge.

"Yes, ma'am," Karen muttered meekly. Rachel saw Mr. Miller nod his head in approval at Karen's changed demeanor. He tipped his hat to Rachel then left the house to put his horse back into the paddock.

When Rachel had finished unpacking the last of their personal items a week later, she realized her friends had been right, work was her friend. She had been so busy unpacking and organizing that she hadn't thought about Barry or noticed the aching hole in her heart the entire time. She had almost...*almost* felt normal while her mind had been preoccupied with other things.

Rachel glanced out the screen door to see what Samuel was up to and spotted him in the large vegetable garden, toiling away under the hot sun. He had taken all his meals with them since they had moved in, and she was growing more comfortable and almost fond of him. Sweat plastered his blue shirt onto his broad back, his strong muscles evident through the material.

She brought herself up short. *Geez, Rachel...Barry's body ain't even cold yet!* The adage leapt into her mind. She felt instantly guilty and thoroughly ashamed. She snapped herself out of her trance and swung open the screen door with a bang to announce her presence. At that moment, Samuel looked up from his work and stared directly into her eyes with an amused look that clearly demonstrated that he'd caught her in the act of staring. Rachel paused, a hot blush sweeping up her neck and over her face. She wanted to turn tail, run and hide, but his blue eyes rooted her to the spot.

For a long moment, they just stared at one another then Rachel found her voice. "W-w-w-would you like some cold iced tea or lemonade while I make lunch? Or is it sweet tea that's the tradition around here?" she stammered, completely flustered.

Samuel tipped his hat. "*Jah,*" he nodded, still staring at her, a brief smile lifting a corner of his mouth. "Lemonade."

"Okay...it'll be ready in a jiffy." She backed up, almost knocking down the screen door in the process. She fumbled behind her, got it open, and backed inside, letting it slam. *What is wrong with me? I'm acting like a nervous schoolgirl with a crush.* Her cheeks felt hot.

She returned to the kitchen and pulled out a large bagful of lemons from the refrigerator, laying them on the counter. After scrounging around in the kitchen cabinets, she located her electric juicer. She set it on the counter holding the electrical cord in one hand while scanning the room. There wasn't a single electrical plug in the entire kitchen. *Rachel, you idiot – no electricity.*

After several more minutes of searching the kitchen cupboards, she found an old-fashioned glass juicer and began squeezing out the lemons by hand, filtering out the pulp and seeds with a small sieve until she had a pitcher one third full of the tart liquid and chunks of lemon peel.

By the time she had squeezed enough, her arms were aching. She added sugar, crushed mint from the garden, lemon slices, water, and ice cubes until she was satisfied that it was just the right balance of sweetness and tartness. She filled a large glass and stepped outside again, walking to the garden where he was still busy hoeing and weeding.

"Samuel?" She offered him the glass, wondering why she suddenly felt so nervous in his presence. Samuel straightened up, mopping his brow with a handkerchief. He smelled of sweat and earth.

41

"*Danki,*" he nodded, accepting the proffered drink. He set it to his lips and began chug-a-lugging it in one long draught. She watched, fascinated, as some ran down into his beard, trickled down his neck and disappeared beneath his blue shirt. He stopped once he had drained the glass. He handed her back the tumbler. "Very *gut*. There was a taste in there that was different?"

"Mint…I crushed some mint leaves in there to give it a little lift. Would you like some more?"

His blue eyes briefly met hers. "*Jah,*" he replied softly.

Rachel ran back into the house and soon returned with the pitcher. She refilled his glass and set the pitcher on a table on the porch. "I'll just leave it here for you in case you want more while I finish lunch," she said, smiling nervously. For a second, she felt the bizarre urge to curtsey, an urge she instantly squelched. She could feel his eyes on her as she turned and went into the house.

"What are you smiling about?" Karen wanted to know, descending the stairs.

The question brought Rachel up short. *She had been smiling?*

"Nothing," she murmured, returning to the kitchen. She pulled out some containers which held leftovers and vegetables. After several frustrating attempts, she got the wood stove good and hot, and soon she was frying slices of roast beef along with some onions and bell peppers in the skillet. She slathered pumpernickel bread with spicy mayonnaise before adding the roast beef, provolone cheese and topping it with lettuce and fresh basil before slicing it in two.

She found him on the service porch washing up. "Lunch is ready." On the counter next to him was a basket of freshly picked produce. She looked at the basket, her eyes lighting up at the cornucopia of beefsteak tomatoes, carrots, onions, peaches, and celery. "Are these for me?" she asked, looking up at him with a shy smile.

42

"*Jah*," Samuel nodded. For a moment, they locked eyes again, but he was the first to look away.

Rachel cleared her throat as she set down the basket and picked out the ripest tomato. "Nothing like home grown tomatoes," she mumbled, trying to fill the awkward silence between them. "Would you like some on your sandwich?"

Samuel nodded and removed his hat then turned to go to the kitchen table. Rachel stepped to his right to get out of his way just as he stepped to her left. They paused then Samuel went right as she went to his left. She giggled nervously at their awkward dance. Finally, she placed her hands on his tan forearms and moved him out of her way so she could go around him to get back to the kitchen. She didn't have to look up to confirm that his face was as red as hers, she could feel the heat of embarrassment radiating from him at arm's length.

"Well, that was interesting," remarked Karen as she sat down at the table.

"Shush," Rachel warned her. "Uh-uh – no you don't, go wash your hands first."

"They aren't dirty."

Rachel watched with amusement as Samuel turned his steely blue eyes on Karen and gave her a look that made her jump out of her chair. She marched to the sink, pumped the water out and lathered her hands with the bar of soap. Rachel smiled to herself while she sliced up the tomato. She liked how Samuel enforced respect for her. Barry had often let Karen slide with her disrespectful behavior, but Amish men apparently brooked no such nonsense. She lifted the bread on Samuel's sandwiches and slid a healthy slice of tomato into each, then added one to her own. For Karen, she just placed a slice onto the plate, knowing how picky she was.

Rachel sat down, wondering if Samuel would bow his head this time or just stare at the table like he had for all the previous meals. She bowed her head, giving a brief prayer of thanks, noticing again that he still refused to follow suit. She brought the sandwich to her mouth but waited so she could watch him bite into his first, curious to see his reaction. This time, she was determined to say and do nothing that would cause him to interrupt his meal with painful memories. Samuel rewarded her with a grunt of satisfaction.

"This is very *gut*," he nodded, taking another healthy bite.

"I used Chipotle mayonnaise and fresh basil," Rachel said, biting into her own sandwich. She ignored her daughter as Karen pulled out basil leaves, onions, and peppers one by one with a wrinkle of her nose and set them to one side. Samuel lifted an eyebrow at this but said nothing. They ate in companionable silence for a few moments. He polished off both sandwiches in record time and drank another large glass of lemonade.

"*Danki*, Mrs. Winston," he murmured, standing up.

"You're quite welcome, Mr. Miller," Rachel replied, pleased that he had eaten well. "I hope you will join us for dinner as well. I'm defrosting some meat I found in the freezer, and I'll be making a Hungarian Brisket."

"Are you sure it's no bother?" His words said one thing, but his eager eyes conveyed quite another message.

She wondered what he had been eating before she arrived. "*The way to a man's heart being through his stomach...*" sprang to mind. Rachel shook it off. "None whatsoever."

Samuel nodded and exited through the service porch, retrieving his straw hat and shoes first.

Karen turned to her, "Mooooooooom," she cooed, taking a petite bite of her sandwich. "Are you trying to win him over with your cooking?"

Rachel was aghast. "Of course not, it's just been a while since I had someone to cook for that actually *enjoys* eating." She watched in frustration as Karen pinched off all the crust from around her sandwich. "Also, Samuel looks like he hasn't had too many good meals lately...well, anyway, he does a lot of manual labor, and a man like that needs to eat well."

"Uh huh," Karen nodded, obviously unconvinced by her explanation. "So, it's Samuel now?"

"Look, just hurry up and finish eviscerating your lunch," Rachel snapped. She finished her sandwich and said nothing while Karen trashed half of hers. Rachel shook her head in disgust. "Waste, waste, waste," she grumbled.

For the next hour, Rachel immersed herself in cleaning up from lunch and prepping the roast to be slow cooked on the stove. She had forgotten how much she enjoyed cooking and how therapeutic she found it. In the last six months, she had done little more than open a box of cereal or fry eggs. Now, her culinary juices were flowing again. She sprinkled her special mixture of kosher salt, sugar, ground pepper, and shawarma spices over the roast, seared it in hot oil, then placed it underneath a layer of sautéed onions, diced tomatoes, and beef broth to slow cook in the Dutch Oven she'd found in one of the cabinets.

Chapter Four

Fools Rush In

With the setting sun behind him, Samuel entered the *dawdi haus* after a long day of physical labor and sagged onto his bed. He shouldn't be interacting so much with the *Englisch* widow and her *dochder*. If the Bishop or his *schwester*, Sarah, saw how it had been these past few weeks, they would surely have words for him. He had violated several ordinances of the *Ordnung* already. Even worse, what was *Der Herr* thinking of him? In his heart, he knew his soul was in mortal danger for all the rancorous feelings and thoughts he had been harboring since the accident. What did his outer behavior matter when his heart and soul were poisoned with rage? He ran his fingers through his sweat-soaked hair and continued staring at the floor, his rumbling stomach and conflicted mind locked in combat. His ingrained, life-long custom of remaining separate was telling him one thing, but his hunger pangs and the delicious aromas coming from the *Englisch* woman's kitchen daily were telling him another. His hunger always won the battle.

After the funeral for his family, Sarah and her husband John had urged him to move in with them, but he had declined. Sarah's in-laws were already occupying their *dawdi haus* and her seven children were crammed three to a room. There had really been no place to put him except on the living room couch. Friends and neighbors had generously donated food for a while, but that had run out after several months as people went on with their daily lives. Every other week, he would join Sarah's family for supper after the Meetings or the occasional Singings then return home with the leftovers, which lasted a day or so. The rest of the time he lived off the canned food his wife Rachel had put up previously. He couldn't very well drive his horses ten miles to Sarah's house and back every night just for a hot meal. As a result, he had lost a lot of weight in the ensuing months.

You need to remarry, Samuel, Sarah and John had constantly needled him. *You need a good frau to take care of you.* The very thought turned his stomach. He couldn't even consider it. His stomach cramped with hunger pains again. He couldn't have continued eating cheese, crackers and living off canned food while keeping up with the demands of the farm, which was why he had sold three quarters of it to his neighbor at the same time he had sold the house. No, selling the farm to a woman who could cook and clean was the best compromise. He would just have to be more careful.

The savory aroma of roasting meat and onions came wafting through the window, making his mouth water again, settling the matter for the night. He would eat Rachel Winston's cooking, and, in return, he would take care of the property that had once belonged to him.

Samuel filled a kettle with water and set it on the small propane stove to boil so he could take a sponge bath, then he filled the laundry basket with his dirty clothes for Mrs. Winston to wash.

***

"Karen, could you go next door and let Samuel know that dinner is ready?" Rachel called, spooning the oven-roasted potatoes, carrots, and onions onto a large platter with a slotted spoon.

Her daughter rolled her eyes, "I just sat down."

47

"Karen....go."

"Ugh." The teenager got up and stomped out the front door to the in-law house, knocking on the door twice.

After a few moments, the door opened.

Karen's eyes flew open. "Wow! You look...uh, nice."

Mr. Miller had changed from his sweat-soaked clothes to clean ones and a nice black hat. "Um, Mom wanted me to tell you that dinner's ready."

Samuel Miller colored slightly at the compliment but said nothing as he followed Karen into the main house. The fragrant smell of pot roast permeated the entire room. He entered and, for a moment, he couldn't move. He stared at Rachel Winston with a strange expression on his face.

Rachel glanced up and froze, wondering why Samuel was looking at her so funny. Then she remembered the black apron she was wearing. She looked down at herself and flushed red, feeling like a thoughtless moron. She had found the apron hanging on a peg in the kitchen in the broom closet and had donned it, forgetting that it had probably belonged to his late wife. The pained look on his face spoke volumes. She swiftly untied it, lifted it off, and set it on a wall peg feeling like an intruder who had gotten grimy fingerprints all over a museum relic.

She cleared her throat, hoping she hadn't offended him too much. "Please come in, Samuel," she encouraged. She felt odd constantly inviting him to sit down at his own table, but he never did so until she did. Samuel hung his hat on his wall peg next to the apron and took his seat, looking nervous for the first time. Rachel wondered why. She carried over the platter piled high with roasted meat, vegetables, and potatoes, followed by a bowl of sautéed snap peas, mushrooms, and a basket of dinner rolls. Samuel stared at the fare as though he had struck gold. Rachel bowed her head for prayer but peeked at him under her lashes. Again, he did not bow his head or close his eyes. His face was an unreadable mask.

"Lord, thank you for this day and all your blessings. Thank you for this food you have provided. Please tell our families that we love and miss them." Rachel murmured. She looked up to find Samuel staring at her, his eyes conveying his appreciation for her prayer.

"*Danki*," he said.

Her heart warmed at his response as she placed a large portion of sliced meat, potatoes, and vegetables on his plate and handed it back to him. "Please help yourself to the dinner rolls. I made them from scratch." She turned to Karen. "Hand me your plate, honey." She served Karen, watching out of the corner of her eye as Samuel took his first bite of the succulent roast, his face registering delight. Rachel preened inwardly, pleased that she had shown him that an "*Englisch*" woman could cook just as good as a "Plain" one. Samuel dug into his meal with gusto. For the next few moments, both she and Karen watched in rapt fascination as he devoured his meal. He made small grunts of pleasure as he chewed, and she knew she had scored major points with her cooking. Her baking skills, on the other hand, were another matter entirely. She had gotten a *Needs considerable improvement* in the baking category at the Culinary Institute. She held her breath as he picked up a dinner roll and attempted to pull it apart so he could spread butter on it. He dug his fingers in, but he may as well have been trying to split a rock bare-handed. She hadn't quite mastered the art of baking in a wood-fired stove. She had a difficult time regulating the temperature.

Rachel could feel the slow burn of embarrassment spread up her neck as he gave the dinner roll a closer look. Her humiliation was complete when he rapped it on the table once or twice with not so much as even a flake coming off. It appeared to be made from plaster.

He held it up. "This is an *Englisch* joke?"

Karen snorted.

Rachel stood up and held out her hand. "No, I just stink at baking."

Samuel laid the roll in her outstretched palm, a smile tugging at the corners of his mouth. "*Jah.*"

"I need help."

"*Jah,*" Samuel nodded in agreement while forking another bite of roast into his mouth.

"*Jah,*" Rachel mimicked in irritation, staring down at her plate. It was one thing for her cakes, pies, and breads to be the butt of jokes by family and friends back home. It was quite another when she was planning to be the innkeeper of an Amish-style inn. The Amish were renowned for their baking. Word would get out and it would kill off potential business.

Thankfully, Karen changed the subject. "Mom, my phone has been dead for a week, and I don't have any way to charge it. When are you going to get electricity in the house?"

Rachel flinched when Samuel's head popped up in surprise. "Well, I was actually going to discuss that with Mr. Miller," Rachel replied, shifting uneasily in her chair.

Samuel paused and wiped his mouth. "Why would you need to discuss it with me? This is your property now; you can do with it as you please."

Rachel took another bite, considering how best to broach the subject. Despite his polite words, she still wasn't sure he would be too keen on the idea of having his former home brought up to date by *Englisch* standards or of strangers traipsing in and out daily. "I'm glad you said that Samuel. I plan to turn the farmhouse into a working bed and breakfast inn, but a very different one, an Amish style inn. I want to offer it as a way for "*Englisch*" people, like me, to experience what it's like to live the way the Amish do. I want to have classes where people can learn how to make and mend clothes, quilt, tend a garden, work with livestock, bake bread, and put up canned food."

"Better take baking off the list," snorted Karen.

Rachel ignored her.

"Then why would you need to bring electricity into the house?" His eyes were curious, not accusatory.

Rachel rushed on. "I will need to have electricity to power the in-room heating and air-conditioning units to make the guests comfortable in the summer and winter months and to conduct business and run a website. My second concern is learning all these skills firsthand so I can teach them to the guests, right? Well, what I was wondering is…um… could you, I mean… would you be willing to make some introductions to your community on my behalf to see if they would be willing to teach me?"

"You wish to learn the Amish way of life in order to teach it to *Englisch* tourists?" he asked incredulously.

Rachel nodded. "Yes, people are fascinated with the Amish, so I think it could be a real draw where they could experience it for themselves firsthand. They could go home with crafts and skills they have learned. Perhaps we could have some women in your community offer special workshops or sell some of their crafts in our little gift shop?"

"I would have to speak to the Bishop and Deacon first," he replied after a long pause. "I'm not sure they would sanction such a request." He looked disturbed at the idea.

Rachel nodded; a bit deflated. "I understand. I would appreciate it if you could just ask them. It's worth a try anyway." She shrugged. "If not, I'll just have to learn the hard way." She picked up one of the untouched dinner rolls from the basket and banged it on the table to make her point. "I just hope I don't get sued by one of my guests for dental injuries."

"Yeah, my dad did all the baking in the house," Karen volunteered.

Rachel stared down at her plate, fighting the urge to cry at the mention of Barry. Just hearing Barry referred to in the "past tense" brought a painful lump to her throat. A long uncomfortable silence ensued.

"Mom, what about the other thing?" Karen asked.

Rachel stared at her, her mind a complete blank.

"*You know.*" Karen's gaze was intense.

"Oh, I'm sorry, Karen, I got side-tracked." She turned back to Samuel. "We're also going to have to bring indoor plumbing into the house. There's no way I'm going to attract guests when they find out there's only one outhouse. I need to get a septic tank installed and convert the largest upstairs bedroom into His and Hers separate bathrooms with private showers and one bathtub."

She watched Samuel stare at his plate. It was obvious that things were changing much too rapidly for his liking, but there wasn't any alternative. The property belonged to her now and she had to make it work.

"Like I said, Mrs. Winston, this is your home now, do with it as you will." Samuel stood up; his dinner only half eaten. "Please excuse me."

Rachel stood up immediately, hurt that he was going to leave before finishing the food she had prepared especially for him. She felt awful and guilty that she had pushed too much on him too soon and upset him. Without thinking, she grasped his forearm. "Please don't go, Samuel, I'm sorry for overwhelming you with all of this. I know...I can only imagine how painful this must be for you."

She saw him stare down at her hand clutching his arm and wondered what was going through his mind. She expected him to immediately withdraw his hand, but he didn't.

"I am not offended, Mrs. Winston. I just think it best if I return to the *dawdi haus* now." His voice had gone hoarse with pain.

Rachel released his arm, sat down with a thump, and nodded silently, trying to fend off her own tears until he had left the room. "Of course," she murmured. "At least take your supper with you. Karen will come by later to pick up your dish."

Samuel put his hat on then picked up his plate of food and his glass before heading for the front door. She sensed him hesitate and felt his eyes on her. She remained in her chair, still staring at the floor, unable to keep her tears from plopping onto the braided rug beneath her feet. Then she heard the screen door creak open and quietly shut behind him.

Samuel shut the door of the *dawdi haus* behind him and sat down heavily. He knew Rachel Winston had meant nothing by taking his hand in her own, but it was strictly *verboten*. Had any of his kin seen it, he would have received a stern reprimand. It had been months since he had felt the touch of a woman, the touch of his own Rachel's hand. Rachel Winston's hands were surprisingly soft. She did not have the rough, calloused hands of a "plain" woman who did most of her chores by hand and whose fingers were calloused from years of quilting. For a passing moment, her touch had both thrilled and horrified him.

He shouldn't be permitting her touch and eating her food as if she were his *frau*. He was letting his human needs get ahead of what he knew to be right. His abrupt departure had also brought her pain, and this greatly bothered him. He was completely torn. In his heart, he had already left his faith; how much worse could it be to take meals with her and her daughter? Was he right to leave without finishing the meal she had made for him, or should he have shown her kindness and stayed? He thought of Karen. He found it strange that the woman's daughter would not even go to her *mudder* to comfort her or stick up for her when she was obviously so distressed. That was what his daughter Sarah would have done had she seen her *mamm* hurting so. Instead, Karen had gone on eating as if she didn't care. With sudden clarity, he realized that Rachel Winston was every bit as alone in her grief as he was.

He made his decision. He stood and walked back out of the *dawdi haus* with his plate and glass and returned to the main house without knocking. Rachel looked up in surprise, her brown eyes still dripping tears. She stared back at him with a questioning look on her face. Samuel walked slowly back to the table and sat down, replacing his plate and glass back in their proper places.

He cleared his throat. "I will make inquiries at the next Meeting on your behalf," he finally said, picking up one of the dinner rolls and waving it at her. "You must learn how to make proper rolls, pies, and loaves of bread if your Inn is to succeed."

Rachel looked ready to weep with relief but instead she gave him a grateful smile. For a long moment, they looked into each other's eyes. "Thank you," she finally whispered, turning back to her dinner. "Karen – you're not eating."

Karen ignored her mother and leaned forward. "Mr. Miller, what kind of meeting were you talking about?"

"It is our worship service," he replied, spearing another hunk of the savory meat.

Rachel looked up with hope. "We need to find a church, which one do you attend?"

"Our services are not in a church," he replied. "Our community takes turns hosting a Meeting every other week at each other's homes and barns.

"Cool! Every *other* week, not every?" Karen grinned.

"Are non-Amish even allowed to attend?" Rachel asked.

"*Nee*, not unless they have committed to becoming Amish and are baptized," Samuel replied.

"Oh," Rachel replied, her shoulders obviously sagging. "We'll just have to find another place to worship, Karen, someplace that needs a soprano in the choir."

"You sing?" asked Samuel, looking at Karen with surprise.

Karen nodded, "Yes, I used to sing in the church band with my dad and in the choir. I was a first soprano." Her voice fell with sadness, but it was fleeting, and she quickly masked it. "I really miss...it."

"We have Singings for our youth," Samuel said. "Perhaps you would like to attend as guests?"

"How come it's okay for me to attend a youth singing, but my mom can't come to your church service?" Karen asked. "That doesn't seem very fair to me."

"The Singing is a social event," Samuel replied, strangely pleased with her reaction.

"Do I have to dress Amish to attend?" Karen asked.

"*Nee*, but you should dress *very* modestly," Samuel replied. "It would be best if you came in a long dress and not blue jeans."

"I don't have one. Maybe I could borrow one of the dresses I saw hanging in the closet upstairs?"

Samuel said nothing, but another flicker of pain crossed his face.

Karen thought about it for a moment longer while Rachel remained silent.

"Okay," she said noncommittally, then added. "Maybe I can finally make some new friends there." She stood up with her half-eaten plate of food and brought the dish to the sink. "I'm heading to bed, Mom."

Rachel looked at her watch. "So early?"

"Well, there's no television, no internet, and my phone's dead. I have no new books to read, and that stupid rooster wakes me up at 4:30 every morning. What else is there to do?"

"Help me clean-up from dinner, that's what." Rachel indicated the kitchen counters that were stacked high with pots, pans, and serving dishes.

"No thanks," Karen grimaced as if she had a choice in the matter.

Samuel caught her eye and gave her a very disapproving look. Karen stared back at him, her eyes widening, but it looked like this time she wasn't going to be persuaded by his displeasure. If she had been his own child, he would have put her over his knee and taken a strap to her backside. The *Englisch* had no idea how to discipline an errant child properly.

He stood up and rolled up the sleeves on his shirt, his eyes never leaving Karen's face. She stared back at him, completely unafraid, but obviously curious about what he was going to do. He walked over to the sink, put in the stopper, and pumped it full of water. "Mrs. Winston, *bitten*, put the kettle on to boil." He pointed to the large copper kettle his wife had always used to heat wash water. Rachel nodded and hefted it onto the stove. As Rachel stored the leftovers in plastic containers, Samuel scraped the remaining scraps into a slop bucket for the pigs, then stacked the plates, bowls, and glasses in the sink, never once taking his eyes off Karen's shocked face, his frown growing more and more pronounced with each passing moment. It was unheard of for an Amish man to do dishes. It was woman's work, but since the loss of his family and before Rachel Winston arrived, he had been doing a lot of chores that were normally left to women. Soon the kettle was singing. Using a pair of heavy-duty mitts, Rachel hefted it over to the sink and poured in the steaming hot water. The moment Samuel began to wash the plates, Karen leapt out of her seat, thoroughly embarrassed, and tried to take his place.

"Okay, okay! I'm sorry, I'll do it!" She exclaimed with a loud groan, attempting to shoulder him aside.

Samuel crossed his arms and planted his feet, his disapproval hanging like a thundercloud over them both. "You will do a *gut* job, *jah*?" He stared at her.

"*Jah*...I mean, yes." Karen refused to meet his eyes. She blushed crimson.

Satisfied, Samuel dried his hands, rolled down his sleeves, and retrieved his hat from the wall peg. He tipped it to Rachel in a show of respect. "*Danki* for a good supper." He returned to the *dawdi haus.*

Rachel joined her daughter at the sink with an armful of pots and pans and they washed, rinsed, and dried them together in silence for a few minutes.

Finally, Karen broke the silence. "Remember when I was little and you used to throw coins in the dishwater so I could find them when I washed, mom?"

Rachel smiled at the distant memory. "Yes, you liked that game so much you kept putting the clean dishes back into the sink so I would keep throwing more money in."

Karen smiled despite herself. "I did, didn't I?"

"I had to stop you after three times."

There was a long, drawn-out pause. "I'm sorry, mom."

"I forgive you, honey."

"Should I apologize to Samuel too?"

"I think he would be satisfied knowing you apologized to me, I'm the one you disrespected."

Samuel lingered in the dark just outside the kitchen window, listening as Rachel and her daughter playfully splashed water at each other. He remembered how his own Rachel would snuggle back in the circle of his arms as she did the dishes and how she used to lay her head on his chest and close her eyes as he nuzzled her neck. Even after five children, she would still giggle when he sandwiched her between himself and the sink so they could kiss. He hurried into the *dawdi haus* and shut the door before the sobs erupted from his throat. He sank to his knees and covered his face with his hands, his body wracked with pain. Until the arrival of this woman and her daughter, he had never allowed himself to grieve for his family. Not even on the day of their funerals. Now he sobbed with abandon, unable to hold back the waves of grief.

When he came to himself, he lay curled on his bed, the pillow soaked with his tears, yet inside he felt lighter than he had in almost a year. The tight band around his chest had dissolved…at least for the time being. He sat up and ran his fingers through his hair, not immediately noticing Rachel Winston standing just outside the door; her face looking worried.

"Are you okay?" she whispered; her eyes full of concern. "I couldn't help but overhear…"

Samuel bolted upright and nodded, not knowing what else to do.

Her brown eyes were filled with compassion and understanding. "Crying helps; I ought to know."

She backed away a step or two. "I just wanted to check on you," she murmured, now a little nervous. "Would you like some decaf coffee and pie?"

A teasing smile lifted one corner of Samuel's mouth. "Did you bake it?"

"No," Rachel grimaced, "its store bought, some kind of local berry I believe."

"*Jah,* give me a moment." Samuel nodded, standing up and straightening his clothes.

Rachel nodded. "No problem, take your time."

He mopped his face with a handkerchief and came to the screen door where she waited on the other side. She had witnessed him in one of his most raw and unguarded emotional moments and it made him feel naked…vulnerable… but he also felt great relief. It was the first time he had ever been able to unburden his heart since the loss of his family. He followed her back to the main house where hot coffee and pie awaited him.

Dessert was over, dishes washed and put away, and night had settled upon the farm. Rachel and Karen had procrastinated for as long as they dared, but the call of nature could wait no longer; it had become too urgent. They stared with dread at the little red structure, grimacing in expectation of the disgusting surprises that might await them.

Karen gave her a push. "You go first."

"Why? So, I can dislodge the creepy crawlies before you use it?"

"Exactly."

"*Chicken.*"

"Mom…just go."

Rachel tiptoed forward and put her hands on the knob, feeling like she was in a B-rated horror flick. You'd think she would have gotten used to it by now…On the other side, God only knew what awaited her…more cobwebs? The spiders were nothing if not persistent.

Karen growled. "Hurry up before I pee myself."

Rachel turned the knob and opened the door. The long squealing creak would have made Alfred Hitchcock proud. A small cloud of dark things silently flew out.

"OMG. OMG!" Karen ran for the front porch.

Rachel swatted at them and ducked. "What? It's just birds."

"Those are bats, Mom. BATS. Flying rodents."

Rachel's bladder was screaming in protest. "I don't care anymore." She went inside, arms flailing about with a feather duster and shut the door, dropping the flashlight on the floor. She was done in moments but decided to give her daughter a little surprise. She got her clothing back in order and then stood still, holding the flashlight under her face, and waited.

Karen's voice sounded strained, "Mom?"

Rachel unlocked the door but didn't step outside, breathing through her mouth so she wouldn't be assaulted by the smell.

"Mom?" Karen's voice was coming out as a nervous squeak. "MOM. Are you done or what?"

Rachel stood frozen, waiting for Karen to open the door. Another twenty seconds ticked by.

"I'M OPENING THE DOOR." Karen flung the door open then screamed at the sight of Rachel's face in a hideous grimace, lit from below. "Get out. O.M.G. You are so *mean*."

Rachel stumbled out, choking on her laughter.

Karen shoved past her, "just remember what payback is."

The door shut and Rachel waited outside, serenading Karen with eerie moans.

Karen began giggling despite herself. "Stop it, you're making this harder."

"Karen...*Kaaaareeeennnn*," Rachel wailed in her best ghostly voice. "The potty monster is rising to meet you."

"Mom. Really. STOP IT."

"He's coming closer...and closer."

Samuel listened and watched from the window of the *dawdi haus*, covering his mouth with his hand so they wouldn't hear him chuckling and figure out that he was eavesdropping. He observed the scene with amusement. Rachel Winston was nothing if not larger than life. If she was like this during profound grief, she truly must have been a remarkable woman when her husband was still alive.

Chapter Five

The Deal

Samuel was not looking forward to attending the next Meeting. As much as he missed his family, friends, and neighbors, he had become acutely aware that the parents of a spinster in his community were pressuring the bishop to marry him off to their daughter, Ruth. She had set her *kapp* for him from the day of Rachel's funeral. The last time he'd attended a Meeting several months ago, he'd overheard several of the womenfolk discussing the rumors when they thought he was out of earshot. He had avoided the worship services for a while as a result.

He entered the home of the Lapp's the following Sunday with hat in hand, steeling himself for the inevitable lecture.

"Samuel!" His *schwester's* voice carried from across the room. She rushed forward to greet him, her husband John, following in her wake. Several female heads turned in his direction. "*Ach*, Samuel, you look better, not so thin. Have you learned to cook?" She meant it as a joke.

Samuel stepped back and greeted his brother-in-law with a nod. They clasped hands. "It's *gut* to see you, Samuel," John said.

"*Es ist gut zu sehen*, John."

That was all they had time for as the service was about to begin. Samuel followed them out to the barn and found a place on a bench amongst the other men. Benches had been set up on either side, one side for the women, the other for the men. The barn smelled of fresh hay, alfalfa, and of course, livestock. After an hour of singing hymns, Bishop Fisher spoke from the book of 1st Corinthians. Samuel sat with his eyes cast downward, grateful that John, who sat next to him, never commented on the fact that he refused to sing, mouthing the words in silence instead.

Samuel barely heard the bishop. He kept imagining he could see the faces of his *frau* and *kinner* among the womenfolk across the room and the thought brought him intense pain. He was still angry with *Der Herr* and refused to participate. As soon as the service ended at 1:00 p.m., Sarah pushed him to the head of the buffet line. Spread before him was a veritable Amish feast. Each table held a variety of meat, vegetable, noodle or potato dishes, and finally the dessert table.

She shoved two plates into his hands and began to fill them, not bothering to ask what he wanted. "Whatever is left over I want you to take home."

"That won't be necessary," Samuel said, ignoring the stares of Ruth Bieler, the afore-mentioned spinster, and her parents. "I have been eating very well since the new owner moved in."

Sarah grimaced at him, the topic of the family farmhouse sale a sore subject. "You should never have sold the farmhouse and most of your acreage, Samuel."

Samuel sighed. They'd had this same argument several times before. "What's done is done."

"But to sell it to an *Englisch* woman!"

"An *Englisch* woman who has asked to learn our ways," Samuel replied, surprised at himself. He had not intended to broach the subject this quickly and wondered at his automatic defense of Rachel Winston.

Sarah stared at him; a large slice of ham loaf poised just above his plate. "What do you mean?"

"She intends to open an inn that will introduce visitors to the lifestyle of our people. She wants to learn how to cook

Amish dishes, quilt, sew, and to can food so she can share this knowledge with her guests."

Sarah let the ham loaf plop onto his plate. She put her hands on her ample hips. "She's *narrish*. Of course, what else could you expect from someone who comes from Southern California?"

Samuel glowered at her. "She's not *narrish*, Sarah, she's trying to make a life for herself and her *dochder*."

"I don't like the fact that you've turned your home into a place of commerce. Or that you're living in such proximity to an unmarried *Englisch* woman and taking up for her. What's gotten into you, Samuel?"

Samuel fought to keep his voice even. "*Der Herr* left me no other choice, Sarah. I did the best I could under the circumstances and Mrs. Winston is a widow, not an unmarried woman."

His sister paused; a large spoonful of potato salad now poised above his plate. "You like her!" It came out like an accusation.

"I like her cooking," Samuel clarified. He juggled both plates in one hand then turned away. "It's *gut* to have three home-cooked meals on a daily basis. *Der Herr* has provided for me."

"You know that you are always welcome to come and eat with us whenever you want and take home all the leftovers," Sarah pouted.

Samuel nodded. "I know that, but I can't travel twenty miles round trip every night just to have supper. It's inconvenient and tiring when I get up early the next morning to take care of the livestock and work the fields."

"You could remarry; the bishop says Ruth Bieler is—"

Samuel snorted. "Sarah Hochstetler, I know very well what you are talking about, and it is too soon. Remarrying is out of the question. This Mrs. Winston is a very *gut* cook and she doesn't mind making a little extra."

"Better even than Rachel?" Sarah blinked at him, her forehead creasing with pain.

"Different, not better and, as it so happens, her name is Rachel, too."

Sarah's eyes grew round. "You never told me that."

"I just have." Samuel walked outside with his sister behind him to the benches and tables that had been set up under the trees for the men. "Would it be alright with you if I brought her to your next quilting bee and the singing? She is anxious to start learning and make some friends."

Sarah crossed her arms, clearly conflicted. "I don't know Samuel; have you spoken to Bishop Fisher about this yet?"

"He's next on my list, but I wanted to ask you first."

Sarah stared down at her apron while Samuel waited. His *schwester* had a heart of gold. Instinctively, he knew she would agree to help. She was always the first to offer a helping hand whenever anyone was in need. It just remained to be seen if that generosity would extend to Rachel Winston.

"*Jah*, but only on a trial basis, Samuel, and only if the Bishop and Deacon Lapp give their blessings first."

Samuel kissed her forehead, the first public display of affection he had shown her in years. "I will go ask now." He left his full plates on the table and approached Bishop Fisher, who was just exiting the kitchen with his own plates of food.

"Samuel Miller, it is very *gut* to see you again." said the kindly man with the silver beard and spectacles. "Let's sit down, I want to hear how you are doing."

His attendance at the biweekly Meetings had been sporadic at best. Samuel shrugged, "I am breathing and working, I'm surviving."

He helped the old gentleman to a seat next to him. The bishop had known him all his life and been the one to marry him and Rachel almost fifteen years ago. He had also been the one to bury his family. Samuel had no doubt that Bishop Fisher had personally taken the untimely death of his entire family very hard. He had been broken-hearted to preside over all six of their funerals at once. The tragedy had been a terrible blow to their entire community and front-page news in *The Budget.*

The bishop laid a gentle hand on his shoulder. "You are much changed, Samuel." He said quietly, studying his face with genuine concern. "Is there anything I can do to help you?"

He sensed that the bishop was about to broach the subject of his remarriage to Ruth Bieler, and he intended to steer the discussion into a completely different direction. He wasn't sure why it meant so much to him that Rachel Winston be received into his community, but somehow it did. Perhaps it was her silent compassion, their shared grief, or perhaps it was because he knew if she couldn't make a successful go of the inn, they would soon all be out of a home, and he'd be bunking on Sarah's couch.

"I am eating better, Bishop Fisher, now that the house is occupied by a woman who cooks."

"*Ach,* is that so? Who is this, this *Englisch* woman? What do you know of her?" The topic of his remarriage had been avoided.

"She is a recent widow, the mother of a daughter, a *gut* cook, and a devout Christian," Samuel replied truthfully. "She has asked to learn our ways."

The bishop looked mildly shocked. "Why? Does she intend to be baptized into our community?"

"*Nee* – she wants to make the house into an Amish inn where the guests will experience living as plain people. She believes it will be a great draw and provide her with much needed income."

"Well, that's the first time I've ever heard of such a thing." Bishop Fisher murmured thoughtfully, munching on a leg of fried chicken. "We've had some *Englisch* converts into the community recently, but never just to run a business."

"It could help if it attracted more tourists." Samuel suggested.

"It is an interesting prospect, Samuel, and one worth discussing with Deacon Lapp. With the economy the way it is, we have all been seriously impacted."

"I will leave it in your hands then and the outcome to *Der Herr*." It left a bad taste in his mouth to utter God's name, but it would have raised suspicions had he not.

"There is another matter I wish to discuss with you, Samuel, but perhaps now is not the time? I will pay you a visit soon." The bishop took up his plate and left him with a friendly wink.

Samuel watched the bishop depart and the chair was soon filled by his *bruder-in-law*, John, followed by some of his oldest friends crowding in around them, all anxious to discuss the news of his new occupant. *They're worse gossips than the womenfolk*, he thought glumly.

"We hear you have an *Englisch* woman living in the house," Mark Zimmer announced. Mark and he had been friends since they attended school together.

"It's not my home anymore, I'm just the caretaker," Samuel reminded him softly.

"Shame you had to do that," Mark continued with a shake of his head. "*Der Herr* gives and takes away, blessed be His name."

The common saying made Samuel want to grind his teeth, but he nodded and said nothing. He was tempted to get up and leave the table. He wondered angrily if Mark Zimmer would have said the same thing so cavalierly had it been his own family that had been taken away from him! He could feel the heat of anger flushing his face. He sensed John's watchful eyes on him, no doubt wondering if he was going to explode and say something that would land him in hot water. Samuel fisted his hands under the table out of eyesight and shut his eyes, struggling with his emotions. The voices of the other men talked around him, but he was oblivious to their conservation. Why did *Der Herr* give me five wonderful *kinner* only to snatch them away along with my wife? How much pain am I to endure and expect to remain faithful? He felt his arm nudged.

"The bishop is returning with Ruth Bieler. I think her parents want you to give her a ride home in your buggy, Samuel," John whispered in his ear.

Samuel looked up just in time to catch the pale-faced, green-eyed spinster coming his way with Bishop Fisher, a look of hopeful anticipation on her wan face.

"Not today," he replied, taking his plates with him before they could corner him. "Sarah invited me to come over to your farm for supper later and I've agreed."

"*Gut, gut,* the *kinner* will be happy to have their *onkel* join us after such a long absence," John called after him as he fled. Out of everyone, John seemed to understand his pain the best, perhaps because he had lost a twin brother to a farming accident while still very young. Samuel managed to evade the Bishop and Ruth by making himself scarce for the remainder of lunch, hiding in the barn with the boys and the livestock. Most Amish widowers were usually remarried within a year, but he did not intend to let them corral him into another marriage so soon. From his vantage point in the barn, he saw Bishop Fisher speaking with Ruth Bieler's parents, shaking his head in apology. They nodded in meek submission and left with their disappointed *dochder*. Shortly thereafter, he saw Bishop Fisher with Deacon Lapp and another elder by themselves, obviously looking for him. Relieved to have dodged a bullet, Samuel exited the barn and approached them, hoping they had reached a positive decision about Rachel Winston. He stood in plain sight, suddenly nervous on her behalf.

"*Ach*, Samuel, there you are." They waved him over. "We have briefly discussed the matter. We are willing to let this *Englisch* woman learn our ways providing she brings no undue attention or embarrassment to the community and there must be no inappropriate interaction with you and her on a personal level."

"*Jah*," Samuel agreed, feeling both relieved at their decision and resentful at the insinuation. "My *schwester* has already agreed to help Mrs. Winston in her efforts as long as it was sanctioned by you."

Deacon Lapp leaned forward with a teasing smile on his face. "Perhaps if you were to give Ruth Bieler some of your attention, none of this would be necessary."

Samuel didn't respond. Ruth had competed for his attention ever since they were young, before he and Rachel were married, but something about her had always bothered him.

"What's done, is done, Deacon Lapp. I have done the best I could with what *Der Herr* has dealt me," Samuel muttered. It was hard to keep the edge of bitterness out of his voice.

"Of course, you have, Samuel. We do not begrudge you a proper mourning period, but life does go on."

This comment turned his stomach sour. Bile rose in his gorge. He tipped his hat in abrupt farewell, "and so must I. Blessings be upon you all." He hurried away, nauseous.

"Upon you as well, Samuel," the elders called after him.

John found him behind the barn and waited in silence while Samuel retched up his meal.

"I'm sorry, John," he said, mopping his face when he could finally speak.

John offered him a dipper of water from the trough pump to rinse his mouth. "I don't know about all this business with the English woman, Samuel," his *bruder-in-law* said as they slowly walked back to the house to find Sarah and the children. "I still think you could have kept the farm, at least long enough to…"

"To what? Marry another woman? Have more children just so *Der Herr* can take them all away again?" Samuel spat, struggling to keep his voice level. "I'm in my thirties, John.

I'm too old to start over." Samuel froze mid-step, visibly trembling with the effort to remain calm. "I lost everything, John...*everything*. What *gut* is a home and farm to me now? If I could, I would have moved away to another community just so I wouldn't have to endure the pain of their memories every waking moment. I'm...I'm beginning to forget their faces." He choked, ready to retch again.

John placed his hands on Samuel's shoulders, his eyes filled with compassion for him. "I am truly sorry, Samuel. Do not let their loss weaken your faith; that would indeed be an even greater tragedy."

Samuel stared back at him, his blue eyes turning icy cold, his lips pressed together in a tense line. There was no point telling John it had already happened. "I'll keep that in mind." He wanted to leave and return home to the *dawdi haus* right now. If only he hadn't already promised them that he would come to their home after church. His stomach was still churning. He was ready to get into his buggy and drive home.

John frowned, "Forgive me," he murmured. "I did not intend to make light of your pain."

"I forgive you," Samuel replied, wishing he could escape. They left the barn and went to the main house where they found Sarah and the other women hard at work cleaning and packing up the left-over food.

Samuel saw Sarah look at her husband then back at him. She frowned. "*Was ist los?*"

"I'm afraid I spoke out of turn," John said, glancing apologetically at Samuel. "Are we almost ready? Should I gather the *kinner?*"

"*Jah*, I'm just about done here." She shoved a heavy paper grocery bag into Samuel's arms. "That should last you for a few days. Put them in your buggy. Can Mary and Martha ride with you so it's not so crowded in ours?"

Samuel nodded, accepting the bag of leftovers. He stood there, wishing he could disappear.

Sarah bustled past him and cupped her hand around her mouth, "Mary, Martha, Mirriam, Willis, John and Isaac Hochstetler... *komm* here." She waited with hands on hips as the girls got off the grass and the boys exited from the barn.

"*Jah, Mamm?*"

"Martha and Mary, you will be going in your *onkel's* buggy. Have you got everything? Do you have the quilt squares you've been working on?"

The girls patted their sewing basket. "In here, *Mamm*, we're almost done with them."

"*Gut*. Hurry along now; the rest of you will ride with your *daed* and me."

"Can't I ride with *Onkel* Samuel?" Isaac, the seven-year-old asked, his brown eyes pleading.

"*Jah*, there's still room enough," Samuel nodded, offering the boy, who was his favorite, a ghost of a smile. "I'll let you hold the reins if you like."

"Yippee," crowed Isaac, and then stuck his tongue out at his older brothers. He grabbed Samuel's free hand and hauled him forward until they reached the buggy.

"In you go," Samuel said, his eager nephew bringing a smile to his face. Mary and Martha climbed in after him and sat in the back, chattering between themselves. He put the reins into Isaac's little hands and paused. Memories of his eight-year-old son John came flooding back: John standing between his legs, in the circle of his arms, learning how to drive Dodger with a look of rapt joy on his face. Both his son and Isaac were so short, they could stand in the buggy without their hats hitting the roof. Samuel placed Isaac between his long legs and encircled his waist so they could hold the reins together. Samuel guided him in backing up Dodger and together they turned him out into the lane. The wind was warm and humid, a typical summer day in Lancaster County. They could smell the freshly culled hay and alfalfa as they passed one farm after another.

"*Onkel* Samuel, why do you look so sad?" Isaac asked, turning his head for a moment so he could look up into his face.

"Isaac, shush," Mary scolded him from the back of the buggy.

"It's alright, Mary, it's an innocent enough question," Samuel replied. He drew Isaac close against him, wrapping his arms about his torso just as he used to do with John. Oh, how he missed embracing his son.

"I've just been very sad since I lost your aunt and cousins," Samuel murmured, struggling to keep his voice even. The steady clip-clop of Dodger's shoes on the pavement was a comforting backdrop to their conversation.

Isaac turned all the way around, his brown eyes growing large and solemn. "I'm sorry you lost them, *Onkel* Samuel," he whispered. He relinquished his hold on the reins, placing them into his uncle's hands. Then to Samuel's utter surprise, Isaac encircled his waist and embraced him. The kind gesture brought tears instantly to his eyes. It had been such a long time since he had held his own children in his arms.

Isaac remained standing, one arm draped over his *onkel's* neck, for the remainder of the ride to the Hochstetler farm, little caring whether he drove or not. They turned into his sister's gravel driveway and the moment Dodger stopped, Isaac hopped off his lap and bounded out of the buggy, racing his sisters into the house. Samuel was unhitching Dodger when Sarah and John's buggy arrived moments later. He took off the traces, halter, and bridle, and led Dodger into the paddock so the horse could roam freely. He pumped fresh water into the trough and set out fresh hay, which the horse dug into immediately. He waited for Sarah by the front porch while John unhooked his own horse and led it into the same paddock. Sarah climbed the steps, linked her arm through his, and together they walked into the house.

"So, tell me more about this *Englisch* woman," she said.

Samuel looked at the chair she pointed to but remained standing, reluctant to submit to his *schwester's* interrogation.

At that moment, Isaac came to his rescue again. He bounded into the kitchen and grasped hold of Samuel's hand.

"*Onkel* Samuel", he said breathlessly. "*Kommen* see the new colt."

"Not now, Isaac. I want to speak with your *onkel*," Sarah protested with a scowl in Samuel's direction.

Samuel allowed Isaac to pull him out the front door. "We can talk later, Sarah, it will keep."

"*Ach*, all right, but don't think for a moment I will forget about it," she called after him.

Samuel joined John and his nephews in the barn. They gathered around the stable where the mare and her young colt were housed.

Isaac grabbed his hand again. "Isn't he *gutguckich*?"

"*Jah*, very handsome," Samuel agreed. "He has a fine glossy coat and well-formed head." He lifted Isaac so the lad could see over the railing. The mare nickered a warning then settled down when she saw there would be no further intrusion into her domain. Samuel took an apple he had pilfered from the fruit bowl out of his pocket and using his pocket knife, cut it into slices. "Have you given him a name yet?"

"We were thinking of Yonnie," Isaac replied, "after my cousin."

A lump formed in Samuel's throat when the image of his young son's face sprang to mind. Yonnie had been John's nickname. "I think that is a very *gut* name, Isaac," he replied huskily. He placed a couple of apple slices into Isaac's hand. "Give Yonnie his treat," he encouraged.

At that moment, he caught John giving him an understanding nod. Samuel nodded in return. Their thoughtful gesture of the horse's name had touched his heart.

The little brown colt stepped forward timidly. He was plainly nervous, but the sweet smell of sliced apple was no match for his shyness. He stopped several paces away and stretched his neck out as far as it would go, his lips extending toward the fruit. Isaac giggled and brought his hand back inch by inch until the colt was within petting distance. Yonnie dipped his soft muzzle into Isaac's hand and picked up both slices at once while several sets of young Amish hands lifted to pet him. Samuel doled out the remaining slices of apple to the rest of his nephews who fed the little horse under the watchful eyes of his dam.

They returned to the house a while later. The smell of freshly baked rolls and shoofly pie filled the air. The younger ones were busy setting the table and making gallons of lemonade and sweet tea.

John's elderly parents sat in the main room. Mark Hochstetler was in easy chair reading The Budget and John's *mamm*, Ruth, was darning socks, reading glasses perched precariously on the end of her nose. They both set down their things and rose to greet him.

Ruth held out her hands. Her hair was snowy white beneath her *kapp*, and she was bowed with age, but her grip was still strong. She looked carefully at him, her shrewd eyes looking him over. "How are you, Samuel?"

"As well as can be expected," he replied politely.

She smiled at him. "I hear that Bishop Fischer and the Bieler's have been discussing future arrangements?"

"I wouldn't know," he replied quickly, hoping they would drop the subject. Sarah bustled forward and put a glass of lemonade in his hand. "Go out on the porch and relax for a while."

Relieved that she had indeed apparently forgotten to talk to him in the hustle of preparing supper, Samuel followed John out to the front porch and sat down on a rocking chair. For the next few hours, they spoke intermittently on topics that weren't close to his heart: fishing, the coming harvest, and the doings of John's children.

When the sun had set, Sarah called them in to supper. Samuel's empty stomach rumbled hungrily at the smell of fried chicken, mashed potatoes, and tomato relish. He had lost most of what he had eaten for lunch earlier behind the barn and now he was famished.

The children waited anxiously as their elders took their seats, and then they took their places beside them and bowed their heads to give thanks.

Samuel glanced around the table from beneath his lashes, his heart aching. It was mealtimes more than any other that tore most at his heart. *It was not so long ago that my own family was gathered around my table. Those days are gone forever.*

Chapter Six

Buddy

Rachel stared glumly out the kitchen window, waiting for any sign that Samuel was returning home. It was early evening but still very warm. She had been fidgety all day with not much to do but read and *putz* around the kitchen. Karen had abandoned her and holed up in her room, doing *heaven-only-knew-what.* Rachel cleaned up from their meager dinner, feeling very lonely and sorry for herself. She hadn't realized how cut off she was from the world until this moment. There was no internet, cell phone or television. She didn't know a soul in the community other than Samuel. She couldn't call any of her friends or family and her conversations with God felt like a one-way exercise in futility.

She could hear Karen up in her room, grumbling loudly about having to take a tepid sponge bath again instead of the hot showers she was accustomed to. Karen was making sure she knew exactly how she felt about it by slamming every dresser drawer in the room at least twice.

Nagging fears plagued Rachel's mind. *What if the Amish community doesn't want to help me? What if I can't make a success of the inn?* She was having serious doubts about their move to Lancaster, but it was too late to change any of that now. Rachel pushed open the screen door and went out onto the porch to wait for Samuel. She had always wanted a house with a wrap-around porch and this one was everything she could have dreamed of. It was broad, with fresh-

ly painted light blue wainscoting on the ceiling to compliment the glossy white tongue and groove floorboards and
a nice, waist-high railing. There were several rocking chairs
and at the corner, a lovely porch swing which looked out
over the flower garden and the back looked over the quaint
red barn. Wrap-around porches were unheard of in Southern California except in very rural areas, custom homes, or
communities of historical cottages and bungalows. She had
often fantasized about how she would serve hearty lunches
or high tea on beautiful tables set with China and crisp lin-
en when the inn was fully functioning. Hopefully, the porch
would soon be filled with guests enjoying the bucolic scenery, playing croquet, reading, or playing checkers.

Twilight deepened and several little lights began to wink
and rise just above the lush grass of the yard. She gasped
and bent over the railing to investigate. More lights began
to appear, rising and falling beneath the trees and shrubs as
if fairies had come out to dance.

Fireflies. At least that had been Barry's word for them. A
pang of sorrow knifed through her heart. She clutched her
aching chest. *If only you were here to share this magical moment
with me! If only you could see this.* She stood for quite some
time, watching the silent light show until twilight faded into
darkness and the lights rose higher then finally winked out
one by one, leaving her alone in the dark, her heart sorrow-
ing.

"That's all, folks!" Porky Pig's voice stuttered in her head.
Looney Toons had been Barry's favorite cartoons.

Depression settled upon her like a heavy blanket. Pain
and loneliness overwhelmed her. She was sorely tempted
to take one of the powerful sedatives her doctor had prescribed and sleep the rest of the night away. She still had
quite a bottle of them left over. She glanced over at the little red outhouse and grimaced. She was eventually going
to wind up with a bladder infection if she kept holding it
all the time. She hated using the thing. The first order of

business was to get indoor plumbing as soon as possible, followed by electricity and Wi-Fi so she could build a website, book guests, and charge her cell phone. For that, she would need to hire tradesmen. Samuel would have to drive her around in his buggy until her car arrived. It should have been delivered over a week ago, but she had no means of contacting the transport company to find out what was taking so long. The last time she had been able to contact them, she had provided the phone number of the closest phone shanty.

"Better not put it off any longer," she muttered. She opened the outhouse door and automatically ducked. This time nothing flew out. She fished out the clothespin that she kept in her back jeans pocket, clamped her nostrils shut and swept the feather duster around the interior before stepping in to complete her business. With her basic bodily functions out of the way for the next few hours, Rachel wandered into the barn with a kerosene lantern to take a look around.

The moment she entered startled doves flew out the barn door. The last time she had been in anything resembling a barn was in second grade, on a school trip to the local dairy. She stepped into the enormous structure and looked around, amazed at the height. The hayloft was at least twenty feet off the floor and stacked high. The glow of the lantern revealed a large spring wagon and numerous farm implements. She walked further in and found her way back to the stalls. Dodger was gone, but the other horse, Molly, was in the stable munching from her feedbag. Further in, she discovered two cows, who lifted their heads and mooed in greeting. Unlike her memories of the dairy, these were well groomed and clean, as were their stalls. She reached over the railing to pet their heads, enchanted by their large violet eyes. She went on to the next stall where she found some goats and sheep that had bedded down for the evening. They rose to their hooves and bleated, crowding the rail in the hopes of getting a handout.

"Just like having my own petting zoo," Rachel murmured to herself with a smile, reaching in to stroke their heads. One of the goats tipped its head up and nibbled on her shirtsleeve.

"Oh no you don't." She pulled her arm away, extricating the cloth with some difficulty. The goat bleated at her in protest. She made her way around a corner where the smell of the pigpen assaulted her nose. A trough was there, filled with the day's leavings. Flies buzzed everywhere.

She wrinkled her nose, "*Blech.*" She'd seen enough. Rachel quickly made her way back to the barn entrance and froze. A small brown mutt with a fringed, two-toned fantail and Dachshund markings sat there, staring at her. His little triangle ears perked up the instant he saw her, and his tail began thumping the ground. He lowered his head but did not growl.

"Oh my gosh, are you ever cute," Rachel breathed. Always a dog lover, she squatted on her haunches, setting the lantern down a safe distance away and held her hand out for him to sniff, coaxing him with a soft voice. "It's okay...I won't hurt you, come here." The dog took a couple of steps forward, then paused, his little foxlike face wary. She made some kissy sounds and then sat Indian style on the floor. "C'mon, little buddy, I won't hurt you." The dog took a few more timid steps then stopped. *Guess I'll have to be the submissive one.* Determined to win the dog over, she lay on her back flat on the floor, stuck her legs and arms in the air as if she was playing "dead," and whined softly. This perked the dog's head and tail up. He cocked his head. "Come here; it's okay," she coaxed softly. This time, clearly intrigued, the dog came up to her and did something she didn't expect. He laid down next to her and rolled over onto his back, mimicking her while staring deeply into her eyes. She rolled over onto her side and rubbed his belly gently, causing the dog to emit a long, drawn out, contented sigh.

At that precise moment, she became aware that someone was watching her. She looked up and found Samuel standing in the barn doorway, holding onto Dodger's reins with an odd look on his face, the buggy just outside. She'd been so intent on winning the little dog over, she hadn't heard him drive up. Not wanting to frighten the dog, she slowly rolled up to a sitting position and gathered him into her arms. He lifted his little face to hers and started licking her neck.

"I suppose you're wondering what I'm doing on the barn floor playing dead with this dog," she said, her face burning with embarrassment. Samuel just stared at her, the look on his face one of shock. "What's his name?" she asked.

"Buddy."

"Buddy!?" Rachel exclaimed; her eyes wide. "That was the name of *our* last dog!"

Samuel looked at her, shocked at yet another coincidence. Rachel stared down into the dog's little face, utterly besotted, and let him lick her some more. "Buddy, it's so nice to meet you." She giggled at the way his cold nose tickled. "My daughter will go ape when she gets a look at you." She got to her feet, hefting the dog into her arms like a baby. Rachel stood before Samuel, wondering why he was looking at her so funny. "Is anything wrong?" she asked.

Samuel slowly shook his head in disbelief, his eyes riveted upon the little dog in her arms.

"I made some shoofly pie for dessert. Do you want to come in and tell me what you think? My daughter refuses to try it."

Samuel nodded absently, still staring at the dog as if it was a ghost.

"Good, I'll put some coffee on to brew and we can talk about some things I need your help with." Rachel turned and carried the dog across the yard then up the porch steps and into the house. She set him down on the kitchen floor and gave him a bowl of fresh water and some table scraps. Buddy sat down, curled his fan tail about him like a cat and began to eat while Samuel continued to stare at him. Rachel went to the cupboard, pulled out a tin of coffee, and measured it into the strainer. Then she went to the sink, pumped water into the pot, and set it on the stove to percolate. When she came back to the table, Samuel was still staring at the dog, who was now licking his chops in contentment.

Rachel set the pie on the table along with two plates, forks, coffee cups, and cream. "Is something wrong? You keep staring at the dog like he's a ghost." She sliced off a wedge for Samuel and set it on a plate before him.

Samuel stared at the dog who was returning his gaze. "I haven't seen Buddy since the day my family…" he paused and swallowed hard, his Adam's apple bobbing beneath his beard. "I thought he had run off. I've been putting food and water out for him every day in the barn, but I didn't know if it was other animals eating it or him. Buddy was my *frau's* dog. He was her shadow…followed her everywhere she went."

"Oh." She didn't know what to say to this. She nudged the pie closer. "Are you going to try it?"

Samuel tore his eyes from the dog and looked down at the pie and grimaced. She had again overcooked it. It was charred around the edges. She could tell he was just being polite when he cut a piece with his fork and put it into his mouth. The moment he tasted it, he made a face and almost gagged.

"Go ahead, be honest. It's awful, isn't it? I told you I stink at baking." Rachel took a bite herself and immediately spat it out onto the dish. "Blech."

Samuel nodded in agreement but manfully swallowed it. "*Jah*…blech."

They shared a smile.

"What am I going to do with all this pie now?" moaned Rachel.

"The hogs will take care of it," Samuel said, pushing his uneaten pie toward her. "If they turn their snouts up at it, you'll know you're in big trouble."

"Funny." Rachel scraped the pie pan into the large slop bucket and put it into the sink. She returned with the coffee pot and poured them each a cup of the steaming liquid and added fresh cream. "*Sooooo* what did your elders say?"

Samuel cleared his throat. "They have agreed to help you learn our ways," he said, "and my *schwester* has also agreed to tutor you in canning, sewing, and especially how to bake."

Relief and joy overtook her. "Thank you so much." She leaned forward and planted an impulsive kiss of gratitude on his cheek. She clapped a hand over her mouth. "I'm so sorry, I shouldn't have done that."

Samuel stared at her in shock. "I better go now."

Rachel stood. "Please forgive me, I don't always think before I act."

"*Danki* for the *kaffe*, Rachel," Samuel murmured, retrieving his straw hat from the peg and setting it back atop his dark wavy hair. He paused then put his hand on her shoulder and gave it a gentle squeeze before leaving the house.

Rachel hung her head, desolate. He had been her only human contact all day and she had spoiled it again. She looked down at the little brown dog as the screen door creaked shut. Buddy was sitting at her feet, looking up at her expectantly, a doggie smile on his handsome little face, his fan tail thumping on the floor. He was irresistible. Rachel scooped him up in her arms. "Want to cuddle in bed with me?" she whispered, nuzzling him. "Phew! You stink! You're not getting into the same bed with me until you get a bath." Rachel made a quick U-turn back to the kitchen and set the dog on the floor. She pumped the sink full of water and put a kettle on the stove to heat. She didn't have any doggie shampoo, so Karen's strawberry/kiwi would have to do until she could get some. Buddy sat waiting by the kitchen sink with his head cocked while Rachel ran upstairs to fetch the shampoo.

Karen sat up in protest. "Hey – what are you doing with my shampoo?"

"Come on down and see." Rachel raced back downstairs with her daughter following close behind.

Buddy looked up at them and smiled, wagging his tail when they reappeared.

"OMG he is *so* adorable," squealed Karen. She squatted down to scratch the little fellow's ears. "Gross, he smells like he's lived in a barn for the past year."

"Exactly, which is why you're going to help me bathe him," Rachel replied. She turned to the stove as the kettle began to sing and poured the hot water into the sink until it was pleasantly warm. "Go find some heavy-duty towels so we can dry him off when he's done."

For once, Karen didn't argue when given orders to do something. She left and reappeared moments later with an armful, which she dumped onto the floor.

"Okay, lift him in."

Karen lifted Buddy into the sink and held him gently while Rachel took a plastic cup and poured water over him. His perky ears instantly went flat, and his expression turned miserable.

"Oh, you poor little thing," Karen cooed with a grin, already in love.

"Okay, hold him fast while I shampoo him and don't let him shake," Rachel said, squirting the shampoo down his back.

It took three washings and some careful trimming to get a years' worth of dust, burrs, and grime out of Buddy's coat. Rachel lifted him onto the floor and together she and

Karen gave him a good rubdown with the towels until he was completely dry. When they were done, he favored them with a maniacally happy smile, wriggling from head to toe in obvious delight at being clean again. His coat was a glossy black with brown markings and soft to the touch. Then he zoomed in circles around them until Karen caught him.

Karen scooped him up. "He's sleeping with me," she announced, carrying him upstairs to her bedroom. Rachel sighed, gathered up the soiled towels, put them in the laundry basket and carried it out to the service porch where other piles awaited. She'd deal with the mounting laundry tomorrow. She stared at the old washing machine, wondering how Samuel's wife had managed to wash loads for such a large family in it. It seemed woefully inadequate for seven people. She made a mental note to purchase two large-capacity washers and dryers as soon as the electricity was installed to accommodate her future inn guests. She was not looking forward to having to hang laundry on the clothesline the old-fashioned way. It may smell a lot better, but it took five times longer to get it done, and she was just one person. She sighed. It was just part of learning how to live "simply" until she could get the needed appliances installed.

Samuel shut the door behind him and leaned against it with his eyes closed, thoroughly shook up. Buddy had disappeared the morning of the buggy accident and remained hidden until this very evening. It was uncanny. He still couldn't get the image out of his mind of Rachel Winston on her back, legs in mid-air, alongside his wife's dog on the barn floor. Under normal circumstances, he might have chuckled at the sight, but the mere fact that the dog had come out of hiding after a year and bonded instantly with a virtual stranger was making his head reel. It was strange the way the dog behaved around her. Buddy sat at her feet and allowed her to pick him up like a *boppli*, the same way his own Rachel used to; something the dog had never allowed anyone else to do. Samuel touched his cheek above the whiskers where her kiss had warmed it, remembering the look of relieved delight on her face when he had given her the news that his community would help her. It was all too much for him to take in. He knew he had hurt her by fleeing to the *dawdi haus* again, but he had no other choice. He didn't want to break down in tears in front of her. Samuel slid to his knees and covered his face with his hands. He had not spoken to *Der Herr* since the day his family was taken, and now he was at war within himself over doing so. His thoughts were as jumbled as his emotions. *Der Herr, why have you brought this woman and her dochder into my life? What is your purpose in all this? Talk to me!!*

There was no answer, only silence. He hadn't really expected one, but the profound silence after seeking God for the first time in over a year only served to renew his bitterness. He rose wearily to his feet and fumbled for the matchbox on the hearth. He lit the kerosene lamp, bathing the small room in a soft golden glow. He removed his suspenders, hat, shirt, and finally his trousers, changing into a long cotton nightshirt. He climbed into bed and closed his eyes, but sleep would not come until many hours later.

Rachel woke early the next morning with a to-do list a mile long. She needed Samuel to take her into town so she could find and hire a general contractor. Her guests might be charmed by eating Amish food and learning how to do crafts "the plain way," but she doubted she could lure any to the inn without indoor plumbing, HVAC, and hot showers.

As had become her custom, Karen was up before dawn to help Samuel with the animals in the barn and to collect the eggs. Rachel shook her head as she stood over the stove preparing their breakfast. It was nothing short of a miracle that her daughter, who had always prided herself on how late she could sleep in, would get up so early on a regular basis. By the time Rachel had the coffee brewing, bacon sizzling, and cottage potatoes fried up, they had both entered the house ready for a hearty breakfast. Karen put the basket of colorful eggs on the counter while Samuel went to the back porch and cleaned up. Buddy trotted behind Rachel with a happy look, hoping to luck out on table scraps.

"You're becoming quite the farmer's daughter," Rachel remarked, watching her daughter carefully put the eggs into their egg cartons.

"I love helping out with the animals," Karen said, carrying six over to her mother in the fold of her apron so she could fry them. She wrinkled her nose. "Except for the pigs and chickens, they really stink."

Rachel watched Samuel out of the corner of her eye as he bent over the sink, noticing again what broad shoulders and muscular arms he had as she carefully plucked the eggs from Karen's apron. Not paying close enough attention, one dropped onto the floor.

Karen gave her a nudge in the ribs. "Mom, put your eyes back into your head," she hissed.

"*Was is los?*" Samuel asked, entering the kitchen, his eyes fixed on Rachel.

Rachel refused to look at him as she wiped up the broken egg; Karen had caught her red-handed ogling him again. Karen smiled up at him. "I was just asking her if she could make me plain scrambled eggs," she fibbed, taking his place at the sink to wash up.

He nodded, "*Ach.*"

Rachel sighed with relief. Was she really being that obvious? She refocused on their breakfast.

Samuel took his seat while Karen brought what was ready to the table.

"Your eggs are almost up," Rachel announced, deftly cracking, and separating an egg into a bowl with one hand. She put in a tablespoon of mayonnaise, a squirt of harissa paste, added kosher salt and some fresh basil, then whisked them frothy and poured them into a frying pan of melted butter. The eggs greeted the hot pan with a sizzle. Was it her imagination or could she feel Samuel's eyes on her? She felt a thrill going up her spine. She scooped the eggs onto a plate for Karen and brought it to the table. Rachel sat, then smiled down at Buddy, who had taken up a position on the floor directly beneath her daughter's chair, waiting for "treats" to drop his way. Now how did he know that Karen was the one in the family notorious for dropping food? Again, Samuel merely stared down at his plate as they bowed their heads and said grace.

"Dear Lord, thank you for this home, Samuel Miller, my daughter, and our adorable new furry angel disguised as a dog, Buddy. Please bless the food we are about to eat and bless this day, amen."

Rachel served Samuel first, heaping his plate full, and poured him more freshly brewed coffee. "I was wondering if you could take me into town today to run some errands since my car hasn't arrived yet?"

Samuel looked up in surprise. "I need to tend the house garden first. It's in need of weeding and hoeing."

"Karen can take care of that," Rachel said with a stern look in her daughter's direction before she could object. "She's been complaining about how bored she's been lately; this will give her something to do."

"But *moooommm…*" Karen protested with a full mouth.

Rachel smiled inwardly when Samuel shot Karen a disapproving look. She immediately backed down, slumped in her seat and said nothing more, but she did slip Buddy a piece of her bacon.

"I need to find a general contractor to start on the improvements," Rachel added.

"Yeah," Karen piped up, "I hate using that outhouse and taking sponge baths."

Samuel nodded, intent upon his breakfast. "*Gut*, I will show your daughter what to do in the garden and then hitch up the spring wagon to the horses."

"Do I *have* to work in the garden?" moaned Karen in a pleading voice. "Can't I just hang with Buddy?"

Rachel was about to give her daughter the standard lecture about her entitlement mentality and lack of cooperation when Samuel beat her to the punch.

"*Der Herr* says in Second Thessalonians 3:10 that if a man will not work, neither shall he eat." He reached as if to grab her plate.

Karen clutched it, stared back at him, then turned her head and silently appealed to Rachel, who remained stonefaced. Confronted by two adults who were in total agreement, she finally stared down at her plate in defeat. "Oh, all right." she moped, knowing she was outnumbered.

Rachel shot Samuel a grateful smile and mouthed the words *thank you.* They ate in agreeable silence for the next few minutes. Rachel finished first and put her plate on the floor for Buddy to lick clean. "I'll just get the kitchen cleaned up while you show her what to do and then meet you outside."

"*Jah*," Samuel nodded, wiping his mouth. He retrieved his hat and went to the back porch, holding open the screen door for Karen. She stomped outside with Samuel right behind her.

Rachel collected the dishes and piled them into the sink to soak. She would finish them when she returned. Little Buddy followed her around the kitchen, his perky little face still hopeful for handouts. She squatted down to pet his silky head. "I bet you're hungry, huh?" she said to him. His tail thumped weakly; his brown eyes filled with hope. Rachel got a bowl and filled it with water then scraped some left-over scrambled egg onto a plate and set it on the floor. Buddy licked it clean in seconds then gulped down some water. He looked back up at her expectantly, instantly forgetting that he had just eaten.

"You sure are a charmer." she murmured, unable to help smiling at him. "Would you like to go for a ride?"

Buddy cocked his head to one side. Rachel grinned in delight and repeated the question to see if he would do it again. This time Buddy cocked his head to the other side. She squatted down and kissed him on the snout. "I guess that means yes," she murmured, nuzzling him. Buddy turned his face up and licked her neck. The screen door creaked open at that moment and Samuel stepped inside just in time to witness the exchange of affection. Rachel turned her face up to Samuel and grinned at him. "Guess he likes me."

She watched his pale face as he nodded at her and wondered why he seemed so disturbed.

"The wagon is ready and your *dochder* is working in the garden."

Rachel scooped Buddy into her arms and slung her purse over her shoulder, then paused to look up at Samuel. "You're my hero," she announced. "You have no idea how much I appreciate the way you back me up with Karen; it sure makes my life a lot easier." She gazed up at him in admiration, suddenly struck by his intense masculinity. Their eyes met and for a moment, they just stared at one another. His eyes were aquamarine and fringed by thick black lashes. He also had a finely chiseled face and perfect nose. *If only he didn't have that awful, scraggly Amish beard, he would be quite handsome,* she mused. Warmth started at her toes and rose swiftly up her body until it bloomed into a hot blush as Samuel continued to stare back at her. Rachel suddenly realized they had been staring at each other for much longer than was appropriate. She cleared her throat and forced herself to look away first. "I guess we better get going?"

Samuel nodded and held the screen door open for her. She walked down the steps and peered around the corner of the house where Karen was stooped over, pulling weeds with a vengeance, muttering under her breath.

"Do you need anything from the store while I'm out?" Rachel asked.

Karen straightened, "Yeah, a gardener."

"Got one," Rachel replied, pointing her finger at her with a smile.

"Not funny."

Since Buddy was too short to reach the bottom step, Rachel lifted him up into the wagon. As if he had done it dozens of times before, he hopped immediately onto the flatbed and waited for Rachel to get in. She raised a leg to climb in, lost her balance, and almost cracked her head on the sideboard. Samuel caught her just in time and helped her in.

"Thanks," she muttered, hoping he didn't think she had fallen against him on purpose. He climbed in after her and flicked the reins. The wagon took off with a jerk. Rachel rode in silence beside him, not touching, but close enough for her to grab onto his arm in case she lost her balance again. Little Buddy nosed between them like a furry chaperone and sat with his nose in the air, sniffing the wind. She set him on her lap and wrapped her arms around him to keep him safe.

They pulled carefully onto the two-lane road and headed for town. It was the first time she had been off the property since they had arrived weeks earlier. Just in time, the "cabin fever" was really starting to get to her. Although it was summer, it was still quite early, so the temperature was cool enough to make riding in the open wagon a pleasant experience, except for the constant jostling. Buddy panted happily, obviously enjoying the ride. Rachel looked about, admiring the beauty of the rolling farmland and the picturesque barns and homes.

It's so green here, she marveled. *Not like the concrete jungle I grew up in.* There were cows and sheep grazing, Amish men driving mule teams in their fields, and other horse-driven buggies passing them on the opposite side of the road. She felt as though she had stepped back in time as a pioneer woman and was riding in a covered wagon, ready to conquer the land. The wind was soft on her face, the silence broken only by singing birds, the snort of Samuel's horses and clopping shoes, or the occasional automobile. A buggy filled with an Amish family approached from the opposite direction on the other side of the road. Rachel raised her hand to wave at them, but the disapproving frown of the Amish man in the driver's seat instantly stayed her hand. She glanced over at Samuel, about to ask him why they had given her such a look, but saw that he, too, was frowning. When the next buggy passed with the same reaction, Rachel began to worry.

"Is something wrong?"

"*Jah*, it is not proper that I am seen driving alone in a wagon with an *Englisch* woman," he replied, tight-lipped.

"Then why did you agree to do it?" Rachel asked, feeling terrible.

"Could you have driven the wagon?"

"No."

"Did you have any other means of transportation?"

"No,"

"That is why I agreed," Samuel replied, sitting a little straighter on the bench. "*Der Herr* knows your situation and that I am acting honorably."

"Now you really are my hero," Rachel replied looking up at him thankfully.

"*Danki.*" Samuel finally turned his head to look her in the eyes with a crinkly smile, her compliment unexpected and heartwarming. She noticed that he did not look away again, not even when another buggy passed by. Warmth rushed through her body as she returned his stare and smiled shyly. Samuel Miller was a very kind and generous man, she realized, a lot like her Barry.

Chapter Seven

In for the Long Haul

Samuel pulled to a stop before the hardware store the Amish commonly frequented, wondering what he had gotten himself into. He had driven alone with an *Englisch* woman and looked into her eyes as though they were courting, which was inappropriate. He just couldn't seem to help himself. Her brown eyes seemed to hold a power over him he was helpless to resist. He often found himself becoming lost in their depths, staring much longer than was *gut* for him. He shouldn't be getting so involved in her life and business, but circumstances conspired to make that impossible. The looks he had gotten from his community this morning as he drove her to town had said it all: extreme disapproval. No doubt, word would soon reach Bishop Fisher or Deacon Lapp and they would come to get an account of his unseemly behavior.

Something about Rachel Winston made him want to help her, to come to her rescue. He had to admit that he had liked it very much when she referred to him as her hero. He looked over to stare at Buddy who was nestled on her lap. The dog had instantly adopted her and behaved in much the same way as he had with his deceased wife.

Samuel climbed out of the wagon first. Rachel pointed to Buddy. "Will he stay if I tell him to?"

Samuel nodded.

"Buddy...stay!" Rachel pointed at the dog. Instantly he laid on his belly and put his chin on his paws, his tail thumping plaintively on the wooden seat. She smiled at him and cooed. "Such a good dog you are."

Samuel followed her into the hardware store, still shaking his head over Buddy's behavior. He looked about in every direction. The store was empty except for them and the employees. He breathed a sigh of relief, grateful that he wouldn't have to deal with any additional wagging tongues. Rachel went up to the counter to get the attention of the manager.

"Excuse me, I need to get a referral for a good general contractor. Can you help me?"

The balding man with glasses looked up and gave her a welcoming grin. He wore a short-sleeved blue shirt with the store insignia on it. "Of course. You must be the lady from Southern California I've heard about?" He stuck out his hand. "Ernest Temmer, glad to meet you. What services do you need specifically?"

"You know about me?" Rachel responded, obviously shocked. "I guess that's a small town for you...uh, I need a septic tank installed, indoor plumbing, electricity, HVAC, phone, and Wi-Fi installed."

Ernie smiled and winked at her. "Word travels fast. I can recommend a couple of fellas to you. They're reasonable and do good work."

Ernest searched through a drawer then handed her three business cards. He looked up and suddenly seemed to notice Samuel standing off to one side. "Well, hello, Mr. Miller, it's been a while since I've last seen you. I was so sorry to hear about your family."

Rachel looked over at him just as he flinched. "*Danki*," he nodded, then tipped his hat and hastily exited the building to wait in the wagon with Buddy. Samuel was so deep in his thoughts that he scarcely noticed when twenty minutes had elapsed. Rachel exited the building and walked up to the wagon.

"Mr. Miller? Samuel." He jerked up straight when she touched his shoulder.

She smiled up at him apologetically. "Could you pull the wagon around to the back? They're ready to load the water heater."

"*Jah*," Samuel nodded and bent forward to reach for her hands to lift her in. Her lashes looked wet, as if she had recently been crying and he wondered what Ernest had told her about his family while he waited. She climbed in. Buddy trotted forward to greet her, wagging excitedly. Samuel could still feel her eyes on him as she patted the dog, but he pretended not to notice. He flicked the reins and steered the wagon around to the back of the building where Ernest was waiting for them at the loading dock with a small crate.

Although he had never used one, Samuel knew what a water heater looked like and this smallish box could not have been one, but he said nothing as they lifted it into the wagon along with some bags of electrical supplies and small flower packs.

"Where is the water heater?" he asked, knowing the devices to be of enormous girth.

"I bought a tankless water heater," Rachel explained. "This way I won't have to worry about it ever running short on hot water when the inn is full. This heats the water instantly as needed." She turned back to the manager. "Thank you, Mr. Temmer, could you send the contractor out to the farm as soon as possible? Give them this number – it's to the public phone shanty down the road if they absolutely need to reach me; my cell phone is dead."

"Will do," replied Ernie. "Just let me know if you need any other help. I know the folks over at the Chamber of Commerce well and they'll come in handy when it comes time to open your inn."

Samuel looked at Rachel. "Now where?"

"I need to go to a Home Depot or Lowes to purchase some appliances then I need to get some more groceries, especially dog food. Can we go back to that Super Wal-Mart?"

"*Jah,*" Samuel replied, glad to be avoiding the Amish market his wife used to go to. It would just add more fuel to the fire if his people saw him helping the *Englisch* woman grocery shop. The gossip mill would go into overdrive about Samuel Miller grocery shopping.

Rachel spent an hour in Home Depot, just long enough to order two sets of washers and dryers, and a commercial refrigerator and freezer. Then they went to the Wal-Mart. He pulled the wagon over to the Amish section of the lot, put on the brake and stepped down.

"Buddy...stay." Rachel pointed at the dog. Buddy laid down and whined.

"That is one amazing dog," she said, climbing down.

"Perhaps you should see about getting dog shampoo too, *jah*? Buddy smells like strawberries."

Rachel blushed. "We had to use Karen's shampoo on him so *jah*...I mean...yes...good idea...I will...along with dog food...oh good grief, I'll be right back."

She scurried into the Wal-Mart and returned an hour later with a shopping cart full of items. She handed the grocery sacks up to him one at a time so he could store them away in the empty egg crates at the rear of the wagon. She paused for a moment, fishing into one bag until she found what she was looking for. She pulled out a chew toy for Buddy and made it squeak. Buddy's chest went down, butt up in the air, his tail waving excitedly like a flag. She threw it into the back of the wagon where he fetched it and trotted back, hoping for another throw.

With the last of the bags loaded, Rachel clambered in and put him back on her lap. Soon they were back on the two-lane road, clip-clopping for home. She sat quietly beside Samuel, cuddling the dog and shrinking in on herself whenever an Amish buggy went past them. This time, he noticed that she made no attempt to wave to the other buggies. They made it back just before lunchtime. The temperature was starting to climb. When they pulled into the driveway, Samuel saw Karen sitting on the front porch swing, one leg tucked under her, the other on the floor, pushing it lazily back and forth while she sipped iced tea, her nose in a book.

"Hey honey, are all the weeds gone? Are you hungry?" Rachel called from the wagon.

Karen looked up. "Yeah, I'm hungry. Did you bring me back Chipotle?" Her eyes were hopeful.

"You should know better. There aren't any for twenty miles in any direction. Help us with these bags and we can go in and start some lunch."

Karen set down her book and got off the swing. "Who's we?" she replied, using the same inflection as her father used to. It elicited an involuntary cringe of pain from Rachel. Karen held up a basket of produce from the garden with obvious pride. "That garden is amazing, Mom! Much better than the one we had back home. Can you make a salad? I'm really craving a Caesar salad."

Rachel surveyed the basket. It had a head of lettuce, some tomatoes, and a few cucumbers. "I think I can whip up a salad with that," she replied.

Samuel hopped down first and then offered Rachel a hand to help her down. "*Danki*," she said. He reached for Buddy, but the dog backed away, looking instead to Rachel for help.

"C'mere," she encouraged, snapping her fingers.

Buddy eagerly came forward so Rachel could lift him down. Soon they all had the shopping bags unloaded. "I'll park the wagon in the barn with your water heater."

"Thank you, Samuel. I truly appreciate the help you gave me today," Rachel said, loading up her arms with the grocery bags. She offloaded some into Karen's reluctant arms.

"Karen, help me put the groceries away and then we'll make some lunch."

"Do I have to? I just spent half the morning weeding and hoeing and I'm tired," she moaned, trudging into the house behind her mother.

"If you want to eat...yes," Rachel snapped, her patience already exhausted.

"Okay, okay," Karen acquiesced, casting a nervous glance over her shoulder at a glowering Samuel. The screen door slammed shut behind her.

With a final disapproving look at Karen, Samuel took hold of the horses' reins and led them into the barn. He unhitched the wagon, then led Dodger and Molly to their respective stalls, brushing them down and filling their feed buckets with oats as a reward. Next, he went to inspect the vegetable garden to see what kind of job Karen had done, fully expecting to find shoddy work. He was pleasantly surprised to discover that she had removed all the weeds and thoroughly hoed each row. She had done every bit as good a job as his fourteen-year-old *dochder*, Sarah, would have done. Despite all her grumbling and complaining, Karen Winston did fine work. Fifteen minutes later she called out for him. "Mr. Miller, lunch."

"Over here," he responded, pressing his hand against the fence. Instantly, he felt a wood sliver slide under his heavily calloused skin. He was sucking on his finger when he entered the service porch to wash up. He took his usual seat. The aroma of sizzling bacon greeted his nostrils.

Rachel Winston turned around and immediately noticed the finger still in his mouth. "Are you okay?"

"Sliver," he grunted.

"Well, sucking your finger isn't going to do you a bit of good," she said, lifting the frying pan off the heat. Without waiting for an answer, she strode forward and pulled his finger from his mouth to examine it. She whistled, "That's some gnarly sliver."

Samuel removed his hand from hers. "I'm fine, it happens all the time."

Rachel gave him a scowl and grabbed his hand back. "It's not fine, it can get infected."

Again, Samuel removed his hand. "I'll take care of it after lunch," he promised.

Rachel grabbed his hand back. "It's your dominant hand; how are you going to manage that?"

The woman was as obstinate as a mule. He swallowed down the grin that threatened to crack his mouth as she continued. "We're going to take care of it now." She turned to her daughter. "Karen, can you fetch me that magnifying glass over there and the first aid kit in my bedroom?"

"But I'm hungry; can't we eat first?"

"*Jah,*" Samuel nodded, taking Karen's side for the first time since their arrival. "It can wait until after lunch."

"Ganging up on me like this just makes me that much more stubborn," Rachel warned them both. "Karen - go get me the things I asked for...now."

Karen stomped off, growling unintelligible words under her breath and returned with the first aid kit and magnifying glass. She got out the hydrogen peroxide, antibiotic ointment, a large needle, and tweezers. "Hold still, Samuel," she said, grabbing his finger.

He glowered but suffered her to examine his finger.

Rachel held out the large needle to Karen. "Light that candle over there and pass the needle through the flame a few times, then bring it back to me." She soaked a cotton ball full of the peroxide and swabbed his finger, removing as much dirt as possible. Then her large brown eyes met his with an apologetic smile. "This is really going to hurt. Do you want a twig to bite down on or anything? Maybe a bullet?"

"*Nee,*" Samuel shook his head, grimacing at the fuss she was making.

Karen turned her back. "I can't watch."

"Well, then how about making those BLATs while I'm doing this?" Rachel suggested.

Karen rolled her eyes. "I have to make lunch, too?"

Rachel shrugged. "No…but then you're just going to have to wait that much longer to eat…" The threat hung in the air.

Karen growled and stomped to the refrigerator, where she pulled out mayonnaise, an avocado and bread while Rachel commenced digging. Samuel flinched when the needle pierced his flesh. He gritted his teeth and bore it in silence while she methodically dug a path through his calloused flesh to the sliver of wood. The deeper she went, the more he wished he had accepted the offer of the twig. He opened his eyes, looking around for something to distract himself from the pain, and finally opted to study her face as she bent her head over his hand. Rachel had fair, perfect skin without a hint of wrinkles, looking more like she was in her twenties than her thirties. His eyes traveled up her face to her hair. He was still not used to seeing the uncovered head of a woman. Only in the privacy of their bedroom had his Rachel let down her long, golden-brown hair. When time permitted, she would sometimes ask him to brush it out for her. He had loved running his fingers through the thick mass and often the hair brushing would lead to more intimate things. He shook his head, dispelling the images from his memory. He concentrated his stare at Rachel's hair. It was dark brown, long, and very wavy. Most of the time she swept it off her long neck into a large hair clip or ponytail. She had thick, brown eyelashes and full lips, which were now pursed in deep concentration. Another painful dig made him wince again; he jerked involuntarily.

"Sorry," she murmured, not deterred in the least. He continued his silent appraisal to take his mind off the pain.

She was shorter than his Rachel and petite. His wife had swiftly lost her girlish figure after giving birth to their five children. As if sensing his eyes upon her, Rachel looked up and caught him staring at her. She blushed and averted her eyes, saying nothing as she wiped away the seeping blood with cotton gauze. "Almost there," she whispered, bending over his finger, her brows knitting in concentration.

"*Jah*," Samuel nodded, gritting his teeth, unable to keep the tears of pain from sliding down his cheeks. This time he closed them, so he wouldn't be tempted to stare at her anymore.

"Okay, I'm there, hang tough for another second."

There was a brief flash of intense pain, then sudden relief when the digging stopped.

"Got it," she crowed, holding up her tweezers with the offending object in them. She held a small bowl under his finger and poured hydrogen peroxide over the wound and patted it dry. Next, she applied antibiotic ointment then wrapped it with a bandage. "All done, now we can eat." Rachel gathered up the bloody gauze, cotton balls, and bowl and set them aside. She went to check on Karen who had done nothing more than remove the bacon strips from the pan.

"Why didn't you make the sandwiches?"

"I didn't know what to put in them," Karen whined, refusing to look in Samuel's direction.

Rachel rolled her eyes in exasperation. Samuel frowned. It was obvious that Karen was just using another stalling tactic to get out of helping.

"B is for bacon, L is for lettuce, A is for avocado, and T is for tomato. *Geez*, Karen, you'd starve to death if I ever left you on your own."

In a jiffy, Rachel had the lettuce leaves, sliced tomatoes, and mayo piled high on the bread. "Hope you like BLATs," she called a bit nervously over her shoulder as Samuel pulled his chair closer to the table.

"I've never had one," he replied.

"You're kidding me, right?" Rachel swung around to stare at him. She held up two plates containing sandwiches. "You don't know what you've been missing."

Rachel sat down and poured them each some sweet tea. "I used the lettuce and tomato from the garden, so it should be extra good. Shall we?" They bowed their heads, and the blessing was given.

Samuel lifted the bread to look underneath. Inside was a large leaf of lettuce, a slice of tomato, avocado slices, and crispy bacon strips. Then he looked back at Rachel, who was waiting for him to take his first bite.

"Go ahead," she encouraged, "and for dessert there's Whoopie pies and no, *I.did.not.make.them.*"

Samuel couldn't help but chuckle; the constant digs at her baking skills were obviously getting to her, even if she agreed with them.

"*Gut*! Very *gut*!" He nodded enthusiastically. He liked these sandwiches.

"I'm really looking forward to going to that Sing along, Mr. Miller," Karen announced. "I really need to have some fun! I haven't had any fun in ages. I hope I can make some new friends!"

Samuel shifted uncomfortably. He had not meant to lead the teenager on with false hopes of lasting friendships. His people generally did not mix with the *Englisch* on a more than casual basis. "This may just be a one-time event, I'm afraid," he said, feeling bad at Karen's crestfallen expression. "You would have to become Amish and be baptized to really become a part of our community."

"The same goes for me, too, I assume?" Rachel responded, evidently hurt on behalf of her daughter. "We live in the heart of the Amish community, but we can't really be part of it, because we aren't Amish."

"That's so unfair," Karen moped, putting down her sandwich. Samuel watched her push away from the table, wishing he had kept his mouth shut. "I'm not hungry anymore, mom. You can give my sandwich to Buddy." She stood then glared at her mother. "Why did you bring me here? I never wanted to come in the first place. I have no friends here and apparently now I can't make any because I'm not Amish!"

Rachel stared at her daughter, stung by the sudden venom in her voice.

Karen balled her fists. "Dad would never have made me move here! Dad wouldn't have made my life a living hell! I hate you!" She turned and stomped up the stairs to her bedroom and slammed the door behind her.

Samuel watched Karen leave with a sinking heart then turned in time to see Rachel hide her face in her hands and crumple into tears.

This was his fault. They had both been so happy just a moment ago and he had spoiled it with talk of his community's rules. He never could handle the tears of a woman. He stood next to Rachel who was sobbing into her arms.

"I'm sorry, I did not mean…" the words died in his throat when, instead of fleeing from him as he expected her to do, Rachel stood up and collapsed weeping against his chest. He stood awkwardly for a moment, his arms akimbo.

He should step away from her, go back to the *dawdi haus*, but he was rooted to the spot. Despite the alarm bells going off in his head, he put his arms around her shoulders and let her cry, his embrace only encouraging her quiet weeping to turn into great gulping sobs that racked her entire frame. Her arms went around his waist as she clung to him, crying so hard she could barely remain standing. For a long time, he just held her and patted her back in silence. Despite his misgivings, he liked the way she felt in his arms.

Her sorrow was as profound as his, but her loneliness was worse. While he had an entire Amish community of friends, neighbors, and relatives waiting to welcome him at any moment, Rachel Winston had no one, not even her daughter. She had left all she knew to provide a home and moved into a community that would prefer to have as little to do with her as possible. For the first time in almost a year, his heart hurt for her more than it did for himself. He wasn't sure how long they stood there, but he allowed her to be the one to back away first.

Finally, Rachel quieted and wiped her tears with a paper towel, flushing beet red, her eyes already swollen. "Thanks," she whispered, refusing to meet his eyes. "I-I probably shouldn't have done that, huh?"

Samuel just stood there, watching her, his arms feeling empty without her in them. He cleared his throat. "It's quite alright, Rachel...I understand."

She smiled at him through her tears. "I know you do, Samuel, better than anyone." She gestured at his uneaten sandwich. "Please, go ahead and finish. I promise not to afflict you with any more emotional meltdowns...at least for today." She made a courageous attempt at a smile, but he could see that her heart just wasn't in it.

"Only if you will eat with me," he found himself replying.

Rachel looked up at him, thoroughly surprised. Their eyes locked. He stared into hers for a long moment. Her thick lashes were spiked and dewy with tears that were also glistening on her cheeks. Without thinking, he took his rough calloused fingers and gently wiped them away, just as he used to do with his own Rachel. Her full lips parted in surprise, her eyes searching his inquisitively.

At that moment, Samuel wanted nothing more than to take her back in his arms and comfort her again. With great effort, he retook his seat. They finished lunch in silence then he went into the fields to work, pondering about what had just transpired between them.

After lunch, Rachel sat on the front porch with some iced tea, watching Samuel work in the distance in the sweltering heat; remembering the feel of his arms about her as she cried. It was the most emotional comfort she had experienced in a very long time. Samuel had seemed content to just stand there and hold her for as long as she needed, not rushing her grief, something no one else had ever done for her since the death of her husband. For months following Barry's death she had longed for him, wishing she could be comforted in his arms as she mourned for him, which, she realized, was very convoluted. Barry had always been her primary source of emotional comfort. He gave her solace during the years she grieved their infertility then the lack of relationship with her daughter in the early years of her adoption. There had been many times that she had wept so hard that Barry had to shush her so Karen couldn't overhear her; however, the heartache at Karen's constant rejection was nothing compared to the emotional agony of losing Barry.

In an adjacent field, Rachel watched a large wagon filled with Amish men and younger boys working together to bale alfalfa. A feeling of intense envy spread over her. The Amish always worked together as a family and community. How wonderful that must be. It was a foreign concept to the world she had left behind. Technology was supposed to bring people closer, but it only resulted in more isolation. Back in California, her daughter had spent every waking moment on social media; she didn't even speak to her friends on the phone anymore…she just texted, TikTok'd, Instagrammed or Snapchatted.

Rachel sighed deeply. What would it be like to be part of a community like that? To have so many friends and family around, always ready to help lighten the load. To have other women to talk to? What would it be like to become a part of that community? *Could I become Amish?* She shook her head to clear it, but the thought persisted. *Don't be silly, Rach. You'd look awful in a bonnet with no makeup.* She continued staring out the window, mentally checking off the pros and cons. *Cons:* no electricity, no music, no air conditioning, no more blue jeans, shorts, tank tops or loose hair. *Pros:* Being part of a wonderful community, quilting bees, canning produce, new friends, learning to become self-sufficient, lots of moral support, not being alone anymore…and the thought that had been niggling at her for some time: Samuel… *I wonder how someone like me becomes Amish?*

⋞⋟

Rachel confronted Samuel that night just as they were finishing supper. "Samuel – how does one become Amish?"

Karen froze in mid-bite. "Ummm, mom, have you totally *lost* it?"

"I'm quite serious, I want to know," Rachel continued, waiting on Samuel who merely stared at her as if she had grown a second head. "Well?"

He swallowed with difficulty. "It would depend upon the reason why you wish to become Amish in the first place," he murmured.

"Well…I'm really lonely for one," Rachel replied slowly, "but mainly I'm just curious right now; what would someone like me have to do to become Amish?"

Samuel shifted uncomfortably. "You would have to become very familiar with our ways, then contact the bishop for an interview,"

"Anything else?"

"You would need to learn Pennsylvania Dutch and High German."

To his surprise, Rachel grinned at him. "*Ich habe vier jahre der Deutschen in der high school.* (I took four years of German in high school.) What else?"

Samuel sat back in his chair, completely surprised. "You would have to be baptized in our faith."

"I've already been baptized once but, since you hold the same beliefs as I that wouldn't be a problem, but I'm still

104

really going to have to think this over," she finally replied. "I'm not sure I'm up for the challenge, but we'll see."

Samuel nodded, "*Jah* – this is not a decision to be entered into lightly. It is *gut* you are giving it serious thought." He wiped his mouth and remained where he was, reluctant to go to the lonely little *dawdi haus.*

Rachel apparently felt the same. "It's a really nice night out; would you like to sit on the porch swing with some iced tea and watch the fireflies with me?"

"*Jah,*" Samuel replied softly, surprising himself. Rachel had no idea what she was asking of him. In his community, sitting together on a porch swing was as good as courting, but she didn't know that, and he wasn't going to tell her. They took their glasses of tea and went out to the porch swing to watch the magical dance of the fireflies together in the deepening twilight while Karen amused herself with Buddy upstairs.

They sat quietly for a few moments, sipping their tea, the swing rocking gently.

Rachel turned to look at him and finally broached the elephant on the porch. "What happened to your family, Samuel?"

Samuel closed his eyes and sighed deeply. "They died in a buggy accident during a storm." The words were out of his mouth before he could stop them.

"A buggy accident?"

He nodded. "They were delivering eggs on the way to my *schwester's* and never got there. My *schwester,* Sarah and her husband, John, grew concerned and went out looking for them." Samuel paused, continuing with great difficulty. "They came upon the accident...the buggy had overturned in a deep ditch that was filled with rainwater...they all drowned, my *frau* and five *kinner* – *Der Herr* took them all away from me."

Suddenly he found himself back on that horrible day a little over a year ago.

He had been in the barn most of the day tending to some needed repairs while a summer thunderstorm raged outside. His *frau* and *kinner* had been gone since early morning, making egg deliveries, and had planned to visit his *schwester,* Sarah and her family.

At 3:00 p.m. he had heard someone calling from across his property.

"Samuel, Samuel!" called a frantic voice.

He went around the corner to find Sarah and his *bruder-in-law* John standing at the entrance to the barn, looks of horror on their faces. John was wheeling his hat in his hands, round and round, *a bad sign.* They were drenched from the downpour.

Samuel stared at them, dread creeping over him. *"Was is do uff?"*

His *schwester* spoke first. Sarah stepped forward and took his arm. "Samuel, you must *kumme* with us."

A crack of thunder boomed overhead, punctuating her words with a sense of doom.

Samuel didn't budge. He already knew. "Is it Rachel and the *kinner?*"

Sarah nodded and took both of his hands in hers, no longer able to keep the tears from spilling down her cheeks. A sob erupted from her throat. Rachel had been Sarah's best friend since childhood as well as her *schwester*-in-law. "They never made it to our home, Samuel. I got so worried when they were late. We went looking for them."

Samuel's throat constricted, he nodded, waiting for her to continue.

"We found the buggy overturned in a ditch; it was flooded half-way up. The emergency crews had gotten there before us but...but..." Sarah pulled the hem of her black apron up and covered her face as she collapsed into choking sobs. "They were too late...we've lost them all, Samuel. Rachel... the *kinner*...all of them."

All Samuel could do at the time was to stare at her in numb horror as she buried her face in John's chest and wept brokenly. Outside the barn, the rain was still coming down in sheets, the rain that had taken his family from him. Something inside him had died in that moment. He couldn't weep. He had gone completely numb. He had followed Sarah and John into the house and sat nodding while they spoke to him, not really hearing or feeling anything.

That had been almost a year ago…he hadn't prayed to *derr Herr* since, his faith in the goodness of God shaken to the core.

"Mr. Miller, are you okay?"

Samuel turned to look at Rachel, returning to the present and found her staring at him, her eyes wide and filled with tears of compassion for him. "I'm so sorry," she finally whispered. "No one should have to bear that kind of grief."

"I lost everyone I loved that day," he whispered, his throat constricting in pain.

"I'm so sorry," Rachel replied, her voice breaking, tears of compassion sliding down her cheeks.

Samuel bowed his head and caved in on himself, grief overwhelming him. He was only dimly aware of Rachel laying her hand upon his back and praying for God to comfort him and give him peace. Although he was angry at God, her prayers still touched his heart deeply.

She waited for him in silence, allowing him to weep for as long as he needed to and didn't attempt to offer him trite words of comfort for which he was grateful. Sometime during the deepening twilight, their fingers intertwined and remained that way until it became too dark to remain on the porch anymore. It was high time he went to bed, but he was reluctant to leave her.

"*Danki,*" he said softly, finally releasing her hand.

"Anytime, Samuel," she replied, and he knew she meant it.

Chapter Eight

Egg Rounds

Rachel's meeting with the general contractor was this morning. Samuel and Karen had already completed their early morning chores, eaten breakfast, and were occupied elsewhere. Rachel waited on the front porch; her eyes fixed on the road. Shortly after 10:00 am, a black Ford F-350 pulled into her driveway.

A middle-aged man with silver hair exited the cab and held out his hand in greeting. "Mrs. Winston? I'm Daniel Gold."

Rachel shook his hand then opened the screen door for him. "Nice to meet you, you came highly recommended. Please come in, would you like some coffee?"

"Love some," he replied, following her inside. He set his iPad and briefcase on the table. "I've already pulled plans from the city and you're in luck. We're only going to have to run electrical lines and plumbing from this house down to the lane to where your Mennonite neighbor already has service, so you'll save quite a bit of money there."

Rachel nodded, relieved as she poured him a cup of coffee. For the next hour, they discussed what she needed in detail, then he set to work going over every inch of the house with a digital tape measure and his iPad, making a detailed floor plan and plat map of the entire property.

"I'll work up the bid," he told her a few hours later, shaking her hand. "I should have it for you by next week."

Rachel shook his hand. "That would be great, thanks." *Now I only hope I have enough money for it all.*

Karen entered the service porch and set her basket of eggs on the counter with pride. With fifty-plus chickens laying an egg a day they were already up to their eyeballs in eggs; there was no keeping up with them. What had Samuel Miller done with all the eggs before they arrived?

Rachel ogled the eggs. "You're going to have to start selling them soon honey or they're all going to go bad."

"Hey that's a great idea, maybe I could make some money."

"Every little bit helps, perhaps you can ask Samuel about it?"

"Good idea," Karen agreed. At that moment, Samuel entered the service porch to wash up for lunch. Rachel jerked her head at Karen as a hint.

"Mr. Miller, the walk-in refrigerator is full of eggs; how would I go about selling them?"

Samuel turned to look at her, "My Sarah had an egg route to our neighbors and the local market," he replied. "You might be able to pick it back up in her place."

Rachel watched Karen put on her best wheedling smile. "Would you mind showing me the route, Mr. Miller, *pleeeease?*"

"*Jah...* better than letting them all go to waste," he nodded, his face a bit sad.

Rachel already had the table set for lunch. "I need to ask a favor as well, Samuel, I need to take some pictures of the property for the website. I understand the Amish don't allow themselves to be photographed so I hate to ask this... but would it be alright with you...I mean...would it bother you if Karen borrowed one of the dresses in the closet upstairs and acted as a model for me?" She held her breath, afraid of what his reaction would be. To her surprise, Samuel nodded.

"*Jah*...it will be alright, my Sarah is with the angels now and has no need of earthly clothing," he replied, his eyes sorrowful.

Rachel stared at him mournfully. It was bad enough losing a spouse...but to lose all his children as well. She just couldn't imagine the pain he was in.

"How much do I charge for the eggs?" Karen asked.

"Five dollars for a dozen."

"Wow really? I'm going to be rich!"

Sudden inspiration struck Rachel. "Honey, I have an idea. Why don't you get into that Amish dress you mentioned? I'll pin your hair up into the bonnet and we can snap some pictures of you collecting eggs, working in the garden, and feeding the animals in the barn."

"Hey, Mom, why don't you dress up too? I can take pictures of you burning bread in the kitchen."

"Very funny," Rachel grinned at her, pleased to be sharing a rare moment of levity. "After I learn the tricks of the trade from Samuel's sister, you will be taking photos of my beautiful bread, rolls, and pies!"

After lunch, Karen ran upstairs to change her clothes. In moments, she returned wearing a pale blue dress and black apron. "It's a little small on me, but it's okay, I guess," she said, handing her mom the white linen *kapp*, hairbrush, and bobby pins. She turned around so Rachel could fix her hair. Rachel brushed out Karen's glossy brown tresses and then rubber-banded her hair into a tight ponytail. Then she twisted it into a coil and pinned it into a tight bun, which fit inside the *kapp*.

"How do I look?" Karen twirled around.

"Like an English girl pretending to be Amish." Rachel replied honestly.

"What's wrong?"

Rachel braced herself for an argument. "You need to lose the make-up, honey. Amish girls don't wear any."

To her surprise, Karen didn't offer an argument. "Okay, I'll be back down in a minute." She flew upstairs and Rachel could hear her splashing in the washbasin. When she returned, she was fresh-faced with no hint of make-up.

"Better?"

"Honey, you're beautiful, you don't need make-up. It doesn't enhance your looks at all, it just covers it up." To her surprise, her daughter blushed at the compliment. Rachel located her old 35mm camera, hopefully the batteries were still good. "Ready?"

"*Jah,*" Karen replied, imitating Samuel's deep voice. They went outside, Buddy trotting along behind them. He spotted some birds on the ground then took off after them, barking furiously.

"Mom look, wouldn't that take a good picture?" Karen pointed to a farmer across the way sitting behind his mules while they pulled the cultivator through his field.

"It would! I suppose it's okay if we take the picture from a distance," Rachel replied.

"Here, I'll do it." Karen reached for the camera. She focused the lens on the farmer and took several photos, then handed the camera back to Rachel. "Let's go to the chicken coop first. I can check for more eggs while you take pictures." She picked up the wire collecting basket and went inside with her mother. The smell of chicken droppings was overwhelming.

Rachel gagged. "How do you stand the smell? Good thing the website won't have smell-o-vision."

Karen shrugged at her with an air of superiority. "You get used to it after a while, I can barely even smell it anymore."

Rachel stared at her, wide-eyed in disbelief. "Amazing."

Karen rolled her eyes in her now familiar disgusted way. "Yes...*Muth-ther*...are you ready yet?"

Rachel nodded and readied the camera. She took pictures of Karen collecting eggs. Soon they moved into the barn where Rachel got another shock. Karen sat down on a stool and on the first squirt got milk into the pail. Next, she took pictures of Karen pretending to feed the sheep and goats and curry the horses. Then they walked outside the perimeter of the house and took exterior photos of the red barn, white farmhouse, wrap around porch, and rolling green farmland. She even took some pictures of Karen swinging from a tree swing under a large weeping willow. Rachel called her over. "Okay, I think I have enough now, you can go upstairs and change if you want to."

"I don't want to change." Karen replied to her surprise. "I kinda like wearing it; besides, maybe I'll sell more eggs if I'm dressed this way." A sudden idea occurred to her. "Do you think Mr. Miller will let me wear this dress to the singing this weekend? I don't want to stick out like a sore thumb."

"You'll have to ask him, honey," Rachel replied, walking with her back to the house.

"Okay, I will." Karen went in search of Samuel. Rachel went upstairs to take photographs of the bedrooms for her website.

The home did not need much in the way of redecoration, just a few additional touches here and there. Samuel's family had meticulously maintained it, both inside and out. The hardwood floors were a lovely golden color and in perfect condition. Each bedroom had handmade braided rugs on the floor and old-fashioned porcelain wash basins on wooden stands. Each bed was covered with a different Amish quilt in jewel tones, so she only needed to put a vase with fresh cut flowers on each nightstand.

Rachel stood in the doorway of the first vacant bedroom and looked around, profound sadness descending on her. Which of Samuel's children had this room belonged to? The room was bare of personal belongings, but she didn't know if that was because the Amish did not decorate their rooms or if he had removed them because he could not bear to be reminded of his loss.

She thought back to her former home in Southern California where she had not allowed anyone to disturb any of Barry's things, wanting them to stay just as he had left them, even if they were lying in the middle of the floor. Her home had become a morbid "Barry shrine" until the day she was forced to box everything up and donate it to Goodwill by her sisters-in-law, Michele, Debbie, Julie, and Monique. It was one of the most painful things she had ever done. Each article of clothing she packed away felt like death by a thousand cuts. She had allowed herself one set of his flannel pajamas as a keepsake, remembering all the moments they had cuddled in bed together on the weekends and opened presents in them on Christmas mornings. If she couldn't bear to get rid of Barry's things, how had Samuel been able to dispose of his entire family's personal belongings? It was beyond her comprehension.

She set the camera on its tripod and took photographs of each room from every angle before proceeding to the next.

Samuel returned from the fields in the late afternoon, sweating profusely. It was another warm and humid day in Lancaster County. Karen met him on the porch steps with a tall glass of ice-cold lemonade.

"*Danki*," he said in mild surprise, accepting the glass curiously. He drank it down in one draught and she quickly refilled it. He looked at her face then did a double take, noticing that she was dressed as a plain Amish girl with no make-up. "*Gut*." He nodded his approval.

She grinned at him. "The lemonade or the way I look?"

"Both."

She sighed with relief. "Mr. Miller, would you show me the egg route?"

"It will have to wait until tomorrow morning when it is cooler," he replied, wiping his forehead with a handkerchief.

Karen's disappointment was palpable. "Oh, okay," she shrugged and trudged away.

Samuel entered the service porch to wash up for supper. He could smell the fried chicken all the way from the front yard.

Rachel was just tossing a large green salad when he entered. She turned around and gave him a broad smile. His heart warmed at the sight of her face. For the first time since they met, she smiled big enough to show off the dimples in both cheeks. She placed the platters of food onto the table, looking around to see if her daughter was within earshot.

She sidled up close to him. "Samuel, I don't know what you're doing but whatever it is, keep it up. Karen is becoming a changed girl."

He returned her smile, and they continued gazing into each other's eyes in silence for a long spell. Rachel took his hand and clasped it warmly. He looked down as their fingers intertwined for a moment then his eyes traveled back up to her face. A wave of tenderness swept over him. Neither moved; he didn't want to break the spell.

At that moment, they heard Karen come through the screen door. It closed with a loud bang. Their hands instantly separated.

Karen washed up and plopped down in her chair. "Yum, fried chicken and mashed potatoes!"

Samuel swiftly took his seat while Rachel passed around the platter of chicken, "Karen, I'm going to need your help with the laundry tomorrow. We're out of clean clothes."

Karen groaned. "What am I, the house slave? I do everything around here."

Samuel's face darkened with anger. Karen refused to look at him, no doubt already aware she had crossed the line again. If any of his *dochders* had dared speak to their *mamm* that way, they would have had their ears boxed. Karen needed to learn proper respect. She had no concept of what real life was for the average Amish child…and he had a *gut* mind to teach her.

"Slave!" sputtered Rachel, her face going red with indignation. "Half of the laundry is yours."

"I never get to have fun anymore. All I do is work, sleep, eat and work." Karen moaned. "I never get to be with kids my own age anymore. I'm cooped up in this house all the time with just you, Buddy, and the chickens. All I do is *work*."

Rachel was on her feet, ready to do verbal battle, but Samuel shot her a warning glance.

"I can remedy that situation," he said, turning to Karen, whose face had turned as petulant as a four-year old's. "If I can arrange it, would you like to spend the night at my *schwester's*? She has six children. One of her daughters is close to you in age."

Karen's face instantly lit up with excitement…just the way he had hoped it would.   "Really? A sleepover with a girl my own age? That would be so great."

"*Jah*, but I will need to speak to my *schwester* first."

"Okay," Karen nodded, suddenly all smiles again.

Samuel held up a warning finger, "But only if you help your *mudder* with no more complaints."

Karen opened her mouth to protest again, then obviously thought better of it and nodded. "Okay."

"I'll get a message to Sarah from the phone shanty, then." Samuel informed her.

Karen's face went blank. "What's a phone shanty?"

"A tiny public phone booth," Rachel explained. "We'll start the laundry when you return from your egg route tomorrow, deal?"

Karen frowned, "Deal."

They finished their supper and Karen helped her mother clean up without being asked, no doubt to score some points with him.

After dinner, Samuel and Rachel went out to the porch swing for their now nightly ritual of watching the fireflies. They gently rocked back and forth for a few moments, sipping tea.

"Tell me about your husband," he murmured, really wanting to know.

Rachel turned to look at him, both shocked and pleased that he would ask. "What do you want to know?"

"How did you meet?"

"At a college and career church retreat in the mountains," Rachel replied. "It was like the lyrics to that song from the musical South Pacific *"...some enchanted evening, you may see a stranger, you may see a stranger...across a crowded room, and somehow you know..."* only in my case it was in the morning at breakfast, and I thought he was so good looking that he would be too stuck up to talk to me."

"But he wasn't?" Samuel guessed.

"No," Rachel blushed, smiling at the memory. "I noticed him from across the room and the next thing I knew he was sitting across from me and introducing himself."

"Then what?" Samuel asked.

At this Rachel blushed. "Well, we went out into the snow that day and horsed around. After that, I became what would be commonly referred to now as a *stalker*." She giggled at the memory.

Samuel stared at her uncomprehending. "Stalker? What is "stalker"?"

"Someone who haunts the footsteps of another in the hopes of establishing a relationship" she replied, blushing red. "I sought him out, followed him everywhere and made sure to sit near him at each meal."

Samuel was not surprised at this admission. Rachel Winston did not seem to be the shrinking violet type; much like his own Rachel who had let it be plainly known that she favored him in their youth.

Rachel continued, smiling at the memory. "It was only a weekend retreat and we had to all go down the mountain and return home after Sunday's morning church service. Barry had been the only male to ever pay me any real attention, so I was desperate not to let him get away."

Samuel found this difficult to believe but said nothing.

Rachel continued her story. "So, since we had bonded over the discussion of our favorite cartoons, losing our first loves and the fact that he had been putting his arm around me and kissing my forehead for the past day, I felt safe in doing what I did next..."

Samuel couldn't even guess at what this would have been. "Which was what?"

"I asked to see his bible and wrote my name and phone number in it."

Samuel chuckled despite himself; Rachel Winston was a forward little thing.

"He called me the next day after the retreat and asked me out on a triple date with his sister, her husband and another couple to see Disney's Fantasia."

"What is that?" Samuel asked, unable to take his eyes off her face as she spoke. She had lit up with joy at the memory.

"A full-length animated feature cartoon set to classical music..." She paused for a moment. "During that first date, something incredible happened but Barry didn't tell me about it until years later."

Samuel waited patiently.

Rachel looked up at him and smiled. "I had excused myself to the lady's room and while I was away, he told me that the 'know it all' friend of his sisters on our date that night had told them all that I would be his future wife!"

Samuel's mouth dropped open in genuine shock.

"Of course, Barry couldn't stand this girl, so he told her that there was absolutely no way that was ever going to happen (just to prove her wrong). The funny thing is, about 3 years before I ever met him, I had written a short story called A Wish Fulfilled in which Jesus, uh, *Der Herr* introduces me to the man he had chosen for me." Rachel raised tear-filled eyes to Samuel. "You'll never guess what the name of that man in the story was…"

"Barry?"

Rachel nodded and bowed her head. "I even illustrated the story and the picture looked just like him. I waited until we had been together about 9 months before I dared show it to him. I was afraid of scaring him off."

"I used to pray for Barry by name before we ever met… it was truly a match made in heaven." Her voice died down to a plaintive whisper. "I just never dreamed I would lose him so soon." A sob caught in her throat.

Samuel took her hands into his and just held them; his heart aching for her. She gave him a broken smile while tears streamed down her face.

They remained for a long time, holding hands in silence, swinging gently back and forth while the stars came out and it grew quite dark. The silence grew awkward.

"Well, I guess it's time we both hit the hay…" Rachel finally said, rising slowly to her feet. She looked at him with grateful eyes. "Thank you, Samuel, it really helps to talk about him."

"*Jah*," Samuel nodded and reluctantly released her hands and shoved his deep into his trouser pockets, shuffling his feet.

"Goodnight, Samuel…and thanks again."

"*Gut nacht*, Rachel."

The next morning Karen was up bright and early, packing the last of the egg cartons into crates and waiting for Samuel to bring the buggy around. Together, they carefully stacked the crates into the buggy, then Karen climbed in beside him, waving goodbye to her mother, who stood watching from the back porch steps. Samuel tipped his hat to Rachel, his eyes lingering on hers for just a moment. Almost instantly, he noticed a pink blush blooming over her cheeks. Her reaction gave him an odd sense of satisfaction. He flicked the reins and reprimanded himself. *Samuel Miller, you are treading on dangerous ground.*

Dodger set off at a steady pace.

Karen sat beside him, squirming with anticipation. Memories of riding with his daughter Sarah on her egg rounds when she was very young came flooding back as he observed Karen from the corner of his eye. *Perhaps Der Herr has sent this family to me so we could all find healing?* He sat upright, shocked he would consider such a thought.

Rachel carried the last basket of dirty laundry to the service porch with Buddy trotting behind her. She stared at the ancient Maytag wringer washing machine. Under normal circumstances, she would have been charmed at the sight of a "vintage" household appliance, but all she could feel was a sense of dread when she stared at the hand crank and wringer on top, which would have to be powered by her own arms. There was also no clothes dryer. Instead, a genuine clothesline stretched from one end of the back yard to the other, bordering the large vegetable garden. Between the wringer and pegging clothes the old-fashioned way, her upper arms were going to get one heck of a workout. She looked around for laundry soap and found a large plastic tub on the floor near the washer. It was filled with white powder and had a scoop in it. Rachel squatted down and sniffed at it. It smelled like laundry detergent, but it must have been homemade; there was no label. "This ought to be interesting," she said aloud.

A few hours later, just as she finished washing the second load and was ready to wring it out, Karen returned home with Samuel, waving a fistful of dollars at her. Her face was wreathed in smiles, "One hundred dollars, whoo hoo!"

"Good for you," Rachel nodded, pointing to the washing machine. "You're just in time to help me peg the first load and hang it on the clothesline."

Karen stared at the wringer, looking rather intrigued. "It looks like a big version of your pasta machine."

Rachel chuckled. "You know I think you're right. I'm pretty sure it operates much the same way."

"I'll be back in the fields until lunch," Samuel told them, taking the horse into the paddock.

"Thank you so much, Mr. Miller," Karen called after him.

"Thank you, Samuel," added Rachel. At this, he half turned, smiled, and tipped his hat.

Mother and daughter soon involved themselves in the novelty of feeding wet clothing into the wringer and watching it come out the other end. When they finished wringing out both loads, Rachel put the next load into the machine and carried the basket of damp clothes out to the clothesline. A warm summer breeze wafted across the yard, bringing with it the smell of alfalfa, hay, and green grass.

"Karen, nothing smells better than laundry dried on the line outside," Rachel told her daughter as she picked up a bath towel and pinned it to the line.

"How would you know?" Karen retorted, copying her mother with the next towel.

"Because this is how my mom did laundry when I was little," Rachel replied.

"Didn't you have dryers back then?"

"Very funny, smarty pants. I'm not that old! Your grandmother just preferred to hang clothes outside to save money…and she made me help when I was tall enough."

After five minutes, the novelty wore off. "My arms are killing me," Karen moaned, massaging them between pinning's.

Rachel winced. "Yeah…mine too. It's obvious we're way out of shape. We better drink a lot of water or we're going to be in serious pain tomorrow."

They got the first two loads hung and soon the sheets were billowing out in the breeze like sails on a tall ship. While they waited for the third load, they sat on the porch swing together, watching it flap and billow in the wind while sipping tall glasses of cold lemonade.

"You know, even though hanging the laundry was a pain, this is kinda cool," Karen admitted, looking over the rolling hills of farmland. The view from the corner where the porch swing hung gave them an incredible view. The breeze was warm but pleasant, and all was quiet except for the birds, the flapping laundry and the occasional whinny of a horse in the paddock.

Rachel leaned forward and looked closer at her daughter. Karen had a serene look on her face. "Really? You're not putting me on, are you?"

"I kind of feel like Half-pint from Little House on the Prairie, doing things the old-fashioned way," Karen replied. She took another sip of the tart lemonade and grimaced as a new thought occurred to her. "If only we didn't have to go potty in that awful outhouse."

"The contractor is going to start work in the next few weeks. We should have indoor plumbing soon; after all, how long could it take?" Rachel checked her watch. "Time to take the first load in; it should be dry by now."

Karen's head fell back with a groan. "Can't I just finish my lemonade first?"

"Sure." Rachel gulped down hers and set the empty glass on a nearby table. She turned to find Karen dipping her tongue into the glass and lapping up her drink one drop at a time. Rachel put her hands on her hips. "At that rate it'll take you five hours to finish."

"Exactly," Karen grinned.

Rachel took away the glass and hauled Karen to her feet. "Let's get it over with."

They stood below the clothesline. Karen buried her face into a towel and inhaled deeply. "OMG, you're right...it does smell really good. What is that?"

"Fresh air," Rachel replied with a smile. "Just don't do that with your underwear, okay?"

"Ewww...Mom...*gross*." Despite Karen's protestations, she still couldn't help smelling every item of laundry as it came off the line. They folded as they went, dropping the finished laundry into the basket.

Chapter Nine

Learning the Hard Way

Karen could hardly wait for the rooster to crow. Today was the day Mr. Miller was going to take her over to his sister's house for a sleepover. She got the chickens fed and the eggs collected and packed into cartons in record time with the promise that they could sell most of them to the local Amish market on the way there.

She had packed, unpacked, and repacked the night before, changing her mind several times before finally settling on two plain white t-shirts, blue jeans, and shorts as well as the blue Amish dress, a black apron, and a white *kapp*, just in case. She had a hard time keeping still at the breakfast table, gulping down her food and fidgeting nervously until Samuel was ready to leave. As soon as he had downed his last gulp of hot coffee, she was on her feet and waiting for him by the door with her suitcase in hand.

"Don't I at least get a hug or kiss goodbye?" Rachel complained, opening her arms.

"I don't do hugs," Karen replied, hefting her suitcase. Her mother's arms dropped but she steadfastly ignored the stricken look on her face. She was still very angry that she had been forced to move across the country and wasn't going to miss any opportunity to let her mom know so. Besides, her mom should know by now that she didn't like being hugged.

"All ready to go, *jah*?" Mr. Miller entered the room, took her suitcase, and placed his straw hat upon his head.

"Yup." Karen bounced up and down on the balls of her feet.

Her mom waved goodbye. "Be a good girl, honey."

"Yeah…yeah…I will." She couldn't wait to get away and have some fun with people her own age. She didn't even care that they were Amish. She was desperate for the company of someone other than her mom.

The Amish market took all their eggs, so Karen was able to pocket another hundred dollars. She glanced over at Mr. Miller who sat beside her in the buggy, saying nothing as he drove Dodger down the two-lane, his gaze fixed on the road ahead. Karen fanned herself. It was warm and muggy, almost stifling. Pennsylvania may have been much prettier than Southern California, but she sure didn't like the humidity. At least when it got hot in Southern California, her clothes didn't stick to her skin by 9:00 in the morning.

They arrived a half hour later. The mom and several other girls, whom Karen assumed were her children, greeted them in the driveway. They gathered around the buggy in their traditional Amish clothing, all smiles, and apparently quite excited.

"*Guder mariye*," Karen said. She had rehearsed the Pennsylvania Dutch greeting all morning.

"*Guder mariye*," they echoed back to her, smiling broadly.

Karen clambered out, but before she could get her own suitcase, the eldest girl retrieved it from the back of the buggy for her.

"I'm Mary," she said, giving Karen a friendly smile. She pointed to her younger sisters. "This is Martha, she's eight and Mirriam is five."

"Hi," Karen said, squatting down so she could look Mirriam in the face. She was so cute with her pink chubby cheeks, blue dress, and white *kapp*. Like a little Amish doll. She turned back to Mr. Miller. "Thank you so much, Mr. Miller. I'll see you in a day or so then?"

"You wish to stay longer than one day?" he replied, a smile tugging at the corners of his mouth.

Karen nodded, anxious for him to leave already. "Yeah, if it's alright. I don't want to be any inconvenience..."

Sarah put a friendly arm around Karen's shoulders and gave her a little hug. "*Ach*, you won't be...that's for certain." Karen caught the wink the girl gave Samuel but wasn't sure what it meant.

Mary hooked her free arm through Karen's and led her into the house. It was very similar to hers. It had similar hardwood floors, braided rugs, and bare walls, but it smelled of freshly baked bread, pies, and cooking fruit. On the long kitchen counter were rows and rows of Mason jars and on the stove were several large pots with steam billowing out of them. The kitchen was sweltering hot.

Mary led her upstairs and showed her to a room with a large bed. Karen was thrilled. It would be so nice to spread out in a full-size bed for a change.

Mary set her suitcase down on the floor. "You'll be sharing this room with me and Martha."

Karen's heart sank. "Oh? Really? Where's the roll-away bed?"

To her horror, Mary smiled at her and said, "There's only the one bed, but don't worry, we don't snore, at least I don't think we do." She gestured to a small dresser. "I cleared half a drawer for you and your things. After you unpack, we'll go downstairs and help my *mamm* with the canning."

"Canning?" Karen repeated, beginning to realize that she'd been hoodwinked.

Mary nodded, "We're making apricot jam."

"Yum," Karen mumbled unenthusiastically.

Mary waited as Karen dumped her clothes into the tiny drawer and shoved it closed with some difficulty. "Don't you wish to fold them? They'll get wrinkled that way."

Karen shrugged. "I don't care." Her sunny mood was gone the moment she realized that this was not to be the "get-away" she had hoped for. She trudged downstairs behind Mary and followed her into the kitchen.

"*Ach,* just in time, girls…get your aprons on." Sarah Hochstetler greeted them, ladling hot jam into the Mason jars.

For the next hour, Karen placed caps and screwed lids onto the glass jars filled with warm jam and set them into pots of boiling water with jar tongs. It was miserable work. By the time ten minutes had passed, she had sweated through her clothes. When they were done, Mary took her out to the porch for a short break where they shared glasses of sweet, iced tea.

"I wish I could take a bath in this," Karen murmured, holding the frosted glass against her forehead. She raised the glass high "I wish I could take the Nestea plunge!" She peered over at Mary who didn't seem to get the joke and didn't look nearly as wilted as she felt. "Aren't you hot? You're hardly sweating."

"I'm more used to the weather here than you are," Mary smiled sympathetically, sipping from her glass. "Is this your first-time canning jam?"

Karen nodded.

"Well, you did an excellent job. You hardly spilled a drop."

The compliment warmed Karen's heart. "Thanks," she smiled, but it was small reward for the misery it had earned her.

Mary drained her glass of tea and stood up. "Time for the horses," she said, taking Karen's empty glass and depositing it in the kitchen before leading her out to the barn.

Karen followed a few steps behind. Somehow, she didn't think it was going to be for an outing of horse-back riding.

Mary handed her a bridle. "Do you know how to put this on a horse?"

Karen shook her head.

"Just watch me and do as I do. With your left hand you hold the top of the bridle like so and slide it up their face until the bit hits their lips. Keep gently sliding until they open their mouth and let the bit slide all the way in, then fold their ears down so you can get the crownpiece behind them, like so."

Karen swallowed nervously. "You make it look so easy."

"The horses know what to do. Now you do it."

Karen patted the horse on his face first then slid the bridle up. The bit went right in, and she got it on one try. "I did it," she beamed, proud of herself.

"*Gut* job," smiled Mary. Now we'll take them into the paddock so we can muck out their stalls.

Karen's arms fell to her side, "Muck?" She knew what that meant: *lots of manure.*

"*Jah.*"

Karen trudged behind Mary, leading her horse into the paddock. At that moment, little Mirriam joined them. She was carrying a pail of water that looked like it weighed more than she did.

"Do you need help?" Karen called out as the little girl waddled closer with her load.

Mirriam smiled up at her. "*Nee.*"

To Karen's amazement, the little girl hefted the pail and poured the water into the trough for the horses, then ran back to the pump to get more.

Karen turned to Mary. "Should she be carrying something so heavy?"

Mary smiled at her. "Why not? She does it every day just like I used to do when I was her age."

Somehow, somewhere this must be a violation of child labor laws, Karen thought to herself, *also cruel and unusual punishment...* She said nothing as they returned to the barn and led the remaining animals out to the paddock. Then the real fun began.

Karen couldn't remember a time when she had worked so hard in her life. She scooped shovelful after shovelful of smelly manure into the wheelbarrow then pushed it to the manure pile behind the barn, which stunk to high heaven and had clouds of bugs swarming around it. Mary told her they let the manure dry out then sold whatever they didn't use to other farmers. *Disgusting.* Mr. Miller and her mom had totally tricked her! Here she thought she was coming over for a social visit and she was being worked like a slave. Her back, arms, and neck were still aching from doing laundry and now she was forced to shovel pooh and pitch fresh hay. She knew Mary had brothers. Why weren't they doing the barn chores?

She sneezed loudly and wiped her nose on her sleeve. As if it weren't bad enough already, her allergies were kicking in. "So where are all your brothers and dad?" she asked.

"They're out working in the fields. Soon we will need to bring them something cool to drink," Mary answered from the other stall. They finished up in the barn, led the animals back in, and then went to the house to collect the plastic jugs of freshly made lemonade and sweet tea.

Mrs. Hochstetler fanned her face as she handed out the plastic cups and jugs. "It must be every bit of one hundred degrees out there today. They're in the hay field." Sarah handed Karen a Playmate cooler. "Hurry along, now. We still have supper to prepare."

"Yes, *mamm*," Mary said, skipping down the porch steps.

Karen followed her until they reached the water pump and paused. She was so hot, she felt ready to faint. She couldn't imagine how intolerable it must have been out in the fields all day long under the full sun. "Can I get some water first?"

Mary smiled at her sympathetically. "*Jah*, of course. You do look flushed. Put your hands under the spigot and I'll pump the water out for you."

"Thanks," Karen replied, setting the Playmate a safe distance away. She bent forward and held out her hands while Mary pumped up and down several times. Ice-cold well water flowed over her hands. She splashed her face and the back of her neck, but it wasn't enough. Finally, she just stuck her head under the spigot and let the water completely soak her head.

Mary giggled at her. "Well, that's one way to get cool quickly."

Karen straightened and smiled back at her, the water streaming down her head and neck and under her clothes in cool rivulets. "*Ahhhh*, now that feels great." She picked up the Playmate, feeling much better and not caring how strange she looked with her dark hair plastered to her skull. Together, they walked out to the hay field where, far in the distance, she could see the mule-drawn hay baler. Heat thermals shimmered ahead of them. Despite her dousing, she soon grew hot again.

"These are my *brudders*," Mary said as they neared the wagon. She pointed from the eldest to the youngest. "This is Willis, John, and Isaac."

Karen handed up the Playmate and gave them each a shy smile. Isaac could not have been much more than ten years old and here he was working in ninety-plus-degree heat with ninety percent humidity using hundred-year-old farm technology. Willis, the oldest, stared at her with unabashed curiosity.

"*Danki*," he grinned as she handed him and his family glasses of sweet tea. They left the food and drink behind and walked across the field to the shady lawn in front of the farmhouse. It felt blessedly cool compared to the heat of the field.

Karen doused her face and neck with water from the pump again but didn't soak her head. They entered the kitchen where they found Mirriam and the middle sister, Martha, busy cleaning and chopping vegetables while their mother was elbow deep in flour.

"There you are, just in time to take over the noodles while I get the chickens."

Karen followed Mary to the sink and swiftly washed up, donning an apron while they took Mrs. Hochstetler's place at the wooden board, coated with flour. Mrs. Hochstetler disappeared out the back screen door.

Mary smiled at her. "Would you like to help me with the noodles?"

Karen shrugged. "Sure, I guess." She looked around, wondering where the package of noodles was.

"Best to tie your hair back so it doesn't get into the dough."

"Dough?" Karen repeated with a blank look. Mary handed her a rubber band so Karen could tie her hair back. "I thought we were making noodles?"

"We are. First, we make the dough then we roll it out flat and cut it into strips. Then they go into that pot of boiling water on the stove."

Karen had never made dough before, so she became quite fascinated when Mary made a well in the large mound of flour and broke several eggs into the center of it. Next, she took a fork and mixed the flour into the well, a little at a time. Soon she was working it with her hands until, as if by magic, she had a ball of dough. Mary dusted the board with more flour then handed her a rolling pin. "Do as I do," she said, making a disc of dough with her hands. With quick strokes, she rolled out the dough into a flat sheet. Karen imitated her as best she could but couldn't get the dough as evenly flat. Thankfully, Mary didn't seem to notice. A few minutes later, Sarah Hochstetler reentered the kitchen, allowing the screen door to slam shut behind her.

Karen turned around, took one look, and screamed, dropping the rolling pin onto the floor in the process. Flour billowed out in a cloud as she stared in horror at the sight in front her. Mrs. Hochstetler had four chickens, two in each hand, hanging upside down by the talons, newly dead. She had assumed that she had just gone to the refrigerator to retrieve packages of chicken.

OMG Karen gulped. *I'm visiting a slaughterhouse.*

Martha hurried forward to relieve her mother of the dead fowl. Karen looked on in fascinated horror as she took them to the stove and dunked them into enormous pots of boiling water. The chickens soaked in the water for several minutes before she fished them out with a large sieve and plunged them into an ice bath then left them on the drain board to cool.

Karen felt a nudge in her ribs. "Let's finish the noodles." Mary gave her the newly cleaned rolling pin.

"Oh…uh…sorry about that," Karen murmured and went back to rolling out her share of the dough. Every so often she would steal a glance over her shoulder to peek at Mary's younger sisters, sitting on stools with heavy towels on their laps, plucking furiously and shoving the feathers into a large pillowcase. When the chickens were completely free of feathers and pinions, the girls rinsed them and gave them to their mother for butchering.

"You're in luck. We're having fried chicken tonight," Mary informed her with a happy gleam in her eye.

Karen had lost all appetite for chicken now that she had seen, up close and personal, how it was processed. "Oh… goodie," she gulped. Soon, the noodles were cooking in the boiling water, but if she had any hope that work was done for the day, she was sorely mistaken. The list of chores seemed never-ending. She found herself longing to be back at home if only to take a nap. She was exhausted. If only she hadn't told Mr. Miller to leave her here for two whole days! By the time Mr. Hochstetler and his sons came in from the fields to wash for supper, she was ready to crawl under the table and go to sleep.

They sat at the long pine kitchen table and bowed their heads for the blessing, which they gave in silence. Karen was grateful for the chance to sit still for the first time that day and rest her eyes. Suddenly she felt herself poked in the side. Her head jerked up with a snort and her eyes flew open to find the entire family staring at her. The youngest ones clapped hands over their mouths to stifle their giggles.

"Did I fall asleep?" Karen asked, sitting up straighter, her face burning.

"*Jah*," the entire family responded in unison.

Karen flushed with embarrassment. "I'm so sorry, I guess I'm just really tired." She looked down and found her plate filled with fried chicken, noodles, and bean casserole. The sight of the golden fried chicken made her remember the dead carcasses in Mrs. Hochstetler's hands and she lost her appetite.

"May I be excused?"

"Aren't you *hungerich*?" Mary asked, biting into a chicken leg with relish. "My *mamm* makes the best fried chicken."

Karen stood up and pushed her chair away from the table as nausea swept over her. She clapped a hand over her mouth and bolted out the front door, searching frantically for the outhouse. She was there in moments and had to pinch her nose shut while her empty stomach heaved.

It's bad enough getting sick in front of an entire house of strangers but to retch my guts out in a smelly outhouse is the worst. I hate outhouses! I hate them! I never should have left California. I should have refused to get on that train with my mother. I should have run away from home where she couldn't find me...

When her stomach finally settled, she stumbled out of the outhouse, plunked down miserably on the grass, and hid her face in her arms, angry tears streaming from her eyes. *This was such a total set-up to teach me a lesson! I am never speaking to my mother or Samuel ever again!* She refused to cry out loud but sat in silence, letting the angry tears fall silently. Soon she noticed plain brown leather shoes standing next to her. She looked up and found Mary looking down on her in genuine sympathy.

"What?" she asked morosely.

Mary sat down on the grass next to her and put an arm around her shoulder. "Are you alright?"

Karen nodded "yes" despite feeling quite the opposite. Mary said nothing more, which was a relief. She didn't try to talk Karen into feeling better. She just sat next to her in silence and rubbed her back, pretending not to mind the fact that her own dinner was growing cold. Karen lifted her arm to wipe her nose on her sleeve, but Mary stopped her and instead produced a handkerchief for her to use. Karen stared at it for a moment. It was a beautiful white cotton square with white embroidery on it. She couldn't possibly blow her nose on that.

"Go ahead, it's quite alright," Mary encouraged her gently. "It'll go right in the wash tomorrow anyway and I have others."

"Thanks," replied Karen and blew her nose. They sat for several more moments in companionable silence while Karen calmed down. "I guess we should go back in now," she mumbled, knowing that she had been gone too long and feeling guilty for making Mary miss her dinner.

Mary stood up first and held out her hands to help Karen up. Karen looked up at the girl, so close to her own age, and felt an overwhelming sense of acceptance. It had been a long time since she'd had a friend.

"I think everyone will understand if you don't eat the chicken," Mary said, tucking Karen's arm through hers. "But perhaps for tonight, you can just try the noodles you helped to make, so you don't go to bed on an empty stomach. They turned out very *gut*."

A slow smile came to Karen's face, "Really?"

They walked up the porch steps together and reentered the house. Thankfully, no one looked up or treated her as if anything unusual had happened. Karen retook her seat and tasted the noodles. They were yummy. Soon she was even helping herself to a small piece of chicken, the best she'd ever had and that was saying a lot considering her mom's cooking skills.

By the time dinner was over, she felt quite different. She enjoyed clearing the dinner dishes and cleaning up the kitchen with the other girls, pretending they were her long lost sisters. She had always longed for siblings, but her mom had been unable to have children of her own, so she had remained the only adopted child. She, Mary, and the younger girls took turns splashing each other with the soapy dishwater, laughing and joking as they dried and put the plates, cups, and silverware away. Karen found herself giggling right along with them, enjoying the rare camaraderie of being part of a large family.

When they had finished cleaning, the girls went upstairs to their room and took turns sponge bathing. Then they put on clean cotton nightgowns and took turns braiding each other's hair, chattering away while crowding onto the bed. Mary read them a story from the Bible by the soft glow of lantern light. Feeling refreshed and wonderfully content, Karen drew her knees underneath her on the bed and looked around at the happy faces of Mary and her sisters. They were so full of innocence and joy, not the haughty, guarded, or jaded expressions most of her friends had back home. Her old friends fretted constantly about fitting in with the "cool" crowd, having the latest clothes, backstabbing, and enduring all the drama about who was dating whom, or if someone had posted something mean about them on social media. Even though these girls did not have luxuries like iPhones, internet, and television, they seemed much happier and contented compared to the friends she had left behind. She felt like she had stepped out of reality and into the pages of Little Women.

Mary read from the Old Testament and, although Karen had heard the scriptures many times before, they came alive as she performed for her sisters, using different voices for each character. There were giggles and solemn faces in all the right places. She felt disappointed when Mary closed the Bible and announced that it was time to go to sleep. She had really been enjoying herself. They ended the evening on their knees together beside the bed, praying silently, then they doused the lanterns, and the younger girls went to the room they shared. Karen laid down next to Mary and Martha.

"Mary," Karen whispered.

Mary turned toward her. "Yes?"

"Thanks so much for what you did for me today."

Mary reached out, took her hand, and patted it. "It must be very difficult to have lost a parent and leave behind all you know."

The compassionate words made tears well up in Karen's eyes and the tight band around her chest began to loosen. She had been holding her tears in for months, but in the darkness, she felt safe in letting them run down her face.

"I didn't want to move here," she choked. "I didn't want to leave my family and all my friends." Then a sob escaped from her throat. "I really miss my dad," she whimpered, the pent-up grief finally bubbling over. "My mom doesn't think I do but I really, really miss him. He was so good to me and funny. He always made me laugh. I never told him how much I loved him or how I appreciated all he did for me and now it's too late…" she couldn't speak anymore. The pain crushed the words out of her.

"Such a heartache," Mary whispered back. This only made Karen cry harder. Normally she would only allow silent tears to flow down her cheeks, but the emotional upheaval of the last few months had finally reached a breaking point inside of her. Karen dissolved into loud choking sobs that shook the bed, allowing herself to grieve fully for the first time in over a year. She wept for the father she missed terribly, she wept for her mom with whom she could never allow herself to get close to, and most of all she wept for herself. She was only dimly aware of Mary and Martha's arms going around her as she fell into a deep, exhausted sleep.

Chapter Ten

A Fresh Start

The following morning, Karen woke up feeling better than she had in a long time, cleansed from the inside out. Although it was still dark out, the faint light of the waning moon was shining on Mary's face through the bedroom window. Karen studied her new friends for a moment. They looked so serene, so at peace. Despite all the hard work they did each day, they seemed truly happy. A pang of jealousy tweaked Karen's heart. She looked out the window as the sky faded from dark blue to pale blue. It was almost dawn. That meant everyone would be getting up soon and lining up for the one measly outhouse. Might as well go now and avoid the line, she reasoned, throwing back the covers and creeping downstairs with a lantern. She finished her business just as the rooster crowed. She saw the dim glow of lanterns lit in the second story windows as the family awakened to start a new day.

She met Mary on the stairs who was bundled up in a shawl. They exchanged understanding smiles as they passed. Karen felt closer to Mary at that moment than she had ever felt to her parents or her old friends. She had shared her innermost feelings to a total stranger and found comfort. Karen returned to their room and stared at the clothes she had shoved in the drawer, trying to decide what to wear. She finally settled on the Amish dress, *kapp*, and apron so she would fit in better. She was just brushing out her long hair when Mary returned.

"Would you like me to pin up your hair 'plain style?'" she offered.

Karen nodded. "That would be great. It's too warm to wear it down."

"Sit on the bed then," Mary beckoned, taking Karen's hairbrush from her hand.

Karen did as she was told and closed her eyes. Mary sat down behind her and brushed out her hair. It felt wonderful to have someone else brushing her hair and Mary was very gentle. After a few moments, it was bound into a tight ponytail, twisted into a bun, and secured with dozens of bobby pins. Then she placed the white *kapp* on Karen's head.

"All done," Mary said, turning to help her younger sisters, who had entered the room while she was doing Karen's hair.

Karen stood and looked around, trying to find a mirror to see how she looked and almost did a face palm. *Duh. Amish. No mirrors.* Next Mary brushed out Martha's hair while Mirriam stood by and waited, her long golden tresses hanging almost to the small of her back. "Would you like me to brush your hair?" Karen offered.

Dimples appeared on Mirriam's rosy cheeks, and she nodded, sitting down in front of her. Karen watched Mary and copied the way she brushed out the hair, wrapped it in a ponytail, and then wound it up into a tight bun.

"*Danki,*" Mirriam said, giving her a hug of thanks. Then she skipped off down the stairs. The other girls followed her and went into the kitchen where Mrs. Hochstetler was already busy at work, making the morning biscuits.

"What do I do?" asked Karen, feeling eager to help, although she was a bit nervous when it came to cooking and baking. She had done neither in her lifetime other than frying eggs and making enchiladas.

"First, we make the baking powder biscuits, then the bread for the day so it has time to rise. Then we make pies."

Karen gulped. "Couldn't I do something easy like fry bacon for breakfast or scramble eggs? I already know how to do that."

Mary checked the stove, "too late, *Mamm* already has ham and potatoes frying for breakfast. Do not worry. I'll show you how. It's very similar to making noodles and you did a very *gut* job on those."

Karen stood and watched as Mary opened the canisters of flour, sugar, baking soda, baking powder and Crisco. They mixed the ingredients for the bread and were soon kneading the dough together while they chatted.

Although she and Mary had absolutely nothing in common, Karen found her incredibly easy to talk to and was enjoying herself. She loved having someone to do all these things with and felt a great sense of belonging and accomplishment. By the time breakfast was on the table, they had four loaves rising in the warm oven. Mr. Hochstetler and his sons came in, washed up, and sat down at the table while Sarah and her daughters served the food. They bowed their heads in silence for the blessing. Having eaten mostly nothing but noodles the night before, Karen was famished. She piled her plate high with homemade biscuits, scrambled eggs, fried potatoes, and ham.

"You are such a tiny little thing, Miss Karen Winston. Where are you going to put all that food?" smiled Mrs. Hochstetler.

Karen returned the smile. "I don't know, but I'm hungry enough to eat a cow." This sent Martha and Mirriam into giggling fits. Karen attacked her food with gusto, barely pausing to talk between bites. After they gave the second blessing, which thanked God for the meal just eaten, a long-drawn out belch erupted from Karen's mouth. She slapped her hand over her mouth and went beet red. "I'm so sorry."

Instead of reprimanding her, the entire family grinned and nodded as though she had just paid them a wonderful compliment. She couldn't help thinking of her mom who would have given her a dirty look and asked her where her manners were. With breakfast done, Mr. Hochstetler and his sons went out to the fields to start their long day of labor while the women cleaned up the kitchen.

"Now what?" asked Karen.

Mary and her mother exchanged bemused glances. "Now we put the loaves in the oven to bake and start on the pies," replied Mary.

Karen went to the sink, rolled up her sleeves, and washed her hands, holding them up like a surgeon ready for his gloves. "What kind of pies?"

"Whoopie and Shoofly."

Karen burst into giggles. "Whoopie? Not Whoop De Doo? Shoofly? What funny names for pies. Why is it called Shoofly?"

Mary led her to a bowl on the counter. "Because it is so sweet the flies can't stay away from them. Shoofly is my favorite. Now, which would you rather do: the crust, the filling, or the topping?"

"Can't I do all of it?" Karen asked. "Do you think I could make an extra one to bring home with me?" *It would be a great way to get back at Mom for tricking me into this situation. She can't bake to save her life, how embarrassed will she be if I come home with a pie that I made myself?*

Mary shrugged. "*Jah*, sure. We can make extra. First, we start with the pie crust." Mary gave her instructions and watched over her efforts, correcting her when the need arose. She was nothing like Karen's mom, who blew a gasket whenever she screwed up the least little bit in the kitchen, the main reason she had never wanted to learn how to cook or bake. Her mother was too persnickety in the kitchen where everything had to be cleaned up as you went. While she rolled out her first pie crust, Mary hummed a soft tune that Karen recognized as one of the hymns she had sung in church as part of the choir.

"I know that song," Karen exclaimed and began to sing aloud while her rolling pin went over the dough in smooth strokes. Mary joined her, singing in harmony:

> *"Amazing grace, how sweet the sound,*
> *that saved a wretch like me!*
> *I once was lost but now I'm found,*
> *was blind but now I see..."*

Karen glanced over and saw Sarah Hochstetler and her two youngest daughters pausing from their work to listen to them sing together, their voices harmonizing perfectly. When their song ended, Mary pointed down at Karen's pie crust and beamed. "*Ach*, worshipping *Der Herr* results in perfect pie crust; just look at that."

Karen blushed, pleased with her first effort. Mary took the rolling pin, rolled the dough around it, then showed her how to unroll it and lay it across the pie tin. "Now, you press it flat on the bottom and up against the edges then poke the crust many times with a fork. Then we will put foil over it and add pie weights. Then it goes into the oven to bake while we make the filling."

For the next hour, they worked on the Shoofly pies and then the Whoopie pies, which turned out weren't really fruit pies, but little cake sandwiches filled with cream. Karen was having the time of her life, especially when it came time to apply the whipped cream filling to the Whoopie pies. She was a fiend for whipped cream and had a hard time keeping her fingers out of it while they spread it inside the little cakes. More than once, Mary had to slap her hand, and soon it became a game between them. With the bread and pies done and cooling, Karen found herself eager for more.

"Next!"

Mary heaved a deep sigh. "It's Wash Day." She turned to Martha and Mirriam. "Gather up all the dirty linens."

The two girls scampered off while Karen followed her out to the service porch, her good mood dampened. She had just done several loads of clothes a couple of days ago and her arms were still aching. Karen was beyond dismayed when she saw the same hand-cranked Maytag washer with the wringer on the top.

Mary and Mirriam arrived minutes later, each carrying a laundry basket filled to overflowing with soiled clothing and bed linens. They dumped them out on the floor for Karen and Mary to sort through then ran off.

"Where are they going?" She squatted down and began separating the darks from the whites. Her parents had taught her to do her own clothes since the age of thirteen, but never had she done more than put them into the wash or transfer them to the dryer. Most of the time, she managed to finagle the timing so her clothes would not come out of the dryer until late at night. That way, her dad, always the softie, would fold her clothes for her, something that she hated to do. Her clothes had never been this filthy, however. These stunk to high heaven because they were saturated with dirt, sweat, and manure. She pointed to the pile of underwear. "I'm not touching that without a pair of tongs."

Mary shook her head at her and laughed. "*Ach*, this is only the first two loads. There should be at least five more after this." Mary bent over the machine, layering the whites evenly inside the washer. "Between loads, we'll have to find time to help with lunch."

"The fun never ends." Karen grumbled under her breath; her happy mood gone. She despised doing laundry. Mary ignored her comments, turning to her younger sisters who had returned with more clothing. The laundry piled higher and higher until there was a giant mound that practically filled the back porch.

"We'll be using all the clotheslines we have today."

Karen stifled a moan, but Mary cheerfully ignored her. She put down the lid and started the machine, then went to the next, filling it with darks. She wiped her hands on her apron. "Let's go help *Mamm* with lunch. The loaves should almost be ready to come out by now."

Karen followed her back into the kitchen, the wonderful smell of baking bread greeting her nose. Her mouth watered even though she had just eaten a couple of hours ago.

They found Mrs. Hochstetler sitting at an antique, foot-operated sewing machine, stitching some dark purple fabric into a dress. Karen drew closer to take a better look.

"That's my favorite color," she grinned, admiring the dark purple. "It's Justin Bieber's favorite color, too."

Mrs. Hochstetler looked up at her with a completely blank expression. "Justin who?"

"Justin Bieber?" Karen repeated, unable to believe she didn't know who the famous singer was. "He's a very famous person..." her voice trailed off into silence as Mrs. Hochstetler continued to smile at her with a bemused expression on her face.

"Karen, the loaves and pies are done," Mary summoned her from the kitchen.

Relieved to be distracted from what had been a rather embarrassing conversation, Karen hurried back to the kitchen and looked inside the oven.

Mary handed her the mitts. "Would you like to do the honors?"

"*Jah*," Karen grinned, her sense of accomplishment returning as she bent over and lifted out the loaves followed by the pies. *Just wait until mom gets a load of the Shoofly pie I made!*

143

"Set the pies on the sill to cool," Mary pointed. "Then we'll make sandwiches and drinks to bring out to the field. She took hold of the loaf pans with the mitts and flipped them over, so the golden-brown bread tumbled out onto the kitchen board to cool.

Karen leaned close and took a big whiff. "I can't believe I made bread and pies today." She grinned at Mary. "I always thought it was so hard because my mom could never do it, but it really isn't."

"Well, I hear that will soon be remedied. My *mamm* says that she's agreed to help yours learn how to bake properly and do other things our way."

For the next fifteen minutes, they packed up a hearty lunch and made sweet tea. By then the wash was finished and it was time to hang it on the line while the younger girls took the food out to their father and brothers in the field.

Mary hefted the basket of whites onto her hip and Karen did likewise with the darks. "Now we peg, follow me."

Karen followed her out back where several clotheslines stretched from the house to the picturesque white barn. A large cloth bag filled with clothespins hung at one end of the clothesline.

"You want to pin the clothes so they will dry as quickly as possible," Mary explained, lifting a large sheet out of the basket. She unfolded it then hung it over the clothesline and pegged the ends as well as the middle. She pointed to the pile of dresses, aprons, overalls, and trousers. "Hang them upside down from the bottom hem so the shoulders dry."

Karen nodded and hung up the first dress, noting how all the clothes were in solid colors of black, dark blue, light blue, maroon, hunter green or dark purple. They had no buttons or zippers, only hooks, and eyes. She had to pause several times to rest her aching arms. She wasn't used to lifting and holding them over her head for such long periods of time and they were beginning to cramp up. To take

144

her mind off the pain, she began to hum another hymn she had learned at church and was pleased when Mary joined in with her. After an hour, they had both loads hung on the line and went back to the service porch to check on the next load of laundry.

"*Hungerich?*" Mary asked, "I sure am!"

Normally, Karen didn't have much of an appetite, something that never ceased to irk her mother, who constantly worried that she was underweight. She nodded, surprised that she was famished. *Must be all this physical labor.* "Starving," she grinned. She followed Mary into the kitchen and watched as she expertly sliced the bread, slathered it with mayonnaise, and piled it high with leftover meatloaf, lettuce, and tomatoes. She started to ask Mary not to include the vegetables then thought better of it. She didn't want to offend her. Mary plated the sandwich then pushed it over to her. Together, they bowed their heads in silent prayer and then dug in. Karen closed her eyes and groaned with pleasure. The bread was the best she had ever tasted, improved by the knowledge that she had helped to make it. She didn't even mind the lettuce or tomato slices since they were homegrown and very tasty. They washed the sandwiches down with large glasses of sweet tea and then returned to finish the laundry.

For the rest of the afternoon, Karen hung laundry, singing hymns with Mary, before prepping for supper. She couldn't remember a time when she had felt so content despite all the hard work. She barely noticed when Samuel Miller's buggy pulled into the driveway or that he had paused to stare at her before entering the house.

Mrs. Hochstetler came into the backyard where she was working. "Karen, your ride home is here."

Karen turned around and stared at him. "But I thought you weren't coming until tomorrow?"

"I thought you might be ready to come home a day early," he replied, confused by her reluctance.

"Oh." Karen wasn't sure what to say to him. Despite her aching muscles and her exhaustion, she really didn't want to leave yet. She liked being with Mary and her sisters, learning how to make pies and bread and how to can fruit. She didn't want to miss the bedtime story or prayers that night either.

Samuel tipped his hat back enough to look at her better, running his fingers through his thick hair. "Well, I'm here now and can't make another round trip tomorrow, so you'll have to come home with me."

Karen hung her head and obediently trudged into the house to get her things, thoroughly dejected. The last thing she wanted to do was go back to the big empty house and be ordered around by her mother. She climbed the stairs to the bedroom and gathered up her clothes, stuffing them into her night bag, and then trudged back down. She found Mr. Miller and his sister standing at the bottom along with Mary, Mirriam, and Martha, who had all come to bid her goodbye, looking as disappointed as she felt. She felt like crying.

"We have enjoyed having you, Karen," said Mrs. Hochstetler, placing two large brown paper sacks into her arms. "You are a *gut* worker."

"What's this?" Karen asked.

"Shoofly pie and the loaf of bread you made. There's also a surprise in the other bag for you, but you are not to open it until you get home."

Karen nodded and forced a brave smile. "Thanks...I mean...*danki* for letting me come and spend time with your family," she struggled to keep her voice even. "I really appreciate it."

To her surprise, Mrs. Hochstetler bent forward so they were eye-to-eye and gave her a broad smile. "*Gern gschehne,* you are welcome. We'll see you soon at the quilting bee and the singing. Please bring your *mamm* with you."

"I will," Karen smiled wanly, not really wanting to include her mother.

Mary also gave her a warm hug, followed by her other sisters. Karen swallowed down the lump in her throat. If she didn't leave soon, she was going to start bawling in front of them. She hurried down the porch stairs and climbed into the back of the buggy. Once safely inside, she let her tears flow freely as Mr. Miller said his own goodbyes, then returned to drive her home.

When they cleared the driveway, she opened the brown paper sack and peeked inside. Folded neatly was a piece of purple cloth. She pulled it out and gasped with surprise and delight. It was the dress Mrs. Hochstetler had been working on earlier that day, the one she had admired. She had made Karen her very own Amish dress in her favorite color along with a black apron. Karen burst into tears.

"*Was is los?*" Mr. Miller asked, lapsing into Pennsylvania Dutch as he turned round to look at her. He was looking at her as if she had lost her mind. It didn't matter. She couldn't understand what he was saying anyway.

"She made me a dress," Karen sniffed, holding it up.

Mr. Miller stared at her, a ghost of a smile turning up the corners of his mouth. "*Ach...jah?*" That was all he said.

Karen refolded the dress and put it back inside the brown paper bag as though it were a valuable treasure. The only part of going home she was looking forward to, was showing off the pie and loaf of bread she had made to her mom.

Rachel was exhausted. It was close to 4:00 p.m. and her daughter and Samuel had not yet returned from his sister's place. She wondered how hard the Hochstetler's had worked Karen and if Samuel's plan had worked its magic on her attitude. She went into the kitchen to begin pre-

paring a welcome home supper, little Buddy trotting happily behind her. He took up his post on the little oval rug
he had claimed as his own at the end of the cabinets. He
would be out of the way but was still able to keep a watchful
eye out for any morsels that dropped by accident. Rachel
squatted down and rubbed his silky ears, cooing lovingly at
him. While Karen had been gone, she had gotten another
four loads of laundry done and she had the aching arms to
prove it.

Samuel had continued to take his meals with her during
Karen's absence despite their lack of a chaperone. Last evening, he again sat with her on the porch swing watching the
fireflies in silence, their fingers intertwining again as they
spoke of their families and lives before tragedy had struck.
She found Samuel to be a good listener and great comfort,
mainly because his pain was as fresh and so much like her
own. He didn't try to make her feel better by mouthing
platitudes or reciting scriptures, instead he let her vent and
grieve freely, and she did the same for him. Last night for
the first time she had leaned her head upon his shoulder,
and he had done nothing to discourage it or shift away.
Instead, he had just wrapped an arm about her shoulders,
much as an older brother would do while they sat watching
the sky grow dark, finding solace in each other's company.

She went to the sink to wash up and began prepping the
roast chicken, oven fried potatoes and green bean casserole
her daughter loved best. By the time the buggy pulled into
the driveway an hour later, everything was almost done.

Karen trudged inside. Instead of looking relieved to be
home as Rachel had expected, her eyes were red and swollen as if she had been crying all the way home. That alone
was enough to give her pause. Karen almost never cried,
the few exceptions being when they had first gotten news of
Barry's death and the day that they had to put their Cocker
Spaniel, Beatrice, to sleep.

"What happened, are you okay?"

"Fine," Karen grumbled, setting her overnight bag on the floor. Buddy ran up to greet her, his tail wagging happily. Karen scooped him up and nuzzled him while he licked her salty cheeks.

"Have you been crying?"

Karen shrugged.

"I made all your favorites, honey: roast chicken with orange marmalade, green bean casserole and oven roasted potatoes."

"I'm not hungry, I had a big lunch." Karen refused to look at her.

Rachel deflated like a pricked balloon. "Did something happen at the Hochstetler's that I should know about?"

"No, why do you always have to jump to the wrong conclusions?" Karen snapped just as Samuel entered the house. He stared at them both, obviously bewildered, looking ready to say something to her daughter.

Rachel shook her head at him to discourage any upbraiding. At times like this it was best to just let Karen be.

Samuel went to the sink to wash up for supper.

Rachel watched as Karen set Buddy on the floor then put a large brown paper bag on the kitchen counter. "What's in there, honey?"

At this, Karen's face brightened a little. She opened the bag. "Close your eyes."

Rachel closed her eyes.

"Now open."

Karen stood before her beaming. In one hand, she held a loaf of bread and in the other, what looked to be a Shoofly pie.

"Well, that was nice of Mrs. Hochstetler to send you home with some treats," Rachel responded.

Karen rolled her eyes. "Mom, Mrs. Hochstetler didn't make these, *I did.*"

Rachel knew the incredulous look on her face must have been exactly what Karen was hoping for because her daughter's face broke into a great big, self-satisfied grin of triumph for the first time since setting foot in the door.

"You *made* those?"

Karen nodded.

Rachel came closer to get a better look. The loaf of bread and Shoofly pie looked and smelled great. Rachel swallowed down her pride. "They look great, honey. They look good enough to be featured on a photo spread for Amish Home & Garden magazine."

"Aren't you just dying to try some?" Karen grinned, making little circles of each with her hands.

"Of course, I'll slice the bread and serve it with butter. The pie will have to wait for dessert unless you want some now?"

Karen wrinkled her nose. "Mom, you know I don't like pie."

Rachel's brow furrowed. "Then why did you...oh never mind." Karen was nothing if not consistently exasperating.

Karen gathered the other paper bag into her arms and headed for the stairs to her room.

"Do you want me to throw that out?" Rachel held out her hand.

Karen hugged it to herself and shook her head. "No thanks. I'm going to take a sponge bath and read for a while before I go to bed. I'm exhausted."

Rachel watched her go upstairs, then turned back to see Samuel standing expectantly in front of the kitchen table, eyeing the roast chicken.

Rachel smiled grimly at him. "More for us, let's eat."

———※———

The next morning, Rachel arose late only to discover that Karen was already gone. A note left on the kitchen counter said that she would be on her egg rounds for the next hour or so. She was now familiar enough with the route that she no longer needed Samuel's guidance. Rachel glanced at her watch: 7:00 a.m. She had overslept. She changed into light khaki pants and a t-shirt then made the dreaded morning visit to the outhouse. She went in search of Samuel and found him in the paddock with Molly.

"Good morning," she said, feeling suddenly shy. "Sorry about breakfast, I overslept."

He patted Molly and walked over until he stood just on the other side of the fence from her, close enough to touch. "*Jah.*" His eyes were kind but the way he looked her slowly up and down was giving her goosebumps. She looked into his eyes, swallowing with some difficulty. "Is it too late to make you breakfast?" Although she was modestly dressed, her shirt and pants clung to her body. His continual appraisal made her nervous. Her voice dropped to a hoarse whisper as he stepped closer to her, his blue eyes intense. "I can have it ready in no time..."

Samuel's gentle eyes continued to rove slowly over her face. His hand came up and caught a tendril of her hair that was sticking out. Gently he tucked it behind her ear. The look he gave her at that moment made her knees go weak.

"I could use a hot breakfast," he murmured, his eyes staring intently into hers. He stepped closer then hesitated, his blue eyes questioning. She smiled shyly up at him. His hand reached out again and cupped her face gently, his thumb gently stroking her cheek. She took a step forward.

"Rachel...I...I mean...we shouldn't..." His voice came out as a whisper, his face looking tortured.

"Shouldn't what?" her whisper was a plea.

"We shouldn't be interacting like this," His voice came out in a raw whisper. His words were saying one thing, but his eyes and caresses were saying quite another. "I would be shunned for how I am behaving towards you if anyone were to find out."

It was like a dump of cold water over her head. With difficulty, Rachel stepped backward and collected herself, offering him an apologetic smile. "You're right, Samuel... we shouldn't. I would feel terrible if I were the cause of your getting into trouble with your community."

The hand that had caressed her cheek slowly dropped to his side. He stared at his feet as his toes kicked a clod of dirt.

Rachel stepped back, no longer able to look him in the eye. "I'll have breakfast done in a jiffy if you're still hungry."

His eyes rose to meet hers. "I am very hungry," he replied, his double meaning clear. He turned abruptly, marched over to a pail of water, lifted it over his head, and then dumped the contents all over himself. He stood there looking at her, dripping wet. The scene was comical.

Rachel burst into laughter, watching as he shook droplets out of his hair with an abashed grin. He walked back over to her; the look of intense desire gone.

"Just ring the triangle on the porch when breakfast is ready, and I'll be right over." He gave her a relieved smile.

Rachel turned around and marched back into the house without a backward glance, praying that Karen would return home in time for breakfast. Her face flamed as she realized that perhaps for the first time since they had arrived that she and Samuel finally might need a proper chaperone.

Buddy trotted to and fro, ignoring his bowl of kibble while she ground coffee, scrambled eggs, and fried links of sausage. Rachel paused, looked down at him and pointed to his bowl. "Go eat your food." Buddy looked over at the bowl then back at her and wagged his tail, as if he didn't understand. Rachel sighed and returned to dunking the sliced bread into the dish of egg, milk, cinnamon, sugar, and almond extract. She'd already learned that the dog wouldn't eat any of his own food until he had given up all hope of getting any of theirs. She had not yet tasted the bread Karen had made the day before and was curious. She left out a small slice to try *a la natural* and took a bite. Even though it was a day old, it was still soft and delicious. "Beginner's luck," she groused.

Just as she was flipping the French toast over, she heard buggy wheels pull into the gravel driveway.

The screen door flew open then shut with a bang. Karen rushed in; her face flushed with excitement. "Mom, I sold every single carton of eggs! Guess how much money I made today?"

Rachel did some quick calculations. "One hundred dollars?"

"Two hundred!" Karen squealed, jumping up and down with glee. "Not only that, but everyone wants me to come back twice a week. I'm going to be rich, rich, rich!!" She was so excited that she grabbed Rachel and gave her a brief hug, a rarity for her aloof daughter.

"That's great, honey," Rachel smiled and then noticed that she was again dressed completely Amish. She examined the dark purple dress. "This is new. Where did this come from?"

Karen stepped back. "It was a gift from Mr. Miller's sister," she replied then sniffed the air. "Is that French toast I smell?"

Rachel nodded. "Yes, I used the bread you made; breakfast is almost ready. Would you ring the triangle, so Samuel knows to come in?"

"Sure."

Karen gave it a few good clangs then skipped back inside. Rachel did her best to appear casual and normal when Samuel entered the room, hoping Karen couldn't hear the thump of her heart whenever he looked at her. She didn't miss the fact that he had changed out of his damp clothes. They bowed their heads in prayer then tucked into their meal.

"I'm going into town today," Samuel said, taking a bite of French toast. "I have to pick up some feed for the livestock." He paused and nodded his head vigorously as he chewed. "This is very, very *gut.*"

Rachel gaped at him, feeling as though she was watching a ghost. Barry used to nod his head just like that whenever he ate something he really liked. She inhaled some of the coffee down her windpipe and immediately began choking.

Karen stared at her. "Are you okay?"

Rachel nodded, swallowed the hot liquid with difficulty then continued to cough uncontrollably. The hot coffee had burned a scorching trail down her throat and the violence of her coughing was searing her chest. Samuel stared at her in concern, not sure what to do. Buddy ran and hid. Karen got up and began pounding her on the back a bit too hard.

"I'm okay," Rachel finally gasped, raising her arms to fend her off. Karen shrugged, sat back down, and resumed eating.

When she was sure she could speak without choking, Rachel turned to Samuel. "Could I come with you? I need to run a few errands too." She knew she was tempting fate by making an excuse for the two of them to be alone again, but it couldn't be helped.

What trouble could we possibly get into in a buggy? It's not like the back seat of a car...

Samuel looked up, his blue eyes focusing on hers. "*Jah,* I will be taking the spring wagon today. I have milk and cream to deliver to the Lapp Creamery."

"What's a creamery?" asked Karen.

"They process milk and cream into ice cream, butter, and cheese," Samuel replied. "Lapps makes some of the best ice cream in the *welt.*"

154

"*Welt?*" Karen repeated.

"World, honey," Rachel translated.

Karen's face lit up. "Could you bring some home?"

"*Jah.*" Samuel winked at her.

When they had finished breakfast, Karen was the first to rise and pick up the empty plates. "I'll clean up if you want to go," she offered.

Rachel turned to stare at her. "Okay now, stop, you're scaring me."

Karen's only response was to roll her eyes and take the dirty dishes to the sink. Rachel finished making her grocery list then turned back to Samuel. "I guess that's my cue to get ready." She stood and went into her bedroom, brushed her teeth and hair, and even dabbed some perfume behind her ears, excited to spend time alone with him.

Rachel found him in the driveway where he had finished loading the last of the milk canisters. He spread a white tarp over them to reflect the sun for the short fifteen-minute ride to the Lapp Creamery. Since she planned to bring back some ice cream with her, she had brought along a large Playmate cooler with blue ice blocks to keep it from melting on the ride home.

It wasn't as hot this morning, so riding on the wagon was pleasant. Samuel waited until they were out on the two-lane road before reaching for her hand. A few times she even caught him sniffing loudly, trying to identify the flowery scent that was wafting from behind her ears. Even if another buggy went by, they were up high enough so no one could easily see their transgression. They barely spoke or looked at one another for fear of prying eyes, but the touch of his fingers intertwining with hers told her all she needed to know. Despite how happy it made her, guilt and a sense of betraying Barry nagged at her.

They arrived at Lapps without incident and while Samuel unloaded the canisters, Rachel shopped in the adjacent grocery store, picking up the items she needed, including molasses, brown sugar, flour, and even a special decorative ceramic pie plate that had the word "SHOOFLY" in the bottom as a special surprise for Karen.

The store was filled with tourists piling their carts high with "Amish made" goods while snapping pictures. She paid for her groceries and went in search of Samuel. She found him waiting next to a group of Amish families and tourists who had lined up for ice cream. The expression on his face as he watched the Amish children made her heart plummet. It was a look of such profound sadness it took her breath away. At that moment, he turned around and saw her watching him. His face was so sorrowful it broke her heart. She stepped up to him, held his gaze and gave him the slightest of understanding nods. She couldn't touch him. She couldn't offer any real comfort, so she expressed it all in her eyes. He returned her stare, his eyes brimming. She pushed her grocery cart over to the spring wagon where he helped her load the bags into the back.

When they were finished, Rachel gave him a gentle smile. "How about I treat us to a scoop of ice cream before we head home?"

"*Jah*," he whispered, still casting backward glances at the Amish children.

On the road home he opened his heart to her about his children for the first time. "I had twin boys, Yonnie (John) and Joshua, ages 14, a daughter, Sarah who was 13 and another set of twins, Hannah and Martha who were ten. Yonnie loved to work with the animals and wanted to breed horses for sale when he was older, Joshua wanted to become a master carpenter. The girls were just like their *mamm...* full of life and laughter – always playing practical jokes on their *papa...*"

"You must have been very proud of them," Rachel murmured.

"I was," he murmured, casting his eyes downward in sadness.

"Tell me more about them," Rachel encouraged. At this, Samuel's face lit up. He talked unceasingly for the entire ride home, laughing at some memories and weeping at others. By the time they got home, Rachel felt a closeness she hadn't experienced in a long time. He had confided in her and shared with her some of his most precious memories and as he reminisced, it was like his family had come back to life again for him.

Karen was waiting for them on the front porch swing with Buddy. "You were gone for almost two hours," she accused.

"Samuel and I had some ice cream," Rachel replied, not wanting to volunteer the fact that he had driven the horses as slow as possible on the way home so they could talk. "He was right. It's the best ice cream I've ever had, even better than Haagen Dazs!"

"Wish I could have been there," Karen groused.

Samuel began handing down the groceries.

"Yes, well there's a little surprise in there for you as well. We also got two gallons of ice cream: Vanilla and Rocky Road."

Samuel lifted down the cooler.

"I'll get that," Karen exclaimed, "So where's my surprise?"

"Buried somewhere in all the groceries, you'll just have to be patient until we unpack everything."

Karen hurried into the house with the cooler, Buddy trotting right behind her.

Rachel smiled up at Samuel. "Thank you for taking me into town." The heat rose in her cheeks as he looked down on her and gave her a thankful smile. There was a long awkward pause then Samuel cleared his throat, tipped his hat, and led the team toward the barn.

Rachel lingered, watching him walk away, her gaze transfixed on his broad back. Karen returned silently and poked her in the ribs.

"*Owww!*"

"Geez, Mom, put your eyes back into your head. Let's go inside."

Rachel said nothing, a bit anxious at what Karen was implying. *Was I being that obvious?* She gathered up some of the grocery bags and lugged them up the porch stairs and into the kitchen. She set the groceries on the counter and tried to concentrate on unpacking, her mind consumed with all he had told her. She was yearning for physical contact and comfort but didn't want to do anything that would endanger his standing with his community. She sensed that Samuel shared her feelings for her more than he wanted to admit. Things would come to a head if they continued in this fashion much longer and the outcome didn't look good for either of them if they succumbed to their growing feelings. He would be shunned, and it would be all her fault.

She was so caught up in her thoughts she didn't hear the screen door open and close. She had no idea that Samuel had entered the house until she heard a floorboard creak behind her. She turned around and found him standing only a few feet away, his arms burdened with the last of the grocery bags. She took the bags from him. "I bet you're hungry." she said too cheerfully, setting them on the counter. "I'll just get this stuff put away and make us some lunch."

"Rachel," he whispered, his eyes tormented.

Just then, Karen galloped back down the stairs and bounded into the kitchen. Samuel quickly stepped away and began unpacking a grocery bag.

Karen looked at her. "Is lunch ready yet? I'm hungry."

"Not yet," Rachel replied, grateful for the interruption. "Why don't you put away the rest of the groceries for me so I can start on it?" She refused to look in Samuel's direction but could feel his eyes on her. He never did seem to find another convenient opportunity to finish what he had started to say and curiosity burned through her for the rest of the afternoon.

Chapter Eleven

Transformation

Daniel Gold sat at the kitchen table, explaining to Rachel the justification for each line item in his construction bid. The more he spoke, the more overwhelmed she became. She stared at him and even though his lips were moving it was as if no sound was coming out. It had become quite clear that the entire process was going to take not weeks but months and every day that went by meant hundreds of dollars going out the door with none coming in. If all went well, the soonest she might have a functioning inn was just after Thanksgiving; providing there weren't any delays, setbacks, or unforeseen problems, or in other words…*a miracle.*

"Do you have any questions?" Daniel asked her after what had seemed like hours.

Rachel swallowed hard, fighting down her rising panic.

"We won't be able to start work until we get your deposit," he gently reminded her.

Rachel nodded and with trembling hands, fumbled around inside her purse for her checkbook. She wrote out a check for one-third of the total bid, feeling like she was signing her soul over to the devil. Daniel Gold left with promises to return the following week to begin work. Rachel laid her head on the kitchen table and covered it with her arms, struggling not to panic.

What am I doing? Maybe I should run out there and tell him to forget everything. You can still stop this. Maybe we can still move back and rent an apartment? I might still be able to get a job as a sous chef... She jumped up and ran to the door, but the words lodged in her throat. Instead, she watched him get into his big truck and drive off.

She drooped and shook her head...*no...I've gone too far to turn back now. I'll just have to see it through.*

Barry would not have been pleased at the risk she was taking with their money but then again, he never had been any good at making the "big" decisions in their marriage. They would never have gotten married, bought a new car, or even a home for that matter had it not been at Rachel's insistence. That was why they had been so well suited for each other. Her decisiveness had been one of the things Barry had most admired about her.

She blotted her wet face with the hem of her t-shirt and looked around the living room, trying to envision it filled with paying guests.

The following week, the general contractor and other tradesmen arrived with their work crews. Having so many people around also helped to keep her and Samuel at a safe distance from each other. He went straight to the fields each day to get the bulk of his work done before the heat and humidity rose too high and they only saw each other at meals and at twilight for their nightly porch swing rendez-vous.

Daniel set up shop on her kitchen table, laying the schematics out for the electrical and plumbing work as soon as she had it cleared away each morning. The men went to work immediately, prepping the downstairs first for the electrical wiring and plumbing. They cordoned off one room at a time, sealing it off with thick plastic sheets to keep the particle dust from the other rooms as they tore into walls and drilled holes in the framing to snake through the yards of conduit, wiring and pipes. Since she couldn't do much of anything at home, Rachel had Karen drop her off at the local library on her egg rounds so she could start building her website. After several hours of intense labor, Rachel stared at the computer screen, surveying her handiwork. She had purchased the domain name of WWW.SECONDCHANCEINN.COM, uploaded the best of all the property photos and wrote captions under each; grateful for her prior years of experience as an administrative assistant and itinerant blogger. The landing page had an exterior view of the white farmhouse, its wraparound porch and red barn that changed views every few seconds with other exterior images of the property that she and Karen had taken. The site header was a static banner that she hoped would entice visitors to book a reservation:

Come and experience the simple pleasures of life at an Authentic Amish Farmhouse. Below this she embedded an introductory paragraph:

"Your stay at the Second Chance Inn will be unique and satisfying. Learn how to bake bread and pies from scratch and how to can food. Rediscover the forgotten skills of sewing, knitting, quilting, and other crafts. Visit with genuine Amish families where you will have the opportunity to purchase their goods without the middleman. Enjoy the pastoral beauty of Lancaster County. The inn offers five charming but simply appointed private rooms. Indoor plumbing and heating for the winter months as well as air-conditioning for the summer months. Two full farmhouse meals a day are included in the price of your room as well as lemonade and snacks on our wraparound porch. Enjoy fresh eggs daily and homemade ice cream from the milk of our very own cows. There are no televisions, phones, or Wi-Fi services. Instead, we offer the time to sit and relax, read a book, rediscover your loved ones, play croquet, checkers or chess and ride horses. Enjoy buggy rides into the quaint town of Bird-in-Hand to do a little shopping. Catch fireflies at dusk and star gaze. The farmhouse has its own private petting zoo of cows, sheep, goats, pigs, cats, and a dog named Buddy. Fond memories

and new experiences await you that will last a lifetime. To make a reservation..."

Rachel sat back in her chair and stared at the screen, a worried frown creasing her face. How was she going to attract customers to visit in the frigid winter months that were coming up? She drummed her fingers on the desk until several other library patrons gave her dirty looks and shushed her. Rachel stared at the screen for a few more frustrating moments, trying to think of what would compel someone to pay good money to stay at a farmhouse in the dead of winter when sudden inspiration struck. She went to a Stock Images site and searched for photos of old-fashioned horse-drawn sleighs, people ice-skating on ponds, decorated vintage Christmas trees, cozy fireplaces hung with stockings and wintery images of beautiful red barns nestled in snow. Then she began to type furiously, almost giddy with excitement.

She had often told Barry of her longing to go to a Connecticut inn in the winter and experience a real "white Christmas" where even a "grandma and grandpa" were provided for those who had none. It had been a pipe dream but now it was her inspiration.

"Longing to have a one-of-a-kind, old-fashioned White Christmas? The Second Chance Inn is now accepting reservations to host one lucky family who would like to experience Christmas in an idyllic farm setting. The inn sleeps ten so you can bring your entire family. Select and cut your own Christmas tree to decorate. String popcorn and cranberry garlands, toast marshmallows and chestnuts, go for an invigorating sleigh ride to our local pond for a day of ice-skating complete with the world's best hot chocolate. Experience an intimate Christmas Eve singing carols before a blazing fire and daily gourmet feasts in our large farmhouse kitchen. Why not have a relaxing and restful Christmas filled with wonderful memories instead of the usual holiday stress trying to do it all yourself? We'll be happy to take care of everything for you...we'll even wrap the presents..."

Now she just had to make sure Daniel's team would have the indoor plumbing installed well before Christmas and that she could also provide everything else on her fantasy list before the website went live. She would have to check with Samuel on the feasibility of the other items. The next step would be setting up an online payment system.

"Mom."

Rachel jumped in her seat with a little scream, eliciting more disapproving looks from the library patrons. Her heart was pounding furiously. Her daughter just loved frightening the dickens out of her. "Karen!" she hissed in admonishment.

"Shush," one middle-aged woman whispered furiously at them.

"We're going," Rachel told her in a loud stage whisper, logging off the computer. She paid the librarian for the time she had used then followed Karen out of the cool library, instantly assaulted by the hot humid air. Once outside, she was able to talk in a more normal tone of voice. It was early afternoon, and the heat was stifling. They climbed into the buggy. It was days like this that she really wished that that her nice, air-conditioned, VW Grasshopper Green Beetle had been delivered so she could use it.

"How did you do today with your egg sales?"

Karen shrugged. "Pretty good, geez...I can't wait until we get air conditioning in the house; I'm so tired of sweating nonstop."

"Me too. Hey, I got a lot of work done on the website today," Rachel volunteered, hoping Karen might take an interest and ask some questions, but she was being her usual uncommunicative self.

Karen waved her long dead but ever-present iPhone at her. "Too bad I can't see it!" She never could resist getting a dig in.

They spent the remainder of the trip home in relative silence except for the clip clop of Molly. Both Rachel and

Karen were drenched in sweat by the time they arrived home a half hour later.

Trucks as well as buggies lined the driveway. Rachel found the crews sitting on her front porch taking a late lunch during the hottest part of the day. To her surprise, several of the workers looked Amish. They tipped their straw hats to her as she mounted the stairs.

"*Guten tag*, Mrs. Winston," they greeted her.

"Are you all Amish?" she asked, eyeing the pick-up trucks.

"*Nee*, some of us are Mennonite," one of them smiled, understanding her confusion. A tall blond man stood and tipped his hat. "I'm Joshua Yoder, the plumber."

The other men introduced themselves as well.

"*Guten tag*, Mrs. Winston, I'm the carpenter. Joseph Stoltzfus is the name."

"Sam Byler. I will be laying the ceramic tile."

Rachel nodded and smiled politely. There was no way she was going to remember all their names. "I'll need for you to look over some tile samples and select what you want so I can put in an order," said Sam Byler.

Rachel nodded and, after a brief question and answer period, selected plain white subway tiles for the bathroom. They were clean looking and best of all, *cheap*. The workmen soon returned to ripping her farmhouse apart and departed at five o'clock sharp with promises to return early the next morning to continue.

After a hearty dinner of roast beef, noodles, and vegetables, Rachel sat in the porch swing with a tall glass of iced tea in hand, watching the sun set across the fields and the fireflies take flight, waiting for Samuel. He had already bathed and exited the *dawdi haus* with a Mason jar filled with flowers from the garden. He set it on the table next to Rachel's glass of iced tea.

"Thank you!" she smiled. She offered him a glass, "Sweet tea?"

"*Jah,*" he nodded, joining her on the porch swing, taking her hand in his. They rocked silently for a while and every so often they would exchange shy but meaningful glances.

Rachel tried to lighten the mood. "I'm really nervous about meeting your family this weekend," she admitted. "I still can't decide how to dress."

"Modest would probably be best," he murmured, his thumb tracing little circles across her palm. She shivered with delight.

"Do you think they will like me?" It was becoming more and more important to her that his family liked and accepted her.

"That remains to be seen, Rachel," he replied honestly.

"Do...do *you* like me, Samuel?"

He turned to look at her, his face serious. "*Jah,* Rachel... more than is *gut* for me."

Her gulp was audible. "I like you too, Samuel, you have become a good friend...you are the only person I can really talk to about Barry..."

He looked down at their intertwined fingers. "I feel the same, Rachel...I often wish..." His voice dropped off.

"What do you wish, Samuel?"

He looked back up at her, his eyes filled with intense longing. "I wish that you would seriously consider becoming one of us."

"Oh," She hadn't been expecting this. Not this soon.

He turned fully to her and took both of her hands in his. "Do you think that this is something you might want to consider?"

Rachel swallowed down the lump in her throat. She desperately wanted to belong to someone again and there was no denying her feelings for him, but could she really do it?

It was such a drastic change and she had just been through a life altering event. Could she really give up everything for him this soon? She wasn't sure she was able to…not yet.

"Yes, Samuel…it is something I have been thinking about very seriously …my heart is willing but I'm not sure I can do it…I'm not sure I would make a good Amish woman."

They sat for a few more moments and finished their tea in silence. The fireflies had vanished, and the stars were peeping out. Samuel stood to his feet and drew her up with him, looking gently down into her eyes. "*Gut nacht*," he whispered, his fingers briefly caressing her cheek.

"Good night," Rachel mumbled, watching him enter the *dawdi haus* in dismay. She waited until the door closed behind him, then slowly trudged into the house and to her room. She hadn't given him the answer he wanted to hear, that was for sure. She cared about him very much, even desired him, but was her growing affection for him enough to change her life so radically? She wasn't sure and it terrified her.

It was too warm and humid to sleep. *What I wouldn't give for a ceiling fan or central air.* She suddenly remembered the cot on the screened service porch out back. She could sleep there instead. After a quick sponge bath, she dressed in her lightest cotton nightgown and took her pillow and a sheet to the screened porch. A soft breeze caressed her bare limbs. She laid on the cot and listened to the buzz of the cicadas and the night song of crickets, replaying over and over the touch of Samuel's fingers on her skin and the look of tender longing in his eyes.

Chapter Twelve

Out of the Frying Pan

Rachel woke with a jerk, sitting up in alarm. Karen was at her side, already dressed and shaking her awake.

"What are you doing on the porch? I've been looking all over the house for you. C'mon Mom, you overslept, we're hungry."

Rachel rubbed her eyes. "What time is it?"

"It's already 7:00 am. We've been up for hours already *a-choring*."

"Sorry," Rachel mumbled, reaching for her slippers and summer robe, still bleary-eyed. "Just give me a few minutes." She stumbled out of the screened porch toward the outhouse. Karen followed her, giving her a play-by-play of all that she had accomplished while her mother slept the morning away.

"Give it a rest, will you, Karen? Go set the table and I'll be in to fix breakfast when I'm done. You really need to learn how to cook!"

Several minutes later, she was back in the kitchen and had a pot of hot coffee percolating on the stove. Karen was already packing eggs into cartons. Samuel arrived minutes later and stared at her; his jaw hanging slack. She looked down at herself. She was still in her thin white cotton nightgown and light robe. She looked up in time to catch his eyes roaming down the length of her. She could feel her face flaming. She tied the robe closer for modesty's sake. "I overslept," she explained, setting the pancake batter aside. "I'll go change. Karen, can you keep an eye on the bacon?"

"*Jah,*" Karen replied, oblivious to it all.

Rachel bolted into her bedroom, flung open the small closet door, and shimmied into a lightweight skirt and blouse. She had not missed the look in his eyes when he looked her over. *I'm a Jezebel,* she berated herself. She took a brush to her unruly hair then clipped it up.

After breakfast, Samuel left to get the buggy ready for the trip to his *schwester's.* Rachel cleaned up then went in search of him, wanting to apologize for being so inappropriately dressed earlier. She desperately needed to talk to him about what was happening between them. It couldn't go on much longer like this. She found him in the stable, putting the harness on Dodger.

"Samuel?"

His head snapped up to look at her.

"We need to talk."

He closed the distance between them in seconds. Startled, she backed up until she was flattened against the paddock door. Samuel's rigid arms went on either side of her, trapping her, his eyes smoldering.

"*Gott im himmel frau. Sie haben keine ahnung was sie tun, um mich?* (God in heaven, woman. Do you have any idea what you are doing to me?)" His voice was raw but not angry.

She felt guilty as sin when she met his eyes. All she had to do was to move one inch closer and she knew instinctively that he would close the distance in an instant and do what any red-blooded, love-starved man would do in his situation. She was sorely tempted to do so, instead, shame bowed her head. "I'm so sorry, Samuel. I never meant for any of this to happen...to let it go so far."

He leaned closer, his mouth mere inches above her own. Her limbs grew heavy with longing as she stared up at him.

"Rachel," he whispered, his warm breath on her face. "I have feelings for you, feelings I am not supposed to have." His fingers caressed her cheek gently. "Either you get baptized into our community soon and we marry, or I'll have to leave for *gut*. A man can only stand so much…"

Cold fear gripped through her heart. She stared at him in terror and nodded, not even sure what she meant by it.

They left the breakfast dishes to soak in the sink and all three of them climbed into the buggy and set off for his sister's farm, an uncomfortable silence between them which Karen seemingly took no notice of. They arrived half an hour later and Samuel pulled his buggy up beside several others that had already arrived before them.

Karen climbed out immediately wearing the purple Amish dress she had been give. Excited to see Mary, Martha, and the other Hochstetler children again. Rachel lingered inside the buggy, staring nervously at the farmhouse. There was a lot more at stake now than just sharing Amish ways with her inn guests. Samuel had given her an ultimatum with a looming deadline.

She looked over at him, afraid that everyone would be able to read her mind and see right through them both and their casual charade.

He gave her a gentle smile. "It will be alright," he encouraged.

She heaved a heavy sigh then climbed out. Samuel kept a respectful distance from her. The screen door opened with a bang and his nieces and nephews tumbled out to greet them.

"*Onkel* Samuel, *Onkel* Samuel." They instantly surrounded him. He hugged each one in turn then introduced them to Rachel.

"Mrs. Winston, these are my *schwester's* children: Willis, Isaac, John, Mary, Martha, and little Mirriam."

"*Es ist schön, sie kennen zu lernen!* (It's nice to meet you,)" Rachel said in her textbook German, shaking each hand in turn.

"We are glad to welcome you at last," Mary exclaimed, giving her a smile, her arm already slung around Karen's neck in a sisterly way.

His sister, Sarah, appeared moments later. "*Willkommen* to our home," she said, opening the screen door.

"*Danki*," Rachel replied entering the house where the other women had already gathered for the quilting bee.

Samuel walked over to the barn where his brother-in-law and several other men were already gathered.

"Samuel, *gut morgan*." John opened his arms and gave him a friendly clap on the back.

"*Gut morgan*, John," Samuel greeted him then tipped his hat to the others.

"I see you brought the *Englisch* woman and her *dochder* with you," Bishop Fisher remarked.

Samuel shifted uncomfortably. "*Jah*,"

"How are things on the farm, Samuel?" Deacon Lapp wanted to know. Samuel hesitated for a moment. The Deacon had no idea the images his innocent question conjured up in Samuel's mind.

I sit on a porch swing every night watching fireflies, sipping tea, and holding hands with an Englisch woman.

"As well as can be expected," he replied.

John slid an arm around his shoulders. "Well, she must be feeding you *gut*, Samuel, because you certainly have filled out more since the last Meeting. *Küssen einer frau kann verblassen, aber ihre gute küche nur selten der fall ist!* (A woman's kisses may fade away, but her good cooking rarely does.)"

John's lapse into an old Amish adage gave Samuel a jolt of alarm. His *bruder-in-law* had hit nearer the mark than he knew.

Rachel sat quietly, sandwiched between two elderly Amish women at a large quilting frame. It had been set up in the main room, surrounded by chairs filled with females of all ages. Rachel hadn't sewn a stitch since she was in middle school.

"Ouch," she stuck her finger in her mouth and sucked at the needle prick. It had only been the hundredth such prick in an hour. Sarah had long since given up trying to instruct her and left her to stitch as best she could on her own. No doubt they would have to rip out and re-do every stitch she did. Rachel fought back her tears. For the first time since she had moved to Pennsylvania, she was grateful for the warm humid weather. Everyone else was sweating just as much as she was, only hers was flop sweat. The women were nice enough and helpful enough, but she knew they were just being polite. They spoke of upcoming engagements, weddings, births, recipes, and gossip involving people she knew nothing about. If she hadn't known German so well, she would have been paranoid that they were gossiping about her. No doubt, Samuel had given his sister fair warning about her language skills...

She glanced up and looked around, sensing someone's eyes on her. A pale, thin, dark-haired woman at the opposite side of the quilt frame immediately looked away. Her face reddened at being caught in the act of staring at her. Rachel struggled to remember her name, but she had met so many *Marys, Marthas, Ruths, Sarahs* and *Katherines* that her head was swimming. It didn't make identifying individuals any easier when they all wore the same clothing and hair style.

Rachel bent her head over her little patch of quilt, rivulets of sweat trickling down her back, and bit her lip as she poked herself again, wondering for the millionth time if it had been a colossal mistake to come in the first place. She felt like a fish out of water and wavered between wanting desperately to go home and knowing that she should stick it out. Samuel's ultimatum played over and over in her mind. For the next few hours, she soldiered on, stitching as little as possible so they would have less to undo.

Her daughter sat at the other end of the quilt frame talking and giggling with the eldest daughter like they had been best friends for ages. An unattractive stab of jealousy smote her heart. *Why is it so much easier for her? I'm the one who wanted to come here in the first place and learn all these skills.*

At noon, Sarah announced it was time for lunch, rescuing Rachel from further shame. She popped up like a Jack-in-the-box, as if she were a child dismissed for recess. She caught several of the women exchanging amused glances as she did so. They abandoned the quilt frame, and she meekly followed them into the kitchen to put out her meager food contribution. She had lain awake half the night fretting over what to bring, finally deciding on her artichoke dip with crackers, a favorite among her friends and family. She had baked it while preparing breakfast and wrapped the hot dish in a quilted carrier to keep it warm. She worked quietly, artistically arranging the crackers in a circle around the hot dish and sprinkling dill weed on the top to finish it off. She looked around to see what the other women had brought. There was ham, chicken, several potato salads, freshly baked breads and rolls, a haunch of cold roast beef, crocks of homemade sauerkraut, baked beans, pickled vegetables, and scores of pies and berry cobblers.

She noticed Sarah Hochstetler glancing over at her artichoke dip. She gave Rachel a polite smile. "*Wie nennt man das?* (What do you call that?)"

"Super fattening," Rachel replied, her joke falling flat. "Uh, artichoke dip," she explained when Sarah gave her a bewildered look. She took a cracker, dipped it into the hot cheesy mixture, and held it up for Sarah to taste.

"*Ach*, I'll have to wait until after the blessing," Sarah apologized, refusing with a polite smile.

Rachel's stomach rose into her throat. "Of course, *Wie dumm von mir.* (How stupid of me.)" She stood holding the cracker with the dip. She couldn't put it back *now*. She glanced around for a moment then popped it into her mouth when no one was looking, hiding her chewing behind her hand.

"I'm Ruth Bieler," announced a voice behind her.

Rachel gulped down the cracker and promptly began choking. Ruth reached around and pounded her gently on the back until the fit subsided. "Can I get you some water?" she offered.

Rachel nodded, still unable to speak, her eyes watering. She tried to quiet herself, aghast at getting caught.

Ruth returned a moment later with a glass of water. "Just take small sips," she suggested.

Rachel nodded and almost spewed her first sip all over Ruth's front as another cough took hold. She kept her lips firmly pressed together, her mouth bulging with water, and waited a good ten seconds before swallowing. "Thank you," she finally choked.

Ruth gave her a shy smile. "You are the *Englisch* woman who purchased Samuel Miller's farm?"

Rachel nodded.

"Would you like to help me set out my food?" Ruth asked shyly. "I need another set of hands."

Rachel's heart immediately warmed at her invitation. Despite being Amish, Ruth seemed to be as out of place as Rachel did. Hardly anyone had spoken to her throughout the morning quilting session. "I'd be happy to. Just tell me what to do."

Ruth immediately linked her arm through Rachel's and walked her back to the service porch where she had stored her cakes.

"That is the most magnificent coconut cake I have ever laid my eyes on." Rachel exclaimed, admiring the three-layer white confection with awe.

Ruth blushed, pleased by her compliment. "*Danki*...it's an old family recipe. Here," she handed a Shoofly pie to Rachel. "Can you carry that in for me while I bring the cakes?"

"Of course," Rachel replied, happy to have made a new acquaintance. She followed her back to the kitchen where the food was being set up buffet style. She put the pie down next to others of its kind. The food was grouped by category: meat, side dishes, fruits, vegetables, breads, and desserts. Rachel looked askance at her lone appetizer, sitting all by itself as though the other dishes had ostracized it from their company.

"What did you make?" Ruth inquired.

Rachel pointed. "It's artichoke dip." She felt as though she were confessing to a culinary crime.

Ruth smiled at her and went up to it. "May I?"

Rachel nodded and watched as Ruth bent forward and sniffed. "It smells yummy. What's in it?"

Rachel opened her mouth to reply, but at that moment, Sarah Hochstetler clapped her hands for everyone's attention. "Time for the blessing." She opened the screen door and summoned the men and children inside, "Time for the blessing."

The living room, dining room, and kitchen became crowded with Amish. The men removed their hats, and all bowed their heads for a moment of silence. It felt strange to Rachel that not even the Deacon or Bishop said anything aloud. There wasn't even an "amen" at the end to signal when they were done. They all seemed to know and lifted their heads together as if on cue. Everyone lined up, the eldest first, then the men, followed by the younger women, children, and last of all the young adults. Rachel saw Karen standing between Sarah Hochstetler's eldest daughter, Mary, and a strapping blond, young man who bore a close resemblance to her.

Rachel stood beside her dip, not feeling quite at home enough to line up for food without first doing something helpful. She held up the filled spoon, ready to plop a generous serving onto the plate of anyone who gave her the least bit of encouragement, but one after another, the Amish went by and politely shook their heads "no" whenever she offered, taking only a cracker or two to be polite. Obviously, they were not keen on trying food they were unfamiliar with. Each rejection made her feel worse, as if they were rejecting her instead of her stupid artichoke dip. She could feel her lower lip trembling, terrified she would break down in tears and make a scene. Finally, one man paused and held his plate out for her to serve him some dip. Rachel could have wept for joy. She put a small spoonful on his plate, not bothering to look up to see who it was.

"*Mehr, bitte.* (More please.)"

The voice was familiar. Rachel looked up and found Samuel Miller standing in front of her, a look of compassion in his eyes. She dug her spoon into the dip, pulled out a larger clump of warm dip and slapped it onto his plate.

"*Mehr, bitte,*" he repeated, the corners of his mouth twitching.

Warm gratitude flooded over her. Rachel scooped out an even larger portion and slapped it on top of the other, fighting back a grin.

"Crackers *bitte.*"

Rachel put down the spoon and with both hands gathered up a large handful of crackers then plopped them on his plate of dip, her smile growing. Samuel had left room for little else on his plate. He had taken fully 1/3 of the dip she had made. He tipped his hat, gave her a little wink then moved on, ignoring the queer looks his kinsmen were giving him. If she hadn't been amongst a room of disapproving Amish, she would have flung her arms around his neck in gratitude. Satisfied that she had done her duty, Rachel went to the very back of the line where she found Ruth Bieler, trying to ignore the whispers and side-glances of the

other women. No doubt they were discussing the impropri-
ety of Samuel's blatant favoritism.

Ruth turned to her. "I hope there's some of your dip left,"
she said. "I'm very curious to try it."

"I don't think you'll have to worry about that," Rachel
whispered, taking a plate off the stack. Despite the healthy
portions doled out to the men, there was still plenty left for
the women, children, and the young adults. Rachel piled
her plate high with as many vegetables as possible and some
lean cuts of meat; however, she did help herself to a generous slice of Ruth Bieler's coconut cake, the first piece anyone had taken. The Amish had shunned her food offering
just like Rachel's dip and Rachel wondered why. They exited the house and sat together on a small blanket under a
shade tree.

Rachel took a bite of roast beef and cleared her throat
to make small talk. "So...which one of those strapping men
over there is your husband?"

Ruth looked down at her plate in shame. Rachel was immediately sorry she had asked such an intrusive question.
None of the Amish women wore wedding bands, so she just
assumed that Ruth was married like the rest of them.

"*Der Herr* has not seen fit to bless me with a husband,"
she murmured, the subject clearly painful. "In our community, a woman past twenty-five who is unmarried and without children finds herself outside, on the fringes and left to
care for her elderly parents alone."

Rachel could have kicked herself. "Mine passed away a
year ago," she said, hoping it would ease things between
them.

Ruth looked her in the eye and laid a gentle hand on
hers. "I'm so sorry," she said, her eyes filled with genuine
sympathy. "How long were you married?"

"Fifteen years but we knew each other for five before we
got engaged."

"How many children do you have? Are they here?" Ruth glanced around, looking for children that were unfamiliar.

"Just one daughter; she's over there with the Hochstetler girls." Rachel pointed. Karen was in a circle of young Amish women, regaling them with God-only-knew-what kind of stories about her former life in Southern California. She just hoped she wouldn't be getting unannounced visits later in the week from perturbed Amish parents.

Ruth tasted the artichoke dip. "Mmmm, this is delicious." She gave Rachel a conspiratorial smile. "They don't know what they're missing." She took another bite. "What's in it? I think I might like to make it someday."

A lightbulb went on over Rachel's head. "Hey, why don't you come over to my house and show me how to bake, can, and sew and I'll show you some of my specialties?" The words were out of her mouth before she could stop them. She barely knew this woman and was already asking for favors.

Ruth's response was genuine pleasure. "I would be happy to." She leaned forward and whispered in Rachel's ear. "It will be nice to have a friend near my age."

Rachel's heart almost broke in two for her. This poor Amish woman was every bit as lonely as she was, simply because she wasn't married and had no children. She had found a kindred spirit. "When can you come over?"

"Tomorrow after I give my parents breakfast and finish my chores. What would you like to learn first?"

"How to bake properly," Rachel replied without skipping a beat. "I graduated from a culinary school but my baking stinks."

Ruth covered her mouth to suppress a chuckle then apologized.

Rachel waved her off, letting her know she took no offense. "No really. Even poor Samuel couldn't get his teeth into one of my rolls. He's now using it as a hammer in his workshop."

"Really?" Ruth's brown eyes went wide, having taken her literally.

"I was joking," Rachel explained. They burst into giggles again. For the remainder of the day, they were inseparable. Occasionally, Rachel would glance up to find Samuel's gaze lingering on her, but instead of smiling approval at her new-found friendship, his face looked troubled.

After cleaning up from lunch, the women returned to the quilting frame and Rachel sat beside Ruth. Outside, she could hear the men and boys engaged in a game of soft-ball on the back lawn and wondered what position Samuel played and if he was any good. The last few years of his life, Barry had been obsessed with Angel's baseball. She had even gotten him a chalkboard sign that read: WE INTER-RUPT THIS MARRIAGE FOR BASEBALL SEASON.

Ruth was as patient as she was friendly and showed Rachel how to quilt properly in nice, even stitches. The quilt they were working on was a lone-star quilt in fall colors and was to be auctioned off in the next few months. The afternoon slowly turned into dusk. The women helped to put away the quilt and frame before moving the furniture back into place to accommodate the young adults for the singing.

"So, what exactly is a singing?" Rachel asked Ruth, watching Karen file in with the other young adults.

"It is a social event for our youth," Ruth explained. "Each community has youth groups which gather regularly. The name of this group is the Nightingales. It is one of the ways our youth begin to court each other."

"Court?" Rachel bleated, her eyes going wide. Karen was too young to court! She watched while the adults gathered at one end and the youth at the other in the large main room. As they filed in, everyone shook hands and exchanged pleasantries before taking their seats. Between the heat coming from the lanterns and all the bodies, the room was uncomfortably warm. A hymnbook was passed around and the moment Rachel saw it, she panicked on Karen's behalf. It was all in German. She caught Karen's eyes, which were round with apprehension.

Just hum Rachel mouthed to her with a shrug.

The singing began. Someone at the other end of the room began to sing the first few notes and soon everyone else joined in.

Rachel was struggling. Even though she could read, speak, and write German, the hymns were unfamiliar to her. She also found it difficult to interpret the words correctly because of the Gothic style script used in the song book. She finally decided that silence was golden and opted to just observe and listen. She had to admit that their voices were beautiful, and it was all *a cappella*. Occasionally, she would glance over at Karen to see how she was doing and was pleased to see her picking up the tunes little by little, encouraged by her new friends. No one seemed to look at her askance if she flubbed a note. Instead, they would erupt into paroxysms of giggles.

The singing went on for a good two hours and when they were done, Rachel was exhausted. The room was now insufferably hot with all the body heat. She wanted nothing more than to go outside and get some fresh air, but she was terrified to do anything else that would put herself in a bad light again.

Finally, the singing ended, and everyone broke for snacks. A table had been set up with bowls of popcorn, potato chips, cookies, sweet tea, and lemonade.

"I need something to drink now," Rachel croaked, towing Ruth Bieler to the beverage table. They filled their tumblers then Rachel went in search of Karen to see how she had liked her first singing.

She found her daughter surrounded by the Hochstetler children, smiling, and talking animatedly, not seeming the least bothered by the fact that she had been unable to sing most of the songs.

"I'll be out on the porch," Rachel told her.

Karen nodded and waved her off. She couldn't have cared less.

Rachel and Ruth took their snacks out to the generous front porch and found two empty rockers. The cool night air was a blessed relief from the hot confines of the living room. They talked about all sorts of things: why Rachel had moved to Pennsylvania, Ruth's family, and Karen. The night sky became dark, and the stars shone brightly when Rachel suddenly noticed that the house had quieted. She stood up just as the front door opened and the young people began to file out. She looked at each face, waiting for Karen and Samuel to appear.

"Well, I best be going, Rachel. I'll see you tomorrow then, after my *choring*," Ruth said, pressing her cheek against hers in a surprise display of affection.

A rush of appreciation filled Rachel's heart. In one of her typical, spontaneous responses, Rachel put her arms around the slender woman and embraced her. "I can't wait." She didn't bother to see what the reactions of the others were. She didn't care.

At that moment, Samuel stepped onto the porch. "Has Karen come out yet?"

"No, I've been waiting for her...oh, there she is." Rachel waved to her daughter who was walking toward the front door with a young Amish man, a silly grin plastered all over her face. Rachel wasn't too worried. Karen had been on the boy bandwagon for many years now. Back in California, she had a new boy crush every other week. It had become a running joke between her and Barry that dinner at the Winston's was the kiss of death to all of Karen's relationships for they often ended soon afterward.

Karen stopped in front of her. "Mom, this is Willis Hochstetler. Is it alright if he drives me home in his buggy?"

Rachel shrugged, seeing no harm in it, oblivious to the alarmed stares Ruth, Samuel, and others were giving her. "Are you sure you don't mind? It seems a great inconvenience when you already live here?" she asked.

"It would be my honor," Willis replied shyly.

"Okay then," she turned to her daughter. "See you at home." Karen bounced down the stairs with Willis who tipped his hat to her with a shy smile.

Rachel watched them walk together to his open buggy, impressed that he first helped her daughter in before climbing in after her. *I guess there isn't a whole lot of trouble teenagers could get into in an open-air buggy,* she reasoned. She turned to Samuel with a sigh. "Well, I guess it's just you and I, Sam-Mr. Miller." She was looking forward to the drive home with renewed hope in her heart. "Good night, Ruth, I'll see you tomorrow."

Chapter Thirteen

At Cross Purposes

Rachel climbed into the buggy followed by Samuel. She exhaled with relief. "I tell you, if it weren't for Ruth Bieler coming to my rescue, I would have run straight back home with my tail between my legs today." She waited, hoping for at least a grunt in response and for him to take her hand in his. Instead, Samuel sat still as a statue next to her, his eyes fixed on the road ahead as the buggy rolled along. Stung, Rachel looked down at her lap, wondering what she had said or done wrong. She glanced over at him, but he was immersed in his own private thoughts. For the entire ride home, they didn't exchange another word. Her heart plummeted. *Why is he giving me the silent treatment?* She was close to tears then winced in sudden pain, sensing the onset of a killer migraine. She was in trouble. It was at least a half hour drive back to the farmhouse and she had left all her medications in her room. The pain grew worse and worse, her peripheral vision narrowing to a small pinpoint by the time they pulled into the driveway. She was so incapacitated by the pain; she couldn't climb out of the buggy.

"Samuel," she whispered, clutching her head. "Help me." Then she collapsed.

He caught her in his arms and lifted her out, his voice filled with concern. "Rachel, *was is los?*"

"Migraine...Axert," she whispered, "Axert." It was all she could manage.

He carried her into the house and laid her on the bed. On the nightstand was a prescription drug bottle. He picked it up and looked at the label. *Axert.* Buddy came into the room and whined, seeking attention.

Samuel poured a glass of water and held the pill to her lips.

Rachel was incoherent with pain, but she managed to get the pill down. She felt Samuel lift Buddy onto the bed. The dog cuddled next to her. The light was doused, and she soon felt a cold compress on her forehead. She waited for the medicine to take effect, comforted by the gentle stroke of Samuel's hand upon her head until she fell asleep.

Samuel hesitated by her bedside, stroking her hair and cheek as he watched over her. In many ways she was like a child, expansive and open with her emotions and larger than life. He felt protective of her but had to be more careful where he displayed it. His behavior with Rachel's artichoke dip had set a lot of tongues to wagging.

The day had not gone as well as he'd hoped, but what really bothered him was the spectacle of Ruth Bieler befriending Rachel at her most vulnerable moment. Something just did not sit right with him about it. Truth be told, he didn't like the idea of the spinster coming over to the farm either, suspecting that it had more to do with him than with her being a Good Samaritan to Rachel. He didn't want to see Rachel get hurt.

The week following his family's funeral, Ruth Bieler's family had made their intentions clearly known to the bishop, who had in turn approached Samuel himself about her. The fact that they didn't even wait a respectful space of time for him to grieve made his anger and resentment that much more acute. His curt response had disappointed everyone, but he was resolute and from that day on avoided Ruth like the plague. Now today, before he even knew what was happening, Ruth had ingratiated herself to Rachel and earned an open-ended invitation to their...her home for the foreseeable future. He had never trusted Ruth Bieler or her motives. Just this once, he hoped he was wrong about her...for Rachel's sake.

He gazed down upon her slumbering face and stroked her cheek tenderly. She was such a vulnerable soul and was so open with her heart, it made him fearful for her. She was the first person he had been able to express his feelings to about his family without feeling judged. He felt like he could tell her anything, no matter how shocking and knew she would understand because she had been through the same thing. Rachel Winston had rekindled feelings in his heart that he had thought forever dead. Her arrival into his bleak life had brought a tiny spark of light and even some hope. Hope that there was life beyond all the death and blackness that had consumed his soul for the past year. He leaned forward and brushed his lips against her forehead before returning to the *dawdi haus*. It was going to be a long sleepless night...

Rachel awoke the next morning, still in her blouse and skirt from the night before, struggling to remember the last hour before she had lost consciousness. She remembered the migraine hitting like a ton of bricks and barely recalled being carried into bed. She sat up like a shot, alarming Buddy. Had Karen ever come home?

She carefully rolled out of bed and walked to the kitchen. It was already late morning. The workmen were all over the house, pounding, sawing, and drilling. She found Karen at the stove preparing breakfast, humming one of the hymns she had learned under her breath.

Rachel greeted her. "Have a good time last night?"

Karen looked round, astonished to see her. A dreamy smile suffused her face. "The best. Mom...they are all so nice and so down to earth. I made a bunch of new friends."

Rachel tried to keep the envy out of her voice. "That's wonderful, honey." She scooted to one side to let Karen pass by with a bowl of scrambled eggs. "You made breakfast!"

"I was hungry," Karen replied. "Mom, the Hochstetler's invited me to come over again next weekend. Can I go?"

Rachel felt another stab of envy and instantly chastised herself. "Sure, honey, if Samuel doesn't mind. Perhaps I can come too."

"Great, *danki.*" Karen gave her a big smile then continued preparing breakfast, still humming.

Samuel entered the kitchen a few moments later from the service porch and took a seat at the table. "How are you feeling?" he asked her, his face filled with concern.

"Better," Rachel replied softly. The memory of him carrying her in his arms to her bedroom made the heat rise in her face. "Thanks for your help last night."

Karen came to the table with a platter of bacon. "What happened last night?"

Samuel and Rachel exchanged brief glances.

"I got one of my migraines last night," she finally admitted. "Samuel got my medicine for me."

"Those are brutal," Karen nodded, taking her seat. They prayed together and began to eat when a buggy pulled into the driveway. A soft rap sounded on the screen door. Rachel was up like a shot, running to answer the door. On the other side of the screen stood Ruth Bieler.

"*Gut morgan*, Rachel," she greeted. They exchanged brief hugs.

"Hi Ruth, I'm *so* glad you came," Rachel towed her into the kitchen. "Sam...uh Mr. Miller, this is my new friend, Ruth. She's going to teach me everything she knows," Rachel giggled.

Samuel stood up; his breakfast virtually untouched. He retrieved his straw hat from the peg and tipped it to both of them. "I'll be in the fields for the rest of the day. *Gut morgan,* Miss Bieler, Mrs. Winston." He grabbed a packet of pastries and hurried out the back door.

"Is anything wrong?" Ruth asked, following Rachel into the kitchen. "Did I come at a bad time?"

"Of course not, please make yourself comfortable," Rachel replied, feeling very hurt and wondering why Samuel had left in such a hurry. He had been *rude* to Ruth. She covered his plate with aluminum foil and gave it to Karen. "Would you bring this out to Sam…Mr. Miller for me?" Not waiting for a reply, she turned back to Ruth. Karen stomped out the door, grumbling about not getting to finish her own breakfast first. "Did you already have breakfast, Ruth?"

"Yes, I ate with my parents," Ruth replied, setting her satchel down on the table. Why?"

"I was hoping you might keep me company while I ate. I was just sitting down to it."

"I'd be happy to keep you company and have some coffee. It smells wonderful. *Was is los?*"

"Italian Roast, the last of my good stuff until I can get to Costco and buy some of their Kirkland brand." Rachel pulled down a coffee mug from the cupboard. "How do you take it?"

"Cream and sugar please," Ruth replied.

Rachel brought everything over on a tray. "The workmen are in another part of the house today, so the kitchen is free. What are we baking first today?"

Ruth smiled at her. "Some Amish staples: Baking powder biscuits, multi-grain bread, and Shoofly Pie."

A rush of appreciation washed over Rachel. She reached forward and clasped Ruth's hand in her own. "I can't tell you how much this means to me, Ruth. I've been so lonely since I moved out here."

187

Ruth smiled at her. "Eat up and then we'll get to work."

After breakfast, Karen took off on her egg rounds and Rachel donned her white chef's apron with her name embroidered in black across it. Together they gathered the needed ingredients for the biscuits and bread. Under Ruth's watchful eye and gentle instruction, Rachel learned the proper way to cut in the shortening, knead with her hands, and turn out a proper dough. When it was ready to go into the oven, Ruth opened the stove door to let out some of the heat. "These wood stoves burn much hotter than the ovens you are used to, so you need to adjust the temperature and timing for each recipe," she explained.

Rachel slapped her sweaty forehead. "No wonder I've been incinerating everything." After a thorough briefing on how to use the ancient stove for baking, Rachel was ready.

Together they cut the dough into flat discs, arranged them on a baking sheet, and popped them into the oven. Thirteen minutes later, Rachel pulled the sheet out of the oven and whistled. "Wow, just look at these golden beauties." She put them on a rack to cool and turned back to Ruth with an eager grin on her face. "Next challenge!"

For the next hour, the two of them worked dough for three different kinds of bread, alternating between punching, kneading, and storing the mounds in buttered bowls covered with clean cloth near the warm oven to rise while they took a break. Rachel wiped sweat from her brow and glanced at Ruth who didn't seem to be sweating as profusely as she was. Between the heat, the humidity, and the hot oven, she felt as though she were in a sauna. "How do you stand the weather here without air conditioning?"

"I was born here; you get used to it after a while, but it is hot today," Ruth agreed.

Rachel indicated the workmen swarming over her house. "Well, when they're all done, it will be nice and cool in here. Until then, how about we make some lemonade?"

Ruth stood up. "*Gut* idea."

She followed Rachel into the orchard and together they collected enough lemons to make a pitcher of lemonade. Rachel also harvested some carrots, onions, potatoes, garlic, and celery for that evening's pot roast. Once inside, the two women rolled, squeezed, zested, and sliced lemons until they had a large pickle jar filled with the tart liquid. Then in went sugar, water, ice-cubes, and fresh mint from the garden. Rachel sat on the porch swing, holding the sweating glass against her forehead, her eyes closed. "I don't think I made a very good impression at the Hochstetler's yesterday," she confessed.

"Give it some time, they may eventually warm up to you." Ruth replied politely.

Rachel's heart sank at Ruth's comment which confirmed her worst fears. She took another long swig then remembered Samuel sweating out in the hot fields. Guilt washed over her. "I should really bring some of this lemonade out to Mr. Miller with his lunch. He's got to be dying of thirst in this heat." She hesitated, uncomfortable at the thought of facing him alone after last night's silent treatment.

"Would you like me to do it for you?" Ruth offered.

Rachel was instantly relieved. "Would you? That would be great." *This way Ruth won't see what's going on between us.*

"*Jah*...sure," Ruth smiled, standing up. She waited patiently while Rachel filled a thermos with ice-cold lemonade. Next, she made some sandwiches with the rolls they had baked and left-over chicken. In went a jar of canned peaches, and packaged cookies.

"He's over there," she pointed, handing the thermos and cooler to Ruth.

Ruth gave her a happy smile that seemed out of proportion for her errand, but Rachel shrugged it off and returned to the kitchen to check on the rising dough.

***

Samuel saw the figure of a woman approaching him in the distance. He shielded his eyes to see who it was, but she was still too far away. His blue shirt was soaked through with sweat, and his tongue felt like cotton, but he wasn't about to go to the house with Ruth Bieler there. He clicked his tongue and slapped the reins, guiding the team toward the approaching figure. When he saw the Amish clothing, he realized it was not Rachel but Ruth Bieler. His heart sank with disappointment and also wariness.

"Hello, Samuel." Ruth waved at him with a shy smile, waiting for the team to stop. Samuel made no move to get down, but merely stared at her expectantly, wondering what she was up to.

Ruth held up the cooler and thermos to him. "I thought you'd like some lunch and cold lemonade."

Her idea, not Rachel's? He instantly chastised himself then tipped his hat, accepting the food and drink. "*Danki*." Why had it been Ruth Bieler and not Rachel who had taken thought for his hunger and thirst while he worked in her fields? It bothered him more than he cared to admit.

"Why don't I lead the team over to that trough under the shade tree there and give them some water while you eat?" Ruth offered with a coaxing smile.

"Alright," Samuel replied, climbing down. He withdrew a dark blue handkerchief from his pocket and mopped the sweat from his brow and the back of his neck while Ruth grabbed hold of the team and led them to the watering trough. She pumped fresh water from the well until it was full.

Ruth took the kerchief from his hands, dipped it into the cool water, and handed it back to him. "Put that under your hat, Samuel, it will cool you down quicker."

He watched her as she laid out his noonday meal on a small blanket as if they were on a picnic outing. "How are the baking lessons coming along?" he ventured.

"*Ach,* just fine. I've already shown her the proper way to make biscuits and we have three loaves rising in the oven." Ruth wiped her hands on her apron. "I best be getting back to Rachel now."

"*Jah.*" Samuel watched her leave, still disappointed at not seeing Rachel.

The screen door opened with a loud creak and Rachel straightened from the stove to greet Ruth, fairly dancing with joy. "Ruth, they're enormous. The loaves blew up to three times their original size. Can we bake them now?"

"*Jah.*"

Thirty minutes later, three perfect loaves of bread emerged from the oven. The smell filled the house. Rachel was elated. Knowing what a bread fiend her daughter was, she ran out to the front porch where Karen was sitting on the swing, her eyes fastened on the road. "Hey honey, the loaves are out of the oven, want some?"

At that moment a buggy appeared. Karen stood up and waved as several young Amish women clambered out. Rachel went forward to greet them. "Can I help you?"

They nodded shyly and smiled, looking over her shoulder at Karen. "We've come for Karen, Mrs. Winston."

Karen ran down the porch steps. "I'm ready." She ran over to the waiting buggy and climbed in back. "I'll be home later, *Mamm.*"

"Wait, where are you going?" Rachel asked, staring in shock as the other girls retook their seats.

"Oh, just hanging out for a few hours with my new posse," Karen grinned, lapsing into her old vernacular. The Amish girls dissolved into giggles. Karen leaned out of the buggy and shouted back at her. "Don't wait dinner for me." Then the buggy took off and they disappeared.

Rachel stood gawking at the now empty driveway, barely hearing the screen door open and shut behind her.

"Rachel?" Rachel turned to find Ruth standing behind her. "It's getting late. I need to get back to my parents soon and start supper, but I can come back tomorrow at the same time if you like?"

Rachel nodded and gave her a little smile, intensely disappointed. She really didn't want to be left alone again. "That would be great, Ruth. I *really* appreciate all the time you spent with me today."

Ruth closed the distance and gave Rachel a gentle hug before retrieving her horse from the paddock. Rachel held the reins for her while Ruth hitched the horse to the buggy then climbed in. "Tomorrow, we'll make more bread and some different pies," she said, patting Rachel's hand.

"Tomorrow," Rachel nodded, waving goodbye as Ruth steered her buggy away. She was completely alone again. Rachel trudged up the porch stairs and went into the kitchen where she found Buddy with his nose in the air, sniffing at the bread cooling on the counter. She sat down cross-legged on the hardwood floor so he could climb into her lap. "Want some bread?"

He looked up at her with his soulful brown eyes and whined.

Chapter Fourteen

Quilt Squares and Food for Thought

"So where are we going?" Karen asked as soon as the buggy was on the road.

"It's a surprise," Mary Hochstetler grinned. "Karen, this is Ella Stoltzfus, Hannah Yoder, and Lilly Troyer. They were all at the Singing the other night."

Karen nodded hello and smiled but said nothing. She had met so many new people in the past couple of weeks there was no keeping track of them, and she was horrible with names. "Ella, Hannah, and Lilly are all engaged," Mary added.

Karen gaped, sending the other girls into a fit of giggles. "Engaged?" she repeated. None of them looked much older than she was. "How old are you?"

Mary pointed to Ella, then Hannah, and last of all Lilly, "Nineteen, twenty, and eighteen."

Karen's eyes went round. "You're allowed to marry so young? Don't your parents freak out?"

"*Nee*," Mary giggled, steadying the horse who was tossing his head as they drove. "Most everyone in our community gets married around twenty-one, some even younger."

Karen sat back in shock as the other girls nodded in affirmation. "Well, my mom would totally blow a gasket if I did."

"Why would fulfilling your role as a godly woman freak out your *mamm*?" Lilly wanted to know.

"Because she thinks the longer you wait to get married the better," Karen retorted. "In fact, my aunts all told me that the longer I waited to get married, the more expensive the wedding presents would be."

They all had a good laugh at that. "Well in our community a girl is considered an "old maid" if she is still unmarried at the age of twenty-five," Hannah exclaimed.

Karen was floored. "No way!"

All the girls bobbed their heads up and down in agreement.

"If we waited until our mid to late twenties to get married, it would be that much more difficult to get pregnant and have *kinner*."

"*Kinner?*"

"Children," Mary translated. "It is the highest calling for us, to bear children and raise them up as God intends."

"I love children," Karen murmured. "I've babysat ever since I was thirteen."

"Do you have any siblings?" Lilly asked.

At this, Karen's face clouded over. It was a sore subject for her. "No, well yes…kind of." She saw the girls exchange confused looks, but they waited patiently for her to explain. "I'm adopted. My mom couldn't have children of her own, so she and my dad adopted me when I was five."

"*Ach*, that is a tragedy that your *mamm* could not have children," Hannah murmured. "I don't know what I would do if *Der Herr* denied me children."

"What did you mean by you 'kind of' have siblings?" Mary gently probed.

Karen squirmed, uncomfortable discussing such deeply emotional matters. "I have a full brother, Benjamin, who was adopted by another family before I was. I also have a half-sister, Vanessa, but I don't know where she is, and I never hear from my brother. *Boys!*"

All the girls stared at her horror-stricken as if they had never heard anything so terrible. Mary laid a hand over hers.

Karen really hated dredging up the past with all the emotional pain that was associated with it. It was a deep pain that she preferred not to deal with. The girls said nothing further about the subject, but she was touched by their response. Ten minutes later the buggy entered the town. "Where are we are going?" Karen wondered.

Mary pulled the buggy up to a fabric store, climbed out, and tethered the horse to the hitching post. Karen clambered out followed by Hannah, Ella, and Lilly. She stared at the storefront and shrugged. "This is the big deal? You're going to sew something?"

"We're here to purchase fabric for their wedding dresses and quilts." Mary explained, linking her arm through Karen's. That piqued her interest. She loved wedding dresses. They entered the fabric store and Karen stared in awe at the bolts and bolts of cloth in every color imaginable. She had taken a few sewing classes back in California but hadn't made anything since the age of seven. Several other Amish women were already in the store.

"You make your own wedding dresses?" Karen gawked. "Don't you just go to a bridal shop, try them on, and order what you want?"

"*Nee*, we make all our own clothes, especially our bridal dress." Hannah smiled. They walked over to a section that held dozens and dozens of bolts of fabric in every shade of blue and violet imaginable. The girls split up and selected the bolts that appealed to them. Karen was confused. Every wedding she had ever been to, the bride had worn white; but they were all looking at blues.

"Blue is the traditional color for an Amish bride," Mary explained.

Karen nodded as if she understood, thinking it was a very strange custom. It seemed to her that out of the entire world's population of unmarried girls, the Amish with their chaste ways would be the ones most deserving of wearing pure white at their weddings.

With their wedding fabric selected, the girls went to the remnant bin and began pulling out bundle after bundle of solid color fabric and putting them into their shopping baskets.

"Is that to make quilts?" Karen asked.

Mary nodded. "In addition to our wedding dresses, we also make the wedding quilt, which will cover our marriage bed. We will have to have a lot of quilting bees in the next few months if we are going to get all of these done before November."

Karen was impressed and emotionally stirred. She watched how Lilly, Hannah, Ella, and Mary interacted with one another. Although they came from different families, it was as though they were all sisters. They helped each other with everything, from making quilts to cooking and laundry. It was like being part of one enormous family with dozens and dozens of siblings and cousins. She had always longed for a big family with sisters and brothers, but her parents had never adopted any other children. She had a large extended family on her dad's side, but they were 3,000 miles away now *thanks to her mom.*

After her dad died, everything went downhill. She had to say goodbye to all her cousins, aunts, uncles, and grandparents. Her mom seemed to resent the fact that she never cried or mourned in public but the pain for her was just too deep. She missed her dad's affection and warm humor terribly. She was too terrified to let her grief out, so she shoved it down along with all the other hurts she had suppressed throughout the years: the feelings of abandonment by her birth parents, the terror of bonding with her adopted mother, the flakiness of her brother who she had spent a year searching for and was horrible at staying in touch with and now the loss of her dad. He was really the only person she had ever been close to who had accepted her just as she was.

She felt an arm slip around her shoulder. "Are you okay, Karen?" It was Mary. The look of compassion on her face almost made Karen want to cry. She nodded, but it didn't seem to convince her new friend. Karen watched with envy as Lilly, Hannah, and Ella took their baskets up to the counter to pay for their fabric, smiling and giggling together with pure joy upon their faces. They lived such a simple life and worked so hard, but they were the happiest people Karen had ever met. *It must be because they do so many things together. They never feel alone.*

"I guess I'm just jealous," she admitted in a low murmur to Mary, hanging her head.

"Jealous that they are getting married?"

Karen shook her head, reluctant to look Mary in the eyes. Her lower lip began to tremble as the tears threatened to spill over despite her efforts. "No, well *yes,* jealous of all of it, having a big family, how close you all are, how you all help each other..." Her voice trailed off when the tears began to stream down her cheeks. *Now she had done it. Mary and her friends would think her a horrible person and want nothing more to do with her.*

"Karen, you don't have to feel jealous of us," Mary whispered. "You would be welcome to join our community if you wanted to."

Her words hit Karen like a ton of bricks. "Me? Become Amish?"

Mary nodded.

"But I thought you had to be born into it."

"*Nee.* We have had a few *Englischers* baptized into our community. It can be a very difficult transition, but those who really want to join are very content. *Englisch* are attracted to our simple lifestyle but very few are ready to live that way."

Karen mulled this over. "What would I have to do?"

"Learn how to keep house, cook, bake, sew, live without modern conveniences, learn our language, and then become baptized into our church. Later marriage and children."

Karen slumped in defeat, utterly daunted by the list of requirements. "I don't know if I could do all that," she admitted. It seemed like an awful lot of hard work just to belong to a community.

"Well, it's not something you have to decide now." Mary smiled with understanding. "In the meantime, we are still happy to spend time with you. You are always welcome to come to our home, if you don't mind helping with the chores."

Karen felt an enormous weight lift from her shoulders. "I don't mind," she smiled; the prospect of getting to spend more time with Mary and her family was very inviting. Anything to get away from that big, lonely house and her mom. Lilly, Ella, and Hannah rejoined them, having completed their purchases.

"How about we get some ice cream at Lapps before we head home?" Mary suggested. They enthusiastically seconded the motion. They climbed into the buggy and while they waited for the automobile traffic to clear, Mary turned to Karen.

"I probably shouldn't be telling you this since you aren't sure about becoming Amish," she whispered in a low voice so the other girls wouldn't hear. "But I think my *bruder*, Willis, is sweet on you."

"Really?" Karen had suspected as much after he drove her home from the Singing but didn't want to make a big deal out of it since they had only shared a buggy ride. She had just assumed he was being nice and neighborly.

Mary nodded. "My *bruder* has never driven a girl home from a Singing in his buggy before... *never*, and plenty of them have wanted him to."

The other girls turned around in shock.

"Mary, *sie sind so eine blappermaul* (You are such a blabbermouth)" gasped Lilly, choking down her laughter.

Karen stared back at Mary, not sure she understood the significance of her brother's behavior or the other girl's reactions. "Oh?"

Mary sighed and gave her a crooked smile. "*Dummkopf*, that's one of the ways that we court."

Karen swallowed hard. "Court? But I only just met him." As many boyfriends as she'd had had in the past year in high school, the fact that a young Amish man, whom she had only known for a few hours, was now wanting to court her was thoroughly unnerving.

"*Jah*, my *mamm* and *daed* were none too pleased about it." Mary continued. "If Willis had already been baptized, he'd be in serious danger of being excommunicated."

Karen had never heard that word before. "What's that?"

"Expelled from the community…shunned."

Her jaw dropped open. "Just for driving me home in his buggy?"

All the girls nodded; their faces deadly serious.

"*Gut* thing for him he hasn't been baptized yet. Now he's talking about *Rumspringa*."

Karen felt like her head was going to explode with all the Pennsylvania Dutch language, rules, and regulations they were filling it with. "What is that?"

"It is a time when we get to run around and experience the world from your point of view," replied Mary. "It's one of the ways that helps us decide whether we want to be baptized into our church and remain Amish or leave the community and become like the *Englisch*. Not all of us *Rumspringa*, but many do."

"What happens if one of you decides to become like one of us?"

"Then they must leave, and we can have nothing more to do with them anymore. They are shunned, dead to us."

"Is that like getting the silent treatment?" Karen asked.

"Worse," Lilly replied.

"Because it is forever," added Ella.

"That's harsh," Karen replied, fanning herself. It had grown very warm inside the black buggy in the warm afternoon sun.

"We're here," Mary announced, pulling up to a hitching post in front of Lapps. They exited the buggy and made their way over to a long line of both Amish locals and tourists waiting for ice cream. Karen's head was spinning. She'd had no idea how hard the Amish life could be until this moment. Shunned over such a silly thing. There was much she found attractive about their life - the closeness of their families, the almost universal contentment with their life, and how they all pitched in to help each other–but there was also much she found to be overly strict.

After a ten-minute wait, they finally got their ice cream cones and headed home. They dropped Karen off first. The sun was beginning its long descent into the west. Karen wondered what her old friends back in Southern California were up to. Probably going to the movies or Disneyland, hanging out at the beach or the mall, and of course texting. She hadn't been able to communicate with any of them in several weeks since her phone and laptop had died from lack of power. She had given them her mailing address but the thought of sending an old-fashioned letter was a foreign concept to them. She might as well have dropped off the face of the earth as far as they were concerned. She paused in the driveway for a moment then decided to go into the barn and check on the cows. Maybe Samuel could use some help with the evening's milking.

She found him on his short, three-legged stool, sitting beside one cow while the others mooed incessantly in their stanchions awaiting their turn.

"Want some help?" she asked, getting the wash bucket and cloth.

Samuel looked up in surprise then nodded, the streams of milk never missing a beat as he squirted into the rapidly filling pail.

Karen sat down and stroked the cow's side to relax her. Then she took the washcloth, got it fully wet and scrubbed the udders until they were clean. The cow shifted her weight and mooed again, flicking her tail toward Karen's head. She blocked it with her arm then continued to pat the cow, waiting for the milk to come down. If anyone would have told her months ago that she would be milking cows and selling eggs she would have told them they were nuts. She grasped the udders and began the rhythmic motion of pulling and squeezing that had become second nature to her. In moments, she had a steady stream of milk squirting into the pail. Except for the cow's swishing tail, she found milking to be quite a relaxing chore.

The first few days she had done it she had been a nervous wreck, worrying that she was doing something wrong or hurting the cow. Now she felt like an expert and was quite proud of her skill. Sometimes she and Samuel would get into a silent competition with each other to see who could fill their milk pail first. Milking was a good time for thinking. She thought back to her conversation with Mary. Would it really be that hard to become Amish? She already knew how to milk a cow and take care of all the other farm animals. She was also learning to cook, bake and can. Perhaps she should just make a list of everything else she needed to learn. She could check it off as she went. If she was still enjoying herself, she could make her decision later. She picked up her full pail, poured the contents into the stainless-steel canister, and moved on to the next cow.

Samuel exited the barn dirty and exhausted. His skin and clothes were covered with a layer of dried sweat, straw, earth, and field dirt. He wanted nothing more than to bathe, eat supper and sit on the porch swing and hold hands with Rachel. He went into the *dawdi haus* to bathe, the aroma of roast chicken making his mouth water. He had never told her, but Rachel Winston's cooking was even better than his *frau's*. He hadn't gone to bed on a half-empty stomach in months. He stripped his filthy clothing from his body and surveyed his once flat stomach. *A woman's kisses may fade away, but her good cooking rarely does.* He smiled as he filled the wash basin with soapy water. Perhaps if Rachel learned what she needed to know from Ruth, he would soon be able to learn if her kisses would outlast her cooking. He closed his eyes and allowed himself to daydream about her as he bathed. Samuel dressed hurriedly, his stomach rumbling, his emotions at war. The closer he and Rachel Winston grew, the more he wanted to take her for his wife. His only hope lay in Rachel Winston successfully transitioning into his community and for that he would have to continue to put up with Ruth Bieler.

Chapter Fifteen

Romance

The following Saturday, a buggy drew up to the house just before Karen was due to leave on her egg rounds. A young man, hat in hand, knocked on the door.

Knowing how Amish men worked from dawn to dusk, Rachel was more than a little surprised to see one standing on her front porch during chore time. "Can I help you?"

The young man swiftly removed his straw hat, fidgeting nervously. "*Jah,* I've come to escort Karen on her egg rounds."

"Who is it, mom?" came Karen's voice from the back porch.

Rachel turned back to the young man. "Who is it?" she echoed.

He flushed crimson, embarrassed at having forgotten his manners. "I am Willis Hochstetler, Samuel's nephew," he replied.

"Aw, I didn't recognize you," Rachel apologized, a bit off balance by his appearance. "Willis Hochstetler," she yelled over her shoulder.

"What?" came a shriek from the back porch, swiftly followed by a string of words that didn't quite rise to the level of curses, but which clearly conveyed the fact that Karen had evidently dropped some eggs. Rachel opened the door wider. "Would you like to come in?"

"*Jah…danki,*" he replied, clearly uncomfortable.

Rachel beckoned to the sofa. "Can I get you anything to drink? Coffee?"

"*Nee, danki.* I do not wish to inconvenience you," he replied, his eyes focused over her shoulder. Rachel turned around to find Karen standing behind her in the kitchen, wearing her purple Amish dress. She had yet to do her hair and it was hanging past her shoulders and creating quite a distraction for poor Willis.

"Willis," Karen beamed, obviously pleased. She came forward, using her apron to wipe egg yolk from her hands.

"I thought you might like some company on your egg rounds before I take you to the quilting bee at my parent's home. If it is alright with you, Mrs. Winston, I can bring her home after supper. My *mamm* also extended an invitation for you and my *onkel* to join us as well."

"Oh, how nice of her. I'd be pleased to come if Mr. Miller doesn't mind taking me. That way we can bring Karen home and you won't have to make an unnecessary trip."

Willis nodded and stared at his feet, obviously disappointed with this arrangement. "*Jah.*"

Karen rushed past her and swept up the stairs to her room. "I'll just be a minute. I just have to fix my hair."

Willis nodded and continued standing, awkwardly wheeling his hat round and round in his hands. Rachel decided to be merciful. "Please have a seat while you wait, Willis," she indicated the couch again. "I'm just cleaning up from breakfast."

Willis obediently sat down, and Rachel returned to her work. Every once in a while, she'd peek over at him, but the tall, lanky fellow did not so much as budge an inch. The words *well trained* came to mind. Ten minutes later, she heard Karen galloping downstairs, her hair back in a tight Amish bun under the white *kapp*. "Okay. Let's go. Can you help me load the eggs in your buggy?"

Willis stood up, replaced his hat, and followed Karen onto the service porch where dozens of egg cartons in crates lay waiting. Rachel paused from her own work to help them. She stood in the driveway watching them drive off together. On the way out, they passed Ruth Bieler's buggy. She had come for her daily visit with Rachel. She took hold of the reins so Ruth could unhitch the horse from the buggy.

Ruth looked over her shoulder at the departing buggy. "Was that Willis Hochstetler I saw with your *dochder*?"

Rachel nodded. *"Jah…*I mean yes." Now *she* was lapsing into Pennsylvania Dutch! "He came to escort her on her egg rounds before going to the quilting bee."

Ruth nodded. "Quite a few of the girls in our community are engaged and working on their wedding quilts. It is an honor for them to include her."

Rachel couldn't help but notice the wistful look on Ruth's face. Ruth had never had a reason to make her own wedding quilt with her friends. Life seemed to have passed her by. Rachel's heart went out to her. "Want some coffee?"

Ruth gave her a wan smile. *"Jah."*

Together they walked into the house arm-in-arm. Rachel glanced over her shoulder and caught Samuel staring at them from just within the barn doors with a frown on his face and wondered why he looked so bothered.

Karen sat beside Willis, excited and nervous as he drove her about the picturesque countryside, taking her on the more scenic back roads than the route she usually followed. They barely spoke, shyness having overtaken both. Willis was very tall with wheat colored hair and blue eyes that seemed to twinkle whenever she could get him to look her in the eyes. He also had incredible dimples that creased the corners of his mouth whenever he smiled. His skin was a rich golden brown from spending hours in the sun, and, though his limbs were long, he was not scrawny but well-muscled. *If only my friends back home could see me now. If only they could see me riding in a black buggy with this hot looking young Amish man!*

If her phone had been working, she would have already taken numerous selfies with him to post on social media. After her last delivery, when they were finally on their way to the Hochstetler's farm, Karen was ready to break the ice.

"Mary says that you are thinking about doing Ramspring?"

"*Rumspringa*," he corrected her. "*Jah*," he nodded, flicking the lines on his horse to make it go faster.

"What exactly is that?" Karen wanted to hear it from him.

"It means "running around" in English. It is where we get to do things like you *Englisch* do before we are baptized so we can decide if we want to remain Amish."

"Do you want to remain Amish?"

"*Jah*, of course," Willis replied without a moment's hesitation.

Karen was confused. "Then why do you want to do *Rumspringa*?"

"Because it is the only way I would be able to see you without risking the disapproval of my family and community."

Karen was stunned, her face blushing crimson at the thought that he would risk so much to be with her when they barely knew one another. "Well, what do Amish people do when they are on *Rumspringa*?"

"We can use cell phones, go to amusement parks, see movies, wear blue jeans…sow our wild oats."

Karen swallowed at this last bit of information. "It all sounds pretty tame to me."

"Not when you are Amish," Willis replied softly, leaning toward her. "We can also do this…" He put a finger under her chin and gently lifted her face to his. The next instant his lips were on hers. Her body instantly came alive as he kissed her, electrical jolts of pure euphoria lifting her almost out of her seat. She had been kissed many times before but never like this. Willis' kiss was electrifying. Her arms went around his shoulders to pull him closer.

A sustained honk from a nearby car separated them instantly. Willis swiftly pulled the reins, so the horse veered the buggy back over to the right-hand side of the road.

Karen stared at him in wonder, "*Wow.*" The chemistry between them was undeniable.

"*Jah,*" Willis replied hoarsely.

Karen inched closer. So, are you allowed to go on real dates when you are on *Rumspringa*? Can we actually go see a movie together?"

Again, he nodded.

"Are you going to ask me?"

His answering grin lit up his face. "When I couldn't sleep last night, I made up a long list of things I wanted to do," he admitted, pulling out a folded piece of paper.

Karen held out her hand. "Can I see?" Willis reluctantly let her have it. She read down the list aloud. "Hey, this sounds pretty good. Movies, baseball game, dinner at a nice restaurant, Hershey Park, roller-skating, miniature golf, bowling, carriage rides…bundling… what is bundling?" She looked up at him to find him blushing furious red.

Willis snatched back the folded piece of paper. "It's an old custom among our people," he demurred.

His evasiveness immediately ignited Karen's curiosity, but she didn't want to push the matter. If she had had a working cell phone, she would have already been asking SIRI about it. She shrugged. "Oh…okay."

The silence grew uncomfortable between them again. She sighed, "I kind of made a list too, only it's just a mental list at the moment."

Willis' eyebrows climbed into his hairline, "Really?"

Karen nodded. "Learn to speak Pennsylvania Dutch, learn how to sew, garden, cook, can, and bake…well, I have already done some of these already. I've made baking soda biscuits and shoofly pies, did some cooking, and helped to can and I'm learning how to sew. That's all I have so far."

"It sounds like you want to become Amish," Willis noted with a happy gleam in his eye.

Karen blushed. "It does, doesn't it?" She wasn't quite sure what to say after that but the warm press of his hand on hers sent her heart soaring. "Maybe you can teach me how to speak Pennsylvania Dutch?"

⊰•❈•⊱

"You seem distracted, Rachel, is everything all right?" inquired Ruth. They were working together to cook and jar the last of the apricots from Rachel's small orchard into jam. Rachel shrugged as she lifted the Mason jars out of the boiling pot of water to cool.

"I guess I am distracted," she admitted. "My daughter seems to be fitting in so much better than I am, and she didn't even want to come here in the first place."

"Watch out!" Ruth exclaimed. It was too late, the hot jar slipped from Rachel's tongs and crashed onto the floor. Steaming hot apricot jam slowly spread across her freshly cleaned hardwood floors.

Rachel wailed in frustration then sank to the floor to begin picking up the shards. If Ruth hadn't been in the room, she would have screamed out a few choice curse words, but it wouldn't do to cuss in front of her Amish friend. Ruth squatted down beside her and gently took her hands before she could touch the hot glass. "It's too hot to handle right now, just leave it."

Rachel nodded sullenly and put a large Tupperware container over it so Buddy wouldn't go near. She collapsed fully onto the floor on her hindquarters, staring at the oozing mess in defeat. "I really stink at this."

Ruth sat down beside her and patted her hand. "*Ach*, if I had a nickel for every jar I ever dropped, I'd be rich."

These words warmed Rachel's heart. She gazed at her friend and gave her a grateful hug. "I truly don't know what

208

I'd do without you, Ruth. Probably would have slit my wrists by now."

Ruth's reaction to this puzzled Rachel. Instead of returning her hug, she offered only a grim nod in response. "*Narrish,*" she grunted, then helped Rachel back onto her feet. "I'll clean up the mess while you get the rest of the jars out."

"Thanks, I need to hurry if I'm going to make it to the quilting bee at Hochstetler's in time." She didn't notice how Ruth's face fell at the mention of it and suddenly realized that Ruth hadn't been invited. She felt like a heel.

Ruth left shortly thereafter; her face pinched with hurt.

Karen and Willis arrived at his family's farm. "Here we are," he said, lifting her down in his strong arms.

Karen looked up at him and smiled. She liked the feel of his large hands about her waist. Willis tipped his hat at her then unhitched his horse from the buggy and took it into the paddock. Karen made her way inside. She found Mrs. Hochstetler, Mary, Martha, Ella Stoltzfus, Hannah Yoder, and Lilly Troyer, as well as their mothers and sisters seated around a large quilting frame in the center of the room. Mary was the first to greet her with a bright, welcoming smile. Karen didn't know what she had said or done to earn such unmerited favor, but every time she was in the girl's presence, she felt like she was someone extra special.

"Karen!" Mary jumped up and skipped over to embrace her. "*Willkommen.* I saved you a seat next to me. You will need to wash your hands before handling the quilt. We are working on Hannah's since she will be the first one married this November."

"Okay," smiled Karen, following Mary to the sink. A variety of Amish dishes that would serve as a cold lunch when they took a break from their work lay on a nearby sideboard. Karen washed up quickly then took her seat next to Mary, ready and anxious to continue her lessons in quilting.

"Have you planted the celery yet for your *dochder's* wedding, Elizabeth?" inquired Sarah Hochstetler, pushing her reading glasses further up the bridge of her nose so she could see better.

"*Jah*, a month ago, there should be plenty for the reception." All the women nodded in approval, smiles wreathing their faces.

Karen leaned over to Mary and whispered. "What's the deal with celery?" She had never liked the stuff (except with peanut butter) and wondered why it would figure so prominently in someone's wedding plans. Maybe it was the appetizer...?

"It is one of the traditional dishes we make for our weddings," Mary replied, expertly slipping her needle in and out of the fabric in perfect, even little stitches. "Just talking about it makes my mouth water for creamed celery."

Karen wrinkled her face. "Creamed celery? *Eeewww*."

Mary giggled. "Don't knock it until you've tried it."

Karen decided to change the subject. "So, what is this design called that we are working on?" She pushed her needle in and out one stitch at a time because she was not as adept at sewing. Her fingers were already starting to hurt. The quilt stretched out on the frame was in navy and light blues on a white background.

"Star of Bethlehem," Mary replied. "Hannah chose it because she loves the Christmas story of our Lord's birth so much."

Karen nodded and bent over her patch of quilt. An hour after she had arrived, they heard a buggy pull up in the driveway. Karen looked up and was dismayed to see her mother enter the room followed by Samuel Miller.

Great! Just what I needed! My mother cramping my style!

She said nothing when Sarah Hochstetler got up to greet her but was inwardly pleased that the greeting did not seem as enthusiastic as her own had been.

Her mom waved at her. "Hi honey, how's it going?"

Karen bent her head over her work. "Fine." She hoped her mom would get the hint...*just pretend you don't know me.*

Samuel Miller walked through the house and out the backdoor while her mom found a seat next to Sarah Hochstetler. Work resumed while the women chattered. With no small degree of self-satisfaction, Karen noticed the frustration in her mother's face and body language as she struggled with the needle and thread.

The women quilted for the next few hours, laughing, and talking amongst themselves. Despite the blisters and calluses forming on her fingers, Karen discovered that she was enjoying herself immensely. She liked the feeling of being part of something unique and special and that she was helping to make it.

"Perhaps one day we will be working on a wedding quilt for you," whispered Lilly with a giggle. Karen glanced over at her mom in alarm, hoping Lilly hadn't been overheard.

"Shush," Karen hissed.

I'm not too happy about Ruth Bieler coming over every day, John," Samuel confessed to his brother-in-law in the privacy of the barn. "I can't quite put my finger on it, but I feel that the woman has ulterior motives for offering Ra... Mrs. Winston help other than mere Christian charity and friendship."

John was taken aback by this accusation. "Samuel, how could you speak ill of one of our own with no evidence to show for it? How could you possibly know what lies in another's heart? Only *Der Herr* knows what is truly within our hearts."

Samuel nodded. "I only tell you this, John, because you are my *bruder-in-law* and my *gut* friend. You don't see the way Ruth Bieler looks at me ...."

John put a hand on his shoulder, his face etched with concern. "Samuel...why would this bother you? Ruth Bieler is one of us; she would make an excellent *frau*. Even the Bishop thinks so."

"I have never had an interest in Miss Bieler, and you know very well why," Samuel replied, refusing to look John in the eyes.

John drew closer, his voice low with concern. "Samuel, do you have feelings for this *Englisch* woman?"

Samuel's silence was all the answer John needed. His eyes widened with alarm. "You know this is forbidden," he whispered. "You were already treading on dangerous ground by selling the property to an *Englisch* to begin with."

Samuel nodded. "I know the *Ordnung* as well as you, John. Mrs. Winston is considering being baptized into our church."

"Be careful, Samuel, be very, *very* careful." John replied, his voice barely above a whisper. "It was hard enough to lose Rachel and the *kinner*. I don't think you want to be excommunicated merely because you have a passing attraction to this *Englisch* woman. Perhaps, it is a *gut* thing *Der Herr* has brought Ruth Bieler into the picture…to save you from making a horrible mistake."

Samuel said nothing in response to John's words. He couldn't deny John's suspicions and he doubted his *bruder-in-law* would believe him if he did so because John knew him better than anyone. Samuel knew he shouldn't have feelings for Rachel Winston, but his heart wasn't listening.

───※───

At noon, the women broke for lunch. They stood with bowed heads for prayer before helping themselves to the dishes spread out over the sideboard.

Mary pulled Karen over to a covered dish. "You're in luck," she grinned, scooping out the contents and putting some on Karen's plate without asking. "Hannah's mom brought some creamed celery."

Karen grimaced. "Do I *have* to eat it?"

"You have to try just one bite because I want to know what you think," Mary insisted.

Karen groaned. "You sound like my mom." She filled her plate with the few items she found appetizing then followed Mary out to the front porch. They each selected a rocker and sat down. The porch overlooked the Hochstetler's flower and herb garden, which was filled with roses, Black-Eyed Susan's, sunflowers, geraniums, and a multitude of herbs. In the distance, Karen could see the Hochstetler's fields. It was so peaceful and quiet, almost like being inside a storybook or a dream. She was so caught up in looking at the beautiful scenery, she forgot to eat.

"Take a bite, you won't be sorry," Mary encouraged her.

Karen tore her eyes from the fields and scooped up a tiny spoonful of the creamed celery. "Okay...here goes nothing." Her lips closed over the still warm food, and she was pleasantly surprised. The taste was nothing like what she had expected and was very good. It reminded her of the creamed corn she used to heat up from cans for meals when her parents weren't around to cook. She swallowed, took another bite, and didn't stop until she had eaten all of it.

"I told you." Mary beamed. "We'll make a plain girl of you yet."

After lunch and clean-up, the women returned to the quilting frame. Karen had been deeply involved with Mary in conversation when there was a loud OUCH from her mother's side of the quilt frame. Everyone looked up at once and over at her mom who was alternating between sucking on her finger and apologizing profusely, her distress evident.

"I'm so, so sorry," she repeated as she stared with horror at the white patch of quilt she had just stained with blood. Sarah Hochstetler hurried away and swiftly returned with a bottle of club soda, baking soda, and a clean rag. She dabbed at it until the fabric was as clean as it had been before her mom jabbed her finger with the needle. No one seemed much bothered by it and continued to work as before, but her mom refused to do anymore work. She sat out the rest of the quilting bee in her chair neither sewing nor speaking to anyone, looking thoroughly dejected. They continued their work until late afternoon when they finally called a halt. It was time to pack up and return to their homes to start supper for their hungry families. Her mom was up like a shot looking anxious to escape.

"You did some *gut* work today," Mary told Karen, handing her a small square of fabric that she had pieced together.

"What's this?" Karen asked.

"This is a quilt square to begin your own quilt with." Mary gave her a conspiratorial smile. "I have a feeling you may have need of one before the year is out."

Karen's face flamed, understanding the innuendo. "*Danki*," she said, tucking it into her satchel before her mom could see.

"We'll be getting together again soon to continue working on Hannah's quilt. Do you think you can make it?"

"*Jah*, unless, of course, Willis has other plans," Karen smiled, glancing across the room when she saw him enter from the back porch.

At that moment, her mother walked up with Samuel behind her. "Ready to go?"

Karen nodded. "Can I just say goodbye before we leave?"

Her mom nodded. "Sure, just make it quick."

Karen scampered up to Willis. "I have to leave now," she announced.

Willis removed his hat and offered her a shy grin. "May I speak with your *mamm* before you leave?"

Karen shrugged. "Sure, why not?"

Willis' long legs closed the distance in a few strides. "Mrs. Winston?"

Startled, her mom turned at the sound of her name then craned her neck to look up at the tall youth who towered over her. "Yes, Willis?"

"May I have your permission to escort your daughter to a day at the Strasburg miniature train museum and lunch tomorrow?"

Karen could tell her mom was impressed with Willis' courtesy. Unlike Amish mothers, she knew hers would see no need for a chaperone for a day outing.

"She would love that, of course." Rachel nodded, giving Karen a little wink.

Willis returned to Karen. "I will pick you up in my buggy around 11:00 am tomorrow then after our chores?"

His intense blue eyes made her heart flutter uncontrollably. "Okay," she smiled, trying to sound calm. "See you then." Karen said her goodbyes to Mary and the other women.

Chapter Sixteen

Hasty Words

Rachel sat in the buggy beside Samuel, miserable over the day's events and wondering if it were possible for things to have gone any worse. It was the second time she had attempted to join in on a quilting bee and the results had been just as disastrous as the first time. The women had barely spoken to her; conversing mostly in Pennsylvania Dutch with each other. While she could basically understand them because she knew German, she still felt left out. Quilting was just not her thing. No matter how hard she tried to fit in, she ended up feeling more ostracized than ever. She wasn't building bridges between his people and herself, she was laying mortar for walls. She glanced over at him as he quietly drove Dodger along the two-lane, his eyes fixed on the road ahead with a deep frown on his face. They didn't speak for the entire ride home and she pacified herself with the excuse that it was due to Karen's presence rather than his mood.

They arrived back at the farmhouse by four o'clock. It was the end of August, so the sun was still high in the sky. She had at least another five hours of daylight to get some work done after supper. The workmen were beginning to pack up their tools. When they pulled into the gravel driveway, she saw a large flatbed truck parked in front of the house with her green VW Beetle sitting on top of it.

"Hey Mom, look! Your car finally arrived," Karen exclaimed.

The cab of the delivery truck was empty, but Rachel found the delivery men sitting on her front porch. They didn't look happy.

"Geez, lady, don't you ever answer your cell phone? We've been trying to reach you for hours," complained the elder of the two. He was stocky with faded tattoos all over his arms. "We're gonna have to charge you another $100 for keeping us waiting."

"Well, why did it take so long?" Rachel wanted to know, more than a little irritated. "It should have been here weeks ago!"

"There was a mix up in the paperwork and it accidently got sent to Minnesota first. We tried to get ahold of you for weeks to let you know about the delay, but you never answered your phone!"

"I'm so sorry," Rachel exclaimed. "My cell phone has been dead for a long time. I've had no way to charge it. Can I make it up to you? How about staying for dinner since it's so late?"

The two men looked at one another then back at her and shrugged. "Sure," the older one agreed, "but it won't negate the $100 charge. That goes to our company."

"I understand," nodded Rachel. "Karen, can you bring these two gentlemen out some iced tea while I get dinner started?"

"Why can't you do it?" Karen shot back automatically.

Karen," growled Samuel, turning from unhitching the buggy to give her a stern look. Karen jumped in response and ran into the house. The men stepped down off the porch and went to the truck to unload her car.

"Another fifteen minutes and we would have left with your car," declared the younger fellow with blonde, closely cropped hair and bad acne. Rachel said nothing, watching silently as they unloaded the Beetle. She had mixed emotions about getting her car back. She was glad for the freedom, air-conditioning, and independence, but she was also a bit sad now that she no longer had an excuse to ask Samuel for rides. Karen returned with two glasses of sweet tea then disappeared back into the house again. The car was unloaded, and the keys handed to her.

Rachel beckoned to the rocking chairs on the front porch. "Please make yourselves comfortable."

With them happily ensconced, Rachel collected her mail. A bill from the General Contractor had arrived. She was almost afraid to open it and see the amount owed. With pounding heart, she ripped open the envelope and peeked. Rachel groaned aloud even though she had been expecting it.

Karen poked her head out the screen door. "What's wrong?"

Rachel jumped. "Uh, nothing. Could you get the table set for five while I start dinner?"

"Do I have a choice?"

"No," Rachel snapped, in no mood for her daughter's snotty attitude.

"What are we having?"

Rachel went inside and surveyed the contents of the refrigerator. "Lamb chops, green beans and garlic mashed potatoes." She shoved the invoice into her pocket.

Fiddle Dee-Dee sang the voice of Scarlet O'Hara inside her head...*I won't think about it today. I'll think about it tomorrow...*

She seasoned the lamb liberally with kosher salt, olive oil, oregano, rosemary, and freshly ground pepper on both sides then left it out to reach room temperature while she got the fire started. Into the oven went a whole garlic head, cut at the top, drizzled with olive oil, and wrapped in aluminum foil to roast.

Karen returned. "Okay, I'm done. I'm going to my room."

No, you're not. I need you to peel these potatoes, cut them into small chunks, and put them into that bowl of ice water while I harvest the green beans in the garden."

"Arrrrgggggghhhh," Karen growled, grudgingly accepting the peeler. Rachel slung a wicker basket over her arm and went out to the house garden where she found Samuel hard at work, hoeing and weeding.

He straightened from his work and looked at her.

"A bill from the contractors came in," Rachel announced sullenly, kicking at a large dirt clod.

Samuel leaned the hoe up against a garden trellis and came closer. *"Jah?"*

"It's a lot of money," Rachel murmured, feeling the tears of frustration and despair threatening to run down her cheeks. "I just can't seem to catch a break. It's going to cost me $20,000 to dig a hole for the septic tank. I'm going to be cleaned out of money at this rate before I can ever open for business," she moaned. "What am I going to do?" She looked at him woefully.

Samuel stared back at her for a moment. He propped the hoe against the house, took her hands in his, and gave them a comforting squeeze. Rachel tilted her eyes up to his, her bottom lip trembling. His hand went to her face and gently brushed the tears away. *"Schlimmer als scheitern ist das scheitern, um zu versuchen."* (Worse than failure is the failure to not try) he murmured.

Rachel sighed then looked around at the garden blankly for a moment. "I came out here for something…what was it?" She looked back at him, a ghost of a smile playing about her lips. "Maybe I should retrace my steps so I can remember?"

"Green beans," shouted Karen from the kitchen window.

They stared at one another in momentary fear. Karen had seen them.

"Green beans," Rachel repeated.

Samuel pointed to a large trellis overgrown with them. "They are over there. I need to get back to work if I'm to be done by supper time," he reminded her with a gentle smile.

Rachel nodded and ran her sleeve across her nose. She carefully threaded her way across the neat rows of carrots, onions, parsnips, and cabbage until she stood right in front of the massive green bean tower. When she had enough, she made her way back to the front porch. "Supper will be ready in an hour," she said, smiling shyly up at him. Their eyes met and held fast for a long moment, causing a rush of warmth to flood her body.

"I'll be ready," he replied softly with a tip of his hat.

The five of them shared a wonderful dinner that night, finishing it off with freshly ground coffee and Rachel's own home-made apple pie. When they left, the deliverymen were so appreciative they refunded Rachel the $100 surcharge.

That night Rachel got down on her knees before her cot on the service porch and prayed earnestly.

Dear Lord, thank You for bringing me here even though it's been so hard. Thank you for bringing Ruth Bieler as a friend into my life when I really needed one and for my daughter Karen being so accepted and welcomed into the community. I ask for you to lead and guide her and provide her with a future and a hope according to your word in Jeremiah 29:11.

Lord, you also know my situation. You know how I'm running through my money. Could you please help me out somehow? Here she paused for a moment, not quite sure what to pray about Samuel. *I have strong feelings for Samuel, Lord. Maybe it's because I'm so lonely and he's the only one I see all the time. I don't even know what to ask here, Lord, but you know my heart and You know what's best. Please lead and guide me. Amen.*

She climbed into bed and only after she had laid there for fifteen minutes daydreaming about Samuel, did she realize that she had forgotten all about Barry in her prayers. Guilt flooded her heart.

I've only been here a few months and already I'm betraying his memory.

The guilt was immediately followed by a renewed sense of intense grief. She put her head under the pillow and cried herself to sleep.

Chapter Seventeen

Life Goes On, Sort Of...

Karen was hardly at home anymore. As soon as she completed her chores and egg rounds, she was either off to the Hochstetler's house or out with Willis, who was now showing up for their "dates" in *Englisch* jeans and t-shirts. He had also traded in his straw hat for a Phillies cap after Karen had introduced him to professional baseball.

Her daughter was living a double life. Some days she would be completely plain, dressed in Amish clothes, busy with her chores, and working on some secret project in her room. On other days, she would be dressed in her regular *Englisch* clothes with full makeup, usually when Willis Hochstetler came calling for one of their *"Rumspringa"* dates. Rachel wasn't sure which Karen scared her more. Amish-Karen where the girls married young, or English-Karen who was constantly in the company of a young man obviously besotted with her.

It was mid-September, and her electricity and internet were finally installed in the Inn. The His & Hers communal bathrooms were completed, and all the pipes laid for plumbing. All that remained was digging and installing the septic tank and tapping into the county line for water. Now that her phone and internet were up and she had electricity, she was inundated with emails and voicemails from concerned family members and friends who had been wanting to know about her and Karen's well-being for the past three months. Her voicemail was full. She sent out a generic email blast giving everyone the basic 411 on her life and letting them know that they could now call her because her cell phone was finally working. She fielded calls for the next three days straight until everyone's curiosity had been satisfied and their minds relieved.

The next order of business was making the Inn website go live so she could book reservations for the winter months and earn some income. She made a few minor edits and added several more photographs to the site. Some featured herself canning fruit with Ruth and pretending to quilt. She also added pictures of the new indoor bathrooms which featured private showers and toilet stalls. Finally, it was done and ready to go online. Samuel had been busy in the fields gathering in the fall harvest with the help of his brother-in-law, nephews, and neighbors.

The unrelenting heat and humidity of August had waned a couple of weeks ago. The weather was turning milder. Rachel was looking forward to her first fall in Pennsylvania. She had only experienced a New England fall on one prior occasion, when she and Barry had spent a sizeable tax refund on a Vermont bicycling trip with the secondary destination of upstate New York and Manhattan during the Columbus holiday. Karen had been only six years old at the time. From that time forward, whenever Southern California experienced crisp fall weather, they would find themselves longing to return to the East Coast.

Her eyes welled up as she remembered how overjoyed Barry had been to eat lunch at Tavern on the Green, visit the Baseball Hall of Fame in Cooperstown, and how beautiful the fall foliage had been on the drive through upstate New York and Vermont. On her thirtieth birthday, he had taken her to Tiffany's on Fifth Avenue and bought her pearl earrings. Afterward, they celebrated with a kiss on top of the Empire State Building followed by dessert at Windows on the World before the terrorist attacks of 9-11 which had destroyed the twin towers. All she had left now were memories, scrapbooks, and the pearl earrings.

She sat sniveling before her computer, tears sliding down her cheeks as she sipped her morning coffee to check email, muttering silent prayers for a miracle. She had registered her site with the local chamber of commerce, Airbnb, the Bed and Breakfast Inn Registry, and posted it everywhere she could think of across social media for the past two weeks to drum up business.

It was the third week of September and the morning had dawned crisp and cold enough to warrant a fire in the hearth, her first since moving in. She had real cordwood, not the phony logs purchased at the supermarket in a flammable wrapper. The wood snapped and crackled gently in the fireplace, and she found the sound of it soothing. Her kitchen smelled of freshly baked cinnamon rolls and fresh bread, a testament to her improved baking skills, thanks to Ruth Bieler. She stopped mid-slurp, her eyes freezing on an email message with the words RESERVATION REQUEST in the subject line. With her heart pounding, she opened it just as Karen walked into the kitchen, back from her egg deliveries. She hurried to the fireplace and warmed her backside.

"Oh, thank you God," Rachel screeched, lifting both arms in the air as if she had just scored a touchdown. Coffee sloshed over the sides of the cup. Buddy scurried away in fear and hid under the dinner table.

"What?" Karen asked, stuffing a wad of bills into her apron pocket, and peering over Rachel's shoulder.

"I just got a reservation request for a family to spend the last two weeks of December here for Christmas."

"But we still don't have indoor plumbing," Karen complained. "They'll cancel as soon as they find out they have to use an outhouse in freezing weather."

"I'm going to use their deposit towards getting that septic tank installed and I'll have to charge the rest." Rachel replied. She hoped she still had enough credit to cover the difference.

Karen shrugged, "*Whatever.*" She turned to go.

"Hey, what have you been up to lately besides seeing Willis?" Rachel wanted to know. She knew that Karen had been working quietly on some project in her room, but her daughter still wouldn't tell her anything about it.

"Just doing some arts and crafts to keep myself busy," she replied evasively.

"I love arts and crafts. Want some help?"

"No, I'm good," Karen replied.

Rachel's heart sank a little. She shouldn't have gotten her hopes up. "Well, okay. Umm, I must run to the store after I send these emails. Do you need anything?"

Karen paused for a moment and was about to shake her head then seemed to reconsider. "Hey Mom, could I come with you and do a little shopping in town?"

Rachel's heart skipped a beat for a moment. *Karen actually wants to spend some time with me?* "Of course. Hey, maybe we get some lunch together, make it a girl's day out? Get our nails done?"

"Maybe," Karen replied, shrugging but not looking the least bit interested.

A knock sounded on the door.

"Ruth Bieler's here," Karen announced with a grimace.

"What's the problem with Ruth?" Rachel hissed, not happy at having her daughter "dis" her one and only friend in the community.

"Nothing, just forget it." Karen stared at her wet face as if noticing it for the first time. "Were you crying?"

Rachel wiped the tears away with the back of her sleeve. "I miss Daddy," she mumbled lamely.

"Really, Mom, it's been over a year, you really need to get over it already." Karen walked away to answer the door, shaking her head. Rachel stared after her, feeling like she had just been punched in the gut. Her daughter was so out of touch with her own emotions she thought anyone else who had them was abnormal.

Ruth held her hands out to Rachel the moment she got a look at her face. "*Was is los*, Rachel?"

"I'm just missing Barry," Rachel smiled weakly, grasping Ruth's hands.

Ruth nodded with a sympathetic look and gave her a fleeting hug. "What did you want to work on today?"

"Well, I need to go into town and run a couple of errands. Would you like to come along? We could do some shopping and get some lunch together? My treat."

Ruth hesitated for a moment as if struggling to decide then nodded. "*Jah*, that would be fine."

"Go ahead and help yourself to some coffee and cinnamon rolls. I just need to respond to these emails and get my shoes on. We can go in my V-Dub? It has heated seats."

"*Danki*," Ruth smiled, helping herself to a cinnamon roll.

Rachel typed furiously, booking the reservation, and notifying her potential guests of the fifty percent deposit due upfront. "Would you mind bringing that covered tray and some rolls over to the *dawdi haus* for me? Samuel must be famished by now."

Ruth brightened at this. "*Jah*, I'd be happy to." She gathered the covered plate, piled another with cinnamon rolls, and went out front just as Samuel was returning from the barn.

"*Gut morgan*, Samuel," Ruth greeted him with a warm smile. "I thought you'd like some breakfast. We are heading out on some errands and won't be back for a while."

Samuel stared back at her for a moment, his disapproval evident. Ruth Bieler knew good and well she was not behaving in accordance with the *Ordnung*, but since Samuel wasn't either and Rachel Winston was clearly ignorant, she wasn't too worried about being caught.

Samuel accepted the food but didn't say *danki* nor tip his hat, which made her scowl. He merely went inside the *dawdi haus* and closed the door behind him. Ruth quickly returned to Rachel who was gathering up her purse, keys, and shopping list while simultaneously yelling up the stairs for Karen to hurry up.

They were soon off. They arrived in town where Rachel's first order of business was the general contractor. Her hands were trembling as she handed Mr. Gold her credit card, praying that the 50% deposit would be waiting for her upon her return from town. He scheduled his men to dig the hole for the septic tank and connect the plumbing for the following week.

"If the weather holds, Mrs. Winston, we should have everything done in about two weeks."

"Does that mean that I will finally be able to take a hot shower?" Karen asked.

"Yes, it sure does," Mr. Gold replied with an understanding smile. They all stood and shook hands. "Not to worry, Mrs. Winston. We'll take good care of you."

"Thanks," Rachel nodded. She herded Karen and Ruth out the door. Across the street was the fabric shop where Karen had wanted to shop.

Karen blocked the door as they were about to enter. "Why don't you go on ahead and do your other errands and I'll meet you later?"

"What? I can't come in with you?" Rachel wanted to know.

Karen replied, "I'll just be a few minutes, I know what I need. Just go ahead, I'll only be a few minutes."

Ruth Bieler stood by, silent and uncomfortable. Rachel crossed her arms, trying not to show her hurt feelings. "What if we want to come in and shop for ourselves?" It seemed like Karen hadn't wanted her company after all, she had just been using her for the ride.

Karen stared at her, her eyes pleading. "Please Mom? It's a surprise. You don't want to ruin my surprise, do you?"

"Let the child shop alone," Ruth nudged her, linking her arm through Rachel's. "It's obvious our company isn't wanted." She gave Karen a little wink and pulled a still reluctant Rachel after her. Karen's story about a surprise hadn't appeased her at all. If it was a surprise, she was pretty darn sure it wasn't a surprise for her. She allowed Ruth to drag her down the street to go window-shopping.

Half an hour later, Karen caught up with them, a shopping bag bulging with fabric. Since the Amish didn't get their nails done, Rachel went to buy supplies instead for her first inn guests, then they all went to Yoder's café for lunch, a favorite among the locals where hearty Pennsylvania Dutch fare was served six days a week. The scent of freshly baked bread greeted them as they entered. A chubby little Amish girl quickly seated them and handed them menus, returning moments later with glasses of water.

"Would you like anything else to drink?" she asked.

"Hot tea for me," Rachel smiled, studying the menu. She had been craving chicken and the smell of it permeated the restaurant. Since her daughter could never eat an entire meal on her own, she ordered the broasted chicken with roasted vegetables and a roll to share with her. Ruth ordered the meat loaf and the same sides. The girl took their order and soon returned with their tea, a basket of freshly baked rolls and honey butter, followed by their meal. They bowed their heads for silent prayer then dug in.

"YUM," Karen exclaimed. "Mom, you've got to learn how to make chicken like this," Karen groaned, closing her eyes in ecstasy. "This is the best ever."

"It is good," Rachel agreed.

They quickly finished their meal, did a little more shopping in the café's gift section, and returned home. Rachel made a beeline to her computer and logged into her account, holding her breath. She prayed silently and then collapsed with relief when she saw that the deposit had gone into her account. The Second Chance Inn was officially in business.

Chapter Eighteen

Fulfilling a Dream

Rachel was ecstatic. The weather held long enough for Mr. Gold's crew to get the septic tank in and finish the plumbing. On a particularly frigid morning in mid-October, the week when all the trees on her property turned brilliant shades of red, orange, and bright yellow, she and Karen got to take their first hot showers and use the indoor bathrooms. *Sheer heaven!*

Rachel could hear Karen all the way from the downstairs celebrating with whoops and hollers of joy and occasionally the hallelujah chorus. Rachel had her own small ensuite bathroom in her room, which had necessitated taking some of the square footage out of the bedroom. Rachel lathered herself up with the lavender soap she had bought special for the occasion and stood with the hot water sluicing down over her. She had forgotten just how good a hot shower felt and allowed herself to indulge for a good half hour. The tankless water heater was a marvel. No matter how much hot water they used, it never ran out. The outhouse was still there, but Samuel was the only one who used it now.

They spent the remainder of October and most of November in preparation for her first guests. Each room had an expensive, in-wall HVAC unit that would keep the room cool in the hot summer months and warm for the harsh winter months. The guest rooms had been freshly painted and stocked with Amish-crafted quilts, soaps and toiletries.

As the weather grew chillier, things between Rachel and Samuel continued to warm up. Instead of sitting outside in the chill air on the porch swing, they sat together on the couch in front of the fireplace and talked, played checkers or read out loud to one another. They discussed their separate childhoods and about the loved ones they had lost. Rachel knew she was falling in love with Samuel, and she was pretty sure the feeling was mutual. He never brought up the topic of her becoming Amish again, but it was always there, hanging like the sword of *Damocles* above her head anyway.

It was the week of Thanksgiving and Rachel was feeling happy for the first time in over a year. She invited Ruth and Ruth's parents over for Thanksgiving dinner and decorated the farmhouse with fall foliage, gourds, asters, and pumpkins. Every room had a scented candle burning with the scents of apple pie or cinnamon orange spice; scents Barry would have gagged over.

With the purchase of the Thanksgiving groceries, Rachel's bank account was close to empty until she received the balance of the holiday reservation payment and that wouldn't happen until the family checked out at the end of December. At least she had a fully stocked root cellar and pantry, and her bills were all current.

The morning before Thanksgiving dawned cold, bone chilling cold. Rachel was bundled up in her warmest sweats and her UGG boots and was still freezing despite the wonderful fire crackling in the hearth and the stove that was now kept going day and night for warmth. She had set the long farmhouse table with her beloved grandmother's china, gourds, and miniature pumpkins. Just as she was slathering dry brine all over the turkey, she heard Samuel come in from the barn for breakfast. Instead of his usual purposeful stride, his feet were trudging heavily across the floor. Rachel went to greet him and her *gut morgan* died in her throat. He was white as a sheet, covered in a thin sheen of sweat, and trembling uncontrollably. He stumbled toward the table and fell onto his knees. Rachel and Karen both lunged to catch him before his head hit the floor and rolled him onto his back. His eyes rolled back into his head.

"Samuel," Rachel cried out. "What's is it? What's wrong?!"

Karen knelt beside her, her brown eyes full of concern. "Mom, what's wrong with him?"

Rachel pressed her hand against his damp forehead. "He's very sick. Feel how hot his skin is?" Samuel's skin was on fire. "Quick, go to the freezer and fill up two, gallon plastic bags with ice cubes. I've got to get his temperature down fast."

For once, Karen didn't argue with her and came back not only with the bags of ice but the ear thermometer as well. Rachel raised his arms. "Put the bags of ice under his armpits while I get his temp." He was shaking with chills so violent she could hear his teeth chattering. He moaned when Karen pressed the icy bags into his armpits then erupted into violent coughing. He sounded heavily congested. Rachel put the thermometer into his ear and triggered the read-out. It was as bad as she feared: 103, dangerously high. "Keep those bags of ice in his armpits no matter how much he complains." She ran to the sink, filled a pail with cold water, and added additional ice, returning with a sponge. She soaked the sponge then squeezed the icy water over his chest. It was so cold her fingers hurt. Samuel moaned and curled into a fetal position.

"Too cold. Too c-c-c-cold," he moaned. Little Buddy sat nearby, intimidated by the action going on around him. His ears were flat against his head, and he was whining.

Karen stared at her in alarm. "Mom, are you sure you know what you're doing? Look at him. Maybe I should take the buggy and fetch a doctor?"

"In this weather? The day before Thanksgiving? Use the computer and Google physicians in Lancaster and start calling them up. See if any of them will make an emergency house call. I'll sponge him down while you do that."

Samuel continued to moan and tremble violently as Rachel bathed his hot skin. After fifteen solid minutes of this, she finally got his temperature down to 100.6 whereupon he went limp and fell unconscious. "Karen, any luck yet? Get over here, we need to get him into bed. Get that quilt off the couch and we'll put it underneath him and use it like a stretcher."

Karen ran into the kitchen. "Mom, are you nuts? We can't lift him upstairs."

"We're putting him in my room," Rachel snapped, ignoring the queer look Karen gave her. They rolled Samuel to one side, spread the quilt under him then rolled him back into the middle. "Make sure the door is open and the path clear before we lift him. Are the blankets pulled back?"

Karen went and double-checked the door. "It's all good," she said, then squatted down to lift the quilt at his feet.

Rachel squatted opposite her. "Lift with your legs not your back! Ready? One…two…three."

"OMG, he's heavy," Karen grunted, her face turning red with exertion. Together they struggled to a standing position and with much exertion, were able to get him onto Rachel's bed in one try. Despite the cold weather, Rachel was soaked in sweat. She removed her sweatshirt under which she wore a long-sleeve cotton shirt.

"He needs a doctor, have you found anyone yet?"

"I'm still looking," grumbled Karen, leaving Rachel to tend to Samuel. She refilled the bowl with cold water from the sink and replaced the melted ice bags with fresh ones. Samuel was drenched with sweat and mumbling as if he were trying to tell her something.

"What is it?" She put her ear close to his mouth so she could hear him better. His eyes opened, then they widened as he continued to stare at her, tears seeping out and tracing lines down his cheeks.

"Rachel," he whispered brokenly, a tremulous smile coming to his mouth.

"Yes, I'm here," Rachel replied. "What is it?" She wiped his face with the cool washcloth. Samuel's hand closed about her wrist. His other arm encircled her and pulled her onto his chest. *What is he doing?* He began to murmur endearments in Pennsylvania Dutch into her ear. She gently tried to extricate herself, but he pulled her closer until the upper half of her body was pressed against his. It was no good trying to get away, he just held onto her tighter. She relaxed in his arms a bit to see if he would ease his grip.

"You're here? You're really here? *Meine süße frau. Wo sind die kinder?*" His voice had become soft...caressing almost. Finally, he allowed her to pull away so he could look at her. She sat up straight and stared at him. Samuel was smiling at her in a way he had never done before...with tenderness and joy and that was when it hit her: *He thinks I'm his dead wife and is asking for his children. He's delirious!*

Her heart sank. "They're all gone, Samuel. They are with *Der Herr* in heaven," she reminded him gently using his own terms. Samuel regarded her silently for a long moment, clearly confused.

His hot hand cupped her face. "Gone? You are not my Rachel?"

She shook her head sorrowfully, wishing she was "*his Rachel.*" His eyes flooded with tears and a wail of pain erupted from his throat. He began to sob so hard it made the entire bed shake. He was inconsolable. *I should have lied to him. I should have pretended I was her.* Rachel was becoming frantic; she didn't know what to do. His skin was turning hot again, a sure sign his temperature was rising. She had to get ibuprofen into him.

"Samuel, take this." She poured a glass of water and held out a tablet, but he wasn't listening. He continued wailing while the walls vibrated with his agony.

"No, let me be, I wish to join my family."

Rachel was desperate. If she couldn't get his temperature down, he would surely get his wish, and she needed him.

Without Samuel, she would be lost. She tried reasoning with him for several minutes, but it went nowhere. He was becoming more delirious.

"Rachel?" He was looking at her again with those hopeful, dreamy eyes and another smile.

Rachel paused before she answered him. Perhaps she could use this to her advantage. "Samuel, *geliebt*, dearest, won't you please help your *frau* make you feel better?" She gave him a sweet smile and held up the water glass and pill.

Samuel stared at her, his facial expression hovering between confusion and relief, thinking his deceased wife had returned to him.

He nodded.

Rachel leaned forward to pop the pill into his mouth.

Samuel's arms went around her and pulled her firmly against him. The next thing she knew, his lips were upon hers, kissing her hungrily. He may have been delirious, but he was still as strong as an ox. There was no resisting his strength. The more she tried, the more it seemed to turn him on. His passion quickly overwhelmed her, and she became vaguely aware that her own arms had snaked around his hot body while his mouth continued to ravish hers.

"Mom! *WHAT. ARE. YOU. DOING!!?*"

Rachel reared back and found Karen standing in the bedroom doorway, staring at her with a mixture of horror and disgust. Samuel's arms remained wrapped around her; his eyes fastened on her. Ignoring her daughter for the moment, she tore herself away from Samuel and held the water glass in front of his lips. "Take this now, Samuel," she ordered sternly. Samuel smiled weakly, opened his mouth, and downed the pill obediently. She pushed him flat, replaced the bags of ice in his armpits, and sponged him down again until his skin grew cooler to the touch. After fifteen minutes, he was finally asleep. The ibuprofen had finally taken effect.

Karen was still waiting in the doorway with a strange look on her face. "Why were you kissing him?" she hissed.

"He thought I was his wife, he was delirious," Rachel replied wearily, sitting down at the kitchen table. She rested her forehead on her arms. She was utterly exhausted.

"That's not what it looked like, you were kissing him right back," Karen accused.

Rachel lifted her head and rolled her eyes, hoping she would sound convincing. "I was playing a part so he would take his medicine. I've probably ingested every germ he had in his body to boot."

Karen glowered at her. "Well, you're a really good actress because it sure looked like you were enjoying it!"

Rachel ignored this last comment, hoping Karen wouldn't notice the blush flaming her cheeks. "Did you find a doctor yet?"

"One…he's on his way here now. He knows Samuel and his family…" her voice drifted off. She looked down and shuffled her feet. "Were you really only pretending, mom?"

Rachel stared at Karen before answering her, stunned by the pain in her voice. Karen and Barry had been very close to each other. Her behavior with Samuel a moment ago must have seemed like a total betrayal.

"Yes," Rachel confirmed softly. Well, it was mostly true after all. She had had no other way to get him to cooperate with her. Still, there was no denying the way she had felt locked in his passionate embrace. His kisses had made her toes curl. She had a hard time not thinking about it until the doctor arrived an hour later.

Rachel and Karen waited in the kitchen as Dr. Yoder performed his examination. He was Mennonite. He drove a car and used a cell phone, but he was a favorite among the Amish for their medical needs. He came out ten minutes later, his stethoscope still hanging around the back of his neck. "Samuel has influenza. There's a nasty twenty-four-hour bug going around. I gave him a shot of antibiotics but will have to culture his throat to verify if it is viral or bacterial. Keep him hydrated, comfortable, and his temperature down. You did the right thing with the ice bags and ibuprofen. As soon as I get the results back, I'll have a prescription delivered." He handed Rachel his business card and wrote his cell phone number on the back. "Call me immediately if there is any change. Right now, I see no need to have him hospitalized, but if he gets worse, he will need to be. The congestion has not reached his lungs."

"Thank you so much for coming on such short notice and before Thanksgiving," Rachel exclaimed, shaking his hand. "I hope it was no great inconvenience."

Dr. Yoder paused and looked down at his feet for a moment. "I've been the Miller's family physician since Samuel and Rachel were wed," he murmured, a sad look passing over his features. "I was the attending physician when his *frau* and *kinner* were brought into the emergency room. No man should have to endure what Samuel has, Mrs. Winston." He patted her hand. "I'm glad you are here to help take care of him. I'll be back to check on him in a few days."

"Thanks again," Rachel replied as the door shut behind him. She wondered how much the house call was going to cost her and if the good doctor would be willing to take payment in the form of fresh eggs.

Rachel watched over Samuel for the next twenty-four hours as he alternated between hot sweats and cold chills, his coughing fits violent enough to send Buddy upstairs to hide under Karen's bed. When night came, Rachel made a bed for herself on an air mattress on the floor next to him so she would be able to tend to him, but there was no sleep to be had that night. She slept only fitfully between his bouts of coughing and checking on his fluctuating temperature. When he was too quiet, she panicked and got up to make sure he was still breathing. She continued to sponge him down if his skin got too hot. He often murmured the name "Rachel" in a plaintive voice, but she knew it was his wife he called for and not herself. She did her best to ignore it but at 3:00 am he was again delirious and insistent.

"Rachel, Rachel..." His arm slid down the side of the bed and groped around for her until his fingers found her head. He caressed her hair. "*Komm zu mir.*" Despite the warning bells going off in her head, Rachel rose and sat wearily upon the bed. "What is it, Samuel?" She felt his forehead. His skin was on fire. She poured more water into a glass and held out another pill, "Time for your medicine, Samuel."

"Kiss me first," he replied, his feverish eyes fastened on her face. His arms reached for her.

He really doesn't want me...he wants "his" Rachel. He doesn't know what he's doing... She knew she shouldn't do it but found herself leaning forward to meet his lips as if drawn by a magnet. *You're playing with fire.* His hands clasped her head and drew her mouth to his. She felt his arm slide down and curl around her waist, pulling her against him. His lips opened her mouth with a passion that both frightened and thrilled her. In all the months they had known each other and grown into friends, exchanging meaningful stares, and holding hands, why did he choose now of all times to kiss her? Was it because he was too delirious to even know what he was doing? She felt helpless to resist him. All common sense, germs, and thoughts of personal hygiene fled from her mind. She returned his kiss with equal ardor, her fingers twining into his sweaty hair. Alarm bells went off in her head as his kisses deepened. *This is going too far...*

"Stop!" she stiff armed him and violently wriggled away until she was on her feet, standing beside the bed and breathing heavily.

He reached for her, clearly not understanding. "Rachel, *was ist falsch?*"

"I can't do this." With trembling hands, she shook out an ibuprofen tablet and held out the glass of water as if it were a shield to thwart him. "Medicine," she commanded hoarsely and this time she would brook no argument. Samuel complied, meek as a lamb, then collapsed back onto the bed. In moments, he was asleep as if nothing had ever happened. Rachel sponged his hot skin again and hurried to the bathroom to gargle with mouthwash and take another dose of Zinc, doubting it would do any good. She wearily returned to her air mattress. Her entire body was trembling, but she wasn't sure if it was a low-grade fever or pent-up emotion. She lay awake for a long time, listening to Samuel breathe; reliving the feel of his hands and lips on her until she fell asleep.

Chapter Nineteen

Fever

"Mom? How come you're not up yet? How's Samuel? Where's breakfast?"

Rachel cracked open one eye and looked up to find Karen standing over her. She must have fallen asleep sometime before dawn. She slowly raised herself to a sitting position and stretched, several joints popping in protest. Her shoulders and lower back were sore from sleeping on the air mattress which had slowly deflated throughout the night. She got to her feet and continued stretching to work out the kinks. She checked on Samuel. He was in a deep sleep, his mouth hanging slack; a low rumble coming from his chest. She felt his forehead, not too hot...a good sign.

"I'll get breakfast going but you're going to have to take care of all the cows until Samuel is better."

Karen opened her mouth to protest then thought better of it and nodded, knowing there was really no choice. "Alright, give me an hour, but I'm going to want chocolate chip pancakes, bacon, and scrambled eggs."

"You'll get what you get, and you won't throw a fit," Rachel responded automatically, quoting her late husband. "Don't forget, I still must get the turkey in the oven and make all of the fixings for supper this afternoon. We're going to have a full house. Ruth Bieler and her family are coming over."

"Shouldn't you just cancel?" moaned Karen. "It's too much work."

"For who?" Rachel retorted, beginning to lose her cool. "I'm going to be the one slaving in the kitchen and tending to Samuel. All you must do is tend to the animals. Besides, it's already too late for that. I spent my last dime on all this food, and it's got to be eaten."

"Oh *allllllllright*," Karen groused, stomping off to relieve the cows, whose mooing had taken on a distinctly distressed timbre.

"Rachel?" Samuel's voice came weakly from the bed. "Where am I?" He looked around and Rachel watched his eyes grow wide in alarm when he realized he was in her bed in her bedroom. "What am I doing here?" Before she could respond, Samuel bent double and began to cough. She pounded him on the back until he was able to clear his bronchial tubes of phlegm. He fell back, exhausted from the effort.

She dipped a washcloth into a basin of cool water at his bedside and gently wiped down his face. "You don't remember anything?"

Samuel shook his head, too exhausted to speak. Rachel wrung out the cloth and gave his face another rinse. "You collapsed with a fever yesterday. Karen and I brought you in here and Dr. Yoder checked you out. He says you are to have complete bed rest and not work until he clears you."

"I should not be in your bed. Take me back to the *dawdi haus*." He erupted into another spasm of violent coughing.

"Samuel Miller, you are too weak to walk, and we are not about to kill ourselves carrying you there. Besides, even if you could walk, how convenient do you think it will be for me having to run back and forth across the lawn in cold weather to check on you constantly?" The exasperation in her voice silenced any further arguments. He continued to stare at her as if he was trying to figure something out. His eyes lingered for a moment on her mouth which made her feel very self-conscious. His brows knit together as if something was bothering him. Rachel could feel her face grow hot as she remembered his passionate kisses. She abruptly stood up, hoping it would distract him enough to forget what he was trying to remember. "Alrighty then, I've got a Thanksgiving dinner to start and breakfast to make for a hungry daughter who is taking over your chores. You are to stay in bed until I come back for you. Is there anything you need at this moment?"

Samuel nodded and struggled to find the words. Finally, he muttered something.

"What?" Rachel was getting impatient.

"Bladder," Samuel said a tiny bit louder. He closed his eyes in mortification, refusing to look at her.

"Oh." She didn't think she could walk him to her bathroom in his condition. He was much too heavy for her to support. She cast her eyes around the room hoping for inspiration when they lit upon an empty canning jar she had used as a vase. She tossed the flowers into a wastepaper basket and handed the jar to Samuel. He looked at her as if she had lost her mind.

"It's either that or nothing. I can't support your weight to the bathroom and you're too weak to walk. If you fall down, and break something, then what?"

He turned his face away in shame. "Some privacy, *bitte.*"

She pointed to the jar cap on the table. "Just screw that lid on when you're done. I'll be back with your breakfast in a bit and then you're getting a sponge bath. You're beginning to smell."

His eyes flew open wide. "*Nein, nein.*"

"No to what? Breakfast or the sponge bath?"

"You will not wash me." His voice was adamant, but his eyes looked frightened.

Rachel had had enough. She was exhausted and in no mood to argue common sense with a stubborn Amish man. She bent over him; her hands splayed upon the mattress. "Samuel Miller, you are a very sick man who I have allowed to stay in my bed so I can nurse you, but...you are really starting to *reek*." She bent closer, her face mere inches from his. "Furthermore," she hissed. "You may not remember it, but you mistook me for your wife yesterday so any further prudishness on your part is totally lost on me. Now pee in that jar and leave it on the nightstand. I'll deal with it after I finish breakfast." With that, she marched out of the room leaving him to wonder what she had meant by him mistaking her for his wife.

Samuel laid back in shock, his emotions in turmoil. He had almost no memory of the prior day. *What did she mean by mistaking her for my Rachel?* He searched his memory, struggling to remember, but the last thing he could recall was trudging into the house for breakfast. He had been short of breath and his chest felt tight...everything after that was blank. He waited until he could hear the familiar banging of pots and pans coming from the kitchen then used the jar as he had been instructed, screwing the cap on tight. His chest and back hurt and he had a pounding headache, but he was determined to get out of Rachel Winston's bed.

With an effort, he pushed the quilt away and swung his legs over the side of the bed and sat up. Instantly, a wave of dizziness swept over him. He closed his eyes and waited until it passed. He looked down at himself. He was in the drawstring underwear that his wife had made him years ago and his filthy undershirt. The thought of Rachel Winston seeing him like this, sick or not, was mortifying. He put his feet on the floor and stood up. Without warning, he convulsed into another spasm of coughing. He slid onto his knees beside the bed, propping himself up with his arms, barely able to catch his breath.

Rachel was at his side in moments. "What are you doing out of bed?" She screeched, sounding much like his own Rachel when she became indignant with him. He could not answer her, still doubled over with coughing spasms. Rachel leaned him forward until he was resting against her and pounded his back until his congestion cleared. He wanted to get up, but he was so lightheaded from coughing, all he could do was kneel.

"Samuel, let me help you." He felt her arms go under his armpits and around his back, and then felt himself heaved back onto the bed. She almost collapsed on top of him from the effort and for a moment, their faces were just inches apart. Samuel flinched. The memory of her body and mouth pressed against his own suddenly materialized before his eyes. For a moment, he remembered the passion it had stirred in him. He shrank back, ashamed and confused.

"I'm fine, just let me be." His voice came out harsher than he had intended. She deserved his gratitude not impatience.

Rachel Winston said nothing, but the hurt in her eyes was obvious. "Stay in bed," she snapped, all business again. She covered him with the quilt and returned to the kitchen. Samuel laid in bed and stared at the ceiling, struggling to remember the events from yesterday. Soon the smells of hot coffee, bacon, eggs, pancakes, and pies came wafting in from the kitchen. His stomach grumbled. The service porch screen creaked then slapped shut.

"Mom, is breakfast ready yet?" he heard Karen yell.

"Almost. Are the cows and livestock milked and fed?"

"Yes."

"Eggs gathered?"

"Yes, yes, it's all done. I'm starved. Can I eat now?" Karen's tone was exasperated. It never ceased to irk him how disrespectful she was to her *mamm*. He continued to listen quietly to the exchange between mother and daughter. There was no affection between them, none. Not like there had been between his Rachel and their *kinner*, and it made him sad. Sad for all that he had lost and sad for Rachel Winston, who obviously yearned for the love of her *dochder*. There was some additional noise as Rachel placed breakfast on the table, a brief pause, then moments later she re-entered the bedroom with a tray of food.

"Hungry?" she asked, avoiding his gaze.

"*Jah*," Samuel whispered, taking in the dark circles under her eyes. She probably hadn't slept much the night before because of him. She set the tray down on the dresser and turned back to him.

"Can you sit up by yourself or do you need help?"

I can do it myself. The words were almost out of his mouth but instead he said, "I need help." *Where had that come from?*

Rachel leaned him forward against her, arranged his pillows so they would prop him up, and then helped him scoot back so he could sit up straight. The scent of lavender from her hair and skin instantly brought the memory of her mouth upon his. He stiffened in shock. Rachel glanced at him, her eyes questioning. He pulled the quilt up high to his chest, trying to keep his face expressionless.

She placed the tray of food over his lap. "Are we good?"

He nodded, his face aflame with guilt.

"I'll be back with your coffee." She was all efficiency. Samuel looked down at the tray. There was a bowl of steel cut oatmeal, already flavored with maple syrup and cream. Rachel returned moments later and poured a cup of black coffee into his favorite mug.

"Rachel," his voice caught her just before she exited the room.

"Yes, Samuel?"

He stared a long moment at her tired face. "*Danki.*"

She gave him a sad smile. "I'll be in after you finish breakfast to give you a sponge bath then I'll be in the kitchen for the rest of the day. Karen will be in later to fetch your tray."

He was about to object but, if he were being honest with himself, the prospect of her hands on his body and feeling clean again was a very welcome idea indeed.

Rachel returned just as he had finished eating, almost as if she had a sixth sense. Karen removed the tray from his lap then stepped aside for Rachel, whose arms were laden with thick towels, a wash sponge, and a vinyl tablecloth his *frau* had used for eating outside. She set these to one side, left the room and soon returned with a pail of warm water and Vicks Vapor Rub. Samuel grew nervous when she closed the door behind her for privacy.

"Are you going to cooperate, or do I have to get rough?" She gave him a mischievous grin to lighten the mood. A chuckle rose in his throat, which quickly morphed into violent coughing. Rachel pounded his back until they subsided. Samuel leaned back exhausted.

"Can you get out of your clothes yourself or do you need my help?"

He shook his head. "I will do it," It took most of his strength, but he removed his undershirt from under the covers and let it drop to the floor. It was saturated with sweat and dirt from his last morning in the barn and he was glad to get it off. Next, he pulled off his drawstring undershorts, which were even filthier. They joined the undershirt on the floor. Rachel picked them up and tossed them into a nearby laundry basket.

"Socks," she reminded him. Those also went into the dirty laundry. "Okay, I'm going to lift the quilt up in front of my face. When I do, roll over to the far side of the bed and pull the plastic tablecloth under you, then the bath towel."

Samuel rolled over to the far side of the bed onto his stomach, pulling the towel and tablecloth beneath him which took every ounce of strength he had left. Rachel dropped the quilt over him and tucked it all around his body. Her icy hands jolted him when they brushed up against his hot skin.

"Your temperature is spiking again."

He nodded, his body trembling uncontrollably from the chills.

"Roll onto your stomach first," she commanded. He did so. He felt the quilt pulled away to expose his back. The air felt frigid. He groaned into his pillow with embarrassment and discomfort.

"Hurry," he gritted, his teeth chattering violently into the pillow.

"Doing my best." First, she bathed him with warm soapy water, scrubbing his back and neck good. Then she rinsed him with tepid water mixed with rubbing alcohol.

"That's c-c-cold," he protested.

"I know it feels cold, but we have to keep your temp down," she replied with compassion in her voice. She toweled him off then, without bothering to ask him for help, she rolled him onto his back and began soaping up his chest, shoulders, and arms. She worked efficiently and silently while Samuel endured it, feeling thoroughly exposed though she kept him covered in all the right places.

"Feet and legs next," she informed him, covering his upper torso with the quilt. She rolled the quilt away to expose his leg to the thigh, then washed and rinsed him good, especially his feet. "Your toenails need trimming," she commented but didn't offer to do it. Even Rachel Winston must have her limits, he supposed. In ten minutes, he was clean except for his personal area and head. He felt much better. He wasn't as chilled as before and it was good to be clean. He looked at her expectantly.

"Now it's your turn." She handed him a soapy washcloth and indicated the area below his midsection. "You need to wash the rest of yourself."

Samuel grimaced, took the cloth, and washed himself as she waited, her face expressionless. They exchanged the soapy cloth for a rinsing one. He was quick and efficient. He handed it back to her.

"Your hair needs washing," she informed him.

"*Jah*," he agreed.

"Are you going to let me wash your hair without complaining?"

He nodded.

246

"I'm going to put your head in the wash basin and shampoo it while you lie in bed." She hurried away for a few moments and returned with two wash basins and a pitcher of steaming water. She rolled a towel and put it under his neck then placed the empty basin beneath his head. She leaned over him and slowly poured the hot water into his hair. She leaned closely over him. Hastily he averted his eyes and stared up at her brown hair which was clipped into a messy bun with half of it spilling down in curly tendrils. Her eyes were fixed upon his scalp, so Samuel felt free to study her features without being noticed.

She had a heart-shaped face and wore no makeup. Her olive complexion was clear with no wrinkles, not even laugh lines. The only imperfection was the dark circles under her deep-set, brown eyes. She bit her full bottom lip as she worked the shampoo into his hair with strong fingers. The sensation of her fingers kneading the soap into his thick hair was an intensely intimate feeling and she was not rushing through it. Her fingers drew slow circles on his scalp, the sensation filling him with bliss. He had not experienced someone washing his hair since he had been a little boy in his *mamm's* house. As she continued to massage his scalp, his eyes wandered down to hers and then locked. She stared back at him for a moment then gave him a tremulous smile. He smiled back at her and reached up to gently clasp his hand over hers. He yearned to pull her down to him so he could kiss those full lips again.

Rachel's fingers paused for a moment. "Everything okay? You look like you're in pain."

"I'm *gut*," he replied softly.

Rachel said nothing but the next thing he felt was warm clean water sluicing gently over his head into the basin. "Karen, can you come and get this?" Rachel yelled.

"I'm coming." Karen came into the room and carefully removed the almost full basin while Rachel slid an empty one under his head, her strong hands supporting his neck.

Another rinse of warm water and soon she was toweling his hair dry.

"You could really use a shave," she remarked, gathering up the sodden towels. "Your beard looks very scraggly." He could tell that she regretted it the moment it was out of her mouth.

Samuel scowled up at her. "My beard is my wedding ring," he replied. "It is not to be touched." Anger was good. It depleted the overwhelming physical desire he was having for her.

Rachel threw up her hands. "Fine, it stays! It was just an observation. I need to get those towels and the oil cloth out from under you."

With his head still wrapped in the towel, Samuel rolled to one side and felt her cool hands reach in to collect them. When he looked up at her again, she was holding out another glass of water and pills. "Time for your meds."

He downed them without further comment. Rachel left the room, closing the door behind her. Samuel closed his eyes and laid naked under the thick quilts, struggling against the feelings she had stirred in him. Feelings of both tenderness and desire. Eventually, he fell into a troubled sleep and did not awaken until Rachel returned to his room at midday to check on his temperature and bring him soup.

He awoke to find her cool hand on his forehead. "Looks like your temperature went down; how do you feel?"

"Hungry," he replied, sitting up. He was about to swing his legs over the side of the bed then remembered that he didn't have a stitch on. He quickly laid back down, his face flaming.

Rachel didn't seem to notice. She set the tray on the nearby dresser and carefully helped him into a sitting position. Dizziness swept over him. He closed his eyes and waited.

Rachel's voice was concerned. "Are you okay?"

Samuel nodded, waiting for the room to stop spinning then sat up. "I need to use the bathroom. I think I can walk there with your help." It came out as an embarrassed mumble.

"Oh, okay, let me help you." She reached to help him stand, but he clutched the quilt tightly around him. Evidently, she had also forgotten about his lack of clothes.

"I need clothing first."

"Oh? *Oh!*" Her eyes widened and then she grinned at him. "Well, that could have been embarrassing, hold on." She disappeared and returned a few minutes later with a heavy woolen robe.

He frowned. "I can't go about with just that."

Rachel's face went red; she had evidently reached the end of her patience. "Just put it on, Samuel. It's faster than trying to get clean underwear and britches on you, isn't it?" She laid it on the bed and turned her back. He got the robe on and cinched it tightly closed, but his naked chest was still exposed.

"Take me to the outhouse."

Rachel stared at him. "I am not walking you outside in your condition, especially now that we have indoor plumbing. You'll just have to use that one." She pointed to what had been a closet and was now a small bathroom.

Samuel was too exhausted to argue and allowed her to lead him in. He had not yet seen it but found it to be clean, very simple and practical. When he was done, she helped him back into bed, propped him up with some pillows and set the tray on his lap. The soup had turned tepid.

"I have to get out the food for Thanksgiving so if you need anything just ring that little bell there on the nightstand." She indicated a tiny silver bell.

He nodded and settled back into the bed.

"*Bon appetit.*" Rachel returned to the kitchen. Samuel regarded his lunch. It was homemade chicken soup with vegetables and noodles. His stomach rumbled loudly as the smell greeted his nostrils. He stared at the bowl of soup, guilt overcoming him. He had seen how his own Rachel would labor for hours to prepare such a meal for their *kinner* when they fell sick. Also on the tray were freshly baked biscuits and butter. With everything else she had to do, Rachel had still taken the time to make a labor-intensive sick meal for him. She had taken care of him as though he were her husband. The thought filled him with intense longing.

Chapter Twenty

The Thanksgiving That Wasn't

Rachel had just gotten the turkey out of the oven when Ruth and her family arrived at the front door laden with wicker baskets. Rachel gave Ruth a warm hug then admired the covered wicker hamper. "What's all this?"

"Pumpkin, apple, and pecan pies," Ruth replied. "We thought you would have your hands full with dinner. Rachel, these are my parents."

Rachel smiled at the elderly man and woman in greeting.

"*Mamm,* Papa, this is my *freund,* Rachel Winston. Rachel, these are my parents, Otto and Hannah Bieler."

"*Willkommen in meinem haus,*" Rachel said in her best German. This seemed to please the elder Bieler's. She beckoned them to overstuffed chairs before the crackling fireplace. "*Bitte macht es euch bequem.*" (Please make yourselves comfortable.)

Hannah smiled at her. She had pale blue eyes and snow-white hair pulled into a severe bun under her *kapp.* She patted Rachel's hand. "It's quite fine with us, dear, if you want to speak *Englisch,*" she smiled. She paused and took an appreciative sniff. "The turkey smells *gut.*" she settled into the overstuffed chair.

Ruth helped to seat her father then turned to Rachel. "Can I help you with anything?" She gazed round the house as though looking for someone. Rachel watched her eyes light up with appreciation when she saw the new ten-foot kitchen island with a solid maple block/marble countertop combination sitting opposite the wood cook stove. It served as a prep and baking surface as well as a place for her future guests to eat at while watching food demonstrations. She had added it on during the bathroom renovations and was quite pleased with the result. Not only did it give her triple the amount of counter space, but it also provided storage for the cookware and small appliances she had brought from California. Hanging to dry on an old ladder suspended from the ceiling were bunches of drying herbs she had picked from the garden. She had found it in the barn, leaning up against a wall, dusty with neglect. She had scrubbed it clean, and Samuel had hung it from the ceiling for her with chains. Now all she had to do when she needed herbs was to reach up and grab a handful of dried sage, oregano, thyme, or rosemary.

"I like this," Ruth said, running her hand over the smooth surface of the maple counter. "It is very well made." She glanced over at the serving bowls filled with homemade stuffing, orange-apple cranberry relish, praline sweet potatoes, garlic mashed potatoes, green bean casserole and a golden-brown turkey. "You've been hard at work I see."

"You've no idea." Rachel gave her a swift hug. "I'm so glad you brought dessert. I ran out of time, what with Samuel coming down sick with the flu and all."

A look of panic came over Ruth's face. "Samuel is sick?"

"Yes, he came down with the flu yesterday, but he seems to be doing much better today. He had enough energy to argue with me about a sponge-bath."

At Ruth's horrified look, Rachel immediately realized her mistake. Otto and Hannah turned in their chairs and stared at her in horror as well. At that moment, Karen chose to enter the room from upstairs.

She looked at the shocked faces in the room. "Something wrong?" she wondered out loud.

To Rachel's dismay, Ruth quickly collected her parents and began ushering them to the front door, neglecting her wicker hamper in her rush to leave. "I'm sorry, Rachel, but I can't expose my parents to flu…their health is already too fragile. *Ach*, you should have told me before we came inside. We will have to leave immediately."

"At least let me pack up some food for you while you wait in the buggy." Rachel offered, fighting back tears of disappointment. *How could I have been so stupid?*

"No, Rachel. I can't take the chance with the germs." Ruth looked both apologetic and fearful.

Rachel went as far as the front door then stopped just shy of the porch, watching with a growing sense of guilt as Ruth bundled her elderly parents into the buggy and sped away as fast as she could. She turned and looked at her empty dining room table set with her best china, fall décor, and all the food she had spent her last dime on. She plunged into instant depression. It was all for nothing. She burst into tears where she stood, hands over her face, shoulders heaving for several minutes before she lifted her head to look for Karen. She caught her just as she was ascending the stairs with a full plate in her hands to eat in her bedroom alone.

Rachel was aghast. "You're not even going to eat with me?"

Karen shook her head and spooned a mouthful of garlic mashed potatoes into her mouth. "I don't want to get the germs either, Mom." Moments later, her bedroom door slammed shut. Rachel slowly trudged into the kitchen, heart leaden, her eyes swimming with tears. *What did I do to deserve all this, Lord?* She lifted the platter containing the turkey, tempted to fling the entire meal into the scrap bin and have a good temper tantrum but common sense prevailed. She set it back on the counter then slid to the floor herself, completely dejected. Buddy took this as his cue to approach and whine plaintively.

I'll eat it if you don't want it, his brown puppy eyes clearly said.

Rachel stroked his little face, the tears blinding her again. She allowed herself a good long cry then got to her feet and filled her plate. She carried it over to the overstuffed chair Hannah had vacated and ate alone in front of the fireplace while he watched every morsel that went into her mouth. She barely tasted anything. Not too long later, the tryptophan kicked in and she found that she could no longer keep her eyes open. She pulled a blanket over herself, curled up in the chair and fell asleep with Buddy nestled under one arm.

Rachel woke with a start and looked around her. The family room was pitch black. The fire had died out, she was still in the chair, and she was freezing. Her chattering teeth and body aches were what had awakened her. Buddy lifted his head, whined in alarm, and jumped off the couch, staring at her with wary eyes. Rachel felt as though a truck had run over her. She began to sneeze uncontrollably. With dismay, she realized that she had finally caught Samuel's flu bug. She felt faint and slightly nauseous. Karen was too far away to hear her, and Samuel was in her room with the door shut. She was completely on her own, running a fever with no help. It had hit her like a ton of bricks.

"Help," she cried feebly, dragging the lap blanket more tightly around her. Her voice was reduced to a croaking rasp. Her head was pounding. "Help." She shut her eyes so she wouldn't have to watch the room spin. Even though she felt chilled to the bone, she could tell her skin was on fire. Every part of her body ached.

Oh, just take me now, God. I've had enough. I quit. Just let me die already!

If it weren't for the violent coughing spasms and sneezing, she could have happily slipped into unconsciousness and never awakened. After what seemed an eternity of unrelenting agony in which the tick, tick, tick of the mantle clock counted down the hours of her growing misery, she felt strong arms slide under her, lift her up, and settle her into her own bed. The next thing she knew, bags of ice were shoved into her armpits. Through tear-swollen eyes, she looked up and caught a brief glimpse of Samuel's face, hovering over her with deep concern. He laid a cool washcloth across her forehead. "I'm doing much better, thanks to you and the antibiotics. Rest now...I'll watch over you," he whispered just before she passed out.

"Mom!" Rachel opened her weary eyes and saw Karen leaning over her. "Don't you have guests arriving next week?"

She sat up with a jolt. "What day is it?"

"It's December 10th..."

"What? What happened to the last week of November?"

"You've been sick all that time!"

I've been sick and unconscious for almost an entire week?! Adrenalin shot through her as panic set in, she had about ten days to get everything ready for her first guests. She threw off the covers and the stench from her body odor made her gag. Evidently neither Samuel nor Karen had the stomach to give her a sponge bath in all that time. She wobbled onto her feet, dehydrated and dizzy but feeling better. No time to convalesce, she had work to do!

Chapter Twenty-One

A Christmas for the Record Books

Once recovered, Rachel went into overdrive to make up for lost time. Thanks to the winter months, tending the fields and garden was no longer necessary, so Samuel and Karen were able to help her in readying the farmhouse in time to receive its first guests.

A new, emotional intimacy existed between her and Samuel. They had tended to each other during sickness just as if they had been married and she knew that come what may, he would be there for her. He often looked deeply into her eyes and caressed her hand when Karen was not around. They maintained a respectful distance in public and especially when Ruth Bieler was around, knowing how gossip could spread like wildfire. The mutual friendship, affection, and attraction between them was approaching critical mass and sooner rather than later, one of them was going to have to make a life-altering decision. Rachel just wasn't sure she was up to the task of becoming Amish, no matter how much she had fallen for him.

The day finally dawned for her first guests to arrive at the Second Chance Inn. Rachel stood nervously before the front window, waiting for Samuel's horse drawn sleigh to appear just like in Barry's favorite movie, *Holiday Inn*. There had been a fresh fall of snow the night before as if special ordered just for her. The snow had made driving the regular buggy hazardous, so he had taken the sleigh. The front porch was festooned with fresh garland and large red bows, and she had placed a holiday wreath on the front door, which had been painted with a fresh coat of red paint. The red barn had a huge Christmas wreath over the hay door. She had hot mulled cider and wine warming on the stove, a blazing fire in the fireplace and a generous farmhouse dinner of roast chickens, scalloped potatoes, Brussel sprouts, and apple cobbler with Lapp's vanilla ice cream waiting for the Inn's first guests.

As painful as it was, Rachel had dug out her Christmas decorations and distributed them liberally throughout the house and bedrooms. Each one held a special memory of her former life with Barry and by the time she had gotten them all out, she had become a weepy mess.

Even little Buddy was sporting a red and white velvet scrunchie collar with jingle bells that tinkled whenever he moved. He had put up with it, but his reproachful look clearly said how much he disliked wearing the jingly article. Rachel surveyed her handiwork, hoping that the next couple of weeks would spell future success for the Second Chance Inn.

Buddy whined and looked at her, his sharp ears perking up. Soon she too heard sleigh bells approaching. It turned into the driveway in the fading light of day. Samuel pulled the sleigh to a halt and helped each family member down: a father, mother, two boys, and a little girl, all red-cheeked from the drive, their faces alight with anticipation. They had come from New York City, Manhattan, to be exact, and wanted to give their children an old-fashioned Christmas. It was exactly the demographic she had been hoping to attract to the Inn. If their experience was good enough, it might result in a stream of steady income from their referrals. Rachel watched as the family took in the sight of the red barn, bright against the freshly fallen snow, the Christmas garland circling the house and the glowing candles in each window. Then they saw her. With happy faces, they all raised their arms and waved excitedly.

Rachel opened the front door with a happy smile as the frigid air greeted her. "*Wilkommen* to the Second Chance Inn and Merry Christmas. Please come inside, supper is ready."

Her guests introduced themselves. "I'm Rhonda," said the mother, "and this is my husband, Charles. These are my two boys, Mitchell and Greyson and my daughter Genevieve."

"Hi! I'm Rachel Winston," Rachel introduced herself with a smile.

As Samuel brought their luggage onto the front porch, Rachel helped them off with their wraps. The woman wore an expensive, full-length fur coat and matching hat. Her diamond ear studs sparkled in the candlelight as she twirled around to admire the roaring hearth, the garland, and the farmhouse table set with a Christmas red tablecloth, candles, and plain white dishes. "It's absolutely beautiful," she said, clapping her hands together like a delighted child. "Everything you described and more. But where is the Christmas tree?" She indicated the empty space before the picture window.

"I thought you and your family might enjoy picking out your own from the local farm and decorating it," Rachel replied. I have lots of corn to pop and fresh cranberries to make garlands with."

"Doesn't that sound like fun, kids?" asked Charles eagerly. The boys shrugged, their faces devoid of the childish enthusiasm of their parents and younger sister.

The little girl tugged on Rachel's red apron. "Can I put the angel on top?" she asked, her pansy blue eyes hopeful.

"Of course," Rachel replied, remembering when Karen had been that small and would sit on Barry's shoulders to do the honors. "Only we have a beautiful sparkly star, not an angel. Samuel will bring your suitcases up to your rooms for you. Why don't you all have a seat at the table? Can I offer you any mulled cider or wine?"

"What's that?" questioned one of the boys, taking a seat. He shoved the white napkin into his collar as his brother sat next to him, both eyeing the roast chickens hungrily. "Hot apple juice," his mother answered, taking a seat across from them, next to her daughter. She admired the kitchen and the suspended ladder full of dried herbs. "It's so homey here, not at all like our loft in the city," she sighed wistfully.

The husband sat down beside her, and Rachel paused, not sure whether she should suggest a blessing, wondering if they would be offended. Finally, she shrugged. Her home and life belonged to the Lord, and she was going to honor Him, guests or not. "Let's join hands and bow our heads," she invited them.

They looked at one another for a moment then took each other's hands and bowed their heads out of respect. Rachel sensed Samuel and Karen step up behind her, lending her moral support.

She closed her eyes. "For food that stays our hunger, for rest that brings us ease, for homes where memories linger, we give our thanks for all of these, dearest Lord. Amen."

"Amen." said everyone in unison, faces beaming. For the occasion, Karen had dressed in her warm woolen Amish dress and apron and helped to fill their glasses and distribute the platters of food. The family talked animatedly, the children asking Samuel, Rachel and Karen nonstop questions about the farm animals, the ice-skating pond, and what size Christmas tree would fit into the front room. Samuel was peppered with questions from both the adults and the children who were fascinated with his people's plain way of life.

259

When dessert was finished, the family retired to the family room to play board games in front of the fire while Rachel and Karen washed up. Rachel could hear the boys freely (and quite loudly) voicing their complaints about having to leave their cell phones, tablets, smartphones, Xboxes, and Gameboys behind in Manhattan but soon they were engrossed in learning Chinese Checkers, Scrabble, The Game of Life, and Monopoly. The latter two were contributions from Rachel's childhood; the Amish would never have had such games in their homes. She smiled to herself, pleased, as the family immersed themselves in the competition, enjoying one another's company the old-fashioned way. By nine o'clock, all of them were yawning.

"If either of your boys would like to help with the cows in the morning, they best go to bed early," Rachel suggested.

Greyson's face lit up. "Can we Mom, Dad?"

"How early do we have to get up?" asked the elder brother, Mitchell, with some trepidation.

"Four a.m.," Karen told them with a grin. "First we wash the udders, then we milk them, and then my mom makes us a wonderful farmhouse breakfast."

The boys looked at her in horror. "Four *a.m.?*"

"Four a.m.," she confirmed. She raised an eyebrow at them. "Is that too early for you city folk?" It was an obvious challenge, and it had the desired effect.

The parents covered their mirth with their hands.

"I'll get up if Greyson does," said Mitchell.

Greyson sputtered. He was trapped and he knew it. He could no more wimp out to his older brother than he could to the innkeeper's daughter. "You're on," he said. "Last one to the barn shovels the manure out, right Mr. Miller?" he appealed to Samuel who was struggling to wipe the smirk off his face.

"*Jah,*" was all he could manage.

"Well, guess we should be heading for bed then," said their father. "Early to bed, early to rise and all that."

"And all what?" Greyson demanded having never heard the colloquialism before.

"You'll find out tomorrow," replied his father.

An hour later, it was just her and Samuel, standing alone before the fire in the dimly lit family room. Rachel looked up and smiled at him, pointing. "You're standing under the mistletoe."

Samuel stared back down at her, attempting to look serious but the corner of his mouth kept twitching playfully. "Amish do not engage in mistletoe activities," he replied softly, closing the distance between them despite his words.

Rachel's breath caught in her throat, her insides turning to jelly. "No?"

"No," he whispered, his hand reaching for hers.

At that moment, a door opened upstairs, and they heard feet descending the stairs. They distanced themselves instantly. Rachel hurried to the kitchen sink, face aflame, fiddling with the pots and pans. Samuel squatted before the hearth and poked the cord wood.

Out of her peripheral vision, Rachel waited as Karen went to the refrigerator, peered in for a moment then shut it without taking anything. Rachel looked over her shoulder and found her daughter staring at her, with an accusatory glare. "Geez, mom, it's barely even been two years."

The words hit her like a punch in the gut which was no doubt exactly the effect Karen had intended. Rachel watched in silence, her face burning with guilt as Karen stomped upstairs and closed her bedroom door. She looked over at Samuel. They exchanged alarmed stares. They had done nothing, yet she felt guilty. Rachel turned slowly back to the sink, filling it with hot water. Shortly thereafter, she heard the porch door open and shut as Samuel returned silently to the in-law house without so much as a goodnight.

The next morning, she awoke early. The sounds of groaning, grumping, and stomping resounded throughout the upstairs as Karen rounded up the boys for milking duty. After ten minutes of needling, they were dressed and ready to go to the frigid barn and learn the essentials of animal husbandry. Rachel got dressed and replenished the wood in the oven and in the hearth.

Around 6 a.m., Samuel, Karen, and the two young men trudged into the now warm kitchen after washing up on the service porch. A fabulous spread of food greeted their bleary eyes. There were enormous homemade cinnamon buns, scrambled eggs, bacon, sausage, orange juice, canned peaches, hot cocoa, and coffee. Mitchell leaned forward and inhaled the scent rising from the cinnamon buns.

"We should let Mom and Dad sleep in," he grinned at his younger brother. "No sense waking them up early while on vacation, right?"

"I heard that," said their father, appearing at the foot of the stairs, wrapped in a warm robe. He sniffed appreciatively. "I could smell the rolls, coffee, and bacon from upstairs. There's no way I'm sleeping through this breakfast."

His wife appeared moments later, also in her robe, with their daughter in her arms. The little girl was clutching her doll. "We're all going to have to go on diets after this vacation," Rhonda moaned with a smile.

Greyson heaped his plate high with food. "Mom, you should come see the horses and the sheep. They are so friendly. I was mucking out their stalls this morning."

"Yeah, I can smell," Rhonda smiled at him, her pride clearly showing.

The brothers took their heaping plates to the table and waited politely for the others. Without being asked, the family bowed their heads and waited for Rachel to repeat the blessing from the night before, smiling happily to themselves.

They finished their breakfast in a leisurely manner, talking excitedly about their plans for picking out the Christmas tree, visiting a maple syrup farm, ice-skating, shopping, sleigh rides and hunting. Karen's chickens were laying less as the days grew shorter and colder, which gave her more time to help around the house. She seemed to enjoy interacting with the Inn guests and had assumed the role of the "cruise director" by coming up with fun activities, crafts, and games for the children. One night she had them all in stitches playing charades and the next night she had the children involved in an impromptu Christmas play. She had even talked Samuel into hanging a long rope from a wood rafter in the middle of the barn so the kids could swing back and forth on the wooden seat.

Rachel spent the remainder of the week leading up to Christmas catering to her guests. She took them to the local village to do some last-minute shopping at the Amish shops for one-of-a-kind, wonderfully crafted gifts. Rachel taught Rhonda how to make bread, cinnamon rolls, and pies from scratch and Karen even showed little Genevieve, or Vivi as they called her, how to quilt a small square. Samuel took the boys and their father out hunting for their first time and returned home with a wild goose and several rabbits.

When she wasn't helping to entertain the family, Karen remained closeted in her room, working on some secret project. Two days before Christmas Eve the family went to the pond and were all fitted with skates by a local rink manager. Rachel played music from her iPhone over some Bluetooth speakers while they skated and played crack-the-whip. She even joined in on the fun. She still had her custom skates from when she had taken lessons in her twenties and took turns skating backward and hauling both the children and adults around the rink at breakneck speed.

She paused for a moment and saw Samuel standing on his skates as if he were waiting for her. She skated up to him, spraying him with ice as she came to a stop on the edge of her blade.

He held out his hands, his eyes twinkling. "Do I get a turn?"

Rachel grinned mischievously at him. "Be careful what you ask for," she replied, grabbing his hands. They were warm and heavily calloused. She began slowly, to get him used to the speed, watching his face carefully. He didn't look down at his feet as she would have expected him to, the way most people did who were uncomfortable on ice skates. His eyes never left hers. She picked up speed. The first corner was coming up and she was going fast. Samuel was rock solid on his skates, standing straight but shifting his weight as needed. His face was wreathed in smiles as she hauled him around the rink by the hands as an old skating tune blared from the tiny speakers. She swung him fast around another corner, eliciting chuckles of delight from him.

"I have never gone this fast before," he smiled at her. "It's exhilarating!"

"If only we knew how to ice-dance," Rachel sighed, swinging him round a corner, skating backwards.

"Ice dance?"

"It's like ballroom dancing on ice-skates," Rachel replied. The skaters dance in each other's arms, doing lifts and turns and are never allowed to break contact."

Samuel looked at her, his eyes warm. "Sounds *wunderbar*." He gave her hands a tender squeeze. The look in his eyes was making her feel dreamy. A hot blush swept up her face as he continued to smile at her.

"Want to do a pair spin?" she challenged.

"How?"

Rachel brought them to a stop and turned him to face her. "Grab my hand," she instructed. "Now, using your toe pick, push forward in a circle as fast as you can – don't let go of my hand. When I say 'now' grab my other hand and pull towards me as hard as you can with your skates forming a half circle. Ready?"

"*Jah!*"

It took a few tries and more instructions but pretty soon they were spinning fast about each other in a circle that had the rest of the family watching with great interest."

Vivi jumped up and down, waving her arms. "I want to do it; I want to do it!"

Rachel grabbed Vivi's hands and soon they were spinning at a dizzying speed.

Mitchell and Greyson grabbed each other, determined to out spin everyone else.

Even Rhonda and Charles gave it a go, but their spin was feeble. When everyone got too dizzy to spin anymore, they returned to circling the pond.

Rachel and Samuel skated again for a few more moments together then reluctantly broke apart when the stares from Karen became too much. "*Danki,*" he said, giving her hand a last squeeze. They reluctantly parted.

Rachel looked around the rink. The family had become comfortable in their skates and were having a great time without her.

I wonder if I could still do any of my jumps?

She had already warmed up for the better part of a good half hour and felt confident enough to give it a try. She began circling the rink, picking up speed, reveling in the pleasure of skating again. Here goes nothing! She put out her arms, speeding into the approach for a flip jump. She was just about to go into her three-point turn when her toe-pick caught on a rut in the ice and sent her flying. The ice rushed up to meet her and she landed heavily on her stomach. All the air whooshed out of her body. Pain engulfed her. She lay paralyzed, face down, gasping for air, unable to call for help. She closed her eyes, struggling to breathe. She had forgotten how painful it was to fall on her diaphragm.

Samuel reached her first. Gently he rolled her onto her back then his arms went under her legs and behind her back. He swept her up into his arms and carried her over to the picnic bench where he sat her down. The family swiftly gathered around her, concerned and unsure what to do.

"Are you okay?" asked Rhonda, her face creased with concern.

Rachel could only nod weakly in response. She waved them off and gave them all a reassuring smile and thumbs up. The family returned to their skating but still cast worried glances at her as she struggled to breathe.

Samuel remained by her side, saying nothing, just holding her hand as the pain gradually subsided. It took several minutes before she could breathe normally again.

Karen skated over and sat next to her. "You okay, mom?"

Rachel nodded, still unable to speak.

That's what I get for being a showoff.

She gave herself a few more moments to recover then reverted into her role as innkeeper. She brought out the feast she had packed for lunch from the insulated bags she had stored in the sleigh. There were grilled cheese sandwiches, homemade tomato bisque in a thermos, hot cocoa, and chocolate peppermint whoopie pies. She spread it out on a folding table she had brought, and the family dug in with gusto…their appetites increased by all the exercise.

⁂

Finally exhausted after another hour of skating, the family clambered back into the sleigh and went home to shower and play games until dinner; primed for what Rachel had promised to be a spectacular feast.

It was Christmas Eve Day. Karen had taken the family out in the sleigh to get the tree while Rachel labored over the Christmas Eve dinner. It was now early afternoon, and she went into the barn, looking for Samuel. She spotted the rope swing, wondering if it would hold her weight. She pulled it back as far as it would reach, sat down on it and let go. She swung forward – a whoop of delight echoing throughout the large expanse of the barn as she whooshed forward.

"It's more fun if you swing from over here," Samuel's voice said.

Rachel looked around to find him standing before a row of stacked hale bales. They were piled up about ten feet high at the far end of the barn.

He beckoned to her. "*Komm her.*"

Rachel scampered forward with childish anticipation, a grin spreading from ear to ear. Samuel clasped her hands and hauled her up the hay bales, bringing the rope swing with him. He kneeled down, and held the rope, so the wooden seat was laying on the top hale bale. "Sit down," he instructed, still holding the rope taught.

Rachel crouched into a sitting position and scooted forward as he held the rope. He grinned down at her. "Ready?"

She squeezed her eyes shut and nodded. Samuel let go of the rope and she descended with a whoosh, swinging in a large arc almost to the outside of the barn. "*Wheeeeeeeeeeeeeeeeeee!*" she screamed as the swing made its return arc back to the bales. Just before she smacked into them, Samuel caught the rope in his hands. Rachel landed with a plunk onto the ground and fell over laughing. "That was so fun!"

Samuel plopped down beside her, chuckling, his entire face wreathed in an enormous smile. She had never seen him look as carefree as he did in that moment. She liked making him smile and laugh and wanted to savor the moment. "Can I go again?"

He stood up, took her hand, and led her back up to the hale bales, holding the rope while she seated herself. Then he did something surprising. He grasped her by the waist and pulled her back even farther then abruptly let go.

Rachel shrieked as loud as her voice could go as she swung through the frigid air, twisting wildly. She lost her grip on the return arc when the wooden seat tilted and dumped her onto her back side, one leg still hooked to the swing as it dragged her across the floor. She collapsed into hysterical giggles, unable to even sit up, her leg still wrapped around the rope.

Samuel was at her side in a moment, asking her if she was all right but she was laughing too hard to respond. The more she tried to stop laughing the harder she laughed. Soon she heard him laughing beside her...not amused little chuckles but big belly laughs. After a good five minutes they both managed to calm down enough to move.

Samuel got up first.

Rachel reached for his hands. "Help me up, my butt is freezing!"

Samuel hauled her onto her feet in one swift pull and pulled her into his arms, still grinning at her. "You make me laugh,"

Rachel grinned up at him. "I'm glad." He held her for a few moments longer then reluctantly let go when they heard sleigh bells approaching. The sleigh had returned with the family, with Karen in the driver's seat. Her face was flushed bright red from the cold and the excitement of driving the team through the snow which had been a totally novel and exhilarating experience for her.

"Mom!" She jumped out of the sleigh, tying the reins onto the rail. "That was so awesome! You gotta try it! It's so much more fun than driving a car but it's freezing!"

"Maybe you can take me for a ride sometime?" Rachel grinned, still on her high from the swing and laughing jag.

"We got a tree!" yelled Vivi, dragging Rachel by the hand to view their prize.

A nine-foot Fraser fir was strapped to the back of the sleigh.

"Samuel and I will take care of getting the tree inside," Rachel welcomed them. "In the meantime, there's hot soup on the stove."

She welcomed them into the house where a large pot of homemade Zuppa Toscana was bubbling in the Dutch oven. The smell of Italian sausage, bacon, and broth permeated the house. On the sideboard was a loaf of freshly baked bread, a green salad, and a loaf of banana bread.

"That smells heavenly," Rhonda exclaimed, removing her fur coat. "How did you know I was craving soup?"

"If I had been out in the cold all morning picking out a Christmas tree this is what I would have wanted," Rachel replied with a smile, happy that she had correctly anticipated their needs.

She spent the remainder of the day helping the family to bake and decorate Christmas cookies and string popcorn and cranberry garlands for the tree. They sang along to Christmas carols from her CD player while they hung the ornaments. The boys had long ago forgotten all about their electronic gadgets and social media and instead, immersed themselves in playful competition to see who could make the longest popcorn garland or the most elaborately decorated Christmas cookie. Their parents shot Rachel happy smiles and approving glances throughout the afternoon, seemingly pleased at how their brood had taken to doing crafts together as a family. By the time evening came, the tree was a thing of vintage beauty. The only source of light was the twinkling Christmas lights, candlelight, and the blazing hearth. The family stood around the tree, breathing in the pine fragrance in silent admiration. From behind Rachel, a single, beautiful voice lifted in song.

"Silent night...holy night...all is calm...all is bright..."

Rachel turned to see Karen, eyes closed, singing in her beautiful soprano. Without missing a beat, the rest of the family and Rachel joined in, tears forming in her closed eyes at the sheer beauty of the moment.

Samuel quietly entered through the front door at that moment and took in the scene. The room was dark except for the glowing hearth and flickering candlelight. The guest family had their arms about one another, and all had their eyes closed as they sang Silent Night *acapella.* He gazed upon Rachel who had lifted her arms heavenwards in worship as they all sang. He stood transfixed, unable to take his eyes off her, watching the tears glistening on her cheeks from the candlelight. She was immersed in worshipping *Der Herr,* something he still couldn't bring himself to do.

She had not turned her back on God as he had, nor treated Him with disrespect. She still thanked Him, praised Him, and included Him.

Shame descended upon him.

Der Herr had sent His only Son into the world on this night to save men's souls...who was he to demand an accounting of God? His life of faith had been a litany of dos and don'ts yet when it came to the ultimate test of his true faithfulness, he had failed miserably. He had turned his back on God and felt justified in doing so yet here was a young mother who had also lost the love of her life and she was worshipping Him with her whole heart and soul.

He continued to watch her sing, mesmerized by the beauty in her face. The song ended. The room became still, filled with a quiet holiness that was palpable. The family opened their eyes, sighed, and exchanged hugs.

"Well..." said Charles Johnson, wiping tears from his eyes. "That was something. That was really something."

Rachel wiped the tears from her eyes. "Time for supper," she announced.

The family entered the kitchen and beheld the long farmhouse table.

"Oh *myyyyyy,*" sighed Rhonda, her eyes going wide. The children stared in wonder.

Pine boughs, cranberry garland, and white candles set in ball jars ran down the middle of the snow-white tablecloth. Each place setting had a cloth napkin wrapped with plain twine, a sprig of holly, and red jingle bells on the ends. The plates were white with drinking goblets of ruby red glass. On the sideboard was the goose the boys and Samuel had bagged, golden brown and steaming. It was surrounded by a variety of roasted vegetables, a bowl of homemade stuffing, orange/apple cranberry relish, and hot wassail to polish off the feast. At the end of the table was a Gingerbread Bundt cake festooned with sugared rosemary and cranberries to replicate a Christmas wreath.

"I feel like I've stepped into a Norman Rockwell painting," exclaimed Charles, rubbing his hands together with glee.

"Who?" chorused Karen, Mitchell, Greyson, and Vivi in unison.

"A famous painter in the early 20th century who typified life in America," Rachel replied, knowing she sounded like Webster's dictionary. "I have a book of his paintings on the bookshelf if you want to look at them later."

"Can I say the blessing this time?" asked Vivi, raising her little hand as if she were in class. "I learned a new one from Karen."

Rachel's eyebrows rose along with that of Vivi's family. "Oh? Why sure."

Rhonda and Charles exchanged bemused glances then bowed their heads.

Vivi glanced at Karen, who nodded encouragement, then began to sing: "Oh, the Lord is good to me, and so I thank the Lord, for giving me the things I need, the sun and the rain, and the apple seed, the Lord is good to me." She sat down with a happy plop.

Everyone clapped hands, delighted.

"May I say a blessing too?" Rhonda shyly raised her hand. Rachel nodded, immensely pleased. Rhonda took the hands of her husband and Vivi into hers then everyone else around the table followed suit. There was a long nervous pause.

"God, I'm not good at praying but I wanted to say thank you for this wonderful place and the time we've had together. Please bless Rachel, Mr. Miller, and Karen for giving us a Christmas we will never forget. And God bless my family... amen."

"Amen," agreed everyone.

Rachel was so moved she could barely talk. She concentrated on carving the roast goose and making sure the family had all they needed before serving herself, Samuel, and Karen.

Even Samuel seemed impressed with the feast she had made and heaped his plate high. When supper was over and the dishes were cleared, Rachel handed a bowl of pierced chestnuts to Rhonda. "There's a copper roaster standing by the hearth. Just put these in and hold them over the fire for about ten minutes."

"You're kidding? Really? Chestnuts roasting on an open fire?" Rhonda grinned.

Rachel held up a Nat King Cole CD. "Of course! This is a Norman Rockwell moment, isn't it?"

Rhonda jumped up and down with glee. "This is so cool," she squealed. The family sat down before the fire and set the roaster onto the hot ashes. The smell of roasting chestnuts filled the room while Nat King Cole crooned his famous melody. The nostalgia was only diminished when the Johnson children decided they didn't really like the taste of chestnuts and spit them out into their paper napkins in disgust.

"Yuck," Vivi pronounced. "Can't we roast marshmallows instead and make s'mores?"

"Yeah," seconded her brothers.

Rachel didn't miss her cue, jumping up to retrieve marshmallows, graham crackers and Hershey's chocolate bars from the pantry. Soon they were all toasting their marshmallows over the roaster's open flame, singing Christmas carols until late.

The night wore on and Rachel had yet to wrap the "Santa" gifts.

As the prearranged time, Rhonda beckoned to her children. "Best be getting to bed now."

"That's right," piped up Vivi. "Santa won't come until we're all asleep, right Mom?"

"Right," Rhonda replied with a warning glance to her older sons who were already "in the know."

Vivi paused on the stairs, yawning. "I know it's too late to send a letter to the North Pole, but could I leave one next to the cookies for Santa?"

Rhonda and Charles exchanged worried looks. "Sure, honey," he said.

Vivi trotted over to the box of crayons and paper she had used earlier to make Christmas cards, selected a thick red one, and wrote a short note. She folded it into a tiny package and left it next to the cookies and milk.

"Good night," she waved to Karen and Rachel. "Mom, will you tuck me in?"

"Of course, pumpkin." Rhonda followed her daughter up the stairs, followed by her husband and sons who were snickering amongst themselves. She gave Rachel a parting wink.

Karen, Rachel, and Samuel lingered in the family room. When all had grown quiet upstairs, Rachel unfolded the note and peeked at it. In childish print, Vivi had written the following:

Dear Santa -
I saw the Polar Express last month. My brothers don't think you're real. I want a bell off your sleigh to prove them wrong.
Love Vivi.

Karen looked at Rachel. "What are you going to do?" Rachel had kept Karen believing in Santa Claus until the age of twelve and she didn't want to see the magic of Christmas disappear for Vivi at such a young age, especially not at her Inn. She turned and appealed silently to Samuel for help.

"We do not tell our children these myths," he replied with a gentle but disapproving look.

"Well, I can't do nothing; she's just a little girl." Rachel pondered for a moment then brightened. "You have sleigh bells."

"*Jah,* but…"

"Would you mind giving up just one? I'll replace it, I promise."

"Please?" Karen wheedled, applying additional pressure, her eyes pleading. "You have no idea what a bummer it is to find out that Santa Claus isn't real."

"These are our first paying guests, Samuel, can you imagine the fallout if their youngest daughter stops believing in Old Saint Nick tomorrow because of us? They might post a review online that we ruined their family Christmas." Her voice was in earnest, but she was grinning at him.

Samuel shook his head and threw up his hands in defeat. "*Ach,* follow me." He threw on his heavy winter coat, woolen hat, and muffler. Together they followed him by lamplight out to the barn where the sleigh bell harness was hanging from a peg on the wall. It was sturdy leather, and the bells were fashioned in pure brass in varying sizes, their surfaces embellished with winter designs.

Karen pointed to the second to largest bell. "This one."

Samuel stared at them then reluctantly took out a penknife and cut the leather ties holding it on and put it in Karen's hand. "There is some bronze polish over my work bench; shine it up real *gut.*"

A huge smile wreathed Karen's face and on impulse, she threw her arms around Samuel and gave him a swift hug before scampering off. "*Dankiiiii,*" she sang out.

Sometime around midnight, Rachel was kneeling on the floor by the tree, wrapping the special Santa Claus gifts for each of the children. All was quiet except for the soft crackle of the dying fire and Buddy who was whimpering in dreams on his side. Karen had already gone to bed and lay snuggled under a mound of quilts. She was completely alone, and it was Christmas Eve. The intense pain of missing Barry overwhelmed her. Tears slid down her cheeks while she filled the stockings with special handmade Amish treats and goods, remembering all the Christmas Eves she and her husband had snuggled together on the couch before their own tree, listening to Maranatha Music's *The Gift*. What she wouldn't give to feel his arms around her just one last time…

At that moment she heard the front door quietly open and saw Samuel standing in the doorway, looking down at her. The pain etched on his face mirrored her own.

She patted the floor next to her, pushing aside the wrapping paper, twine, and tape. He sat down beside her Indian style, staring sadly into the fire.

"I miss my *kinner*," he murmured, turning to her. Tears were swimming in his eyes.

An enormous lump came to Rachel's throat. She nodded, taking his hand in hers, unable to speak. They held hands for a long time, leaning against one another and staring into the fire in silence. Words were inadequate for such a time as this. The fire eventually died down to a soft glow. Finally, Samuel stood, drawing her up with him. He bent forward and placed a gentle kiss between her brows.

"*Frohe weihnachten*, Rachel," he murmured.

"Merry Christmas, Samuel," she whispered.

He gave her another sad smile then returned to the *dawdi haus*.

Rachel rose before everyone else the following morning. She got the wood stove reheated first then the hearth. She had prepared her special orange zest Challah French toast the night before and took it out to reach room temperature while the oven heated up. She fried up Applewood smoked bacon, ladled out fruit compote, poured orange juice, and heated hot cocoa, and lots of hot coffee. As soon as the oven was hot, she popped the baking tray of French toast in. She set the farmhouse table with candles and red and white candy-cane plates. Around 7 a.m. she heard the children rousting their groggy parents out of bed, eager to see what lay beneath the tree. Samuel had already gone to the barn to take care of the animals and was just washing up on the service porch when the family and Karen tumbled down the stairs. Rich Mullin's song *"You Gotta Get Up, It's Christmas Morning"* greeted them from her little Bluetooth speakers, reminding her of all the Christmas mornings when Karen was a little girl and Barry would prepare his family's traditional *Capirotada* (bread pudding) for breakfast.

"Santa was here! Santa was here!" squealed Vivi, taking in the pure white wrapping paper and simple twine her mother had requested via email prior to their arrival.

Rachel poured the parents each a generous mug of piping hot coffee brewed with cinnamon sticks and stood back as the family gathered around the tree to open their presents.

Vivi went to inspect the Santa cookie dish and screamed. *"Santa gave me a jingle bell. A real bell off his sleigh just like I asked him for last night. Look mommy!"* She held up the red drawstring pouch that contained the gleaming brass bell. It was threaded with a white ribbon that said "BELIEVE" on it which had been left over from a previous Winston Christmas. It had taken her over an hour the night before to find it amongst her Christmas boxes but the reaction from little

Vivi had made it all worth it. Vivi took the bell over to her parents, jumping up and down in glee. She was rewarded with a grateful smile from Rhonda over the head of her daughter.

For the next half hour, the family opened and admired all their presents while the French toast baked. Rachel, Karen, and Samuel gathered around her prep table. On top of the counter was a medium sized flat parcel wrapped in plain brown butcher's paper and twine with a small tag that said MR. MILLER on it.

Samuel looked at Rachel. "*Was is los?*"

"Oh, that's from me," Karen replied, putting it into his hands. "I've been working on it for weeks." She bounced up and down, barely able to contain her excitement. "Open it, open it!"

Carefully, he unwrapped the package to reveal a black book that resembled a photo album. He opened the cover and Rachel watched as his blue eyes grew large with shock then filled with tears. His lips trembled as he continued to thumb through the book, tears dripping onto the pages.

"How did you do this?" he choked, trembling from head to toe.

Rachel mistook his reaction and reached for the book. "Karen, what is this?"

Samuel covered his face with his hands, shoulders heaving in silence as Rachel turned the album around. She gasped when she beheld the first page.

"It's his family, Mom," Karen whispered, all excitement gone, her face creased with anxiety. "I found photos of them from various sites on the internet where people took photos of Amish auctions in the area. Remember when the doctor was here? Well, he helped me to identify some pictures of them, so I just used them to find these other photos. I-I-I thought Mr. Miller might like to have something to remember them by."

Rachel's eyes strayed back to Samuel who was struggling to compose himself, dreadfully afraid her daughter had done something forbidden to offend him. Rachel looked at each page, her own eyes filling with tears as she looked at his children. Karen's gift was beyond price. She had given Samuel the most precious of all presents that had, in some small way, restored his lost family to him. She gazed at the photos, admiring the beauty of his children and the simple joy on their faces. It was plain to see the love between him and his wife in the one photo where they were captured together. A pang of jealousy knifed through her for a split second. That Karen had managed to find photographs of them at all was a feat in and of itself.

"Karen...this is absolutely beautiful...amazing," Rachel whispered, tears running down her own face. "I think you and I both misunderstood his reaction, didn't we, Samuel?"

Samuel finally looked up at Karen, his face raw with pain but his eyes kind.

"You're not mad at me are you, Mr. Miller?" Karen quivered. "I know it violates the *Ordnung*...but I thought you wouldn't mind."

Samuel shook his head, still unable to speak, obviously in emotional turmoil. He could not have been prepared to see his family like this. Rachel knew it was forbidden in his culture to take photos of themselves. No doubt he was struggling against a life-long doctrine that had been ingrained in him since childhood and the mingled pain and joy of seeing his family again. He seemed to be struggling about whether he should accept or refuse Karen's gift. Finally, he relaxed a little; the struggle seemed to be over.

He patted Karen's hands to reassure her. "*Danki. Danki*," was all he could manage, blowing his nose into his handkerchief. He took the photo album back from Rachel and went over each page again and again, still weeping in silence.

At that moment, Rhonda appeared at their table and took in the scene. "Oh, I'm so sorry, I didn't mean to interrupt such a special moment," she said upon seeing his tears.

Samuel got up abruptly, tucking the photo album under his arm. "If you'll excuse me," he mumbled and exited through the back door.

Rachel turned back to Rhonda and gave her a falsely bright, reassuring smile. "It's quite alright; I just don't think he was prepared for such a special gift."

Neither was Rachel. She couldn't get the image of his expression out of her mind when he had seen the photograph of his wife or the way his fingers had caressed it. The auction photographer had captured her at the exact moment their eyes were locked together in a loving glance. "Excuse me for a moment," she choked. "I just need to check on something." Rachel managed to walk to her bedroom and quietly shut the door before she burst into sobs.

Ten minutes later, Rachel returned to the kitchen to serve breakfast. Fortunately, the rest of the family had been oblivious to what had happened earlier. They talked animatedly about the presents, food, and activities they had enjoyed in the past week.

After breakfast, the children went out to throw snowballs at each other, build a snowman and to ride on the new sled that had been a special gift from "Santa." She could hear their squeals of joy from within the house. While she cleaned up from Christmas breakfast, Rhonda and Charles cuddled together before the fire on the overstuffed couch, reading a book together. Her guests were due to check out the following week to spend New Year's Eve in Manhattan.

Rachel fervently hoped their experience at the Inn had exceeded their expectations. She needed great reviews and referrals to generate new reservations. Nothing beats word-of-mouth to create a constant revenue stream. She had taken photos throughout their stay and gotten their written permission to post them on her website as examples of what other guests could expect. Rhonda had often perched at the kitchen island, sipping coffee as Rachel prepped meals or baked. They'd talked together quite a bit during the past week and had become good friends...Rachel was going to miss her.

The next week the family reluctantly checked out with promises to come back during spring break as well as summer. Rachel, Samuel, and Karen helped to load their luggage into the sleigh for their return trip to the train station. The children had become quite attached to Karen and each gave her a hug goodbye.

Rhonda stood for a last moment before Rachel and impulsively hugged her. "I can't tell you how much this Christmas has meant to my family," she whispered, tears welling in her eyes. "I thought I had lost them all to social media and technology, but these past two weeks have brought us all together like nothing else ever has. It was just...wonderful. We have lots of friends and work colleagues who would love to come here. I'll write you a great review as soon as we return and post it everywhere."

"I'm so glad," Rachel replied, a lump forming in her throat. They hugged one another before Rhonda's family climbed into the sleigh. Samuel steered it around and took off. The entire family turned round to wave goodbye to her, oblivious to the fact that the harness was missing one large jingle bell.

Chapter Twenty-Two

Paradigm Shift

Rachel had just finished stripping the guest beds when she heard Karen behind her.

"*Hey moooom,*" Karen began, her voice lifting in that certain way that told Rachel she was about to ask her for a big favor.

"No," Rachel automatically responded, running her fingers through her matted hair. Ruth was going to arrive within the next hour, and she still had not showered.

Karen paused for a long moment, her silence drawing Rachel's attention. She turned around and stared at her daughter who was fidgeting nervously. *Oh, oh...this must be a biggie...*

Finally, Karen seemed to find her tongue. "I've been giving it a lot of thought, and I think I would like to be baptized into the Amish church."

The bundle of dirty laundry in her arms dropped to the floor unnoticed as Rachel gawked at her daughter. She couldn't have been more surprised if Karen had declared that she wanted to become an astronaut and fly to Neptune. She studied her daughter's face, wondering if this was an elaborate practical joke. "You're kidding me, right?"

Karen shook her head.

Rachel narrowed her eyes, suspicious. "Why, Karen? Would this have anything to do with a certain Amish boy you've been keeping company with?"

Karen took a deep breath then slowly expelled it, suddenly defensive. "Well, why not? I've been living like one of the Amish for months. This was all your idea to begin with, mom. I didn't want to come here but you made me and now I'm trying to have a life."

"What about all your friends back home?" Rachel replied.

"I haven't spoken to them in months. They stopped calling and texting me when my phone went dead for so long. I just gave up on them. I don't even miss them anymore. Besides, all my new friends are Amish. They're really nice and I like them…*a lot.*"

Rachel stared at Karen hard. "So, this isn't all because of one particular new friend by the name of Willis Hochstetler?"

Karen blushed crimson. "Maybe a little…"

Rachel wanted to reach for Karen's hands and hold them in hers, but she knew if she tried Karen would only snatch them away. "Honey, there is a big difference between doing things the way the Amish do and becoming one of them. It is a very difficult life…"

Karen crossed her arms and lifted her chin in the air. "Just because you failed at it doesn't mean I will. I know it's hard but there are a lot of things about it I like."

Rachel winced. *Touché*, she thought. She may have learned some basic skills thanks to Ruth Bieler, but it was Karen, not she, who had more easily adapted to their lifestyle.

Karen squared her shoulders and looked her right in the eyes. "I'm turning eighteen soon, mom, so I really don't need your permission to get baptized, you know. It's my decision to make, not yours."

Her words pierced Rachel's heart like a flaming arrow. She watched in silence as Karen marched out of the bedroom then paused in mid-step and turned back around to face her. "I don't see what your problem is. You've been trying to do the exact same thing yourself so you can be with Samuel; *don't think I haven't noticed!* I've been thinking about

282

this a lot and made up my mind. You can be happy for me and give me your blessing or not. Either way, I'm going to be baptized as soon as I turn eighteen." With that final pronouncement, Karen turned heel and marched downstairs while Rachel looked on in astonishment. She felt as though she'd been punched in the gut. Karen's announcement had totally blindsided her.

What could she do about it? She stood for a long moment. *Nothing*, she concluded.

Rachel sighed in defeat. She supposed there were worse things a single parent could be told by their teenaged daughter than their wanting to become Amish.

Rachel picked up the sheets from the floor, ignoring the hot tears dripping down her cheeks. *It isn't the end of the world*, she kept telling herself as she carried them downstairs and stuffed them into the new front-loading washer. *It's not the end of the world*...then why did she feel so...so... *abandoned*?

She found Samuel waiting for her at the bottom of the stairs. A weird look upon his face.

"Hi Samuel," Rachel greeted him, her mood sour.

He nodded, his face looking rather grim. "Rachel," he hesitated, obviously struggling with what he was trying to say. He shuffled his feet. "Could we speak privately, out on the porch?"

Rachel set the laundry basket down on the floor. "Sure," she replied, following him outside into the chill air and wondering what was bothering him so much.

He sat down on the porch swing and removed his hat, wheeling it round and round in his hands in a very agitated way. Rachel waited while they swung back and forth for several moments, wishing she had on her coat.

"You're baking has much improved since you arrived," he finally said.

"Thanks," Rachel murmured. *Surely, he wants to talk about something more important than my baking.* She became nervous, wondering if the deadline was up for his ultimatum.

"...and you have learned many other skills as well, *jah?*" He continued.

"Yes...is there a point to all this?" Rachel prodded gently, her teeth beginning to chatter.

Her question seemed to finally give Samuel the courage he needed.

Samuel turned to look her right in the eyes. "Is it really necessary for Ruth Bieler to come here anymore to give you lessons?"

Rachel stared at him, completely shocked. "*What?*"

Samuel was deadly serious. "Is it really necessary for Ruth Bieler to continue to come here anymore?" he repeated. "You have already learned everything you wanted to learn..."

Despite her effort to remain calm, Rachel's voice came out too loud. "What are you getting at, Samuel? Ruth Bieler is my *friend!*"

Samuel's face grew hard. "I don't like her coming over here almost every single day. I want it to stop. I have my reasons."

Rachel could feel the heat rising in her face. "Well, I don't think that's any of your business!" she snapped. "She's my friend...my *only* friend, Samuel! She befriended me when no one else would!" She stood to her feet, furious with him for the first time. "I can't believe you would ask me to do that to her...the only woman friend I've made since I moved here!!"

She marched back into the house letting the screen door slam behind her in his face, fuming. She had a mind to give Samuel the silent treatment for a good long while. She slammed the pots and pans in the kitchen around for a good ten minutes. Buddy made himself scarce.

Ruth arrived not much later and entered Rachel's house, no longer needing to knock. "Rachel, are you home?" she called from the front room.

Rachel ran in from the service porch to greet her.

Ruth smiled at her. "Did I come too early?"

"No, I'm just running late," Rachel said, giving her a hug. "I had to strip all the beds. My guests left yesterday."

Ruth sat down at her usual spot at the counter, removing her warm woolen cloak and neck scarf. "You seem preoccupied. Is there something bothering you?"

"You've no idea, but we can talk about it over our coffee. On second thought, would you mind going into town with me on a few errands? I need to get out of here and I could really use some advice."

Ruth smiled, wondering what Rachel was so upset about. "*Jah*, I would be happy to," she replied.

Rachel grabbed her purse and cell phone. They climbed into Rachel's car which had been pulled inside the barn. It had been quite a while since she had last used it, so it gasped and struggled and finally started after much effort.

Rachel let it idle long enough for the seat warmers to activate then backed out of the driveway and carefully pulled onto the road.

"Karen just told me that she wants to become Amish." Rachel snorted in disbelief. "My daughter, the techno-geek who pretended to do homework for two years while goofing off on Facebook wants to live like the Amish! The same child who has spent nearly every waking moment of her teen life on her cell phone or laptop!"

Ruth glanced over at her. "I take it you're not too happy about her wanting to be Amish?"

Rachel's face turned crimson. "Oh, it's not that at all, I just can't believe it. I had to drag her out here against her will and she fought me every step of the way. She even hid out at a friend's house the night before we were supposed to board the train. If Kayla's parents hadn't told on her, I wouldn't have found her in time."

Ruth waited for her to continue.

"On top of that, Samuel and I got into a heated disagreement this morning," Rachel froze and snapped her mouth shut, looking at her with a horrified expression. She hemmed and hawed for a few moments then continued. "I guess I'm just surprised that out of the two of us, she's the one who has adapted to your lifestyle more easily," Rachel admitted, her voice ending on a sad whisper. "I guess it's easier when you're young and not so set in your ways like me."

Ruth looked at her, eyes wide in disbelief. "You wish to become Amish?"

"That wasn't my original plan. I was just hoping to learn the skills I needed so I could pass them along to my guests. Then one thing led to another with Sam...er, well...I mean, I began to give the idea some real serious thought..." Rachel paused for a long time. "Well, it just hasn't been working out as well as I hoped it would."

Rachel grasped Ruth's hand in her own. "Ruth, you are my only friend. I don't know what I would have done these past months without you. You were the only one to really talk to me...to make me feel welcome."

Ruth cleared her throat, uncomfortable. "So, what are you going to do about your *dochder*?"

Rachel slumped. "She turns eighteen in a year or so, so there's not a whole lot I can do about it. She's never listened to me in all the years since we adopted her. If I object, it will only make her that much more determined to do it."

Ruth gawked. "Karen is not your own?"

"No, I couldn't have children. Barry so wanted to be a father and the only way we could have a family was to adopt. We went through infertility testing and determined I could never get pregnant, so adoption was our only choice. Karen was five when we got her."

Ruth visibly paused while this information began to sink in. She looked at Rachel. "How can I help?"

Rachel smiled back at her through teary eyes. "I don't know...a shoulder? An open ear...I just really need a friend right now. Ruth, you're my *only* friend!"

Ruth held her hand for the duration of the ride into town although they spoke little after that.

They went to the market where Rachel purchased some needed items and returned an hour later to the house where lessons in sewing ensued. Although Rachel had said that she needed to talk, she barely seemed capable of sewing while tears continuously dripped down her cheeks.

The hours passed swiftly. It was almost 1:00 p.m. when Rachel finally glanced at her watch. It was way past lunch time. "I wonder where Samuel is. He must be getting hungry and thirsty." Rachel turned to Ruth, her eyes pleading.

"Would you let Samuel know about lunch when it's ready?" she asked. "I just can't deal with him right now."

"Sure," Ruth replied, curtly.

"Just tell him I'll have his meal brought over to the *dawdi haus* when it's ready." Rachel added.

Ruth stood to her feet and immediately went out the front door in search of Samuel. She found him in the barn. "Samuel," she called and waited for him to acknowledge her. Samuel paused and straightened from his work to stare at her, his eyes wary. "Rachel says you are to take your meals alone in the *dawdi haus* from now on." The lie was out of her mouth before she could stop it. Hopefully Rachel would still be too upset to question Samuel about it later.

Samuel just stared at her, his face an unreadable mask. "Fine," he finally mumbled and turned back to work.

Ruth returned to the house where she found Rachel sitting at the kitchen table looking miserable. "I told him," Ruth told her. "Why don't you fix up a tray and I'll bring it over there for you?"

Rachel nodded and gave her a sad smile. "Okay."

Fifteen minutes later they finished making the meatloaf sandwiches, a thermos of hot coffee, and some canned fruit. Rachel placed the tray into Ruth's hands and waited silently as she walked through the front door to the *dawdi haus*. She walked as fast as she dared, the plates rattling on the tray as she approached the door. She rapped twice. He opened the door a crack and just stared at her. She looked at him expectantly, waiting for him to open the door for her.

Samuel paused, a frown passing over his face as he glanced at the front windows of the main house. Ruth held her breath, her heart pounding with fear that he would confront Rachel and learn the whole truth. He stepped toward the main house, a determined look on his face.

"Samuel." Her voice was sharp with panic. "*Das ist* heavy. Please open the door and let me place it on the table."

Finally, he relented and held open the door so she could enter. She placed it on the table and waited.

Samuel just stared at her; his brow furrowed. "*Danki*," he finally murmured, signaling it was time for her to go. He turned round and angrily pumped water into the sink to wash his hands.

Ruth backed up, wiping her sweaty palms on her dress. "Well, good appetite," she said before letting the screen door close softly behind her. As she crossed the snowy front lawn, a sleigh drove up. A young Amish man exited, and froze when he saw her staring at him. It was Willis Hochstetler. Moments later, Karen flew out of the house, dressed in a warm woolen dress and cloak. She climbed into the sleigh and with a flick of the reins the two of them drove off in a hurry. No wonder the girl wanted to be baptized Amish. She was carrying on with Samuel's nephew!

Ruth hurried back into the house and almost bumped into Rachel who was standing right inside the front door.

"Did Samuel say anything when you gave him the food?" she asked, her brown eyes anxious for information.

"*Nee*," she replied. "He just seemed angry about something but wouldn't say what. I need to get going now, Rachel. My parents are waiting for me…see you tomorrow?"

Rachel nodded then turned away, but Ruth could plainly see the tears filling her eyes.

Chapter Twenty-Three

Estranged & Betrayed

It was the end of January and Samuel was growing anxious. Every time he attempted to see Rachel, Ruth Bieler intercepted him and made it quite clear that he was no longer welcome in the house or in Rachel's presence. The woman always seemed to be around. She appeared in the early morning and didn't leave until the sun went down. The rare times he had gotten a glimpse of Rachel Winston from a distance she had turned away and fled back inside, her face an unreadable mask.

Alone on his bed at night, sleep evaded him. It had been weeks since they had last spoken. There was no lying to himself any longer, he yearned for her. He missed her. Their mutual sorrow may have been what initially drew their hearts to each other, but he couldn't deny the attraction he felt for her or the deep friendship that had grown between them. Rachel Winston had rekindled the flame in the heart he had long thought dead. Why had it all changed so abruptly after her guests had left? He missed sharing meals with her and Karen around the table. Instead, they were delivered to his doorstep where he ate alone. Instead of facing him, she was using Ruth Bieler as a go-between, who seemed all too happy with her newfound role. He couldn't put his finger on it but something about it irked him mightily.

Samuel flung off the bedcovers, dressed hurriedly and went to the barn to take care of the animals. When he got there, he found Karen already at work milking the cows.

"*Gut morgan*, Mr. Miller," she said, giving him a happy smile.

"*Gut morgan*, Karen." he replied, retrieving his milking stool. "You're up earlier than usual."

"*Jah*, I have a lot to do before the Meeting."

"*Jah*? My s*chwester's* family seems to have become your second home," he remarked. He had not been blind to the frequent trysts Karen and Willis had been making since they met at his sister's house during the summer. While he ate all his meals alone in the *dawdi haus,* Willis had become a frequent dinner guest in the Winston household and vice versa. He wondered if Rachel had any clue as to what the shared buggy and sleigh rides, singings, and little gifts in the mailbox for Karen were adding up to. In her world, it probably would have been overlooked as a simple crush, but in his community, it was much more serious. There had also been talk that Karen was about to be baptized into his church, but she had not confided in him, and he no longer felt comfortable enough with Rachel to ask her.

"Mr. Miller?" Karen's voice came from the next stanchion over. "Could I ride with you to the Meeting this morning?" A low rumble of thunder sounded outside the barn.

"Will your *mudder* be joining us?"

Karen shook her head at him. "I don't think so; she went to bed with one of her bad migraines last night. She's probably just going to sleep in this morning."

Another low rumble of distant thunder sounded outside, causing the cows to moo nervously.

Samuel sniffed the air; it smelled like rain. "Looks like we're in for a stormy day; best take an umbrella and cloak with you today."

He left the barn and strode with renewed purpose to the main house. This time he was going to talk to Rachel face-

291

to-face without interference. He rapped on the front door and waited but there was no response. He knocked again, much louder this time. Still nothing. He grasped the door handle and twisted the knob, but it was locked. Another clap of thunder rumbled. It was louder and closer this time; the sound of it rolled over the valley.

"Mr. Miller, can you help me? This is too heavy for me," called Karen's voice from within the barn.

He went back inside, hefted the galvanized container of fresh milk, and took it to the refrigeration unit. "The house is locked up; do you have the key?" he asked.

"I keep it around my neck on a string."

He was stunned. "Why is it locked?"

"I was told that she wanted it locked up from now on," Karen replied, handing it to him.

"By your *mudder*?"

"Ruth Bieler said my mom wanted it locked."

Samuel swallowed hard, digesting this new piece of information but saying nothing. They entered the house.

"I'll be right back; I have to change my clothes before we leave." Karen hurried upstairs, leaving him alone on the bottom floor. Now nothing stood between him and Rachel Winston. With a quick glance up at the empty stairs where Karen had disappeared, he went to Rachel's bedroom and opened the door. He was violating a hundred different edicts of the *Ordnung* by entering her room like this, but he no longer cared. All he wanted to do was to clear the air. Rachel lay in bed, snuggled under several quilts. Her wavy brunette hair lay strewn across her face and pillow. He approached the bed, determined to do nothing more than wake her with a gentle touch. Still deeply asleep, her mouth slightly parted, she looked incredibly vulnerable. He stood beside the bed and reached out his hand to sweep away the hair from her eyes.

"Samuel Miller *was machen sie?*" hissed a voice behind him.

Samuel straightened and turned around, the heat of guilt flushing over him as he beheld Ruth Bieler standing in the doorway, her face livid.

She beckoned him with her hand to step away from the bed and he obeyed. Had he done anything else she would surely have cause to accuse him before the elders. She had already seen enough to do so. His heart hammering, Samuel stepped away and docilely followed her into the family room.

Ruth turned and stared at him, a strange look on her face. "Samuel, even though I should tell the bishop about what I just saw, I won't. I think Rachel has already suffered enough ostracism already."

Samuel nodded silently, a combination of fear, anger, and suspicion roiling inside of him. What was Ruth Bieler doing here so early?

"I came to see if I could talk Ra-Mrs. Winston into joining us at the Meeting, but it's obvious she isn't up for it," he said.

Karen hurried downstairs. "It's pouring," she announced, pausing on the landing. She looked at the two of them, her face questioning.

"What about breakfast?" Samuel asked, stalling. "Neither of us has eaten and it will be a long time until lunch."

Ruth held up a covered basket. "I brought some cinnamon rolls, sausage, and coffee in a thermos just in case. We can eat on the way."

How convenient, almost as if she had this all planned. There was nothing he could do under the circumstances. He was already treading on thin ice as it was.

Karen held up an umbrella. "Okay, let's go!"

To Samuel, she seemed every bit as anxious to get to the Meeting as Ruth Bieler, no doubt because of his nephew, Willis.

Karen and Ruth waited under the shelter of the porch while Samuel harnessed the horse to the buggy then made a run for it as the freezing rain pelted down. Karen scrambled into the back and Ruth took a seat beside him. Samuel flicked the reins and the buggy jerked to a start. The rain lashed down hard. Every few minutes, a flash of lightning and a crack of thunder would spook the horse. The rain was melting the snow making the road hazardous. He had a lot to deal with to keep Dodger under control so that the horse would not bolt in front of traffic or careen into the ditches that ran along either side of the road. It was with great relief when they arrived safely at the bishop's farm where the Meeting was held that week. No longer preoccupied with keeping Dodger in check, Samuel's heart filled with sudden terror. He reluctantly exited the buggy, watching helplessly as Ruth Bieler made a beeline straight for the bishop.

His heart thudded to the bottom of his stomach. She was going to expose him.

Rachel flew upright, the clap of thunder outside going off like a bomb. The windows shuddered and the rain pelted against the windows as the skies opened. Buddy raised his head and whined, trembling in fear. Rachel pulled him against her and rubbed his silky ears until he calmed. She squinted at her alarm clock. Eleven-thirty. She was sure she had set it for 6 a.m. yesterday before Ruth had left for home, but she must have slept right through it because of the migraine medication. Since the Meeting was at the bishop's farm this week, she had wanted to attend with Samuel to see if she could make amends. Samuel had been avoiding her for weeks with no explanation as to why, and she was more than ready to put an end to it.

Rachel rolled out of bed and winced. The medication had taken away most of the pain, but it still lingered. Her head was still throbbing. She made a quick circuit of the house. It was empty and silent except for the storm raging outside. She went into the kitchen. Not even a note from

Karen to let her know she had gone to the Meeting without her. Everyone had just abandoned her. She plunked down at the kitchen table, depressed.

I might as well not exist as far as Karen or anyone else is concerned, she thought to herself. Samuel had been avoiding her for a month and Karen was being her usual antisocial self. Tears of self-pity rolled down her cheeks as she tried to cheer herself up. At least Ruth Bieler was still her friend; she wasn't completely alone. They had spent almost every day together in the past month, baking, sewing, and gossiping. It was almost like being in junior high again with a best friend who slept over on the weekends except that Ruth always had to return to her parent's home to take care of them every afternoon.

Rachel felt bad for Ruth. It must be horrible to watch all your friends getting married off and having children while you were stuck taking care of your aging parents all alone.

Ruth had been invaluable in showing her how to do things the Amish way. Rachel no longer dreaded how her pies, breads, or rolls would come out and had even come to feel proud of her baking skills. Rachel went to her computer and checked her email. More messages from the contractor and workers demanding payment. She was out of money. The Johnsons final payment had just managed to tide her over for the holidays, but now she was past due on several bills. Beginning January 2nd, her email and cell phone had been inundated with calls from bill collectors. The Johnson's still had not left a review on their stay and Rachel had received no further bookings for the Inn. If she didn't make some income soon, she was going to lose everything. Her depression deepened.

"What do you want from me, God?" she wailed, looking up at the ceiling. "I lost Barry, our home, the comfort of my family and friends, and now I'm about to lose this Inn. Please, tell me what to do."

Lightning exploded outside the kitchen, shaking the windows.

Rachel shrieked.

Buddy ran off with his tail between his legs and squeezed his body under the nearest piece of furniture. Ordinarily, Rachel loved the thrill of thunderstorms, but this one was freaking her out. The storm cell had parked itself over her house and the bolts were coming down fast and furious. Another scream of fright tore from her throat at the next loud crash. Rachel ran, scooped Buddy up from his hiding place, and ran back into her bedroom with him, crawling under the blankets to wait it out while her migraine intensified.

Samuel steered the buggy into the driveway that afternoon, his heart leaden with the news he must deliver to Rachel. Ruth Bieler had told Bishop Fisher, Deacon Lapp, and even his own brother-in-law of his countless indiscretions. Their faces had all become extremely grave. They agreed that he was playing with fire and inviting excommunication and shunning. If he wanted to remain a part of the community, he had to break all ties with Rachel Winston, immediately. He would have to move out of the *dawdi haus* and in with his *schwester*. He pulled up to the house, his throat constricted in pain, wondering how on earth he was going to break the news to her and what it would do to her.

Samuel glanced over his shoulder at Karen who was oblivious to his dark mood. She and Willis had been almost inseparable that day and he had overheard them whispering amongst themselves about "future plans." That was also going to give Rachel a horrible shock.

He pulled the buggy as close to the front porch as he could and stepped out. Karen was out of the buggy in a flash and charging up the porch stairs to avoid the pelting rain. He was just about to go up the front stairs when Ruth's buggy appeared behind his in the driveway; she had followed him home. What on earth was she doing here? His mood went immediately from morose to angry. Thunder rumbled ominously, matching his mood.

"I have nothing to say to you," he said, the moment she got out of the buggy.

"Samuel, I had no choice! I couldn't let you throw away everything on an *Englisch* woman who has no intention of becoming one of us."

Samuel's eyes narrowed. "How do you know this?" he demanded, oblivious to the rain soaking them.

Ruth squared her shoulders. "I am Rachel's only friend; she tells me *everything*." she replied smugly.

The words struck his heart like flint, causing actual physical pain, but they also rang hollow. He wasn't sure what to believe. He turned his back on Ruth and went into the main house, looking for Rachel. Ruth followed him.

⟶⟶⟶⟵⟵⟵

Karen burst through Rachel's bedroom door. "Mom, what are you still doing in bed with Buddy?"

Another burst of lightning and thunder was her answer. "Hiding," Rachel whispered. "This weather is making my migraine worse." She opened the quilt and beckoned to her daughter. "Want to join us? Remember how we used to cuddle up in bed and watch thunderstorms together?"

Karen wrinkled her nose at her. "I'm too old for that now," she replied but sat on the edge of the bed. "*Mamm…*"

"Mom," Rachel corrected her with a sigh. "Can you please just call me mom for a change, like you used to?"

"Okay…mom. I have something important to talk to you about."

An ominous sense of foreboding settled over Rachel. She lowered the quilt down to her shoulders and squinted at her daughter. "What?"

Karen cleared her throat. "Well, you know how I want to be baptized into the Amish faith, right?"

Rachel nodded and waited; not sure she was going to like what Karen was going to say next.

"You know that I like Willis Hochstetler, right?"

Again, Rachel nodded and winced again. The migraine was becoming acute despite the drugs she had taken earlier. Her eyesight was narrowing down to a tiny black tunnel, a sure sign it was going to be a bad one. Still, she waited.

"Well, after I'm baptized, Willis and I are going to get engaged."

Rachel was horrified. "You're telling me this, not asking?" The steel vise tightened around her head.

Karen lifted her chin and stood her ground. "When I turn eighteen, I won't need your permission, mom. Most of the Amish girls here get married in their early 20's. Willis and I want to get married next too in the next year or so."

"This is ridiculous!" Rachel blurted out angrily despite the pain it caused her. If Karen thought that she was going to let her marry someone she had only known a few months, she had another thing coming. Despite the debilitating pain, she forced herself to clamber out of bed. "Is Samuel here yet?" she demanded.

Karen went pale. "I think he's in the living room…what do you want to talk to him for?"

Rachel shielded her eyes from the painful daylight. She stumbled into the family room. "Samuel, Samuel?" Her voice came out in a squeak. "Did you know anything about…"

She froze, mouth gaping open in shock. Ruth Bieler's body was pressed full length against Samuel's. Her arms were about his waist, and she was looking into his eyes with a desperate look on her face.

"…Rachel can't give you any children, Samuel, but I still can, she's *barren!*"

Rachel's legs gave way. She barely felt the pain when her kneecaps slammed into the floor, it was so completely transcended by the migraine splitting her head apart. In slow motion, she watched both Ruth and Samuel turn to look at her in shock. She had entered the room just in time to catch them in a full embrace. Bile rose instantly into her throat. She struggled to her feet, clapped a hand over her mouth and fled outside into the pouring rain, lightning and thunder pounding around her. She was half-blinded by the rain and the migraine. She stumbled down the porch steps, slipped then fell onto her stomach in the gravel. She was soaked in seconds. With monumental effort, she struggled to her feet again and careened into Samuel's horse and buggy, ignoring the shouts of alarm coming from the house.

"Rachel!"

"Mom!"

She could barely hear them over the roaring in her ears.

Ruth and Samuel. Samuel and Ruth!

They were embracing each other!

She wants to have his children.

Karen is becoming Amish and getting married.

I'm going to lose the inn!

Karen's fearful face suddenly appeared before her. "Mom...stop, come into the house. You're getting soaked."

Rachel shook her head. It sent waves of pain and nausea shooting through her. "No, no, I've lost everything...everything," she moaned. "Barry...you...Samuel...bank is going to foreclose...can't take anymore." She knew she was babbling. There was a brilliant flash of lightning followed immediately by another clap of thunder. Dodger reared and neighed with terror, kicking his forelegs in the air. Karen backed away in fright. Rachel climbed into the front of the buggy and with her last ounce of strength took hold of the reins and violently slashed them upon his back. Dodger wheeled about then took off, throwing up a spray of water, gravel, and mud behind him.

She could hear the screams of Samuel, Ruth, and Karen behind her, but she paid them no heed. The horse and buggy sped down the driveway and pulled out into the road without pausing for any cross traffic. The blare of car horns made her ears want to bleed. The speed of the turn caused the buggy to lift and teeter precariously upon two wheels until it finally righted itself. Another clap of thunder sent Dodger from a canter into a panicked gallop. He neighed in terror. They hit a small bump which launched Rachel into the back of the dark buggy. She lost her grip on the reins. The pain in her head was excruciating; she was close to blacking out.

The buggy was careening wildly through the flooding streets. Dimly through her pain, Rachel could hear the urgent honking of car horns and the squealing of tires as motorists tried to avoid her runaway buggy. She felt no fear, just profound despair.

Everything is gone. Barry is gone. My money is gone. Ruth, my one and only friend, betrayed me... Samuel betrayed me...

As she lay on the floor of the buggy in utter pain and despair, she had a sudden moment of clarity. Ruth's friendship had been a farce all along. She had just been playing at friendship to win over Samuel and it looked like her plan had worked out perfectly. He had been embracing her.

Twin lights appeared ahead and from a distance, Rachel heard a klaxon horn sound a loud warning. She struggled to sit up and looked around, unable to find the reins which were dragging too far out of reach on the ground. She looked up and saw the lights of the tractor-trailer fill her view as the horn blasted a warning.

Rachel closed her eyes in surrender.

Time slowed down. Her heart labored.

"I'm coming Barry," she whispered. "Please, please be there waiting for me..."

The lights and horn blasts filled the buggy. The horse screamed and reared, then her world tilted crazily and went black.

"Ruth Bieler take your hands off of me." Samuel forcefully pried himself from her grip and shoved her backward. Rachel was already out the door and climbing into the buggy. He had to stop her before she could get away. Ruth stepped in his way.

"Samuel, the elders have warned you! You'll be excommunicated if you continue down this path. Think of what you're doing." Her voice was shrill, but her eyes pleaded with him. "Isn't it bad enough to have already lost your *frau* and *kinner*? Do you want to be shunned and lose the rest of your family and community as well?"

Samuel glared at Ruth, his heart pounding. "I love her," he declared loudly, his eyes smoldering with defiance. "If I'm forced to make a choice then I choose Rachel Winston." The next instant he was out the door and in the driveway where he found Karen standing in the pouring rain, staring after the buggy that was carrying her mother away. Ruth followed behind. All three screamed at Rachel to stop to no avail.

Karen turned to him, her eyes round with fear. "I couldn't stop her, Mr. Miller, she didn't seem to understand anything. I'm scared, I don't know what to do."

"Call 911," he yelled as he ran to the barn. He dashed inside and found his other horse, Molly. Within moments, he had a halter on and was riding bareback out of the barn, determined to find Rachel before it was too late. He could barely see with the rain stinging his eyes. Several times, Molly stumbled and skidded on the slick payment, almost throwing him off. The lightning strikes and booming thunder were dangerously close.

He rode Molly hard but could see no sign of a buggy in front of him. Traffic on the two-lane from their farm had slowed to a crawl. How could she have gotten such a vast lead on him? Thunder crashed again and Molly reared, whinnying loudly in fear. He rode her along the right side of the road, dangerously close to the ditch. Up ahead he could see a large tractor-trailer that had jack-knifed. Cold dread filled his heart. He urged Molly on and finally approached what looked to be the scene of a horrible accident.

He jumped off her back and saw a buggy lying upside down in the deep ditch, its wheels spinning in the air. Fast moving water flowed through it. Dodger was lying on his back, neighing wildly, and kicking his legs. It was too deep for him to get out unassisted. Emergency vehicles were already arriving.

The gorge rose into Samuel's throat. History was repeating itself. Memories of another broken buggy and injured horse lying in a flooded ditch assaulted him. The face of some nameless police officer telling him that none of his family had survived.

He ran and slid down into the ditch and freezing water as the emergency personnel converged upon the scene, sirens blaring. The water came up to his hips. He had to tear aside the heavy cloth of the buggy with his bare hands to see inside.

Rachel lay below him, her lower body half-submerged and pinned by the buggy in the icy water, her body twisted like a rag doll. Her face was white as death, her lips blue and she wasn't moving. A cut on her head was bleeding. Water lapped over her chin. With a bellow of anguish, he held his breath and plunged beneath the surface to free her, but he couldn't budge it off her. Her legs were pinned tight. The water continued to rise. He rose, took a deep breath, and submerged again, struggling with the reins, the cloth and the frame that held her in a death grip. He surfaced again, coughing violently, desperation setting in. The freezing water was numbing him through and through. He held her cold face in his hands to keep it above the rising water.

"Rachel," he bellowed, "don't leave me, please don't leave me!" He had never had a chance to tell her that he loved her or how much he cared about her. She would die without ever knowing how he really felt about her. He looked to the dark clouds and screamed his prayer aloud to the heavens above. *"Help me, Der Herr! Please help me! Don't take her away from me!"* Above him, a brilliant flash of lightning illuminated the area around the buggy. The air around him exploded with a thunderous roar. Molly neighed loudly and reared again but remained where she stood, sweating and trembling with fear. Rachel remained unresponsive. Her face was cold and still in his trembling hands. Hot tears ran into his beard. He would not leave her to die alone. If he couldn't save her then he would perish with her. He wrapped his arms around her as best he could, kicking against the current to keep them both afloat while Dodger continued to thrash and scream beside them.

Time seemed to halt as his body grew numb. In the next moment, he heard men jumping into the ditch beside him.

"Help us, she's going to drown!" he bellowed.

Several pairs of hands reached in and together they lifted the frame of the buggy, freeing Rachel's body from the wreckage. Samuel had to be physically hauled out himself, all his strength gone. He rolled onto his back, utterly exhausted and unable to rise. He watched as the emergency teams carefully lifted Rachel's body out of the water. She was completely limp. They set her upon the gurney and shoved it into the back of a waiting ambulance.

He crawled toward her, but he was blocked by a ring of emergency personnel.

"Is she alive?" his voice was barely a croak. An EMT bent over her. He placed an oxygen mask over her pale face. A second EMT ripped her shirt in two then he pressed two paddles onto either side of her naked breast.

"CLEAR!" he shouted. Rachel's body arched up then fell back onto the gurney.

"Is she alive? Someone, *sie so gut*, tell me." He struggled to roll over but felt himself pushed gently down. He looked up into the eyes of a police officer.

"Sir, please calm down, we're doing everything we can."

We've done everything we can; we lost them... echoed the words from his past.

Samuel collapsed with a moan of anguish then darkness descended upon him, pulling him beneath its irresistible depths. Rachel Winston was dead and lost to him forever... she had perished in the same manner as his wife and children.

Chapter Twenty-Four

Rescued

A hand roughly shook her arm which seemed to belong to someone else. She was floating in a deep black void that she didn't want to leave. It was peaceful here and absent of pain. The hand shook her again, more forcefully this time. In response, her body floated closer to the surface of its own accord. Soft light filtered in, pale at first then growing brighter as she rose higher. Her lungs were bursting. She needed air. Any moment now, her mouth would open, and the dark waters would pour in, pulling her down into their depths for the last time.

A violent cough shook her body, but water did not rush in to fill her lungs. Instead, she felt the rush of cold air and tasted medicine in its flow. Rachel wearily opened her eyes and tried to focus. All she could see was a blurry face through a plastic mask. Her chest ached as though some-one had been pounding it with a hammer.

"What happened?" she croaked. Suddenly there was a rush of activity around her. She felt something tighten and squeeze her upper arm then came the prick of a needle. A small beam of bright light bounced from one eye to the other. All around her, she could hear whooshing, clicking, beeping, and talking. Her head was throbbing, but she managed to find who was squeezing her hand unmercifully.

It took a few moments to focus but soon she recognized her daughter Karen, who was looking at her with sheer terror.

"Where am I?" Rachel wondered.

"You're in the ambulance." Karen replied, her voice choked with tears. "Don't you remember anything, mom?"

Rachel shook her head, causing waves of nausea to course through her. She waited until it passed then slowly opened her eyes again and looked at the good-looking doctor in the glowing white lab coat. He placed his hands on her forehead and the nausea disappeared, replaced by a blissful sense of calm and peace. "Sleep now, Rachel, you are in my hands."

Didn't he mean good hands? Was he the Allstate man?

With that she drifted off into a deep sleep, a smile on her lips.

The next time she woke, it was to the sound of birds singing outside her window. She sat up and stretched, allowing herself the luxury of an obnoxiously loud yawn.

"Rachel."

She sat up, her eyes scanning her hospital room.

"Rachel, please lie back down, I'll get the nurse."

She turned in the direction of the voice, fully awake for the first time in what seemed like years. But the face wasn't Samuel's. It was just like him, only younger and clean-shaven. She laid back down and drew the sheet up to her chin. "Where's Samuel?"

The face stared at her, clearly bewildered, then a rueful grin split his mouth from ear to ear. He rubbed his smooth jaw with his hand and chuckled. "I'm right here," he replied. He bent over her and the next thing she knew his lips were upon hers, his kiss dearly familiar.

She brought her fingers up to his face, trailing them along his clean jawline. There was no trace of his Amish beard. It was Samuel Miller; he had a cleft in his chin, and he was *beautiful.*

"What did you do to yourself?" she whispered. His "wedding ring" was gone. Fear swept over her. "Have you been shunned on account of me?"

Samuel clasped her hands between his. "I made a choice, Rachel, I chose you."

She stared at him, blinking back her tears. Then he did something that completely shocked and pleased her. He climbed into the hospital bed next to her and took her in his arms. "I left of my own free will." He took her face between his hands and turned her to face him. "When I found you and the buggy in the ditch, I fell apart. When they were shocking your heart back to life on the road, I thought I had lost you forever."

Rachel's throat constricted in pain as she beheld the fear in his eyes.

Samuel continued. "I could not bear the thought of remaining in this world without you, so I begged *Der Herr* to save you and that if He did, I would take you as my *frau* even if I had to leave all else behind."

Tears flooded Rachel's eyes and spilled over, tears of wonder. "You gave it all up for me? Your family, friends…everything?"

"You are my family now. Rachel - I found purpose and love again when you came into my life," he replied softly, stroking her face. "You brought *Der Herr* back into my life in a way I never expected…I have gained more than I have given up."

Rachel sat next to Samuel in the buggy, still unable to get over how good he looked with a clean-shaven face as they rode home from the hospital. She was shocked to learn that she had spent the better part of a month in an induced coma. Her chest and bronchial tubes were still sore from her long intubation. She had almost succumbed to pneumonia a few times and had been on a respirator until her lungs were clear and she could breathe on her own. The pain was a small price to pay in exchange for sitting at Samuel's side, knowing that he loved her enough to give up everything for her and that Karen really did care about her. She was also relieved to learn that Dodger had not been seriously hurt in the accident. Now her only worry was how she was going to afford to live. The hospital bills had put her deeper into debt and she still faced losing the Inn. She sighed and reminded herself that in the vast scheme of things, it didn't really amount to much when Samuel and Karen could just as easily have been visiting her grave site instead of driving her home. Samuel had willingly walked away from his Amish community, so now it was just the two of them having to figure it all out together. She pushed her dark thoughts to one side and snuggled closer to him, unable to resist caressing his smooth cheek.

They turned into the driveway of the Inn that wouldn't belong to her much longer and slowly trudged into the house. Buddy scampered in to greet her, wagging, and whining at the same time.

Rachel scooped him up and looked around the kitchen. "Take a good last look, Samuel. It won't be long until it goes on the auction block for nonpayment."

"That is not going to happen," he replied firmly.

"Well, unless one of us wins the lottery, I don't see how that can be helped," Rachel replied morosely. "Between my hospital tab and all the debt I've incurred, I'm going to have to declare bankruptcy."

"Huh uh," grinned Karen, appearing in the kitchen.

"*Nee*," Samuel replied. He smiled at her and for the first time she noticed the dimples that had been hidden under his beard. "*Der Herr* has provided."

Rachel set Buddy down and stared at them in disbelief. "What do you mean?"

"I've been keeping up with your email since the accident, mom, and the Inn is fully booked for the next two years starting in the spring. I got them all scheduled, and their deposits are in your bank account. The Johnsons really came through."

Rachel stared at them slack-jawed. "What do you mean?"

Karen sighed, trying to be patient. "They sent an email apologizing for taking so long to post a review, but they had all come down with the flu after returning home. You should read the review, mom, it's awesome! Not only that, but they've told all their friends, co-workers, and extended family. I even used my egg money toward some of your bills." Karen added.

Rachel's eyes filled with tears as she looked at her daughter with new eyes. *Karen used her own money to help me?* She was overcome that Karen had given out of her own funds to help.

"I've also paid some of the bills; enough to keep the wolves at bay, out of my own funds," Samuel added. "No wife of mine is going to be indebted or file for bankruptcy," he finished with a self-satisfied smile.

Rachel stared at him in shock for a few moments then his words hit home. Her mouth went slack. "Samuel Miller, is this a marriage proposal?"

"What a silly question." he replied, reaching under the coffee table. Was he going to put a ring on her finger? Rachel waited, but no ring was forthcoming.

He placed a large flat wooden plaque into her hands. Rachel burst into tears the moment she saw it. Samuel was so surprised by her reaction, he lapsed into German. "*Warum weinst du?*" (What are you crying for?)

Rachel brought her hand up to her mouth, trying to choke down the sobs as she admired the gorgeous white and black painted wooden plaque. On it was the silhouetted image of an Amish buggy and horse. Above, in bold black letters, were the words:

SECOND CHANCE INN
PROPRIETORS:
SAMUEL AND RACHEL MILLER

THE END

Greeting from the author!

Greetings fellow book enthusiasts!

Thank you so much for reading Second Chance Inn! Sit down with your favorite hot beverage and fur baby (if you have one) and come along for the buggy ride.

The idea for this book came from the thought *"what would I do if I ever lost the love of my life, my husband?"* Second Chance Inn is a fictionalized account of what could have been.

Back in 1982, my first love (unrequited), died of a brain aneurysm when I was 22. I was devastated. Many elements of my life (such as this one) have been incorporated into this story of love, loss and love rediscovered.

If you would ever like to connect with me, you are more than welcome to email me at: mmgiron@yahoo.com (I won't share your information with anyone.) Or to follow me on Facebook: Author Marlayne Giron, Instagram: #mmgiron.

I'd also be VERY grateful if you could write a review online. Getting feedback from readers is both very exciting and gratifying and one of the best rewards for an author!

You can also check out my website named after my first book: https://thevictorbook.com

I hope to hear from YOU!
Marlayne

ACKNOWLEDGEMENTS

First to my Lord and Messiah, Yeshua from whom comes all beauty and creativity. Thank you for gifting me with the love of books and writing!

To my husband, Michael, who patiently puts up with all my creative endeavors with good humor and above all, unconditional love and support.

To my dearest friend, Mary, who despite all the pressure of her daily responsibilities, always takes the time to answer my questions and give me wonderful feedback!

Made in the USA
Columbia, SC
14 October 2023

24473329R00190